1982 JANINE

Born in 1934, **Alasdair Gray** graduated in design and mural painting from the Glasgow School of Art. Since 1981, when *Lanark* was published by Canongate, he has written, designed and illustrated seven novels, several books of short stories, a collection of his stage, radio and TV plays and a book of his visual art, *A Life in Pictures*.

In his own words, 'Alasdair Gray is a fat, spectacled, balding, old Glaswegian pedestrian who has mainly lived by writing and designing books, most of them fiction'.

Also by Alasdair Gray

Novels
Lanark
The Fall of Kelvin Walker
Something Leather
McGrotty and Ludmilla
Poor Things
A History Maker
Mavis Belfrage
Old Men In Love

Short Story Collections
Unlikely Stories, Mostly
Lean Tales (with James Kelman and Agnes Owens)
Ten Tales Tall & True
The Ends of Our Tethers
Every Short Story by Alasdair Gray 1951–2012

Poetry
Old Negatives
Sixteen Occasional Poems
Collected Verse
Hell: Dante's Divine Trilogy Part One

Theatre
Dialogue – A Duet
The Loss of the Golden Silence
Homeward Bound
Sam Lang and Miss Watson
McGrotty and Ludmilla
Working Legs
Goodbye Jimmy
Fleck
A Gray Play Book

Non-fiction
Why Scots Should Rule Scotland
The Book of Prefaces
How We Should Rule Ourselves
A Life in Pictures
Of Me and Others
Independence

1982
JANINE

BY

ALASDAIR GRAY

CANONGATE BOOKS
EDINBURGH 2019

This Canons edition published in Great Britain, the USA and Canada in 2019 by Canongate Books Ltd, 14 High Street, Edinburgh EH1 1TE

Distributed in the USA by Publishers Group West
and in Canada by Publishers Group Canada

First published by Canongate Books in 2003
First published in 1984 by Jonathan Cape

canongate.co.uk

1

British Library Cataloguing-in-Publication Data
A catalogue record for this book is available on
request from the British Library

ISBN 978 1 78689 396 3

FOR BETHSY

There are boxes in the mind with labels on them: To study on a favourable occasion; Never to be thought about; Useless to go into further; Contents unexamined; Pointless business; Urgent; Dangerous; Delicate; Impossible; Abandoned; Reserved for others; My business; etcetera.

Paul Valéry

TABLE OF

CONTENTS

Introduction

1982, Janine, Alasdair Gray's second novel, is a text that resists interpretation as completely as its predecessor, *Lanark*, invites it. Not only is this a novel that stands in a fictional dock, accused of the most experimental of imaginative crimes, it is also a book that positively resists the reader. Do not, I beg of you, pick it up lightly; do not, I urge you, be deceived by its come-hither appearance and easy way with words, into believing that *1982, Janine* will let you go before you have been shaken up and rubbed down. Trust me, you will leave go at the end sore and nauseous, in need of balm and a vomit.

Why should we trouble ourselves with difficult books? Why should we not slurp fictional mush and be spoon-fed undemanding narratives? For the simple reason that if literature doesn't have a capacity for awkwardness, then it cannot convey anything of the unreality of what it is to be in this world. Alasdair Gray himself has invoked Joyce's view that 'great art should not move us . . . only improper arts (propaganda and pornography) move us, but true art arrests us in the face of eternal beauty, or truth, or something like that.'[1] *1982, Janine*, with its peculiar mixture of propaganda, pornography and, if not exactly eternal beauty or truth, at least something like that, is thus a stop-go experience. The reader will get up a fair speed over a few pages, only to be arrested by one of Gray's typographical exercises, meta-fictional games, narrative time loops, or simply a sticky patch of glutinous – and yet lovely – prose.

So rebarbative is this book, that even between its own covers are premonitory warnings addressed directly to me: 'Why am

[1] Public interview with Kathy Acker at the Institute of Contemporary Arts in London, 1986. Reprinted in *Alasdair Gray: Critical Appreciations and a Bibliography*, ed. Phil Moores, The British Library, 2002.

I diluting an enjoyable wicked fantasy with this sort of crap?' asks our protagonist, Jock McLeish, as he digresses from describing Janine, his mind-spun succubus, to a homespun version of Berkeley's Argument from Illusion, before analogising further 'like a publisher attaching a brainy little essay by a French critic to *The Story of O* to make the porn-eaters feel they are in first-class intellectual company.' And while *1982, Janine* is not quite a work of pornography, I am surely worse than a French critic; namely, an English writer.

But to introduce *1982, Janine* it isn't enough to merely say 'Novel this is Reader, Reader this is Novel', and then expect the two of you to forge a quick and easy intimacy. Gray has said that this is his favourite among his own books, and moreover that 'I made a novel I had not foreseen.'[2] Perhaps it is this very quality of a text, worked up from a central conceit as a form of fictional bricolage, that makes it so disorienting. So, we are introduced to Jock McLeish, an alcoholic installer of security systems, who lies tippling whisky on his bed, in his room, in a family hotel somewhere in the lowlands of Scotland. We then accompany him as he attempts to stave off the truth about himself by indulging in a series of pornographic playlets; preposterous productions for which he himself is director, screenwriter, casting director and lighting technician. When McLeish's Janine 'hears two unfastened studs of her skirt click with each step she takes.' she is not alone. '"That's a sexy sound," the voice says, and giggles.' The voice is a Russian doll, Gray inside of McLeish, and you, dear reader, inside of Gray himself. You will hear those two unfastened studs click again and again throughout these pages, and each time they will act as a tocsin, reawakening you to the recursiveness of McLeish's fantasies, at once playful and deadly serious, both mucky and yet oddly jocose.

What are we to make of the sexual imaginings in *1982, Janine*? (And make of them something we must, for they constitute too much of the text to be dismissed as mere filler.) Gray himself has said '. . . this particular story started discoursing of improper things: sex fantasies I had meant to die without letting anybody know happen in this head sometimes . . .'[3]

[2] Ibid.

[3] Ibid.

Can he be serious? After all, it's one thing to allow such 'imaginings' to spill on to the pages of a private journal, altogether another to labour over them and then publish. Such committed fans of the novel as Jonathan Coe, have felt moved to dismiss them: 'I have always found the sex in *1982, Janine*, incidentally, among the most boring ever committed to paper.'[4] An opinion he then qualifies: 'It's only the fantasy sex that is boring. The "real" sex, the sex that is supposed at some point to have taken place outside of Jock McLeish's head, is described with a plainness and honesty and lack of sensationalism that makes it deeply sympathetic and compelling, if entirely unerotic.'

I cannot concur. While all pornographic prose suffers from too much – and too well lubricated – a movement, towards one inescapable ending (they all came happily ever after), McLeish/Gray's Sadean 'imaginings' have more than one obvious virtue. First they act as the primary means of repression, ensconced with Janine, Helga, Superb – and not forgetting Big Momma – our protagonist can evade the reality of his relations with Helen, Sontag and most especially Denny. Secondly, the 'imaginings' are at once baroque and highly contrived, acting as a projection of McLeish's negative politics. The meticulously imagined scenes of violation and humiliation are compounded with corporate structures of sexual exploitation, culminating in the distinctly Burroughsian 'Forensic Research Punishment and Sexual Gratification Syndicate'. Thirdly, despite McLeish's avowed anti-Freudianism ('I believe that under the surface we are very like how we appear above it, which is why so many surfaces last a lifetime without cracking'), the 'imaginings' serve to demonstrate that the boy's sexual repression is father to the man's sexual bullying. McLeish's treatment at the hands of Hislop – his putative father – and his fixation on the famous image of Jane Russell in *The Outlaw* (and let us not forget that the real Russell was herself the erotic plaything of a deeply disturbed man), are festering fungi beneath the mulch of his conscious mind. In drunkenness, in despair, they swell with alarming alacrity.

And lastly, while by no means certain that I myself am a

[4] '1994 Janine' in Moores (Ibid.)

closet sadomasochist, I find McLeish's 'imaginings' a sufficient turn on. Sufficient, because shorn of their denim raiment and elaborate staging, these are really fantasies about the oedipal intensity of sex from the perspective of a motherless (in the sense of abandoned) boy. McLeish's dream women are – for the most part – fecund, as he eulogises it: 'The sweetest line in the world was the profile of forgethername's belly curving out suddenly from her navel and then down in a swooping line to oh, I can never go there again, never never never again. Entering there was such sweet *homecoming*, I can never *go home* again.' (My italics). And later in the novel, he more explicitly characterises the female body as 'THE LANDSCAPE OF HOME'. Forced by Sontag to confess to a perversion, McLeish admits to being a paedophile – which he is not – purely because 'I found it less frightening to tell a lie than admit to a woman that I had a mad passion for women.'

Looked at this way the 'imaginings' are the purest of sexual fantasies, being concerned entirely with the natal and procreative character of copulation, the white worm of life-desire, which is condemned forever to swallow its own tail. It is surely not without accident (although the intent was doubtless unconscious), that while McLeish remains childless, his entire life is haunted by possibilities of pregnancy. Besides, to banish the 'imaginings' to the status of a boring aberration is to undermine the whole ground of Gray's novel; the author himself was so preoccupied with the female crux that the boards of the first edition were decorated with a repeating pattern of Ys, alternately right-way-up and upside down. This was, of course, evocative of the 'imagining' wherein McLeish's dream women were posed with their wrists tied above their heads. A reverie, the painful denouement of which – it's resolution in querulous, querying cunnilingus – is indicated in the text by the reversal of the Ys.

This brings us, logically enough, to the typographical exercises in *1982, Janine*. Gray, as perhaps the finest artist/writer of his generation, is always a conspicuous 'maker' of his own books, rather than merely an author. With this novel the use of enlarged and justified type for the beginning of chapters (which are indicated solely by numbers within the body copy), the employment of a rubric for the outside margins, and the chapter summaries in the table of contents, combine to give the text a biblical appearance. But this is standard for Gray, and I would argue just one of the methods he employs to both position his books as ur-texts – primary books from which others derive – and to resist modernity. As Angus Calder has remarked,[5] to label Gray's various devices – typographical and other glosses – 'postmodern' is ridiculous. And A. L. Kennedy – acting as Gray's proxy – writes of Sterne's *Tristram Shandy*: 'The book is wilful, exuberant, bawdy, gleefully plagiarising, eccentric & humane. It delights in its fiction, freely acknowledging the conversation that joins author & reader & using every device that late 20th-century critics label *post-modernist*.'[6]

In fact, Gray's word games are emphatically pre-modern. Rather than attempting to undermine the notion of objective truth by playing with the shattered fragments of the past, Gray shows us how our notions of reality are forced upon us by the relation in which they stand to one another (a technique he shares – albeit in a different form – with Borgés). Thus, the 'invented' plagiarisms, the bowdlerised jacket quotes, the typographical conundrums, and even the manner in which McLeish's fantasies are many layered – all of these serve to impress upon the reader the emotional and philosophic truth of Gray's fictions. In *1982, Janine*, this reaches a climax in Chapter Eleven, 'The Ministry of Voices', where Jock McLeish's descent into delirium is chronicled by no fewer than four distinct narrative voices occupying the page at once. Gray again: 'On one margin the voice of his body complains of the feverish temperature he's condemned to, while in the middle his deranged libido fantasises and alternates with his deranged conscience denouncing him for having such fantasies. On the other margin, in very small print, the voice of God tries to tell him something important, tell him he has missed the point of living in a voice he can hardly hear, because it is not thunderously denouncing . . .'[7] For the reader this is, once more, hard work, not least because the shapes the type forms on the page seem to mirror the fantasies of invagination which plague

[5] 'Politics, Scotland and Prefaces' in Moores (Ibid.)

[6] *The Book of Prefaces*, Bloomsbury, 2000.

[7] Ibid.

McLeish. It is with something like relief that you gain the blank pages that follow, symbolising McLeish's own sleep, and possibly the sleep of reason as well.

The presence of God in Gray's work – God reasonable, God magical, God immanent and transcendent – is another of the markers of the pre- rather than the postmodern. As Gray puts it, 'God is one of the most popular characters in fiction.' By which I think he means to say 'in reality'. But if Gray's sensibility in *1982, Janine* is pre-modern, and his text is built up out of what De Quincey termed 'involutes' (those proto-Freudian compounds of memory and desire), yet the dateline title of the book is no accident.

Not only is the novel taking place in the mind of McLeish, on a bed, in a hotel, in a small lowlands Scottish town (or so we are led to believe), this is also emphatically 1982, a point at which Scotland could be said to have reached just one of its many nadirs. McLeish is created, by Gray, as an antithesis of himself: the honestly self-interested, almost Social-Darwinian right winger: '. . . in Britain,' McLeish soliloquises 'almost everyone of my income group is Conservative, especially if their fathers were trade unionists. Not that I've entirely rejected the old man's Marxist ideas. The notion that all politics is class warfare is clearly correct. Every intelligent Tory knows that politics is a matter of people with a lot of money combining to manage people with very little, though of course they must deny it in public to mislead the opposition.'

In 1982 this is horribly salient, with 40,000 British workers losing their jobs weekly, unemployment well past the two million mark, the steel and coal industries on which Scots industry depends being decimated, while at the head of it all stands a Premier intent on abandoning the Neo-Keynesian, Butskellite consensus of the post-war period, by slashing a billion pounds of public expenditure. In the slough that came after the refusal of the limited devolution offered by James Callaghan's Labour Government, the Scots nationalists (among whom, surprisingly, McLeish includes himself) are foundering in the river of rust which cinches the waist of Scotland (much in the manner that a leather belt cinches one of McLeish's dream women).

Nevertheless, while McLeish's Hobbesian credo provides

some of the pithiest and starkest observations in the novel, it is never wholly convincing. Gray has confessed that in creating a mirror image of himself, he has simply provided another self-portrait, and this rings true. By far the most credible portions of the book, are those that limn in – using the characters of McLeish's father, and his friend 'Old Red', as well as the Edinburgh Festival interlude – the utopian socialist Scots nationalism for which Gray himself is well known. Such is the intensity of conviction, and the way in which the authorial voice lurking over McLeish's shoulder addresses the ordinary reader, that this 'socialist unrealism' – if I may be permitted the coinage – is what carries the day. That, and a bellow of tortured identification with his own benighted fellow countrymen. As McLeish puts it: 'The truth is we are a nation of arselickers, though we disguise it with surfaces: a surface of generous, open-handed manliness, a surface of dour practical integrity, a surface of futile maudlin defiance . . .' It is these agonies of sad self-revulsion that elevate McLeish to the status of a personification of Scotland in 1982.

And if *1982, Janine* is the-book-of-the-state-of-the-nation, it is also the book of the state of its author. It would be invidious to detail all the correspondences between McLeish's life and experiences and those of his creator (aren't all fictions forms of emotional autobiography?), but suffice to say, they are there. Gray hadn't wanted to use an artist or a writer as his protagonist, but anyway, such models weren't available to him for a long time. It may seem strange, writing now in the eye of a thriving – if stormy – renaissance in Scots letters, but Gray himself didn't know more than one professional writer (Archie Hind) before the age of thirty-five. Placed in this context, the work and the life that went into the creation of this book – and Gray's first novel *Lanark* – was curiously unprecedented. It is by no means overly ambitious for Gray to have given this book a biblical format, because for him – and for the generation of Scots writers who was to follow – it was indeed a foundational text.

So, tumultuous, inventive, heart-rending. Both pre- and post-modern. A conventional narrative gussied up as an experimental work of fiction, which is at the same time a deeply experimental work hiding a little novella in the pleats of its skirt. A series of sadomasochistic fantasies, that reach their climax with the still, small voice of God. A landmark work for newly emergent Scots literature, and in my view one of the finest postwar novels in English. It is definitely one of the books I would choose to take to my desert island – and I already have. The name of the island is Britain.

Alasdair Gray, your friend in the south salutes you.

Will Self
London 2002

1: THIS IS A GOOD ROOM.

It could be in Belgium, the U.S.A., Russia perhaps, Australia certainly, any land where a room can have wallpaper, carpet and curtains patterned with three different sorts of flower. Brown furniture covers most of the flowers. There isn't much space between the wardrobe, the 1930s dressing-table, the chair with the tumbler of whisky on it, the double bed where I lie (not undressed yet) between a big carved Victorian headboard and footboard. There is also a modern washbasin, a nice bit of plumbing, the pipes sunk in the plaster instead of wriggling over it like in some rooms I've been. But there is no bible. All American hotel bedrooms have bibles so I am definitely not in the States. A pity. I hate feeling limited. I could be hundreds of men just now, a commercial traveller in wool or tweed, a farmer, an auctioneer, a tourist, one of those lecturers who appear in obscure halls to tell six middle-aged housewives and a retired police sergeant about the Impact of Van Gogh upon the Spotted Thrush during the Last Days of Pompeii. It does not matter how I earn my bread. The topic has ceased to sicken me, I don't think about it. I am not being mysterious. Behind the bluebells on these curtains is the main street of a town that was fairly prosperous when these bedknobs were carved – Nairn, Kirkcaldy, Dumfries, Peebles. It is actually Peebles or Selkirk. If it is Selkirk, this is Wednesday. If it is Peebles I will be in Selkirk tomorrow night, Janine.

Janine is worried and trying not to show it but she's been trying not to show it for a long time, so though she wants her voice to sound casual it comes out husky when she says, "How long till we get there?"
"About ten minutes," says the driver, a fat well-dressed man who stop. Stop. I should undress first.

My problem is sex, not alcohol. I am certainly alcoholic, but not a drunkard. I never stagger or stammer, self-control is perfect, the work is not affected. It's well-paid work, I needed an education to get it, but now I can do what is needed and even answer questions without thinking. Most work today can be done like that. If you lobotomised half the nation it would carry on as usual. The politicians do our thinking for us. No they don't.
"But Prime Minister, for the last twenty years the interest rate/inflation/unemployment/homelessness/strikes/drunkenness/breakdown of social services/crime/death in police custody have been steadily increasing, how will you tackle this?"
"I'm glad you asked me that, Michael. We can't change things overnight of course."
No, the only people who need to think nowadays are in stock exchanges and the central committees of some eastern communist parties. Nobody lasts long in those organisations without a bit of active cunning. The rest of us do what we're told and follow our leaders and so we should. What would happen if most people tried to act intelligently on their own behalf? Anarchy. Some trade unions try it. Read what the newspapers say about them. In Russia trade unions aren't allowed. So what can we do with this intelligence we don't need and can't use? Stupefy it. Valium for housewives, glue-sniffing for schoolkids, hash for adolescents, rotgut South African wine for the unemployed, beer for the workers, spirits for me and the crowd I left downstairs

fifteen minutes ago. But when I try to remember that crowd several loungebars come to mind, all with some wood-panelling, fake warmingpans, a door leading to a lobby leading to a street in Dundee or Perth or Peebles and all with people who say:
"And every month we have this searching approach to formal review."
"Formal review?"
"Yes. Formal review."
"You know the sort of man I am. I get an idea in the morning, I think it out in the afternoon. Next day I order the materials and the job's done by the end of the week. And if someone gets in the way I push past them. I push right past them."
"But you're straight. You're straight. People respect you for that."
"I don't care what their religion is as long as they're on the pill."
"HAHAHAHAHA. HAHAHAHAHA."
People who talk give themselves away all the time. I don't talk. I stand listening until their voices become a cheerful noise and then I want privacy. I want my bed, and Janine.

Janine is worried and trying not to show it but she's been trying not to show it for a long time so her voice is husky when she asks, "How long till we get there?"
"About ten minutes," says the driver, a fat well-dressed man called Max who looks happier with every minute that passes. He takes a hand from the wheel and pats her thigh reassuringly. She winces, then after a moment says, "You told me that in the office before we left."
"I've no idea of time, that's my trouble. But don't worry about me, worry about Hollis."
"Why? Why should I worry about Hollis?"
"Hollis is the recreation officer and you want the job, yes? But don't worry, you'll get it all right. You're dressed just right for Hollis."
"My agent told me to dress this way."
"Your agent reads Hollis like a book."
But Janine is not happy about the white silk blouse shaped by the way it hangs from her I must *not* think about clothes

before I've imagined Janine herself. But clothes keep trying to come first. Do I like women's clothes more than their bodies? Oh no, but I prefer their clothes to their minds. Their minds keep telling me, no thankyou, don't touch, go away. Their clothes say, look at me, want me, I am exciting. It would be perverse not to prefer their clothes to their minds. A woman in the loungebar downstairs, not young but good-looking, had buttoned flaps on her breasts and thighs and buttocks which seemed to be inviting my hands to fumble and undo her all over. I like the clothes women wear nowadays. When I was young most girls wore bright skirts and frocks which, along with their size and hair and breasts and voices, made them seem like superior, more delicate animals. I prefer them dressing like cowboys and carpenters and soldiers. Jeans, dungarees, boots and combat trousers don't look practical on them, but suggest they are ready to get down into the dirt with us men. I find that exciting. Some men, the unsuccessful lecherous kind (but we're all that kind) get angry with women who dress excitingly and say they deserve whatever happens to them. Meaning rape, of course. I don't agree though I know why they feel that way. They hate being excited by women they can't possess. But real women don't frustrate me because I have this dirty imagination. I have Janine, Superb, Big Momma and Helga. I also have a sense of justice. Yes, I need justice on my side. If Janine is going to deserve what happens to her she must do more than wear a silk shirt shaped by the way it hangs from her etcetera. Start earlier.

Janine, barefoot, is slightly smaller than most women but in her shoes she is slightly taller than most men and can be read sexually from a great distance: slender waist, knees and wrists, plump hips and shoulders, big etcetera and dark, copious hair expensively disarranged. She is clever in a fragmentary way, bad at judging people but good at judging her effect on them. With make-up she can look like almost any female stereotype from the dumb adolescent to the cool aristocrat. Just now she looks like Jane Russell in a forties film, *The Outlaw*: eyes dark and accusing, lips heavy and sullen. She looks sullenly across a desk at her agent who says

"Janine, you are wonderful when you keep your mouth shut. You are great in parts where you don't need to talk. But you will never, never, never be an actress."

She stares at him a little while longer then says in a low voice, "Last week you told me something different."

"Last week my judgment was upset by your . . . obvious charms. I'm sorry."

He shrugs his shoulders but doesn't look very sorry. He offers a cigarette. She takes it but ignores his offered lighter, using instead a match from her handbag. She inhales carefully then says, "Yes we've done a lot of things together in the last few days. Your wife can't have seen much of you, Charlie. How is she?"

"Janine, I have tried to get you work, you know I have. But who wants a talking actress whose voice has only one note?"

"I'm asking about your wife Charlie. The one you married three months ago, remember? Your second wife. How much alimony are you paying the first?"

"Listen, Janine, I'm your friend – "

"I'm glad, Charlie," she says, and names a sum of money. And adds, "Give me a cheque now so I can cash it before the banks shut. That will stop me phoning your wife for exactly one month. And if you don't get me work that pays good money by the end of the month I'll want another cheque for the same amount. Regard it as insurance against fresh alimony."

She leaves his office with the cheque in her handbag. At the door he says heavily, "Janine, let me see you tonight."

"Why Charlie, you're still interested in me, how sweet. But if you want call-girl service you'll have to pay extra now, and you can't afford it. So just you go home to your wife."

She is triumphant, this bad wee girl who certainly deserves a spanking. So does the agent, but he doesn't interest me, he's only there to make Janine believable. I was wrong when I said I needed justice on my side, all I need is revenge. On a woman. Revenge for what? The answer to that question has nothing to do with the pleasurable expansion of the penis. I refuse to remember my marriage. I will pour into the mouth of this head another dram of stupidity. The questioning part of this brain is too active tonight.

My problem is sex, or if it isn't, sex hides the problem so completely that I don't know what it is. I want revenge on a woman who is not real. I know several real women and if they got near my lovely, punishable Janine they would shame me into rescuing her. When I was a boy I rescued her all the time, she mainly existed for that. When I had freed her from the Roman arena, the pirates or the Gestapo, she vanished. I couldn't believe in her any more. She was a decent girl in those days, like the girls in my class at school, and I was decent too. But the balls sank into my scrotum, the wet dreams began, I gained a crude notion of what to put where, and now Janine has only one thing in common with the attractive women I know, she never stays long with me if she can leave. Apart from that she is fantastic: completely sexy and calculating and sure of herself. Real women can be sexy and calculating with a man, if they don't love him, but they are never sure of themselves. Inside they are like me, terrified, which is why they need to grab things. When women or men give away affection or money, and give easily without an eye on the future, these people (who can be quite plain and unsexy) are for that moment completely sure of themselves. The fools probably feel they will never die. But I am making a world where Janine's agent phones a day later and says in a bright, urgent voice,
"Would you like to meet a millionaire?"
"Tell me more, Charlie."
"There's a country-club just outside town, men-only membership, but respectable. And exclusive. Only big lawyers and property men can join, the kind who like to get away from the wife and kids now and then for a round of golf etcetera."
"What does etcetera mean?"
"Sauna, massage and good meal."
"Any women on the staff of this respectable men-only club?"
"That's why I'm calling you. Their recreation officer has signed up these broads to put on sexy floor shows. But they're amateurs and nobody in the place understands real showbusiness so the manager has contacted me. I've told him I'll find a professional to rehearse these girls for five or six weeks and get them performing some real smooth routines."

"What's he paying?"
Charlie tells her. She says, "But . . . I mean, for money like that they can get anybody! Somebody famous, I mean."
"Honey, they want someone efficient who won't draw attention to them. Remember those wives and kids. I have told them I might get them the director of *Caught in Barbed Wire*, and that she's a very discreet lady."
"But I never directed – "
"Of course you never directed it but they don't know that. The director's name didn't appear on the credits because there are no credits. Come to the office at three this afternoon and meet the club manager. If he likes you he'll take you to look the place over."
"Hm . . . How should I dress for him?"
He tells her. She says, "No professional director dresses like that!"
"Honey, I told you, these guys know nothing about show-biz. Dress like that and they'll be too busy looking to ask questions."
"The set-up stinks, Charlie."
"Don't worry, Janine, I'll find someone else," and he hangs up.

Broads. Real smooth routines. Honey. This set-up stinks. These people are American. Years out of date, perhaps, but American. I can't help it. Seen from Selkirk America is a land of endless pornographic possibility. Is that because it's the world's richest nation? No. There is less poverty and more sexual freedom in Scandinavia and Holland. It's because my most precious fantasies have been American, from Cowboys and Indians and Tarzan till . . . *The Dirty Dozen*? *Apocalypse Now*? I forget when I stopped needing new ones.
"Don't worry, Janine, I'll find someone else," and he hangs up. She dials back at once but the line is engaged. She dials repeatedly for three minutes and gets him at last. She says, "Charlie, I said the set-up stinks, but that doesn't mean I'm not interested. For money like that of course I'm interested!"
"Glad to hear it. You're in luck. I've been trying to get Wanda Neuman but she's out. All right, be here at eleven."

"Charlie, you mentioned a millionaire."
"That's right. The club has a couple of them, so dress like I said."
"What do they call this club?"
But again he has hung up.

Four hours later Janine is worried and trying not to show it but her voice is husky when she says, "My agent told me to dress this way."
"Your agent reads Hollis like a book."
But Janine is not (here come the clothes) happy with the white silk shirt shaped by the way it hangs from her etcetera I mean BREASTS, silk shirt not quite reaching the thick harness-leather belt which is not holding up the miniskirt but hangs in the loops round the waistband of the white suede miniskirt supported by her hips and unbuttoned as high as the top of the black fishnet stockings whose mesh is wide enough to insert three fingers I HATED clothes when I was young. My mother made me wear far too many of them, mostly jackets and coats. When I complained that I was too hot she said the weather could change any moment and *she* wasn't going to have me off school with a bad cold. I had three classes of suit. The best suit, the newest, was for Sunday and for visiting relations. The second-best suit was for going to school. The third was for "playing rough games". Yes, she expected me to play games, but I had to come home and change into my oldest suit first, and that was often too small to run about in comfortably. Of course when you're a child most games happen on the way home from school or in the playground, so this clothing programme reduced my social opportunities. We lived in a mining town where a lot of boys wore dungarees to school and could play when they liked. I envied them. In summertime some of them didn't even go home after school but rambled in gangs through the surrounding country, fishing and tree climbing, getting into trouble with farmers and coming home at sunset to grab their own supper of bread and cheese. Their mothers (my mother thought) didn't look after them properly. When the evening meal was finished and my father had gone out to a union meeting (he was a timekeeper at the pithead, a strong union man) I would start

changing into my oldest suit and my mother would say, "Have you done your homework yet?"

"No. I'll do it when I get back."

"Why not do it now, while you're still fresh?"

"The sun's shining, it's a nice evening."

"So you're determined to hew coal when you grow up?"

"No. But it's a nice evening."

"Hm!"

And she would fall silent. Her silences were very heavy. I could never pull myself from under them. I could never leave her alone in one, that would have been cruel. Drearily I would get out the school books and spread them on the kitchen table. She would sit by the fire with a piece of knitting or sewing and we would be busy on opposite sides of the room. The wireless would be playing very quietly ("and now the strains of *Kate Dalrymple* introduce Jimmy Shand and his band with thirty minutes of Scottish country dance music"). The room would grow lighter. Later she would brew a pot of tea and quietly lay on the table beside me a milked and sweetened cup of it with a chocolate biscuit in the saucer. Without lifting my eyes from the books I would grunt to show that I could not be so easily soothed, but inside I was perfectly happy. My happiest moments were passed with that woman. She kept me indoors but she never interfered with my mind. Between the pages of a book I had a newspaper clipping to carry my thoughts miles and miles away, an advert for *The Outlaw* – MEAN! MOODY! MAGNIFICENT! above a photograph of Jane Russell, her blouse pulled off both shoulders, leaning back against some straw glaring at me with this inviting defiance. My feelings were more than sexual. I felt grateful. I was amazed by myself. Nobody else, I realized, knew all the rich things I knew. The clean tidy room, the click of my mother's needles, Jane Russell's soft shoulders and sulky mouth, the evening sunlight over the town in the bend of the river where the colliers' sons were guddling trout, a mushroom cloud in the Pacific sky above Bikini atoll, Jimmy Shand's music and the taste of a chocolate biscuit were precisely held by *my* mind and by nobody else's. I was vast. I was sure that one day I would do anything in the world I wanted. I thought it likely that I would marry Jane Russell. I was ten or twelve at the time and believed sex and marriage were nearly the same thing. Now I am almost fiforget that forget that forget that where did I leave Janine?

In a fast car trying not to be afraid, her vulnerable breasts in a white silk shirt, accessible arse in a leather miniskirt, shapely thighs legs feet in black fishnet stockings and, ah! white open-topped shoes with stiletto heels. Standing up in them Janine is on tiptoe, she must raise and tighten her bum, press back her shoulders, lift her chin. Each shoe is tied on by three slender white thongs with small gold buckles which fasten straight across the toes, diagonally over the arch of the foot, and encircle the ankle so that (how happy I am) if the car slows or stops she can't slip them off, fling open the door and run. The car does slow, a little, leaving the freeway for a sideroad through a plantation of fir trees which cast a very cold shadow. "Nearly home!" says Max happily. The car stops before a tall gate in a security fence. Through the wires Janine can see a gatehouse and a patch of sunlight where a man in shorts, singlet and peaked cap is dozing in a deckchair. Max sounds his horn. The man stands, peers towards the car, salutes Max and enters the gatehouse.
"What kind of country-club is *this*?" asks Janine, staring at a board on the gate. It carries the name of a government district and FORENSIC RESEARCH ASSOCIATION. TRESPASSERS WILL BE PROSECUTED. GUARD DOGS. DANGER.
"The rich kind," say Max. "Our members are mostly lawyers and policemen, so for tax-avoidance purposes we pretend we are doing something useful."
"Neat!" says Janine, smiling for the first time that day.

The gate clicks and swings inward. The car passes the gatehouse and emerges from the trees on to an unfenced road curving over a golf-course. Tiny figures move on a distant green beside a white building with windows glittering in the afternoon sun. This is all so securely and expensively what Janine wants that she gives a little sigh of relief thinking, 'I'm an actress so I can't help imagining things.

Max, the lout, is excited, the lout, because I'm sexy, but that's natural, it needn't have bothered me. Did I sweat?' She takes a powder-compact from her handbag, gives her face a straight professional look in the mirror and puts it away thinking: nothing wrong there. Max chuckles.

"Admit," he says, "back there you thought I was a rapist white slaver, right?"

"Well, you said this place was just outside town. And well, it just isn't."

"I'm a bad judge of distance because my work demands that I travel a lot."

But Janine is not interested in Max and his work. She says, "How many members has your club?"

"Twelve."

"Twelve? But . . . I mean . . ."

"Ridiculous isn't it? Our staff outnumber us nearly five to one. But we like it that way. We can afford it."

The thought of such wealth makes Janine feel almost dizzy. The car stops on a bed of granite chips before some wide white steps. Max, quick on his feet, gets out and opens the door on her side wanting to take her arm, but Janine ignores him for now she is pleased with her shoes. Not many women could climb steps with dignity in nine-inch high heels. Janine does it, and when the glass doors at the top open automatically she steps firmly on to the blue carpet of the club foyer feeling she deserves a round of applause. Which is perhaps why the man walking toward her affects her like a round of applause. He is stout (not fat like Max) and soberly and expensively dressed, and he smiles at her, not in a boyish lecherous way (like Max) but with the mature admiration of someone who appreciates her exactly as she appreciates herself. He shakes her hand saying quietly, "Miss Janine Crystal."

She says, "Mr Hollis?"

Max laughs loudly and shouts, "Oh no, this is our president, Bill Stroud."

Stroud says, "Our recreation officer is not quite ready for you. I would like to discuss your salary and answer questions before you meet Hollis. But first of all, drinks and lunch perhaps? Do you wish to visit a washroom?"

"Thanks, but I'm fine. And yes, I'd like lunch, if that's all right. And . . . wow. I mean wow, this place is something special."

Another glass door has opened and they are crossing stop. Stop. I want rid of Max. Stroud says, "Max, you laugh too loud, you have enjoyed Miss Crystal's company enough for today. I am sure you can find someone to entertain you in the gymnasium."
Max's face goes expressionless. With a slight nod to Janine he walks quickly away. In the gymnasium Big Momma stands with no no no no no shortcuts. Take the long way round. I may be awake for hours.

Another glass door has opened and they (Stroud and Janine) are crossing the soft green carpet of a circular room which seems open to the sky, for the glass ceiling is only slightly tinted to soften the glare of the sun. There are low coffee-tables with magazines and armchairs, and to one side some small restaurant tables. A section of wall is a cocktail bar where a man on a high stool chats to a waitress. Elsewhere the room seems walled with palm trees and tall grasses which lean out over the carpet, and when Janine sits down with Stroud at a table set with cutlery for two she notices the door is hidden by greenery. She thinks, 'This is like a dream. I feel I'm sitting in a jungle.' Why the hell does Janine need all this interior decoration? I don't need it. I'm expected to stay in first-class hotels when I travel but I always choose small family places like this. I don't save money that way, my firm pays the bills, but I feel more at home in small hotels. Years ago in London a client took me for a business lunch in the Athenaeum, or was it the Reform Club? Anyway, there were chandeliers, marble pillars, real leather armchairs, a dome (I think) and waiters in evening dress. I acted perfectly calmly but inside I was hard, watchful, critical. Janine is also acting calmly but inside she has been warmed and softened by this luxury, she really loves it and I despise her for that. No I don't, but I would like to. She has no right to enjoy things I can't. She says aloud, "This is like a dream. I feel I'm sitting in a jungle."
"A comfortable jungle," says Stroud handing her a menu. "Not all parts of the club are so comfortable."

The menu is in French. She hands it back saying sweetly, "Please choose for both of us. I like anything that's nice."
Stroud says, "Suppose we begin with – "
I don't know French. Why quote what Stroud says? I'm losing interest. Drink. Think.

What did my mother think as we sat on opposite sides of the kitchen, and she knitted and I mixed profit-and-loss arithmetic with a stormy wooing of Jane Russell? I've never wondered what happened in her head before. She was a tall, rather quiet woman. All the neighbours trusted her, even those who disliked each other. She had a sharp sense of humour but listened carefully to what they said and seldom passed it on. While I was working and brooding near her my feelings of harmony, of luxury, were sometimes so strong that I am now nearly certain she was deliberately putting dreams into my head, dreams of power and possessions and far-ranging life. She managed her own life perfectly, as far as I could see, but didn't enjoy it much. Why do I think that? She only spoke to me about my homework and what clothes to wear. Except one Friday afternoon when I came home from school and she was at the door saying cheerful goodbyes to her closest friends, five women I had called "Auntie" when I was younger. They were leaving one of the gossipy little tea-and-biscuit parties women kept giving each other in those days. She was more silent than usual as she cleared away the cups, then suddenly muttered in a low, fierce voice, "I hate bloody women."
I was astonished. I said, "Why?"
"Have you ever heard them talk?"
I didn't answer. Since I was a baby I had heard them talk about their children, husbands, recipes, dress patterns and love-stories in the *Woman's Own* and *People's Friend*. What they said never interested me, but the noise of it was a comforting background music which I liked much more than male talk about sport and politics, which made a snapping, argumentative, menacing noise. But that was the only time I noticed my mother was not completely satisfied, before she oh forget it forget it forget it.

I know now that what was wrong with her was too much

energy and intelligence. Cleaning a room and kitchen, serving a husband and son, entertaining the neighbours did not use her up. I doubt if working in a shop, or as a secretary, would have used her up either. Or travelling around supervising the installation of security systems, like I do. A lot of nonsense is talked nowadays about "job satisfaction", as if many people could have it. The things which make most jobs bearable (not satisfying – just bearable) are extra, intoxicating ingredients like: pop music on a loudspeaker, a pay-cheque, hope of promotion, hope of a wild night of love. I take straight alcohol, which has started working again. My two heads are beginning to hum to each other, above and below. Good Penis! Good Doggie! Are you awake?
– Yes master.
Will you sit up and beg for meat again?
– Yes! If you show me something tasty.
Stroud signals to the waitress at the cocktail bar, a tall blonde who approaches in a languorous amble which emphasises the movement of her hips.

The tall blonde waitress must amble because her skirt won't let her walk any other way. It is a button-through white satin (no) white denim (no) white suede (yes) like Janine's, but longer, and so tight that although half unfastened her knees appear through the slit in front slowly, one after the other, and Janine can hear the soft rasp of her thighs pressing past each other, but it is not the skirt that strikes Janine with confusion. She thinks, "Silk blouse, net stockings, white high heels exactly like mine, yes even her mouth and eyes are made up just like mine, that's why she's staring at me that way. God, I hate these frigid bitches who dress like whores and then stare at me as if I was dirt."
But now the waitress takes pad and pencil from her waistband and attends completely to Stroud ordering the meal, and in spite of the girl's height and hair-colour Janine's feeling that she is watching *herself* increases, filling her with a numb, dreamy excitement. The excitement has a spice of fear in it but not much. If you wake late for work one morning, spring from bed, dress quickly, then rushing to the front door find it blocked by your car standing in the

middle of the living-room, the furniture moved back against the walls; if you discover this you will not feel afraid at first, you will think that you have not really wakened at all. And when a careful examination shows the car as solid as usual, and undoubtedly your own, because your key opens the door, and if you find the room solid too, with the wallpaper pattern undisturbed, making it unlikely that a jocular friend has suddenly become a millionaire and hired a team of expert workmen silently to knock a hole, insert the car, then swiftly reconstruct the wall exactly as it was – if the consistency of things shows you are in a world like the usual, apart from one inexplicable oddity – then only a pessimist will return to bed hoping to fall asleep and wake again in the usual world he understands. I would walk round the car, open the door and adventure out, fearful, of course, like all explorers in a strange world, but hoping for something new and better. I would have to see everything as a child does, letting the things themselves teach me what they were, knowing my grasp of them was secondary and slight. Why am I diluting an enjoyable wicked fantasy with this sort of crap? – like a publisher attaching a brainy little essay by a French critic to *The Story of O* to make the porn-eaters think they are in first-class intellectual company. How the waitress is dressed gives Janine a queer dreamy feeling, that's all I meant to say, Janine can't stop staring and when she ambles away Stroud chuckles and says, "She hates you."
"Why?"
"Jealousy. You're dressed like one of the staff but she's got to serve you as if you were a member."
"My agent told me to dress like this."
"He did? A pity. I thought you were delicately indicating that you wished to work here. I was pleased."
Janine notices a small plump quick waitress serving a man at a nearby table. The waitress can move quickly because her skirt is unbuttoned almost to the waistband. Stroud says, "All our waitresses and new girls dress like that. Hollis is something of a button-freak."
"Do Mr Hollis's preferences have to interest me?"
Stroud takes an envelope from his pocket and lays it on the table between them. He says, "Perhaps the time has come to talk about money. Would you open this and count what's

inside? If you join us it will be your first week's salary. If you decide to leave now it will be compensation for your trouble."

Janine hesitates then takes from the envelope a flat wad of clean new notes and counts them. The money is more than her agent suggested, more than Janine imagined possible. She knows Stroud is watching her closely. She thinks, 'If I was a cat I would lick my lips, but I'm an actress, and smart. There must be several millionaires in this club if they'll pay this money to get a girl like me on their books.'

She puts the notes back in the envelope and snaps it into her handbag saying, "I don't mind taking a friendly interest in Mr Hollis's preferences, if that's what you want."

Stroud smiles and says, "Then he'll be glad to see you any time."

And I have placed this last bit of dialogue very carefully. Later, when Janine is trapped and trying to escape, she will remember that she was given a chance to leave and refused because of money. We all have a moment when the road forks and we take the wrong turning. Mine was when Helen told me she was pregnant and I said I needed a week and later the doorbell rang and, forget it, I opened the door and Mr Hume and his two sons walked straight past me and, forget it, stood in the middle of my own room, yes, my own room and FORGET IT. FORGET IT.

"Do Mr Hollis's preferences need to interest me?"

The money. Count. Hide licklip. Look cool.

"I'll be glad to take a friendly interest in Mr Hollis's preferences, if that's what you want."

The meal, then audition time, and Stroud is ushering her along a softly lit brown-carpeted corridor to a door marked *recreation room* which he opens, standing aside to let her through, and entering she is dazzled by lights from low down shining straight into her face. She senses a wide dim space on each side, a desk ahead with one or two people silhouetted against the white sources of the light, a continuous purring noise, perhaps a film projector? She looks back to the door as it shuts with a double click. No Stroud. A voice cries, "Come on in, Miss Crystal, show us how you can walk."

Heart thudding, eyes narrowed to slits against the glare she walks slowly toward the light thinking, 'Act calm. I felt like this in the car with Max, and with Stroud when I saw the waitress, but I acted calm and it was all right.'

She hears two unfastened studs of her skirt click with each step she takes.

"That's a sexy sound," the voice says, and giggles.

'Keep cool,' thinks Janine. 'Pretend this is an ordinary audition.'

End of first part.

2:THIS IS SPLENDID.

2:THIS IS SPLENDID. I have never before enjoyed such perfect control. I have abandoned Janine at the exact moment when I nearly got too excited, and I have remembered nobody real except my mother who never spoils my dramas by making me ashamed of them. Why? Because I am now exactly the man she wanted me to be – heavily insured with a company car when I require one, expense account, index-linked pension and no connection atall with the real women she would have despised: Helen, and Sontag, and the editor, and the whore under the bridge, and my first of all girlfriend o, forget *her*. I have total security at last, security until death. If there is not a revolution first. And there won't be. We will go to war before we have that so there is plenty of time (if I am careful and keep perfect control) plenty of time to order and taste all the imaginary women on my mental menu. An astounding achievement, if I manage it. A secret miracle known to only me.

Most pornography fails by not being dramatic enough. There are too few characters. The author has only one sort of climax in mind, and reaches it early, and can only offer more of the same with variations which never excite as much again. Even in *The Story of* O, with its long slow drugged-sounding sentences twisting softly round the heroine like furry snakes, I never enjoyed anything which came later as much as the first two pages. To preserve excitement without masturb (I hate that word) without shooting my load (I hate that phrase) (I hate the *thing*, I hate orgasm, I'm lonely afterward) to preserve excitement my Janine must travel toward her climax through a world like a menacing forest, and just before she reaches it I must switch to heroines in other parts of the forest, women travelling toward climaxes which are different, but connected. I will work like a historian describing in turn Germany Britain France Russia America China, showing depression and dread growing within each for domestic reasons, but distracted by challenges and threats from abroad until the heads of government move to their controls in the hidden bunkers, and make certain declarations, and then the tanks start rolling through the streets with evacuations, concentration camps, explosions, firestorms, frantic last-minute propaganda and the awful togetherness of total calamity before the last, huge, final, bang. *That* is how a big piece of pornography should go. Sadistic? It would be, if de Sade were not so disappointing. He gives much the same masturbatory climax on every tenth page and fills the space between with a lot of pretentious excuses about nature being ruthless and cruel so why should we not be? Blethers. Nature is nothing but a name for the universe and how it behaves. You need ideas to be cruel and only men have ideas. Parts of the universe bump and break each other but storms and earthquakes are not cruelty. Not even animals are cruel. Yes, cats hurt mice for fun sometimes, but only because they are pampered parasites with a hunter's instinct and no need to eat what they catch. It is men who have made cats cruel. Only man is evil. So now I will visit one of my imaginary mice in another part of the forest oh, a great cruel gamekeeper, me.

Superb is my nickname for her, being short for superbitch. But she needs an ordinary name too. I fancy something short and coarse, like Joan. Or Terry. She washes and dries her long black hair then phones her mother. She says, "Mother, hello. I'm not coming tonight."

After a moment her mother says, "Thanks for telling me."

"Mother, listen, you're the only one I can trust. You see I've met this . . . this man. He's the best thing that ever happened to me. He makes me feel a real . . . woman, you know? So I'm not visiting you. I'm going to stay with him for three whole days."

"Why tell me all this?"

"Because I want Max to think I'm with you, like I arranged."

"So?"

"He might phone and ask for me. He's pathetically dependent when he isn't talking to the press about tougher penalties for lawbreakers and wider powers for the police."

"So what do I say if he phones?"

"Tell him I'm resting, put the receiver down, wait a couple of minutes, then pick it up and tell him I've a headache and don't feel like talking. He'll believe you. That's what our marriage is like nowadays."

After a while her mother says, "Terry, I don't like Max, you know that. He's a male chauvinist fascist bastard as I told you when you got engaged to him – "

" – And you were right mother so when I met – "

" – so why not leave him? If the marriage is so bad why not clear out?"

"Mother, I've no money. You walked out on father but you're a businesswoman. You're able to support yourself."

"Come and work for me. You type, I can always use a typist."

"Mother, you know that's impossible. I can't stand being bossed, even by you. If Max decides to divorce me, fine. He can afford big alimony. But he's got to blame himself for it, not me. He mustn't know I've been fooling around . . . Are you listening?"

Her mother says something in a low voice. Terry says, "I didn't catch that."

"Forget it."

"Did you say I was a selfish, frigid little bitch?"

"That's right."

"I'm not, I'm not little atall. And I'm not frigid either. Two

weeks ago I thought I was but that was before I met Charlie. The point is, can I depend on you? If Max phones, will you make the right noises?"
"I suppose so."
"Thanks, mother, that's all I need to know."
Superb puts the receiver down. What a splendid bitch I am making her.

She lifts her legs on to the bed, shifts about till she's lying comfortably, then phones again. She says, "Charlie, it's all right. I'm coming."
Charlie says, "Honey, that's good. When?"
"I'll leave in just sixty minutes."
"Why not now?"
"I've this husband, you know. He likes us to eat together. We don't do much else together."
"How do you look?"
"Fresh and clean. I've had a bath and I'm wearing new jeans. I took half an hour getting into them, I had to lie on the floor and pull and pull and pull. So don't say I don't love you."
"What about the top?"
"Nothing special. White silk blouse."
"No bra?"
"Of course I've a bra."
"Honey, you've got to take it off."
"You bad mad boy!"
"Terry, when I open the door to you tonight, the blouse yes, the bra no. Take it off in the car on the way here."
"What will you give me if I do that?"
"Everything you want."
"You can't, Charlie. You've got the energy, and the dirty mind, but there's only one of you."
He laughs and says, "You're a comedian, Terry. One day I'll have you performing professionally."
"Don't go on about that, Charlie. I'm no actress. The only performances you'll get from me will be strictly private and exclusive, like tonight."
"I'm going to surprise you, though. I'm going to turn you into a professional. And you'll love it."
"Charlie, I have to go. Max will be here any moment. See you in just two hours."

"No bra, remember."
She laughs, kisses the receiver and puts it down. Helen never talked like that, she was too inhibited.

Superb leaves the bed, pulls on her silver wedge-heeled sandals, I never talked like Charlie, I was too inhibited, pulls on her gold wedge-heeled sandals and stands examining herself in a tall mirror. The woman who stares appraisingly back is, no doubt at all, not a young woman, but a very very exciting woman. She thinks, 'Calm down. Get the dinner ready. It's too soon to get high.'
She goes downstairs and Max is sitting in the lounge staring at the blank TV screen. This worries her for a moment though he is nowhere near the telephone extension. She says sharply, "I didn't hear you come in!"
"Why? What were you doing?"
"Phoning mother."
She goes into the kitchen. He follows and stands listlessly in the doorway while she sets a salad briskly on the table.
He says, "Please, Terry. Stay here tonight."
"You know mother is expecting me, Max."
"Terry, I'm begging you to spend this weekend with me."
"Why?"
"I feel you're avoiding me."
"Whose fault is that?"
"Maybe I'm not the greatest lover in the world – "
"Right. You're not."
" – but I'm the man you married. Surely with some co-operation – "
"Mother expects me, Max. Sometimes you spend a week-end doing forensic research and I spend a weekend with my wonderful sympathetic mother. It's too late to talk me out of it. My case is packed and in the car."
They sit down to eat. He says, "I'm checking the car in for an overhaul tomorrow."
"But you got a replacement? Surely."
"Yes, it's in the garage."
"So what's the problem?"

They eat in silence but Superb is excited and sneaks a glance at her reflection on the darkness outside the window.

She is struck by its contrast with the reflection of Max sitting opposite. She thinks, 'Not forty yet, just three years older than me but a tired old man already. He and I could belong to different generations. I'm as young as Charlie is, the way I look just now. Charlie could have plenty of young women but he doesn't need them, doesn't want them with me available. He's lucky. So am I.'

Why does this imaginary stuff seem familiar?

IMPORTANT DIFFERENCES BETWEEN SUPERB AND MY FORMER WIFE.

1 Superb has long black hair. Helen had light brown.

2 Superb (though not fat like Big Momma) is a plain well-built woman with big etceteras. Helen was, is, she isn't dead, more slender, more elegant, slightly haggard when depressed but beautiful when I first saw her, beautiful when she left me twelve years ago.

3 Superb has a sharp tongue. Helen went quiet when she was hurt or angry.

4 Superb is a greedy sexy bitch who knows how to get what she likes. Helen was a gentle woman I want not to remember, shy of sex and with no greedy appetites (could I be wrong about that?)

5 Superb is imaginary. Helen was real. Why can't I keep them apart?

'Not forty but a tired old man already.'

(And now I'm almost fiforget that.)

Not forty but yes, Helen saw me as a tired old man good for nothing but his job. Security installation, an expanding field. I looked tired and uninteresting to her because she looked tired and uninteresting to me. We were killing each other quietly, gently, in the respectable Scottish way. The wife-beaters and rabid bitches are mostly among our unemployed and poorly paid. Then Helen met whatsisname and grew younger yes, and beautiful yes, and I was growing interested in her again when forget all that.

She was right to leave me but forget all that because Superb is a greedy bitch with long black hair and a well-built sensual body whose arse is deeply cleft and she wears these tight jeans which show it and she is thinking, 'Charlie could have plenty of young chicks but he doesn't need them with me available. Yes, I'll take off this bra in the car like he said, he deserves that, we'll meet with no boring preliminaries like: What sort of day did you have?'

Max asks quietly, "Why dress like a whore?"

She stares at him. He says quietly, "Why dress like a whore to visit your mother? You can't tell me those jeans are comfortable."

With an effort she manages to say just as quietly, "It happens, yes, that these jeans are very comfortable. And very fashionable. And I happen to feel good in them. I'm sorry you don't like that. You've no doubt seen a lot more whores than I have – "

"You're right. They look like you."

" – Coarse language doesn't suit you, Max. You're too much of a momma's boy. And I'm a momma's girl so you know where to phone me if you think up some last-minute insult you'd like me to hear."

She gets up at once and opens the door leading to the garage. He follows her. She feels her face flushed, her heart thudding, the question "Why dress like a whore?" resounds in her head. She thinks how she looks from behind, strutting on tiptoe on the steep-soled sandals, buttocks thrust back toward him under the tight white denim. She hears him say, "Terry, I'm sorry I said that. You look great. Really great. I just wish you'd stay the weekend."

She stops and looks at a sparkling new pale-grey Mercedes. She sighs loudly and says in a weary voice without looking at him, "The keys."

He hands her the keys. She opens the door and says, "Get my case from the back of the Ford."

She gets into the driving seat. He fetches a case and lays it on the seat beside her. He starts to say something which she interrupts with a firm, "Good night Max."

He raises the garage door and touches the switch that opens the gate at the end of the drive. She can see him in the car mirror, standing looking after her in the lit garage doorway and getting smaller and smaller until she turns on to the road, and that is the last she sees of him for at least a month. A month that feels like several years. But she hears from him much sooner than that.

Half an hour later she stops the car in a lay-by. Some trucks whip past on the road and when their lights fade she crouches down, unbuttons blouse, slips it off, removes bra then slips on blouse again, fastening just the two lowest buttons. Can I now have her sit back and light a cigarette, smoking with one elbow out of the window (it's a warm night) and feeling the cool silk support her breasts? Yes. The row with Max has upset her, she wants to calm down, she thinks, 'Let Charlie wait another five minutes, it'll make him that much keener.'

How long has she known Charlie?

A week, and now her life is an adventure.

Have they made love yet?

No, and never will, though wearing a mask he will rape her in an hour or two if I keep control of the situation.

Where did she meet him?

At a singles club like the one in Motherwell where I was too nervous to speak to anyone. But Superb is in America rich and free. She wants adventure and joins a dramatic society no no no a yoga group in a town with a singles club. After three or four weeks, when she feels Max is used to her yoga evenings, she visits the club instead. Charlie approaches. He tells her, over drinks, that he is a theatrical agent, that she looks really good, and asks if she has ever thought about becoming an actress. She laughs at him and says, "There's no need to hand me that crap. I like you without it. I think you look good too."

Are women ever as direct and open as this?

Not British women. Not Scottish women. We are all timid and frigid here.

Could I be wrong?

Yes. Confident, tactful, attractive men can inspire openness in women anywhere. Courage encourages courage. I once had a good friend who taught me that. Nobody else ever taught me that. The parents and educators of this damned country teach cowardice, herding us toward the safest cages with the cleanest straw. If I had a clever son I'd be terrified if he showed signs of courage, especially if he was honest too. People in charge nowadays don't want clever brave honest men, they want security systems. I'm clever but a coward and as dishonest as the rest of us, I've never been unemployed. And my Superb, this adventuress, smokes and remembers how she met Charlie and is not greatly worried when she hears a car pull in behind her, especially when she sees it is a police car.

A police car pulls in behind her. Two men get out and walk forward with their hands on their guns (this is America). (But it could be Ulster.) One of them says, "Janine Crystal!"

"That's not my name."

"Get out, Janine. And keep your hands well in sight."

"You're making a mistake," she says sharply, but opens the door and gets out. She is puzzled but not alarmed. Max is a policeman. If she gives his name and phone number they'll check with him and let her go. But it will ruin the weekend. She is not on the road to her mother's house, how can she explain that to Max? A white beam of torchlight strikes her face. Dazzled she feels something cold snap round her wrist, the other wrist is wrenched back and with another cold snap her arms are handcuffed behind her. "Pigs! Bastards!" she hisses as the lightbeam lowers to explore her body, breasts nude under tight silk, no, tight satin. Let her also be wearing a long scarlet belt of the sort that goes tight round the waist once, leaving enough leather to loop loosely a second time. The second loop lies like a necklace on the mound of her belly snug in its white denim why have women's stomachs had so little erotic publicity compared with bums etcetera? The slimming adverts keep telling them to get *flat* stomachs. All right in men, I wish I had a flat stomach, but a *woman* with a flat stomach? Ugh. The sweetest line in the world was the profile of forgethername's belly curving out suddenly from her navel then down in a swooping line to oh, I can never go there again, never never never again. Entering there was such sweet homecoming, I can never go home again. But Superb's thighs, how is she standing? Astride, of course, weight mainly on right leg. The jeans are short and show a lot of ankle, she has a couple of silver bangles on one. Her gold, no her silver wedge-heeled sandals are open-toed to expose nails varnished a bright cherry scarlet. Her face? Astonished, enraged, like Jane Russell again, I can't avoid Jane, but ah! new earrings have just occurred to me. Each delicate lobe is pierced by four slender silver hoops of different sizes, the largest 7 inches across, the smallest 1½. I love her like this.

I love her like this and wish I could prolong the fantasy of possessing her without putting her into increasingly complicated and perverse positions. I wish I could excite myself with memories of real lovemaking. Sontag could excite herself that way. She told me she masturbated by caressing herself while remembering a nice time with a former lover. But my past is a pit full of regrets. My few nice memories of love with real women conjure up remorse and rage at what I have lost so the policeman with the torch chuckles and says, "She certainly isn't hiding anything."

The other says, "Will I make sure of that?"

"Yeah. Take your time."

And although Superb wriggles, curses and spits, strong fingers thrust slowly into pockets over her buttocks and breasts, pockets with hardly room in them for a credit card. Does this contact stimulate her nipples? I doubt it. In porny literature nipples erect anywhere, any time at the slightest touch, but I can't remember nipples having a part in my own lovemaking, not even with forgethername during that summer when we were so busy and happy together. Wait. The editor, yes, though not fat had breasts so plump that her nipples were sunk in them and were only found after a while like lost little islands, each the tip of a submarine mountain in a bland globe of ocean. When discovered and gently tickled sometimes (not always) they did indeed increase and arise. Let Superb be so ignorant of her body that she is appalled to discover her nipples erecting pleasurably at the policeman's touch. She goes icy calm and says harshly, "Is this why you joined the force?"

"No, lady, it's just one of the fringe benefits."

He lets her go, walks to the car and looks inside. The other policeman is speaking into a walkie-talkie set: "We've got the car all right, and the woman, I think. Her clothes don't match the description but she could have changed, of course."

"Hey, look at this!" shouts the other, waving Superb's brassière, "it was on the front seat."

"Right, we're bringing her in," says the man to the walkie-talkie. Walkie-talkie sounds British and out of date. There must be a newer name for it which I can't remember. Disconcerting.

She is pushed into the back seat of her own car which is driven off by the policeman who searched her. She says once or twice, "You're making a mistake," and gets no answer atall. She decides to mention Max as soon as she thinks of a story to tell him about how she got to where she was arrested, unless the mistake can be corrected at the police station. What if she phones Charlie from there and he comes in and testifies that she is not and never has been a woman called Janine? There is no danger of anyone knowing her at the station, she has never let Max introduce her to his professional colleagues. Meanwhile her nipples tingle with embarrassment at the thought of being gaped at by a lot of strange policemen, possible? I don't know, I hope so. These thoughts occupy her so completely that when the car stops she has not seen that the building beside it, and the door she is pushed through, lack the surroundings and sign of a usual police station.

But she is led across a hall with MISSING and REWARD FOR INFORMATION posters on display, and into an office containing three desks. A small stout man sits telephoning at one, a big woman types at another, the policeman escorting Superb puts her suitcase on the third, he has carried it from the car. He says, "Here she is, chief."
The small stout man puts down the receiver, smiles and says, "Hullo Janine."
"That is not my name."
"Can you prove that?"
"Yes of course I can, but . . ." she hesitates, thinks a little then says, "Listen, if you knew my name you'd definitely let me go. I can promise that. My husband is a very important man. He rented me this car a couple of hours ago from some garage, you must be looking for the previous user. But I don't want him to know I'm here, he has heart trouble, the doctors say he must not be upset or troubled in any way. I can ask my mother and a friend to come here and identify me if

you like, but since this is all a mistake I don't see why it's necessary. Show me to anybody who knows this Janine woman and they'll tell you she definitely isn't me."

"So you'd like to take part in an identity parade."

"Yes. I suppose so. Yes."

"Good. I was arranging one for you when you arrived just now."

This man (who is Stroud, yes, Stroud) stands, comes round the desk, leans on the front of it and lights a cigarette, watching her closely. She says, "Please take these things off my wrists."

He smiles at her in an amused, friendly way and shakes his head meaning: No. He clearly enjoys the sight of her like this, she blushes hot but feels she must keep talking and says, "You can at least tell me what I'm charged with, I mean what this Janine person is charged with."

"Theft," says Stroud, "and drug-pushing. And murder. And whoring. But the last isn't so important."

Superb stares at him. He mentions the town where Max works and says, "Know it?"

"Yes I know it."

"Know the chemist at the end of Main Street?"

"No. There are several chemists on Main Street."

"He's a nice old man who patronises the more specialised kind of call-girl. His favourite, Janine Crystal, plays all kinds of kinky tricks on him. She was seen going into his shop at lunchtime and soon after he shut up shop for the day. An hour ago he was found in his backroom, dead by suffocation. A lot of important drugs are missing from his store, also twelve thousand dollars in cash which he removed from his bank this morning, nobody knows why."

Do I find these details interesting? No. Go faster.

"Also twenty thousand dollars in cash which he removed from his bank this morning, nobody knows why. Do you find these details interesting?"

"I find them fascinating, really fascinating," says Superb sarcastically, "But they have nothing to do with me."

"You've nearly convinced me of that. Janine always carries a big suitcase when she visits her clients. Do you mind if my colleague looks through yours?"

"She can look all she likes," says Superb, "I only hope her hands are clean."
The woman opens the case and slowly unpacks it, holding up each article for a moment before laying it down. Superb sees her take out and lay aside housecoat, nightgown and bedroom slippers, and thinks, 'Soon I'll be out of here. Maybe in an hour I'll be with Charlie again.'

She thinks, 'Maybe in an hour I'll be with Charlie again,' then her skin tingles and a dreamlike feeling comes to her, for the woman is holding up a white denim, no white suede button-through skirt – surely that isn't hers? – and she puts it down and holds up black fishnet stockings, suspender-belt and black halter bra. And impossibly high-heeled black shoes. And straps with buckles. And a black leather hood with zips. And a cane. And bottles with pills and powders in them, with paper packets carefully labelled. And a large roll of money. Superb hardly notices the way the others are looking at her. She hears her voice say automatically, "My name is Terry Hunsler, my husband is Max Hunsler the police superintendent for the fourteenth division. Please contact him and tell him where I am."
Stroud chuckles and says, "You're a real actress Janine but it's time you relaxed a little. Look after her, Momma. Get her ready for the parade."
Superb leans forward, frantically shaking her head and tugging at the bracelets binding her wrists. Low cries pour from her lips: "No no no," she moans, "please no!"
"Yes yes yes honey, but don't fret about it," says a soft rich husky voice, and between the strands of hair that hang over her tearwet face Superb sees the woman Stroud has called Momma walking toward her looking like the biggest woman in the world. Huge wide hips and thighs are churning slowly toward Superb under a blue denim skirt that seems as large as a belltent, but the head above the great plump shoulders is small and young like a little girl, a greedy little girl who has just seen a plate of tempting cakes at a party. But she is looking at Superb. End of second part.

3:DAMN SONTAG FOR LAYING WASTE NEARLY ALL MY SEXUAL FANTASIES. She was so knowing, so inquisitive, such a determined instructress. She saw herself as a sexual missionary to Scotland. I was Scotland, something frozen and dumb which she was going to liberate. "Tell me about that," she would say greedily, "it is important to know. Besides, it is such fun. Come, whisper to me, I cannot be shocked. What is it you would really enjoy? I may even dress up for you."

I could not tell her at first. I wanted to keep fantasy and reality firmly separate because surely that is the foundation of all sanity? And my highly unsatisfactory sex life with Helen ended when she learned some of the things I imagined doing when we were lovemaking. But Sontag refused to take my silence for an answer. At last I told her I had a mad passion for small children. This was untrue, but I found it less frightening to tell a lie than admit to a woman that I had a mad passion for women. She was very excited by this and pestered me for details which I could not possibly imagine. At last she said, "You have deliberately misled me," and frowned for a long time with one finger pressing her lower lip. Then she sighed and said, "Come, I will make it easy for you. We will begin at the beginning. What is the first sexual excitement you distinctly remember? I am referring to infancy of course."

Infancy! I was about to tell her I had no sexual excitements as an infant when I remembered a very odd dream from when I was five or four or maybe even three. I imagined I was in a gang of boys of my own age who were riding across country on the shoulders of grown men. We made these men race each other, striking them with sticks to drive them faster, and I took special delight in forcing my man to jump the biggest ditches and plunge through the thorniest hedges. I cannot remember if this was a sleeping dream or a daydream but the feeling of exciting power it gave me was certainly erotic. I thought Sontag would find this homosexual revelation more interesting than my pretended paedophilia but she merely said, "Oedipal. Typical. Now tell me the earliest fantasies you had of intercourse with your mother."

I burst out laughing which made her very angry. She could never understand why I found her ridiculous when she felt most logical. She prided herself on her logical powers. Was she French or German? Her father was one, her mother the other. She told me that as a young girl, a week after her first menstrual bleedings, her mother took her to a doctor and, though it was illegal, bribed him into fitting Sontag with a contraceptive coil. This was before the days of the pill. As they left the surgery her mother said to her, "Now you may behave as stupidly as you wish."

That was logical of the mother but must have been very chilling, very isolating for Sontag. She was about ten years younger than me but sometimes, when she grew silent, I noticed her face take on a lonely, pinched, ancient look. There was not much warmth in her. Her conversation, especially conversation with women friends, was mostly hectic gossipy analysis and speculation about love affairs. They went into great psychological and even anatomical detail, but without much humour or sympathy. They sounded like men discussing football or politics. Would my mother have found that sort of chatter more interesting than the cosy gossip of the aunts, who never said a harsh word about their husbands and never admitted sex existed outside the lives of film actors? I think she would have heard it with the same silent contempt.

I was a locked box to Sontag, something to be prised open so that she could pick out the contents one at a time, label them and fling them away. No. That is unfair, she only threw away the parts she tired of. I'm grateful to her, she became Janine for me. "Yes, buy these clothes and I will wear them," she said. I wanted her to linger with me for hours around shops, discussing this and that until we both agreed upon what was nicest and I paid for it. But, "I cannot waste time on that kind of thing," she said, "you have my measurements. You must do it all yourself."
I visited several women's shops with the same sense of terror and trespass which I bring to obscene bookshops. I wanted to buy her a button-through denim skirt, but they were out of fashion that year. At last I found a shop run by a man who made leather clothes to order, and he had a specimen white suede miniskirt better than anything I ever imagined and just the right size for Sontag. She hears the two unfastened studs click with each step she takes. "That's a sexy noise," the voice says and giggles. I've been through that bit. Sontag became Janine for me and I should be grateful, we enacted a very jolly little rape together. I didn't hurt her, I don't hurt people but. I loved feeling ruthless and in charge for once. And afterwards, when I lay completely emptied, she said, "I must warn you not to become too preoccupied with these fantasies, they are likely to bore me very soon."
Honest woman. I wish she had been more of a prostitute. I would have paid Sontag anything to enjoy again in the flesh that illusion of ABSOLUTE MASTERY which real life has never never never allowed me in any way whatsoever. Sontag became Janine for me, briefly, but she refused to become Superb.

She refused to become Superb whose mind is full of Max. *Max put my case in the car*, she thinks, *Max planted those things in it, Max has planned all this, Max knows about Charlie*, and the thought fills Superb with such numb astonishment that

she hardly hears the big woman say, "They call me Momma because I take such good care of my girls."
She is marching Superb along a softly lit brown-carpeted corridor by a hand which grasps her shoulder firmly but caressingly. The other hand carries the suitcase. She says, "Aren't you glad to get away from all these men? I didn't like the way there were looking at you, Janine."
"My name is Terry!" says Superb through clenched teeth.
"Keep talking like that," says Momma, giggling, "it's sexy. It suits you."
"You are absolutely wrong about lesbians," said Sontag when I told her this bit, "we are not atall hard and cruel."
We, Sontag?
"Yes. Half my lovers have been women. These affairs are less exciting than with the opposing sex but they are more comfortable. I sleep and eat too much and get fat during them."
Shut up Sontag, I insist that a fat cruel lesbian procuress disguised as a policewoman pushes my superb tightjeaned tightbloused superbitch through a door, locks it behind them, then drops the key in a bulging pocket of her denim skirt. Can I have that skirt unbuttoned a little? Yes, enjoy yourself, have it unbuttoned enough to show the insides of her thighs when she stands astride but try not to get too excited.

The room. Some mats and cushions lie on a polished modern floor marked with yellow lines. A long wall of big mirrors doubles its apparent breadth. Near the door is a desk with two telephones. "This is our paradeground," says Momma, going to the desk and placing the case on it, "you'll stand with your toes on that yellow line, and we'll get some other chicks to stand beside you, then we'll bring a witness to tell us if you're the bad girl we think you are."
"Let me speak to a lawyer," says Superb unsteadily, "I'm entitled to a lawyer."
"At this stage hookers like you don't need lawyers," says Momma, opening the case.
"I'm not a hooker!" cries Superb but Momma lifts out the suede miniskirt and looks at it affectionately, shaking her

head and saying, "Wow. For a non-hooker you own some real professional gear."

Is gear an American word? It doesn't matter, don't stop because, "That isn't mine!" says Superb, trying to keep hysteria out of her voice. "My husband, Max, planted it on me, he must have! He must have!"

"So you've never worn it?"

"Never. Never."

"Let's have some fun. Give me a thrill. Try it on and see if it fits."

Superb, wide-eyed, shakes her head meaning: no. Momma takes skirt, stockings, suspender-belt which is that lacy kind advertised in the highbrow colour supplements, crumples them together, tosses them to the floor at Superb's feet then goes behind her and murmurs in her ear, "Like me to remove these handcuffs?"

And Superb, wide-eyed and numb with terror, shakes her head slightly meaning: no. Because suddenly the wrists linked behind her feel like security, for what may her hands have to do when they are free? In a wallmirror she sees herself standing straight upright, legs pressed tight together, very white against the dark blowsy figure of Momma standing astride behind her, deftly unbuckling the red belt and letting it slide to the floor. Then Momma caresses Superb's breasts through the silk of the blouse. Does she fondle Superb's nipples? Do they erect at Momma's touch? Indeed she does and indeed they do. Yet Superb trembles and cries, "No! Please!" on two sharp notes like cries of pain. "Just look at you in that mirror," whispers Momma, "standing there so sweet and scornful. I bet you give that husband of yours one hell of a time. But you're too stiff, honey, it's good you came here. We'll teach you to relax. We'll have you bending like a flower in the wind," and if there is no lesbian like Big Momma in the world then there is no God either because there ought to be, "We'll have you swaying like a flower in the wind," whispers Momma and slowly pulls the blouse off Superb's superb brown shoulders, then suddenly drags it down and leaves it a wreath of crumpled white silk around Superb's hips. Superb sees herself brown and nude to the waist. (Why brown? Suntan. This is in California.) She sees herself brown and nude to the waist, each heavy breast sagging sideways with its own sweet weight, sweet is a word I use too often. She stands exposed like a slave in a market, brown and nude to the waist, what is her hair like, apart from black and thick? A wild tangle framing her face, the silver earrings glittering in it, the mass of it spread halfway down her back. I want to thrust my face into that hair and tug it with my hands but I can touch no part of her because she is imaginary. Only Momma can touch that nude sweet scornful body because Momma is imaginary too, so Momma unlocks the handcuffs, and Superb covers her breasts with her freed hands, and Momma kneels behind her and reaches round Superb's sweet belly to unzip her jeans. A telephone starts ringing.

A telephone on the desk starts ringing because I refuse to let Momma have more fun with Superb than I do. Momma groans, stands up, goes to desk, lifts telephone, sighs and says, "Yeah?" and a moment later tells Superb, "This call is for you."

Superb stares at her.

"I said, it's for you. Come here. Take it."

Superb approaches, shivers, takes receiver. A male voice says, "Terry, it's me, are you all right?"

"Max," says Superb weakly, "Max," and starts laughing wildly, then stops and says unsteadily, "Max?"

"How are you, Terry?"

"Max, you know where I am? You know what's happening here?"

"Only in a general way," says Max.

"Max, what kind of police station is this? When will they let me out? What are you trying to do?"

"I'm trying to save our marriage, Terry."

"Max . . . You're insane."

"No, but I'm desperate. I nearly lost you tonight, Terry. I pled with you not to go, remember? I put off doing this till the last possible moment, because I love you, Terry. That's why I can't stand to be with you during your course of treatment. It would upset me too much. But it's the only thing that can save our marriage."

His voice aches with sincerity. Sontag was furious when I

told her this bit. She shouted, "What compels you to invent such a despicably feeble villain?"
I shrugged my shoulders. She picked at her lower lip with a finger and said, "I begin to understand you. Your dreadful mother, in her efforts to make you a member of the middle classes, destroyed your capacity for male companionship. She desolated your homosexual potential. How unfortunate. You lack the balls to invent a villain worthy of your villainettes."
Give me TIME Sontag. I've a wicked Doctor in mind.
"I cannot hang around for ever listening to these stories, I have my own life to lead. Phone me in a week, perhaps. I am still quite fond of you."
But Max says, "I love you, Terry. I'm with you in spirit, so please remember that no matter how bad things get they'll come right in the end. Perhaps I should ring off now."
But Superb whispers into the receiver, "Don't go, Max, please, please get me out of here," because

Because Big Momma has taken off her denim waistcoat and blouse. Brassière too? Yes, let these huge globes swing freely as she strips off skirt, shoes, pantihose. No knickers. She fastens on the skirt again by the waistband, why am I so keen on unfastened buttons? The answer is obvious as she stands astride astride, lovely word, astride astride so that Superb can see the great rough triangular bush of golden-brown furze between her pendulous belly and cunt. For Momma is blonde, the only blonde I know with close-cropped ash-blonde hair on her small round girlish-looking head and a triangular bush of golden-brown furze. And her girlish face smiles sweetly as she lifts with her right hand a short length of thick rubber tube from her skirtpocket and softly smacks with it the palm of her left. Shut up Sontag there must be at least ONE lesbian like this in the world. Superb's knees tremble, she holds the receiver as if it was saving her from drowning and whispers through it, "Help me, Max, I think she's going to beat me."
"Listen Terry," says Max gently and urgently, "that won't happen until you've seen the doctor. They break the new girls in very gradually and they know you're my wife. You won't be whipped till the second or third week if

you do exactly what you are told . . . Terry? Are you listening?"

"She hasn't hung up on you, Max," says Momma on the other telephone. She sits at the end of the desk, and I must not imagine her too clearly for I am in danger of finding her more exciting than Superb. Why are large women also exciting? I suppose every human body is a potential sexual landscape and a very big body suggests the possibility of getting lost in it, running wild in it, enjoying fruit too heavy and abundant to be snatched away. There was a barmaid I enjoyed watching in a Glasgow pub. She wore a denim waistcoat over a shortsleeved blouse like Momma, and when she reached forward her deeply dimpled elbows were short of the tips of her breasts. She always looked bored and indifferent. Her buttocks were so heavy that she resented having to stand, having to move. Yet one customer, a slightly less fat woman with close-cropped blonde hair, wearing a black trousersuit, stood gazing at her with an expression of humble adoration and trying, without success, to engage her in conversation. I merely glanced at this other woman yet she gave me a surprisingly sweet smile and shrugged her shoulders in a resigned way. It was a signal to a fellow sufferer. My face must have had the same expression as her own. I wish I had spoken to the woman in the black trousersuit. She may have loved the barmaid but she didn't hate men. Maybe we could have consoled each other. But I never know what to say to strangers. I stopped going to that pub. I don't like people reading the expression on my face.

"You won't be whipped till the second or third week if you do exactly what you're told . . . Are you listening, Terry?"

"She hasn't hung up on you Max," says Momma on the telephone extension.

"Shut up Momma, this call is private," says Max. "Listen carefully Terry, I'm going to ask you a question, and if you can honestly give the right answer *now*, I'll get you out of there this minute, though it will cost a fortune and all my friends will laugh at me. Terry, are you listening?"

Superb can only nod but Momma says, "She's listening."

"Terry, have you something for me?"

After a pause Superb says, "Max . . . Max, you must *know* I don't have anything just now."

"That's the wrong answer," says Max. The telephone goes dead.

"That's the wrong answer," and one final click.

"My God, isn't that just like a man?" says Momma putting down her receiver. "You're standing half-naked and he wants *you* to give *him* something. Honey, you're better off with a woman."

"You call yourself a *woman*?" says Superb with an aghast laugh.

"I've done all I can to prove it," says Momma cupping her hands beneath her breasts, the rubber tube is on the desk beside her, "but I admit I'm unusual. I don't have penis-envy. You know about penis-envy?"

Superb can only stare at her. Momma says, "Doctor Freud discovered penis-envy. He thought us girls were jealous of men because men have this THING between their legs, you know? But penis-envy doesn't worry me because I have this other thing."

She touches the tube on the desktop beside her. Sontag told me all about penis-envy in order to explain that it didn't exist. She said that Freud, being a man, wanted women to feel inferior and publicised penis-envy to persuade them they must always feel inferior. But the editor believed in penis-envy. She had a twin brother and first noticed his difference when she was very small and being bathed with him. She started girning and pointing and said, "I want one of those."

Her mother said, "I think there's a spare one in my hand-bag."

And went away, then came back and said, "I seem to have lost it. You'll have to manage without."

So penis-envy is possible, even without Freud. It must be upsetting to learn that half your parents have a fifth limb you never knew about. But no more upsetting than learning that the other half lack a limb you take for granted. In both cases the reaction must sometimes be, 'Perhaps I'm a freak.' And most mothers teach their sons to be ashamed of their penis. I don't blame them. The churches teach us to be ashamed of our penis. They think our whole bodies are wicked. Arts and advertising teach us to be ashamed of our penis. From Aberdeen to London the fronts of Victorian insurance offices are decorated with carved nude women representing truth, fertility and the graces beside an occasional man in robes or armour representing science or fortitude. In art galleries the proportion of cunts to pricks is fifty to one, and without the male homosexual magazines the proportion in pictorial publications for men *and* women is nearly the same. Yes, art and advertising exploit women's bodies for money, but to do so they promote the idea that these bodies are beautiful and good. Economics teach us to be ashamed of our penis. The penis has engendered more people than our organisations can use, it is the root of unemployment and poverty. If the labouring class reduced itself by birth-control the middle class would be forced to raise wages to attract their own members into it. Yet now that contraception just might, with sufficient use and support, free the world of the terrible weight birth brings to bear on it, the liberated women start teaching us to be ashamed of our penis. And they have the police on their side. The penis is a criminal hiding from the law. If you don't believe me, sir, piss in the street and see what happens to you. It is widely agreed that the sight of an adult male penis in a public place has a terrifying and corrupting effect upon women and children. If this is true then men also are a very unlucky sex. No wonder some of us feel our penis is not an original part of us but an unwelcome addition. Not that I want to see legalised nude sunbathing in the public parks. I am a gentleman of the old school. I nourish my fifth limb in total privacy. It is seven or eight years since a woman shared it.

"What is your earliest memory of sexual intercourse with your mother?"

Honestly, Sontag, I cannot remember. My mother was not a person but the climate I grew up in. All I remember about sex with her is, sitting on the opposite side of a room which felt like a prison (there was sunlight outside, down by the river the colliers' sons were guddling trout) a prison that gradually became comfortable, expansive and palatial as I imagined the games I would play with Jane Russell when we were married. Momma picks up the rubber tube and says, "With this thing I can have any girl I like squealing and squirming like a streetwalker being worked over by the toughest cop on the beat. But don't worry. If you do exactly what I say I'll be as gentle as I can. Nod your head if you want it the easy way."

Superb is now so passive that she has nearly vanished as a character. Her reserves of bitchcourage, bitch stubbornness are stupefied by the novelty of her situation. I am tempted to have her suddenly attack Momma and wrestle for the key in the skirtpocket. Momma would win, of course, and summon to assist her a slightly younger woman not quite as fat as herself and wearing dungarees with the legs cut off round the tops of her thighs. But if I introduce a new woman every time I encounter a difficulty I'll soon have a gymnasium full of more women than I know how to handle. The house of happiness is entered through the gateway of self-restraint. Who said that? Plato? Mad Hislop? Chairman Mao? Maybe I thought of it myself. So Superb glares bitterly but nods her head meaning, yes she will do exactly what she is told.

Big Momma still sits wearing this skirt which hides nothing but has a useful pocket and protects her bum from the coldness of the desktop. She lights a cigarette, crosses one leg carefully over the other and says softly, "Step out of those sandals. Peel down those tight jeans and anything else you've got on underneath. Be as slow as you like."
Superb is not interested in giving a slow striptease. She kicks the sandals and removes anklerings, jeans, knickers as briskly and casually as she can, folding them carefully along with the crumpled blouse into a neat pile on the floor. Then she slips the anklets on again, because Momma wants that, and faces the desk with a bored expression, legs together and one knee slightly bent, breasts compressed by folded arms. What is her body like apart from strong, large-breasted, average height? She could be like the editor who had a long straight graceful upper body swelling downward into hips which swelled out into the thighs of rather short plump legs. She was like a plumper than usual Botticelli Venus above the waist and a smaller than usual Rubens Venus beneath, a strange body but lovely when naked. She looked ordinary in clothes because she was ashamed of her

legs and disguised them under wide skirts and dresses with higher waists than her own. She deliberately made herself ordinary, for if a man looked at her in the street she grew uneasy, thinking he was laughing at her short legs. Once, when we were getting drunk together, I explained she ought to dress *for* her body and not against it. She said, "You want me to dress like a tart."

I said, "Only idiots think attractively dressed women are tarts. You mix with fairly intelligent people, they would be pleased if you dressed less timidly."

She said, "Why don't you dress less timidly?"

I said, "My friends are perfectly satisfied with my clothes."

She said, "Liar. You're like me. You have no friends, only colleagues and an occasional one-night stand with women as lonely as you are."

I said, "You are trying to change the subject. My clothes are well cut and fit me perfectly."

She said, "They are also terribly dull."

"Men don't need to look interesting."

"Neither does this woman."

I said, "There is a difference between us which has nothing to do with gender. I don't need friends, but you would be happier if you were less lonely. You are, and I really believe this, a very fine-looking woman. If you would spend just a bit of imagination on your appearance folk would know you were willing to give yourself socially, not just sexually. They would notice you and want to be with you, women as well as men."

She said, "You don't need friends?"

"No. I am perfectly happy without them."

She giggled and said, "You liar. You poor, poor liar."

I said nothing because I was close to becoming angry. She said, "Tell you what, let's do a deal. Buy me the sort of clothes you want me to wear and I'll spend the same sum on clothes for you."

"What sort of clothes would you buy me?"

"Jeans and corduroy slacks. A leather jacket. Coloured T-shirts. Perhaps a caftan to wear at home."

"I'm too old for that sort of nonsense."

"In America and the continent even grandfathers dress like that and nobody thinks them ridiculous."

"This is Scotland."
"Then the deal is clearly off."
Her figure would be lovely for Superb if it did not remind me of her loneliness, her habit of telling me to leave as soon as we had made love, her sadness which is starting to infect me although I haven't seen her for eight or nine years. Someone told me she had a stroke which paralysed her right side and keeps her indoors, I ought to have visited her, I meant to visit her. Let Superb have Marilyn Monroe's body no, she was vulnerable and friendless too, Jayne Mansfield's JESUS, NO head cut off in car accident, give Superb Jane Russell's body and face. Remember nobody but Jane Russell, I mean Superb, and mother, I mean Big Momma, why did I confuse my mother with Momma, there is NO CONNECTION ATALL, my mother was a respectable woman (until she ran away from home) and no lesbian (she ran away with a man) she was tall and not a bit fat, I got Momma's body from that Glasgow barmaid and the whore under the bridge AND MOMMA'S NATURE IS BASED ON NOBODY REAL ATALL. My mother may have hated women, sometimes, but they trusted her. She never enjoyed humiliating people in her imagination the way I do. I'm almost 100 per cent certain of that. So I am not 100 per cent certain of that?

Finish the whisky in the tumbler. Nobody can be 100 per cent certain of anything. The mechanics of the universe make it impossible to look at anything without altering it. She must have found some satisfaction in thwarting my friendships, keeping me beside her, encouraging my studies, but she cannot have enjoyed the thrill I feel as Momma stubs out the cigarette, points to the small scatter of Janine's clothes on the floor and says softly, "Put these on. Start with the suspender-belt."
But can I imagine my Superb obeying that order? Even if she hesitates first, and sees Big Momma pick up the rubber tube in her right hand and once again suggestively smack the palm of her left? Of course I can imagine it. Mad Hislop was a small man and he terrorised six boys, one bigger than himself, into standing in a row, holding out their hands, and receiving six blows each from his three-thonged Lochgelly

tawse. And five of the boys wept real tears, though the biggest merely scowled. Hislop glared at us then said in a tone of supreme contempt, "Lassies! You're nothing but a bunch of big lassies. Excepting you, Anderson. There's a spark of manhood in you. Get back to your seats."

And we went weeping to our seats except Anderson, who sat down radiantly smiling. The more I think of my childhood the queerer it seems although it was perfectly ordinary. So Superb scowls furiously but yes, she picks up Janine's suspender-belt, holds it round her waist then cries out, "It's too small! I *told* you these clothes aren't mine!"

But Momma smiles sweetly and says, "Make them stretch. Pull hard. Imagine you are a poor little orphan girl with nothing else in the world to wear, because as from now, that is indeed the case."

And tears stream down Superb's cheeks as she fastens the lacy Reger suspender-belt although a lot of it disappears into the crease it makes in the flesh round her waist. She pulls on the black net stockings although some of the mesh splits as she tugs them up to attach the suspenders. As she thrusts her arms into the satin blouse, which is sleeveless, the armholes split down the side. She can only fasten the waistband of the miniskirt. And Big Momma, still seated on the desktop, gently teases her clitoris with the end of the rubber tube, is that anatomically possible in that position? and watches Superb dreamily through half-shut eyes and murmurs, "Put on the shoes."

"I *can't* put on the shoes. I can't bend down in these clothes, I can't even sit."

"I'll help you."

Momma leaves the desk. She kneels and carefully fits and buckles on to Superb's foot one of Janine's shoes murmuring, "You won't need to sit. For the next three hours you'll be flat on your back."

"What do you mean?"

"I'm only joking, honey, don't you know that?"

She fits and buckles on the other shoe then stands back with legs astride astride astride and hands on hips like an artist considering an unfinished painting. Superb now stands higher on tiptoe than she ever imagined possible, legs pressed tight together, terrified of falling. Her calves ache, she wails softly, "This hurts!"

"The effect is worth it. You look irresistible. But you don't need *that*."

Big Momma reaches forward, strips off the skirt and casts it aside.

"Nor this either, I was mad to put you into it."

She tugs down and rips off the blouse, drops it, then embraces her gently and warmly, kissing her unresisting tearwet mouth and whispering, "Shoes and stockings, that's all you'll wear from now on. Unless the Doctor orders something different. O forgive me, honey, I don't want to give you to any man atall."

And watching Superb with a look of sad longing she backs toward the desk, lifts the receiver and says into it, "Get me the boss," and after a moment says, "She's ready for you. Forget the identity parade. If you don't come quick I'll take her myself."

And as Momma puts the receiver down Superb is trembling. A strange thing is happening. In spite of the pain in her legs, the suspender-belt cutting her waist, the prickle of the tears drying on her cheeks, her body is aroused, she wants to open and be entered, grasped, held tight by, who is the boss? Who is coming?

Me. Not Max, Hollis or Charlie but me. This bed suddenly rises up like a magic carpet, soars through the ceiling, zooms out of the cone of the earth's shadow into bright sunlight over the Atlantic and, California here I come! But just as the bed is descending on America it doesn't. It suddenly stops still. The mattress widens and hardens into a floor, the floor of the gymnasium with a mat in the corner where Superb is spread on her back like a starfish, a great pillow under her hips so that the rosy heart of her naked sex is completely exposed. Momma has caressed her into excitement, she needs me now and as I clasp and slip warmly into her I am entering Jane Russell the editor Janine Sontag Big Momma Helen forget her forget her and I am at home again. At home again. At home again. No. No. No. No I am not. I am not. I am alone. Alone. Alone. I am absolutely alone.

O hell hell hell hell hell hell hell hell hell hell
hell hell hell hell hell hell hell hell hell hell hell
hell hell hell hell hell hell hell hell hell hell hell
hell hell hell hell hell hell hell hell hell hell hell
hell hell hell hell hell hell hell hell hell hell hell
hell hell hell hell hell hell hell hell hell hell hell
hell hell hell hell hell hell hell hell hell hell hell
hell hell hell hell hell hell hell hell hell hell hell
hell hell hell hell hell hell hell hell hell hell hell
hell hell hell hell hell hell hell hell hell hell hell
hell hell hell hell hell hell hell hell hell hell hell
hell hell hell hell hell hell hell hell hell hell hell
HELL HELL HELL HELL HELL HELL HELL HELL
HELL HELL HELL HELL HELL HELL HELL HELL
HELL HELL HELL HELL HELL HELL HELL HELL
HELL HELL HELL HELL HELL HELL HELL HELL
HELL HELL HELL HELL HELL HELL HELL HELL
HELL HELL HELL HELL HELL HELL HELL HELL
HELL HELL HELL HELL HELL HELL HELL HELL
HELL HELL HELL HELL HELL HELL HELL HELL
HELL HELL HELL HELL HELL HELL HELL HELL
HELL HELL HELL HELL HELL HELL HELL HELL
HELL HELL HELL HELL HELL HELL HELL HELL
HELL HELL HELL HELL HELL HELL HELL HELL
HELL HELL HELL I lost control, I lost control.

4: I AM NOT A BAD MAN, I AM A GOOD MAN.

4:I AM NOT A BAD MAN, I AM A GOOD MAN. I did what my mother wanted, what my ex-wife wanted, what her father wanted, I once had a friend who liked me and now National Security Installations are perfectly content with me. My salary proves it. I contribute to Oxfam, the Salvation Army and Cancer Research although I do not expect to benefit from these organisations. On crowded trains and buses I offer my seat to cripples and poorly dressed old women. I have never struck a man, woman or child in my life, never lost my temper, never raised my voice. Since the age of thirteen I have not shed a single tear. Surely, inside the privacy of this body and the secrecy of this skull I have earned the right to enjoy any woman I want in any way I can? But

But I should not have answered Big Momma's telephone call. I should have sent in Stroud, Hollis, Charlie and Max wearing silk dressing-gowns and masks, and before they did anything to Superb I should have switched my attention back to Janine. There is a male tradition that women enjoy rape but that is wishful thinking. Nearly all bodies can respond to another with a few spasms of automatic pleasure but that is not enjoyment. I have been raped and it was pleasant at the time and afterward I felt like a miserable nothing, I wished I was dead. What depressed me was the impossibility of gratitude. When forget her and I were not lovemaking or asleep we lay merely holding each other, amazed and grateful to be holding each other. I wish we had never left that bed. When dressed she did not look ordinary, like the editor, she looked poor and messy stop. Stop. When dressed, I thought I was smart in that suit but no I looked prim and dull which is why I chose GLAMOUR, chose Helen. Liar. Helen chose me oh, I will gnaw the fingers of this hand to the bone.

Ouch

That hurt. Calm down. Where was I? Thinking about rape.

I wish I could sleep but people who dream with open eyes don't need much sleep. Three hours a night is the most I can manage though I doze a lot in trains, planes and taxis. There is something in rapid movement which lets the mind relax. It's a common experience nowadays. Apart from a few frightened old women we all believe that if we travel fast enough something in the future will stop us falling down. But this bed is standing still so I must think about rape. After Superb had been thoroughly raped in my absence I had meant to return and prepare her for other sorts of astonishment, but alas I did the job myself and now I feel like a miserable nothing. The editor made me feel like this whenever we made love. We had to be drunk first. Each knew what the other wanted but was terrified all the same, terrified of not giving pleasure, terrified of not receiving it. I first met her on a matter of business, the second time by accident in the street and both times she asked me to her flat for coffee. After coffee came sherry and when that was used up we finished her whisky and all the time we talk talk talked. She probably found that as boring as I did but we were hoping for something better. At last I stepped out for ten minutes to buy us another bottle of whisky so I cannot remember who made the first pass. It was probably me. The man usually does. We did it on the hearthrug and there was always a stocking or suspender-belt I never managed to remove from her. Afterward I wanted to sleep of course and

so did she, but she always told me to leave the house first. "What will the neighbours think if they see you leave here in the morning?" I told her I would lie low till noon before leaving. Her neighbours were a divorced friend, a one-parent family and two elderly homosexuals. And this was in a period when casual sex was supposed to be common, but no, "Leave! Leave *now*! You *must* leave me *now*!"
She wept and grew hysterical until I left without one farewell kiss, without her even seeing me to the door. The second time I quietened the hysterics by making love to her again, but afterward she drove me out in exactly the same way. So I went slowly through the streets to my empty bed and lay on it all night and most of the following day. I felt too empty and feeble, too raped to even go and buy another bottle of whisky.

Of course I know why she had to chuck me out like that. If we had slept sweetly in her bed, and made love again in the morning, which is the best time, and she had seen me to the door, and we had parted after a farewell kiss, I would have made her feel a miserable nothing by not arranging to see her again. I was not sure I liked her enough to see much of her. Two people can come together with the most delightful intentions and continue out of mere habit. My marriage was like that. So the editor raped me three times to stop me raping her. Helen raped me once when she was getting ready to leave.

For nine whole years (I can hardly believe this now) for nine whole years we shared the same bed without making love. Then she joined a drama group (I'd been nagging her to do that for a long time) and starting looking beautiful again and coming home around midnight. She said that after rehearsals the club members went to somebody's house for a drink and a chat. One night she came back between three and four in the morning. As she undressed and got into bed I pretended to sleep but she must have known it was a pretence. At last I said, "I know what time it is."
She said nothing. I said, "That drink and chat must have turned into a regular party."

She said, "What are you suggesting?"
"Nothing."
"Are you suggesting I've been unfaithful to you?"
"No."
"For one night in all our years of marriage I sit up late discussing the theatre with a couple of friends who appreciate me and at once you accuse me of being unfaithful! Do I complain about your collection of disgusting magazines?"
I said nothing and suddenly she embraced me like in the early days, embraced me so warmly that my whole body came alive again. I made love too quickly, and no wonder after all those years, and when I wanted to start slowly and gently again she drew away and wept and told me she was in love with whatsisname. A boy in the drama club. They had made love for the first time that night and he wanted to marry her. I stayed silent. She said, "You hate me, I suppose."
I felt stunned and stupid but I certainly did not hate her. There was no evil in Helen. There is evil in me, which is why I deserve whatever pain I get. She said, "I can't promise not to see him again. If you try to stop me I'll have to leave at once."
I said in a tired voice, "Take your pleasure wherever you can find it, Helen," and reached to embrace her, but she switched the light on, dried her eyes and said, "I'm sorry but we mustn't do that again. I'm going to sleep in the spare room."
I should have offered to go there myself but could not move. When she left the bed it felt like the loneliest place in the world. I had not realised how much I had been nourished by the mere warmth of her body. I've been insomniac ever since.

Did Sontag ever rape me? Only intellectually. "This combination of brothel and police station which you have devised is not, I hope you realise, a fantasy. A form of it exists in all nations except perhaps Scandinavia and the Netherlands."
"Nonsense, Sontag!"
"Are you aware that the Parisian police commissioner has publicly advised raped women not to take their complaint

unaccompanied to a police station, since they are in danger of being raped again? Are you aware that in Germany – "
"Don't talk about the concentration camps!" I commanded, my fingers above my ears.
"I will not, but you have read of the death by hanging of the Meinhof girl in that strangely insecure German maximum-security prison. Did you know that the official investigators found dry semen between her thighs? Did the warders fuck her then hang her, or hang her then fuck the corpse?"
"The official investigators decided that she hanged herself."
"They had no explanation for the semen. They did not deny the medical evidence, or explain it, they ignored it, and the television reports ignored it too. Beria, the head of the Russian secret police, had women who attracted him arrested and taken to jails where he abused them as he pleased. Then they were executed for treason. There are equally selfish men with far too much power in America. Of course the system they manipulate is a different one, but this forensic research club you have invented almost certainly exists, though it is probably more frequent in South America than the North."
"There is nothing like it in Scotland," I said desperately, "nothing like it in Britain."
"In Ulster – "
"Don't talk to me about Ulster!" I shouted, my hands over my ears again.
"Very well, I am perfectly aware that recently on the main British island only men have been kicked to death in police stations. However, a girl I know was arrested on suspicion of being friendly with a terrorist – on suspicion, mind you, for she was not. They locked her naked in a London prison cell, a very *cold* one, and kept her under surveillance by male warders for three whole days."
"I find that hard to believe."
"You sound like a Conservative sometimes."
I nearly smiled.

Sontag thought I was some kind of socialist because she knew my father had been in a trade union. She did not know that in Britain almost everyone of my income group is Conservative, especially if their fathers were trade unionists.

Not that I have totally rejected the old man's Marxist ideas. The notion that all politics is class warfare is clearly correct. Every intelligent Tory knows that politics is a matter of people with a lot of money combining to manage people with very little, though of course they must deny it in public to mislead the opposition. The bit of Marx I reject is the prophetic bit. He thought that the poorly paid would eventually organise themselves and overpower the moneyed people. I'm sure they won't, and I'm not going to join a gang of losers. This is selfish of me and probably wicked, but like everyone else I would rather be thought wicked than stupid. A man with money in the bank who speaks out for the poorly paid always sounds stupid or a hypocrite. I heard one, once.

I was at a meeting of Scottish businessmen and we were relaxing afterward in the bar. A fairly young man asked the head of a big brewery firm, which also owned a lot of pubs, "How much do you pay your bar managers?"

The head told him. The young man said, "How can you get dependable men for a wage as low as that?"

The head said, "We can't, but we do very well with undependable men."

The youngster wanted to know more. The head said, "The managers increase their income by keeping down the wages of the barstaff. The barstaff increase their takings by cheating the customers. If a customer complains loudly about short measures or watered whisky we sack the manager and get a new one. There is never a shortage of willing managers, never any shortage of customers."

The youngster said, "That strikes me as a thoroughly rotten system."

The head said, "I'm inclined to agree with you. But it is a profitable system, and perfectly legal."

"So you like this system."

The head shrugged and said, "Not particularly, but my likes play no part in the business. To pay higher wages I can reduce profits and drive away the shareholders, or raise prices and drive the customers into the pubs of our competitors. In either case the firm is swallowed by those who have continued to pay their employees as little as they can."

The younger man said, "But you own more than just the brewery and the pubs."
At this moment I noticed he was intensely agitated, perhaps drunk. The head of breweries said, "I'm sorry, but I don't understand the relevance of that remark."
"You own a lot of farming land, and half a TV company, and a highland grousemoor, and a house in London, and a Greek island."
The head said, "That is not strictly accurate. I am a director of certain companies which own these things. The only things I personally own are my houses. But accurate or not I fail to see how this connects with our previous topic, which was the wage of the average Scottish barmanager."
The young man said, "Yes, I'm sure you fail to see that connection," and turned to walk away. The head of breweries reached out a hand, gripped a piece of the young man's sleeve and did not let go. The head was a big man of the type who keeps himself fit by some kind of sport. His face had gone slightly pink but his voice stayed quiet, clear and steady except when he said *son*. He said, "Listen, *son*, maybe you prefer the Russian system where all land and all business belongs to the Communist Party, which is nothing but a large limited company without one single competitor. Allow me to inform you that Russian bosses also have their town house, their country estate, their holiday home in a more comfortable climate. *And* they are a lot less tolerant of kids who go about shooting their mouths off. *And* I doubt if the pubs are any better than ours. Go away and think about that."
He released the young man and was left with the head of a firm which marketed catfood and with the security expert, who was me. The two bosses smiled at each other (I admire how cool these people can be) but I saw that inside they were rather ruffled. The brewery man said, "That young chap has a lot to learn. I'm referring to his manners."
The catfood man said, "Don't judge him too harshly. He has just realised that his chance of promotion is rather slim."
The brewery man said, "I thought there might be something like that behind it. What did you think, Jock?"

These people like to call me Jock. They would be pleased

if I used their nicknames but I never call them anything. Breweries and catfood knew I came from folk who owned almost nothing so, "That young chap has a lot to learn. I'm referring to manners . . . What do you think, Jock?" and they watched my reaction. I finished my whisky with a thoughtful frown, tapped breweries on the shoulder with a forefinger and said, "I think I'll buy us a drink. What do you want?"

He stared at me, guffawed, then slapped me on the back. He said, "Jock, I suspect you are a bit of a bolshie. I'll have a bloody big brandy, if you don't mind."

For a moment I was glad to have restored good feeling without sounding like a sycophant, then I noticed I had sounded like a sycophant. Breweries would soon be telling his colleagues, "I had a dram last week with old Jock of the National Security crowd. He's a bit of a bolshie but he's utterly dependable and knows his job thoroughly. And he's no sycophant, thank God." My offer of a drink had reassured him, as it was meant to do. Why are men in strong positions such gluttons for reassurance? They can never have enough of it. They control almost everything yet they want to be admired and loved because they are also jolly good fellows. Well, to those who have shall be given and I bought the bastard a brandy and a Glenlivet Malt for myself. Breweries said thoughtfully, "It might become profitable to improve our pubs if the customer started boycotting them to drink at home. But you know how incapable the average Scot is of enjoying the company of his wife."

As this was supposed to be a joke catfood chuckled and I frowned and nodded once. I am not supposed to have a sense of humour. It amuses those above me to see how little humour I have. It intimidates them slightly too, and my self-respect is founded on that. And I prefer hobnobbing with bastards under bright lights to skulking in the shadow with beaten dogs. But I dislike the bastards as much as I despise the dogs and I don't care for myself much. I am a Conservative because I like bright lights. But I can do without them. Death won't frighten me.

I once met another man of my type, a sergeant in the

Argylls who played the pipes for banquets in the officers' mess. He told me queer stories of these officers' antics when the ceremonial part of the evening broke down: twenty drunk men in glazed shirtfronts, bumfreezer jackets and tight tartan breeks forming a human pyramid to discover if the youngest had the courage to climb to the top and unscrew the bulbs of a chandelier thirty feet above a stone-flagged floor; with even dafter homosexual antics of a sort I thought were only practised in the more eccentric Masonic lodges. This piper was a solid quietspoken man so the officers trusted him and suggested he should train to be an officer too. In Britain this suggestion is not often made to one of lower ranks. The piper refused it. The training would have cost nothing, but he could not have afforded to follow the customs of the officers' mess where the lower officers are supposed to buy drinks for their seniors, but not the other way round. New officers cannot afford to be jolly decent chaps if they have only their wages to live upon. And I was suddenly reminded of something told me by a bus conductor in the days when bus-drivers and conductors were different people. The driver was better paid, being more highly skilled, yet there was a tradition that good conductors 'looked after' their drivers by buying them pie-suppers and bottles of lemonade. Who spread the story that the Scots are an INDEPENDENT people? Robert Burns.

> Is there, for honest poverty
> That hangs his head, and a' that?
> The coward-slave, we pass him by –
> We dare be poor for a' that!
> For a' that, and a' that,
> Our toils obscure and a' that,
> The rank is but the guinea's stamp –
> The man's the gowd for a' that.

The truth is that we are a nation of arselickers, though we disguise it with surfaces: a surface of generous, openhanded manliness, a surface of dour practical integrity, a surface of futile maudlin defiance like when we break goalposts and windows after football matches on foreign soil and commit suicide on Hogmanay by leaping from fountains in Trafalgar

Square. Which is why, when England allowed us a referendum on the subject, I voted for Scottish self-government. Not for one minute did I think it would make us more prosperous, we are a poor little country, always have been, always will be, but it would be a luxury to blame ourselves for the mess we are in instead of the bloody old Westminster parliament. "We see the problems of Scotland in a totally different perspective when we get to Westminster," a Scottish M.P. once told me. Of course they do, the arse-lickers.

Well, a majority of the Scots voted as I did, even though politicians from both big parties appeared on television and told us that a separate assembly would lead to cuts in public spending, loss of business and more unemployment. But the usual sporting rules for electing a new government had been changed. "If you win the race by a short head you will have lost it," we were told, so we won by a short head and lost the race. Then came cuts in public spending, loss of business and increased unemployment and now Westminster has decided to spend the North Sea oil revenues building a fucking tunnel under the English Channel. If we ran that race again we would win by a head and neck so we won't be allowed to run it again, cool down cool down you are goading yourself into a FRENZY my friend, think about fucking Superb, think about fucking Janine, don't think about fucking POLITICS.

"You sound like a Conservative sometimes," says Sontag and I nearly smiled. But if I had told her the truth about my politics she would have spent hours trying to convert me and I was having a hard enough time protecting my fantasies from her. If she succeeded in connecting them to ordinary life she would make me feel responsible for every atrocity from Auschwitz and Nagasaki to Vietnam and the war in Ulster and I REFUSE TO FEEL GUILTY ABOUT EVERYTHING. Thinking is a pain because it joins everything together until my mother father Mad Hislop Jane Russell mushroomcloud miniskirt tight jeans Janine dead friend Helen Superb Sontag editor sad lesbian police Big Momma and the whore under the bridge surround me all proving that I am a bad man, I am what is wrong with the world, I am a tyrant, I am a weakling, I never gave what they wanted, I grabbed all I could get. So I did not smile, I groaned and said, "Forget politics, Sontag, and let us get back to sex. You are such an expert in sex, Sontag."

This was untrue. She had read a lot about sex and liked to practise very complicated gymnastic couplings which struck me as more bother than they were worth and made her very angry with my incompetence, but what she enjoyed most was being upside down in an armchair with her legs spread wide over the back while I stood behind it working on her cunt with my tongue. It was a position which allowed me the least possible body contact and did not excite me at all, though I could do it for what seemed like hours while she hung on to the chairarms looking ecstatic and moaning softly to herself. Then we would cuddle in bed while I told her my dirty story. She said, "How can I forget politics when your fantasy has such a convincing political structure?"

"I have other fantasies which are completely unconvincing, completely impossible."

"Tell me one."

I told her about a Miss World beauty contest whose final adjudication is to take place in Thailand. The hundred most beautiful girls from every country on the globe are travelling there in a jetplane which is hijacked by order of an Arab oil sheik and brought down in his private airfield. The girls are then forced to give a beauty parade without those hideous one-piece bathingsuits they normally wear, and twenty queens are chosen by an examination based on more than eyesight. As I described it Sontag grew excited and for once we had a passionate, uncomplicated little fuck together.

"Yes," she said afterward, "it was satisfying to think of the stupid bitches who compete in that sort of contest getting what they deserve, but semi-prostitution followed by real abduction has always been commonplace and the other details came from the everyday news. Your only original touch is the scale of the operation. What a lot of sex you have gone without to have to think of such things."

But I had not told her the whole story. While the twenty winning queens are enjoyed in a harem by the sheik and his four sons, the eighty losers must serve the queens as slaves. The queens are allowed to wear as much jewellery as they like and a single garment. Miniskirts abound. The slaves go naked but are allowed cosmetics and time to make themselves attractive, for if one of the men grows tired of a queen he can replace her by stripping her skirt off and bestowing it on any slave who excites his fancy. The privileges of being a queen, the pains of being a slave are so exotic that the naked girls are continually competing for the masters' attention, while the clothed live in fear of the naked and humiliate them to make them less attractive. The dominant men find this entertaining. Probably big harems were organised like that and certainly most societies are, thank God I now belong to those who are in no danger of being stripped. In my Beauties of the World harem the sheik's youngest son falls in love with Miss Poland to the exclusion of everyone else. She uses her power over him to get weapons and arm the other girls for a breakout, slaves and queens alike, but the plan is betrayed by three of the queens. Miss England thinks nice girls should not handle guns, Miss Russia thinks men are too clever to be defeated, Miss America finds life in the harem more interesting and exciting than elsewhere. The sheik's son suddenly finds Miss America's eagerly compliant stance more enticing than Miss Poland's defiant one so Miss Poland is stripped and punished to warn and entertain the others. If I had told Sontag that she would have certainly seen I was Conservative.

Yet her question sticks in my head, "What makes you invent such despicable villains?" There is a mystery here which makes no sense to me. I am attracted by most of the women I meet, I fear and despise most of the men, I have had only one friend of my own sex in the world yet I am excited by fantasies of worlds where men have total control. My job may be a cause of this. Everyone sees life through their job. To the doctor the world is a hospital, to the broker it is a stock exchange, to the lawyer a vast criminal court, to the soldier a barracks and area of manoeuvre, to the farmer

soil and bad weather, to truck-drivers a road system, to dustmen a midden, to prostitutes a brothel, to mothers an inescapable nursery, to children a school, to film stars a looking-glass, to undertakers a morgue, and to myself a security installation powered by the sun and only crackable by death. In everyday life the installation encloses and controls me but in imagination I stand outside manipulating it and peering in upon, Janine?
Not yet. Superb.
I am going to unrape Superb and abolish that gymnasium and these policemen, who are not necessary. Also that suitcase with the miniskirt in it. She is sufficiently sexy in those tight white denim jeans. On second thoughts I want her in dungaree overalls. And I will drop the business of the car being serviced as Max follows her into the garage pleading with her not to leave him this weekend but she stop.

Stop. If I start imagining Superb again I will lose control again and hate myself again because I HATE cruelty, I hated Mad Hislop, I hated most of all a total stranger old enough to be my father who walked past me with his two sons into the middle of my own room and WHISKY quickquickquickquickquick on to the floor, get the emergency bottle out of the, damn this lock, case under the bed. Raise lid, grasp bottle, unscrew top. Good stuff. Take it from neck. Again. Again. Dip this foul brain deep in cleansing alcohol. Again. Oh warmth, stupidity, my dear dear friend why am I still hurt by the insults heaped on me by that bloody old man? who was only doing his best for his daughter, he thought. Why was that the worst rape I ever suffered? Why do I still care? He is dead, I am old, we are all cowards. He must have felt very stupid when he discovered the truth. Certainly I did. Certainly Helen did.

Carefully pour glassful. Get in bed. Sip slowly. The parts of this mind are blissfully disconnecting, thoughts separating from memories, memories from fantasies. If I am lucky nothing now will float to my surface but delicious fragments.

5:I AM THE EYE BY WHICH THE UNIVERSE BEHOLDS ITSELF AND KNOWS IT IS DIVINE.

5:I AM THE EYE BY WHICH THE UNIVERSE BEHOLDS ITSELF AND KNOWS IT IS DIVINE. We walked in a wood with bright sunlight shining through the leaves. Between the trunks on our right there was fallen brown bracken with an occasional new stem upholding a coiled green tip, and a drift of bluebells, and the cluck-gurgle of the river. On the left was more withered bracken above a slope of moss and primroses. It had rained recently. Everything glittered and the scents of bracken, pine, primroses and wet earth were extra sharp, and the track had many puddles in it. Father and mother, holding a hand on each side, swung me over these puddles. "More more!" I shouted as we approached each one, by which I meant higher and further. I was three years old, perhaps nearer two, but I was the eye by which the universe beheld itself and knew it was divine. The puddles were clear mirrors full of branches and sunlight, the bluebells were like openings into an underground sky, I have never since seen anything as yellow as these primroses when the light touched them. Later I rode my father's shoulders. I preferred riding him because he raised me higher than my mother could, and my weight was no burden to him, so I leaned sideways and patted her head with kingly condescension. What was the colour of her hair? Did she look up and smile at me? I forget but I know I was perfectly happy, and in sunlight.

I wish I was the sun, living at the perpetual height of noon, staring down at the middles of the great continents. Does sunlight enjoy touching the bodies it allows us to see? If it does a lot would be understood: why life began, for instance. Oh I wish I was the sun. How delighted all women would be to feel me, each one undressing without shame and opening far more to me than to any mere man, on private beaches and patios and lawns the deliciously young, the ripely mature, the small girls, the aged grannies all languidly turning to let me toast them equally on both sides. Only Scotland would be veiled from me. By these miserable clouds. I feel cold and lonely suddenly. Mirrors reflecting mirrors are the whole show. Who said that? Mad Hislop.

Mirrors reflecting mirrors are the show where ignorant armies clash by night that thicks man's blood with cold. A great many resounding phrases have started bubbling into this head lately. I must have picked them up from Hislop, who was perhaps my real father. He recited all the great poets by heart, apart from Burns, who he despised. He planted in me a sincere hatred of poetry. Since leaving school I have not opened one book of it, apart from Burns. The maths and technical teachers were ordinary easygoing people who hardly ever used the belt, I did well with them, but Hislop stalked about the classroom with hands in pockets spouting verses which made no sense to boys who sat as still as stones dreading the moment when he would pick on one of us.

"Hereto I came to view a voiceless ghost, whither oh whither will its whim now draw me. Why are you staring at me like that, bright youth?"

I was staring at him because he frightened me and I thought he would punish me if I looked anywhere else.

"I don't know sir."

"You don't know. Is that because you are an idiot or a liar?"

"I don't know sir."

"Show me your exercise book. Hm. Five spelling errors

and an almost total absence of punctuation. You are an idiot. What are you?"

"Idiot sir."

"Don't mumble. Answer loud and clear when I ask a question. What are you?"

"I AM AN IDIOT SIR."

"Then I will provide an exercise to focus your mind. I have no favourites in this class. Go to the blackboard."

This is a nasty thing to remember.

If I remember nothing but pleasant fragments my life will be completely happy. Three great pleasant things once happened to me, forget her and Helen and Sontag. Sontag was the most fun. I did not love her enough for pain to come of it. She arrived suddenly a year after Helen had left. I was in a very bad state. All my work at that time was in Glasgow so there was no travelling to divert the mind and I had not yet learned to be continually drunk. Are there many people without illness or disability who sit at home in the evening with clenched fists, continually changing the channel of a television set and wishing they had the courage to roll over the parapet of a high bridge? I bet there are millions of us. The doorbell rang and a small woman stood on the mat smiling and saying, "Hello, I was passing and had a minute to spare and I thought is he still living here? I will call up and see. So I came up and here you still are!"

She was attractive in a slightly forced, strident way, like how I imagine Janine, and at the sight of her the desperate feeling inside me relaxed though I could not remember having seen her before. I said, "Come in. Have you time for a coffee?"

She followed me into the kitchen and as I spooned the powder into the cups she said, "This place is very neat now but also rather bare."

I said, "I've chucked out everything I don't need and I need very little."

"But how do you feed yourself? I am sure you do not do it healthily. I suppose you eat out of a fryingpan all the time."

I told her I had once done a lot of frying but stopped when,

one morning in a hurry, I discovered that raw eggs cracked into a cup slip down very easily, and uncooked bacon does not taste bad if sufficiently chewed.
"But that is horrible! It is a miracle that you are alive. The human stomach employs far more energy digesting the albumen of a raw egg than the egg itself produces. When you eat a raw egg you are actually starving yourself. And chewing raw bacon will inevitably give you tapeworm. The flies lay their eggs under the rind. Frying is a poisonous way of preparing food but at least it kills the eggs of the flies."
I told her that I usually ate out. She sipped the coffee without enthusiasm and said, "I must make you a really good meal. Unluckily the house where I now live swarms with women and children, you would not be comfortable there. I will make up something in pots and bring them here to heat up. I will also bring some real coffee."
I thanked her and said that since she was supplying the culinary skill I ought to provide the raw material, and I would certainly do so if she gave me an exact shopping list. She said, "No. I will work better if I shop also, you cannot possibly know the best places to buy things. But you may provide as much wine as you like, I will not complain of that."
We agreed upon a day and a time and at once she hurried away leaving my coffee almost untasted. But on the doormat she turned as if to tell me something and instead went quite still, saying nothing. So I kissed her. Then she broke away and ran downstairs without another word. I returned to the television set feeling excited and hopeful. In four minutes a complete stranger had made my hellish dull life worth living again.

That was a miracle. The miracles of Christ don't interest me. I don't care if they are true or false. The only miracles which matter to me were worked by women.

Weeks later I said to her, "What gave you the idea of visiting me that first time?"
"Helen suggested it."
"Helen? Do you know Helen?"
"Did you not know we were friends?"
"No."

"But she and I taught in Bearsden Academy. I came here with two or three others for afternoon tea one Sunday. That was when I first met you. Have you forgotten?"

"Why did Helen suggest you visit me?"

"I met her in town by accident – we had not seen each other for two or three years, and went for a coffee and a chat. We were both a little lonely. I had just separated from Ulric and she was quarrelling with the young man she had left you for, so naturally we discussed sex in general and also in particular. Do you understand?"

"Yes."

"Helen said she thought you would be a good man to seduce. So I came and did so."

"Did she say why I would be good to seduce?"

"No. It was a casual remark made at the moment when we separated."

I tried to cuddle Sontag then, I passionately wanted to hold her tight, feeling it would be like embracing Helen too. But that evening I had not tongued Sontag long enough to be allowed a cuddle. She got up and started briskly dressing, saying, "I am still quite fond of you but sex is not everything. It will be better if in future you wait till I phone you before we meet."

A long time after that, when Sontag had definitely finished with me, I stood in a bus queue beside a gaunt, slightly eccentric old lady with an attractive figure. She looked at me with an air of inquiry and suddenly I recognised Helen. When we spoke she smiled and looked younger. I said, "Thank you for sending Sontag to me."

But she did not remember doing that. She said, "Have you married again?"

"No."

She frowned and said, "Why not? You're the sort of man who needs a wife. You would be very good to her if she was ordinary enough."

This remark confused me. I said, "Are you married?"

"Oh no, I'm not the marrying type. I stayed with you for such a long time because I thought you needed me. Of course I was a bit of a coward in those days, terribly conventional."

Her bus arrived and she went away on it leaving me utterly confused. During our marriage I thought I only stayed with her because she needed me. And I too was a coward, and conventional. It took ten years together, and as many separate, to discover that Helen and I felt exactly the same way toward each other and what good did it do? What good did it do? What good did it do? Come on Jock it is time you entertained yourself again.

Superb, telephoning, says firmly, "What I need to know is, if Max calls you tomorrow, will you make the right noises?"

"I suppose so."

"Thank you mother," says Superb and puts down the receiver. She rearranges herself on the bed then dials another number. She says, "Hullo Charlie. We're all right. Mother will cover up for me. I'm leaving an hour from now."

"Why not leave right away?"

"I've this husband, remember? We still eat together. That's about all we do together."

"How do you look?"

"Fresh and clean. I've had a shower, and washed my hair, and I'm wearing these new white denim dungarees bought just today, so don't say I don't love you."

"What about the top?"

"Nothing special. A demure little blouse."

"Bra?"

"Of course not. I know you don't like them."

"Terry, take off that blouse."

"You bad mad boy!"

"Terry, when we meet tonight, I don't want you wearing anything but those dungarees. Right?"

She must dress this way for three reasons.

1 The colliers' sons, who played rough games my mother did not like, wore dungarees of the bib and brace type, so this garment has an exciting flavour of forbidden games which is enhanced by DUNG, the first syllable of the name.

2 The colliers' sons' dungarees were black to hide the dirt. Superb's are white so that I can see clearly how dirty I make her.

3 (a) If Charlie embraces her from the front he can put a hand under the braces to caress her shoulderblades and feel lingeringly down the spine to where my (no) his other hand has unfastened four buttons over a hip and slid inside to explore the two hills of her bum.

(b) If Charlie embraces her from behind I (no) he can put his hand under the bib to caress her breasts while my other hand has unfastened four buttons over her hip and slid inside to explore the hillock of her belly, feeling delicately down it to the rough mat and soft step before the sweet door of home.

A distant door slams and Superb says, "Charlie, Max has just come in, I'll see you at six."

She replaces the receiver and goes downstairs.

Max sits in the lounge staring at the blank television screen. She walks past him to the kitchen where the table is already set saying, "Come and get it."

They sit eating. He pleads with her to stay with him this weekend. She refuses. He suddenly says, "Why dress like a whore?"

"Say that again, Max."

"Why dress like a whore to visit your mother?"

She smiles sweetly and says, "What are you afraid of, Max?"

He glares at her. She rises, strolls to the garage door, turns, spreads her arms sideways and shakes her hips in a sexy little shimmy. She says, "Do whores really look like this?"

"They certainly do!"

She pouts, unfastens the bib of the dungarees, removes her blouse, drops it on a chair and refastens the stiff fabric over her nude breasts. Legs astride, hands on hips, she smiles at Max tauntingly and says, "Think I'll get more customers like this?"

Why can he not spring upon her, force her to the floor and enjoy her thoroughly? Because we cannot rape someone we know well. I can't, anyway. Neither can Max. He has risen to his feet and stands dazzled, daunted by the bonny perfection of her challenge. All he can say is, "My GOD Terry you're not going to drive to your mother's house like that?"

"Why not Max? It's a warm night. And I promise not to

pick up any hitchhikers unless they're very young, very handsome and very, very strong."
She goes into the garage. He follows. As she lays her hand on the car door he embraces her from behind, folding his arms round her waist, pressing his face into the back of her neck. She sighs patiently and stands absolutely still. He whispers, "Terry, I'm sorry I said that, you look great, really great. Please stay with me this one weekend, Terry. I need you."
She remains perfectly still until he releases her. She gets into the car saying, "Some other time, Max. Momma expects me."
She drives off dressed exactly as her lover wants her, all nude and ready under the one-piece denim dungarees.

At six o'clock exactly (to hell with 18.00 hours, I hate digital clocks) she drives into a multi-storey car park knowing that Charlie has checked in two minutes earlier. She sees his car before docking her own in a nearby space. She recalls his last words on the phone: "I don't want you wearing anything but those dungarees, right?"
An excited little smile comes to her face. "*Right*," she whispers, and slips off her shoes before leaving the car. A feeling of cold gritty concrete underfoot, a feeling of fear as she quickly crosses a cold space to the red rolltop twoseater. Car parks are inhuman places, bleak warehouses for machines, a setting for any kind of evil. But Charlie opens the door to her, she slides into what she thinks is safety, the door closes, they kiss. His hands touch her briefly all over. She whispers, "I'm exactly like you told me to be."
"Good," he says, withdrawing a moment.
"Where are you taking me?"
"Nowhere yet."
He reaches across the car, snapping shades down over all the windows. A dim red light above the windscreen makes her suntanned skin look warm negro, the dungarees look pink. The two seats are upholstered in thick fleece with very high backs which he folds down flat. I suppose the gearlever between the seats can be unscrewed or folded down so that he can take her in his arms, unbutton, undo her etcetera. Will I imagine their lovemaking in detail? Certainly not.

Thousands of people must enjoy imagining what mouths, hands and pricks do to other mouths, breasts and cunts because long descriptions of this activity fill magazines sold on station bookstalls. It strikes me as innocent stuff but no fun at all, mere sliding anatomy. Yes yes yes the greatest and most essential good in the world is two people feeling safe enough, at home enough, to give and take delight in each other's bodies without haste, worry or greed. Once I could enjoy such lovemaking for over an hour, it led to sleep from which I emerged into more of it. I grew so thin and lean that when I went home one weekend my mother asked if I had taken up football? When I said I had not she looked at me closely then said, "Aye well. Just you be very careful," and we dropped the matter. So I cannot read these descriptions without feeling completely separated from what I most enjoyed. In this bed in Selkirk or Peebles I only find entertainment in sexual dramas between selfish bitches and sneaky plotters, between lustful bullies and their slaves. But it will not bore or overexcite me to imagine that Charlie, in his smart red rolltop woo-grotto, makes love to Superb like I made love to Helen in the two years after we married. During the last fortnight of a magnificent summer – a summer more rich and strange than any millionaire, president or king ever enjoyed – I loved her shyly, wonderingly, without ever once touching her. I was unable to believe she cared a damn for me. But after she came to my closet, after the threats, tears, hypocrisy, the false smiles and falser speeches we lay side by side in a bed legalised and blessed by the Church, I was still almost unable to touch her. Sometimes I placed an arm across her shoulders feeling a lonely pity for us both. We were victims of a complicated trick which nobody had planned. But I could not, would not make love until she indicated that she wanted it, and then I roused myself by caressing her as if she were the slave of a completely selfish lust, and I entered her vindictively with a penis which I thought of as a truncheon or redhot poker. Let Superb be so sick of her husband's timid caresses that Charlie's hard truncheon and redhot poker technique is exactly what she wants. He applies it hard to her twice and afterward, dozing in his arms, she murmurs, "Mmm I needed that, honey. You're so good, you know."

Helen seemed to enjoy that sort of lovemaking. It was over quickly but she held me tight afterward when I allowed her to. Sometimes the coitus made me feel so vigorous and hopeful that I had to rise, dress and go for a walk through the dark streets wondering how to improve this life of mine. Should I leave her? Should I emigrate? Could I not find a woman to love who would respect me and whom I could respect? Sometimes after a difficult day the lovemaking pleasantly exhausted me and I lay in her arms feeling that life was not a bad business. One evening I came home and saw on the living-room table a pile of photographic bondage magazines, *Hogtie*, *Harlots in Harness*, *Knotty*, that kind of thing. Perhaps I blushed. Certainly my face went hot. Helen said, "These were in your desk. I wasn't spying, I was looking for a spare envelope. If you wanted to hide them you should have locked the drawer."

I said, "Yes, I suppose I should."

"Why did you buy them?"

"They help me."

"With what?"

I decided not to mention masturbation. Helen wanted sex only two or three times a week, I needed it more often. I said, "They help me with you."

"How can they?"

"They help me to come. Ejaculate."

After a long pause she said flatly, "You don't love me."

"I love you more than anybody else I know."

"But when we make love you have to imagine doing horrible things to me."

"Only for fun."

"I need a cup of tea."

She left the room. I took the magazines out to the midden and buried them under old bottles and potato peelings knowing she could see me from the kitchen window. Later, when I bought new ones, I did keep the desk drawer carefully locked. But after that day we did not make love again till nine years passed away. Why? She had liked my lovemaking till then, I certainly had not forced it on her. Perhaps she was shocked to discover that my brisk truncheon was more than a tame animal she summoned to serve her.

Perhaps she had fantasies of totally dominating me. Certainly she hated feeling subordinate. So do I.

I hate feeling subordinate so Superb, comfortably truncheoned, lies in a lazy dwam while Charlie sits up, places a rug over her and raises the back of his seat saying, "There's no need for you to move."
"Where are you taking me?"
"A quiet little place in the country."
"My bag is still in the other car."
"Leave it. This quiet little place has everything a woman can possibly want."
"It sounds like heaven."
He drives off and Superb falls asleep. I suppose a bossy woman can relax with a man of the same type if she thinks she can get rid of him whenever she likes.

She wakes when the car stops. The rug is gently removed and Charlie leans down to kiss her. He says, "We're here."
"I don't want to move."
"Lie on your front."
"Why?"
"I've a surprise for you. A present."
She turns over. She feels him grip her right arm and something cold is clicked round it above the elbow, then her left arm is pulled hard back and with another click she discovers that her elbows have been handcuffed behind her. She cries, "Hey that *hurts*, Charlie!" and starts struggling on to her knees but his hands, suddenly rough, force her face down into the fleece again pressing hard on her shoulders as he kneels astride her. Where are the dungarees? In a tangle round an ankle, she is otherwise naked. "Charlie," she gasps, "what are you trying to do?"
His answer makes her forget the pain in her elbows.
"Listen Terry. Listen hard or you won't understand a thing. We're in the basement of an organisation which will pay me big money for bringing you here. But before I hand you over I'm going to give you something extra special to remember me by."
And his hands cruelly grasp her buttocks and DANGER OVEREXCITEMENT DANGER OVEREXCITEMENT,

THINK OTHER THINGS QUICK WHAT? ANYTHING, THESE I HAVE LOVED THE ROUGH MALE KISS OF BLANKETS, GOOD STRONG THICK STUPEFYING INCENSE SMOKE and jellies soother than the creamy curd.

Whan that Aprille with his shoures soote sharked up a list of lawless resolutes where wealth accumulates and men decay bird thou never wert.
I am an idiot.
"You require an exercise to focus your mind. I have no favourites in this class. Go to the blackboard, pick up the chalk and write out three simple words which I will dictate to you. For each mis-spelled word you will receive a stroke from my famous Lochgelly. Are you ready? Station. Passion. Cushion."
I was not a very bad speller, these words did not usually bother me. I wrote,

STATION
PAS

and stuck there. *Passion* suddenly seemed highly unlikely. I compromised and wrote,

PASTION

A girl giggled. In Hislop's class the girls were expected to giggle at certain times, especially the attractive girls. I now knew I was going to get one of the belt at least and the word *cushion*, fully formed in my mind's eye, suddenly seemed altogether incredible. I wrote CU and could go no further. Hislop sighed and sat down at his desk with elbows on lid and face in hands like a weary and defeated man. He said, "Was it for this the clay grew tall? Perhaps one of you ladies, Heather Sinclair, will show him how to spell cushion."
So the best speller in the class came out and corrected passion and completed cushion while Hislop produced the famous Lochgelly and told me to hold out my hands. I should never have held out my hand. It allowed him to look dignified while he was hurting me. But nobody ever disobeyed Hislop. When he gave two strokes of the belt he used both hands and drew it from behind his shoulder so it was almost as sore as the legal maximum of six delivered with one hand from the elbow. I cried out at the first blow

and at the second crouched almost double over my crippled hands. He said, "Now look me in the face!" and his voice had that hysterical edge to it which is why we called him mad. I looked at him. I was not sobbing but I was weeping, the tears he despised were flowing down my cheeks. He said, "You are nothing but a big soft lassie. Get to your seat!"

The worst thing he could call a boy was a lassie yet the girls quite liked him. He was gentle and polite with girls, almost courtly, he never patted them playfully or placed an arm round their shoulders when correcting their exercises like some men teachers did. And women liked Hislop. I did not tell my mother that he had belted me because I believed that getting hurt that way was a shameful thing, but a classmate must have told his mother who told my mother, for she suddenly said, "I heard poor Hislop was hard on you last week."

I shrugged my shoulders. She said, "Don't think too badly of him. He's very good to his wife."

Mrs Hislop was a bedridden invalid. Out of his not very large salary Hislop paid an old woman to attend her while he was not himself at home.

Could my mother and Hislop possibly have? Could *he* be my real? Oh no no no but. But I was once in a railway carriage with an old man who would not stop furtively staring at me. At last he said, "Excuse me, but you have a strong resemblance to someone I used to know. Is your name Hislop, by any chance?"

I said it was not. He said, "But you're from the long town?"

That was the local nickname of the town I grew up in. I said, yes I was from the long town, and a Hislop had been my English teacher, but my father was the timekeeper at the pit.

He said, "Oh that explains it."

I said, "Explains what?"

He frowned. A moment later he said that Hislop belonged to the old breed of Scottish schoolteacher, hard but just; if a boy in his class showed the slightest spark of talent or manhood he would move heaven and earth to encourage it; many a lawyer and doctor from the long town owed their university degrees to Hislop. The Hislop he spoke of seemed a few years younger than the one I remembered who had encouraged nobody very much, but perhaps there were no sparks of talent in my class at school. And the old man had avoided my question, he had not told me why my father being timekeeper explained my resemblance to Hislop the English teacher, a resemblance which I never heard anyone else refer to. It lies in the mouth and eyes and can easily be explained without the notion of paternity. If you are much impressed by someone you do come to resemble them. That is why people who live together can acquire a family expression which embraces husband, wife, children, yes even the dog or cat. So there may be a look on my face which belongs to Hislop because he taught it to me. True, I am the same height as Hislop and both my parents are taller people but that it not unusual. True, when my father the timekeeper died I discovered from documents that he had married three months before my birthday. But in Scotland premarital sex is as common as anywhere else in the world. A registrar once told me that since the start of the last century, when the public records first made it notorious, over half the marriages in our county have taken place after pregnancy. But surely SIX months after pregnancy is a bit unusual? I married Helen six weeks after she stopped bleeding. My father the timekeeper was a man who always did what he thought was right. In spite of his socialism, or else because of it, he was the most decently conventional man I have ever known. He never drank, never swore, never said a hard word against a private individual. Why would a man like that wait half a year before doing the decent thing by the mother of his child? What was my mother doing, what feeling, in that half-year? I am a completely ordinary man but my birth is as mysterious to me as my death and I will never learn the truth of it now.

"Don't think badly of poor Hislop, he's very good to his wife," but Hislop acted very strangely toward me. The two sorts of boys he most tormented in his classroom were the energetic ones who disliked what he taught and could not sit still, and the poor puzzled ones who hardly understood a word he said, especially not his sarcastic little jokes. "The antonym of *blunt*, Anderson, is not *jaggy*. The antonym of *blunt* is *sharp*. You have heard the word *sharp* before? Of course you have. So your employment of local slang is either a conscious or unconscious effort to destroy communication between the provinces of a once mighty empire. Are you a linguistic saboteur or are you an idiot?"

And he pressed his lips together and shook with an almost silent little chuckle. I was not clever but I was not a dunce and not rebellious. I was one of the middle people who normally get by without praise or blame. Yet I am 60 per cent certain that I was given the belt more than anyone else in that class. And each time he gave it he told me he had no favourites. He never said that to anyone else. Why?

One day Hislop did not come to school because his wife had died. For a fortnight we were taught English by the headmaster, an ordinary old man who used the belt lightly and seldom, without dramatic tension. Even Anderson the dunce started learning a few things. On the second Friday the headmaster said, "Next week Mr Hislop will be back. He has suffered a terrible bereavement, so I hope you will all be very good boys and girls and give him no trouble. Our school, you know, is very fortunate to have Mr Hislop on the staff. He was a very brave soldier during the war. He spent three years in a Japanese prisoncamp."

These words told me something I had never before suspected: the other teachers knew what a hell Hislop made in his classroom. The headmaster was trying to convey what my mother meant when she told me Hislop was very good to his wife: "Eat all the shit he gives you, the poor bugger can't help dishing it out."

And we got the message. The headmaster's words impressed even me. On Monday when Hislop entered the room I gazed at him with something like wonder. He no longer seemed a monster. He looked small, lonely and haggard, very ordinary and dismal.

And his eye travelled at once to mine, and his hand shot toward me and crooked its index finger twice. I got up and went to him on trembling legs, and when I got close he bent down and whispered in a voice nobody else in the room could hear, "How dare you look at me in that condescending fashion? I will have no favourites in this class. Hold out your hands, and double them."

I did so in a daze of astonishment. Did I cry out at the first blow? Almost certainly, but afterward I did not flinch and certainly did not weep. I was so full of icy hatred that I probably forgot I had hands. Yet when he stopped I did not lower them, I glared at him with a rigid grin I can feel on my face at this very moment, and I stepped toward him and raised my hands till they almost touched his chin and I whispered, "Again!"

He went soft. He smiled and nodded, slipping the Lochgelly over his shoulder under the jacket. He said gently, "Go to your seat son. There's a spark of manhood in you."

And I saw the whole horrible pattern of Mad Hislop's soul. He was not essentially cruel, just insane. He really believed that teaching small people to take torture from big people, and crushing their natural reaction to it, was a way of improving them. If he was my father (which I doubt) he must have felt belting me was a sort of loveletter to my mother: "You have borne me a child, I am making a man of it." He was probably depressed by the amount of torture he had to inflict to produce that steady glare of hatred which proved he had made the thing he called a man. But he never doubted that the effort was worthwhile. How could he? As I returned to my seat, frozenfaced and loathing him, it was obvious that I had become more important. The other boys stared at me in perfect stillness, astonished by my newfound toughness, apart from two other tough guys who smiled crookedly, meaning: You're one of us now. On the girls' side of the room there was a slight whispering agitation, a definite stir of interest, and for a moment I hated them almost as much as I hated Hislop. Women don't despise themselves for weeping, why do they admire men who won't or can't? Why are so many of them attracted by bullies and killers? Why are so many MEN attracted by bullies and killers? Shit. Shit. Shit. Shit. Shit. Shit. Shit.

I suppose Hislop produced the man he wanted for I have not wept from that day to this. Wrong. I later wept two tears, one at each eye when, seated before a television set some time in 1977, Scotland's victory over Czechoslovakia made it certain that we would compete in the World Cup. I have never been to a live football match in my life but as the Scottish supporters cheered and started singing 'Oh Flower of Scotland', a song I hate (why don't they sing 'A Man's a Man for a' That'? we don't live by its sentiments but we ought to live by them) as the Scottish supporters started bellowing that cheap bit of spineless chauvinism an irrational heat in my eyeballs produced on the surface of each one a lateblossoming bead of brine. These did not defile my cheeks. I did not let them spill. I sniggered meanly, like Hislop reacting to one of his own jokes, and tilted my head back, and stayed perfectly still until the tears dried by evaporation.

"The Lord Chastiseth whom he loveth," says the bloody old Bible. Perhaps that is how God behaves but sane people don't. Nobody beats the people they love unless perverted by anxiety or vile examples. In which knowledge I now, in perfectly cold blood, return to my Superb who is being raped up the arse by Charlie. Since the best whisky in the world cannot fill my mind with happy memories I must get back to a fantasy and keep control of it this time. On second thoughts, leave Superb and Charlie for a while and make a completely fresh start. Goodbye to school for ever, I hope.

6: BRIGHT TUNEFUL

PIANO MUSIC. Firm hands with redlacquered nails grip the wheel of a smoothly speeding car. Ahead of the windscreen a busy sunlit road bends to a curve. Hitchhikers stand on the verge holding out cards chalked with placenames. The firm hands slow down the car past two bearded men bound for Los Angeles, a boy and girl waiting sadly for Chicago, two girls enthusiastic for New York, and stop it beside a solitary girl in short short short white shorts and heliotrope blouse unbuttoned almost to her navel who holds a card saying ANYWHERE. Dark abundant hair hangs down her back. This is Janine, but a more eagerly smiling Janine than the one who sat in the car with Max. She wears white sandals, no stockings, carries rucksack. As she bends to enter the car I have a plan view of her white bum vanishing under the roof of a red twoseater which zooms off along the roadway. I ought to be a film director. I can imagine exactly what I want.

The hard throb of a kettledrum mixes with the bright piano music. Seen through the windscreen from in front the hands on the wheel belong to Helga, who is tall, slender, handsome, cool, Nordic, with long straight blonde hair, and high cheekbones, and eyes long and narrow with ice-blue pupils. Janine is talking to her vehemently, with many grimaces and nods of the head which shake down a heavy dark curl over one eye. Helga, driving fast but carefully, only shows how her passenger fascinates her by a small sideways glance and enigmatic smile.

A high view of busy motorway with red twoseater leaving it by a small sideroad. A high security fence on one side shuts off a thick wood. The car passes (but does not pass through) a wide-open gate in this fence. It slows down, then parks on grass verge. Cut music.

Faint birdsong and sound of wind among trees. From beside the open gate I see two women leave the car by opposite doors, hear the slight clunk of the doors shutting, see them meet behind the car and kiss. Then hand in hand they walk quickly back along the fence toward me, tall slim handsome blonde, small plump pretty brunette. Janine is not wearing shorts, a clumsy notion, her long loose black skirt, unbuttoned to mid-thigh, is tossed sideways by the breeze the same way that it sways her dark hair. As the women near the gate I see that their faces are dreamy and slightly openmouthed. They are too shy and excited to look at each other. A rear view of them pausing hand in hand, staring through the gateway. A rough track curves into the wood. It is Helga who takes the first step forward. She leads Janine across the track and under the thickleaved branches on the far side. The women enter the lushgreen sunlit windshaken leaves as if entering a thick mist or running river, they disappear almost completely into it. My mind's eye starts to follow them slowly, rising as it follows so that, just as I reach the gate, and it swings shut, I cannot see who has pushed it. I hear the click of a lock, the scrape of a turning key. Along strands of wire at the top of the gate (between which I can see the foliage where the women vanished) appear the words **CAUGHT IN BARBED WIRE: A Superbitch Production.**

Good. From now on I will subdue my lust for what I create by keeping the eye of imagination as cool as a camera lens, the ear of imagination as discreet as a small microphone. Eye and ear move through the words and wires. They cross the track and stealthily penetrate screen after screen of leaves. A distant bird chirps. I hear whispers, then a blissful moan. I have forgotten to imagine what Helga is wearing. Is my interest in the sexual provocation of women's clothes waning? Please God, don't let that happen. Helga must wear tight jeans because of the boy with the catapult. Another blissful moan. The last screen of leaves parts. I look down on a patch of grass where

Janine is laid out among her loose dark hair. Strands of it stray across eyelids ecstatically closed, lips ecstatically moaning, are caught between breasts spilling out of the satin blouse ecstatically unbuttoned. It is a loose blouse with a few big white buttons. The black velvet skirt hugging her plump hips is fastened by buttons of the same kind and Helga's firm hand deftly undoes them then slips caressingly between Janine's parting thighs to tenderly explore moist secret valley while Helga's tongue probes thick hair to find Janine's delicate little ear. Lightly Helga nibbles lobe then murmurs, "No bra. No panties. You little devil, you were looking for this."

"Mm. I didn't expect to be so lucky. Don't stop."

"And won't you undress me?" asks Helga who (apart from big pocketflaps on buttocks and breasts) is dressed tight where Janine is loose and wears cowboy boots while Janine has kicked off her sandals. Janine whispers, "Later. I'm lazy just now. Do some more nice things to me."

Bright spots of sunlight through the moving leaves dance over their lovemaking.

I must interrupt them soon though I would prefer to join them. It must be wonderful to be among two women who are lazily enjoying each other and want to share a stiff prick. Pricks are made for cunts. Sontag sometimes wanted a sexual trio, but with two men. She told me so. I said, "Ah."

"Have you no nice manfriend with whom you would like to share me?"

"None atall."

"Never mind, I know many people. I am sure I can find someone suitable."

"Oh."

"Do you not like the idea?"

It suddenly struck me that Sontag, with two men simultaneously entering her from opposite sides or at opposite ends, would be in no position to give bossy little lectures while lovemaking. Perhaps another man and I could turn her into a pure instrument of pleasure. I grew excited and said, "That idea might be worth investigating."

She smiled and said coyly, "I am corrupting you!"

"Oh?"

"You have never before admitted to wanting a homosexual liaison."

"I don't want one. You will be between the other man and me. I refuse to lay a finger on him."

She shouted angrily, "That is ludicrous! That really makes me laugh! Why must you suppress all feeling for your own sex? Do you not realise that you cannot satisfy a woman if you do not love yourself, and you cannot love yourself if you recoil from your own sex?"

"That sounds like trigonometry."

"Yes yes but you will not evade me by making a joke. It is inhuman not to love people of your own sex, a man of your age *must* have wished to do it once or twice. And caressing another man is much the same as caressing yourself."

"I never caress myself."

"You must. You masturbate."

"Yes, but without touching myself."

"Impossible!"

It struck me then that most women do find it impossible to masturbate without using their hands. This made me feel slightly superior. I smiled and shrugged my shoulders. Sontag scowled and said, "How do you do it?"

I told her that I imagined an exciting adventure with a woman. At the climax I came against my mattress as if it was the woman.

"Aha! You use your mattress like a woman, which is why you wish to use me like a mattress. Thankyou, but no."

Sontag scored many little verbal triumphs like that over me. They made neither of us much happier.

But she had uncovered something which surprised me. Until she suggested it I had never thought of pleasing my own body with my own hands and the notion filled me with almost fearful distaste, distaste very like my distaste for touching or being touched by another man. I know from experience that embracing a woman brings sweetness mixed with anxiety and leads to pain, but I feel automatically that bodily contact with a man is purely repulsive, why?
"Hold out your hands and double them."
I refuse to blame poor Hislop for everything wrong with me. He was the only bad teacher I ever had and I had him for less than a year. And my father the timekeeper never hit me, never even touched me after the time when he carried me on his shoulders. He was solemn and conscientious, deliberate in his speech and not much fun, but physically very gentle. Were the fights to blame? On my way to or from school, when I had a slight disagreement with another boy, one of us sometimes ran out of sensible words, lost his temper and used hurtful words which the other, in order not to seem weak, used back. Left to ourselves we usually separated shouting insults as we went, but if other boys were near they surrounded us in an excited ring and we had to swipe at each other until one or both burst into tears or we were mercifully separated by a passing adult. I had some ugly encounters of that sort between the ages of seven and twelve, but not more than most boys. In every school there are Mad Hislops among the pupils who like tormenting folk. I hear there are bullies even among girls. Bullies usually attack smaller children who lack friends. I don't know why, but they never attacked me. Yet I still had a physical dread of football. I though it was midway between a primary school punchup and the Second World War. All these things show my early cowardice and dread of the male body but do not explain it. Some questions will never be answered. Forget them.

Helga's hand softly explores and caresses Janine's secret moist valley, Helga's teeth lightly nibble a pink earlobe among Janine's dark tangle of hair, bright spots of sunlight through the shaking leaves dance over their lovemaking and I wish I could keep things as sweet at this. But since I cannot join these ladies I can only stay with them by conjuring up an evil spirit. The blissful whispers are cut by a nasty falsetto giggle. Janine's eyes blink open. Helga rolls aside, kneels, gazes sharply around. "I'm up here," says a voice.

Along a thick bough twelve feet above their heads sprawls a small barefoot person wearing dungaree overalls a size too big for him rolled up to the knee, and a wristwatch with a very thick metal-studded strap. He could be a child of ten but has the bald wrinkled head of a gleeful old man. He says, "Don't stop, I like what you do."
"Little *bastard*!" spits Helga, rising to her feet and looking round for a stone to throw. Janine sits up, brushing back her hair and fumbling with her blouse.
"Leave your tits the way they are, Hugo likes them like that," the bad boy says. Helga fails to see any stone.
"Come on, honey," she says, pulling Janine to her feet, "he's crazy. Let's get out of here."
"You can't!" says the bad boy, "I've locked the gate."
He holds up a key that shines like silver in the sun. Helga stares at him then says, "Wait here," and pushes through the branches that screen the track leaving Janine stooping to fasten her skirt. The boy says conversationally, "I don't know why you bother. In a few minutes you'll have to undo it again."
"Just who do you think you are?" says Janine.
"Hugo calls me Cupid. He *loves* the trespassers I catch for him."
Helga returns muttering, "Yes, he's locked the gate."
Hands on hips she stands astride staring up at Cupid who now sits astride the bough, hands on hips and grinning cheerfully back. She speaks in a voice that tries to sound sensible and casual at the same time: "All right, son, you've had your fun with us. Now open the gate."
"Bluejean dolly, my fun with you is just beginning."
"Listen kid," says Helga, "I can climb a tree as well as you! I don't want to, it'll mess my clothes and I hate using violence on an infant, but when I get hold of you I'll thrash

you till you wish you'd never been born. So just throw down that key!"
"No, I'll lose my bounty if I do that."
"What bounty?"
"A piece of your arse."
Helga grabs a branch and pulls herself into the tree. Stop. This is America. Go back.
"What bounty?"
"A piece of your ass."
Helga grabs a branch and pulls herself into the tree.

Cupid drops the key into the bibpocket of his dungarees, takes out a small plastic box and pulls up an aerial from one side of it. He says into it, "Hello Hugo? Hello Hugo. Hello there, two she-trespassers are in at the side gate, I've locked it, they're just the right age and just your type. Hurry. They're under the chestnut tree. A bluejean wildcat is climbing up here to get me, I'm gonna make her squeal for you."
Helga is almost level with him by now. One foot has just left a lower branch, a leg is hooked over a branch above, her weight swings from upstretched arms clutching a branch higher than the bough where Cupid sits. He pockets the radio, pulls out a big metal fork with a thick elastic sling and takes slow aim saying, "Where will I give it to you honey? I use lead slugs!"
Helga freezes, swinging. Her wide-open mouth and eyes show that she feels she is all target, she stares at the bulging crotch of Cupid's dungarees. He says, "From here I can see one halfmoon curve of your big sweet ass. Will I start with that?"
Suddenly Helga pulls herself upward. There is a twang, she shrieks, then two more twangs and shrieks and a wild threshing of leaves as Helga goes down the tree in something more like a scrabbling fall than a climb. She lands on her feet but with jeans ripped to the knee, her shirt pulled out of them and wrenched off both shoulders (unconvincing) wrenched off one shoulder. And now, getting rapidly nearer, comes the noise of a truck and barking dogs. Helga grabs Janine by the arms and says, "Listen, I'm running, one of us *must* get away, you run too but a different way honey and stall them, stall them if they catch you I'll be back –"

Helga flees from the clearing but Janine does not. She is more dazed by astonishment than terror. Her hands automatically push back her hair and smooth her blouse and skirt as we hear the truck engine stop and see Hugo push through the branches. He is fat bald muscular, naked to the waist and wearing corduroys tucked into combat boots. He has a thick black beard, dark glasses and a revolver in his belt. Two silent Alsations stalk by his side and four yapping terriers. Janine stares up at him, apprehensive. He smiles kindly down at her then reaches forward with both hands and tears the blouse down to her hips exposing enough. Enough enough enough. Cut to:

Helga sprinting across open ground, distant barking of dogs. Then Helga wading through waistdeep weeds, hair and shirt dishevelled, face and breasts shiny with sweat, the only sound is distant birdsong and her loud gasps for breath. She comes to a big coil of barbed wire extending left and right as far as she can see. It is the sort I remember from old war films, higher than a man and supported at intervals by cross-shaped girders. I think they were a sort of tanktrap. This wire is very old and rusty, brambles and convolvulus entwine the lower parts. On the other side is a line of trees and behind the trees the top of an embanked motorway with traffic whizzing along. So Helga, no longer gasping quite so violently for breath, tucks her shirt back into her jeans, quickly rolls the torn ends of them up to her knees, pulls with her hands two strands of wire as far apart as possible, and cautiously inserts one leg. And here control will certainly be lost unless I think other things for a while.

But I am glad to be enjoying myself in the open air, I've had too little of that. My happiest memories are swinging over a puddle full of sunlight in a sunlit wood and being carried over fields in a kingly way on my father's shoulders. "It is inhuman not to love people of your own sex," said Sontag. I certainly loved my father the timekeeper. He took me walks that were sheer delight, perhaps because my mother was with us. Then the walks became dull, perhaps because she stayed at home. Dad developed a bad habit of stopping beside every flower or tree which caught my eye, producing a pocket botany book and laboriously looking up the name. This made walks very boring so I insisted on staying at home with my mother, and after that Dad went walks by himself or with his friend, Old Red.

Dad spoiled several good things with his serious helpfulness. One day, long before I was old enough for school, I was playing on the kitchen floor when I found some discarded envelopes in the wastepaper basket. My eye was caught by the brightness of the stamps which suddenly looked like windows into clearer, more exciting worlds. One of them, it must have come from my mother's cousin in New Zealand, showed a longbeaked wingless bird poking the grass of a field on the far side of the world, and on the British stamps the crimson behind the king's elegant profile seemed the best red I had ever seen. I wanted these magic little windows which nobody else wanted. With a pair of nailscissors I cut the stamps off the envelopes and trimmed away the perforated edges which I thought an unimportant frill. I then glued the stamps to a page in a discarded pocket diary. My mother must have given me the scissors, tube of glue and diary but they came so exactly when I needed them that I don't remember her giving them at all. There was no interval between wanting the stamps, cutting them free from the dull torn crumpled envelopes and putting them safely in my own little book. It was all one pure action, one pure thought. That night I showed Dad what I had made. He examined it with nods of the head, then explained that I should not have used glue. Real stamp collectors used a special kind of paper hinge. Also, real collectors did not cut off the perforated edge, for this destroyed the value of the stamp. All the same, he was pleased with me, I had made a beginning and that (he said) was the important thing. On the following Saturday he went by train into Glasgow, we thought to see a football match, but he returned in the early afternoon carrying a parcel and looking excited. He said, "This is all for you, Jock. I got them from Ferris's stamp shop. I know Bill Ferris."

He unpacked a huge new stamp album with a blank page in it for every country in the world. And an envelope full of assorted stamps of all nations. And a fat green Stanley Gibbons catalogue to help identify them. And a packet of hinges, pair of tweezers, neatly folding magnifying glass and tiny porcelain bath in which stamps could be detached from envelopes without damaging the perforations. My mother said something about expense. Dad said the money spent was an investment in my future: when I got to school my stamp collection would help my geography. He spread his big and intricate adult toys all over the kitchen table and tried to teach me how to play with them but it was too much, too difficult, too bloody boring. He was not discouraged. He said, "We'll take it in easy stages. We'll do ten minutes' work on it every evening after tea, you'll soon master it." I never mastered it. I probably complained too loudly. I cannot remember what became of the album, the multinational stamps, the fat green catalogue. A couple of days after he died I found the folding magnifying glass in a small bureau drawer beside his First World War medals.

Poor Dad. I suspect he was a lonely man. He did not mean to crush my delight in my little book of magic windows and he certainly prepared me for LIFE – which is a spark of delight buried under routines disciplines possessions plans and compromises which are meant to protect it, help it grow, make it useful to other people, and which eventually smother and kill it. But I'm not dead yet. Helga wades waistdeep through weeds, hair and shirt deliciously dishevelled, face and breasts shiny with sweat, and comes to the coil of barbed wire. She stops, gasping for breath, then quickly tucks her shirt back into her jeans, rolls the torn legs of the jeans up to mid-thigh and carefully with her hands pulls apart two strands of the wire and of course my Dad was a lonely man. One week I had three letters from him which I never read.

He usually sent me one letter every month, but several years after my mother left him this spate of three arrived with a day between each. Since I had not answered a previous letter (though I had certainly read it) I was afraid these letters were accusing me of neglect. He had never accused me of neglecting him, never made a self-pitying remark in his life, but I did neglect him and did pity him, so three envelopes marked with my name in his firm book-keeper's hand lay on the mantelpiece like unanswerable accusations. Helen said, "You are being very stupid, very inconsiderate."

I said, "I agree."

She said, "Your father may not like me but he is a thoroughly nice man."

I said, "My father likes you a lot and yes, he is a thoroughly nice man."

She said, "So open these letters *now*, he may be in trouble."

I said coldly, "I know I am being irrational, but I will not open these letters till I have replied to the one before them. I may do that tonight."

And I went off to work. When I returned that evening Helen was looking distressed. She said, "I've read his letters – please give him a phonecall, he's very unhappy."

"Oh?"

"He finds it difficult to sleep – he's having nightmares about your mother. He keeps dreaming that she comes to him in a terrible state, all bleeding and accusing him of hurting her – killing her."

The roots of my hair tingled. My scalp tightened so much that for a moment I felt my heart beating in it. We had not heard that my mother was dead. For all I know she still is alive. I went to the phone and dialled my father's nearest neighbour. He could easily have afforded a telephone, I had offered to pay for that myself, but he said only invalids and businessmen needed telephones. The neighbour brought him to the phone and in a very cheerful ordinary voice Dad said, "Hullo son."

I said, "Hullo Dad, I'm coming down to see you tomorrow."

He said, "Tomorrow? We're both working men. Come down on Saturday, we can spend more time together."

My heart sank at that but I said, "Right, I'll be down early on Saturday morning."

"Good. How's Helen?"

"Fine."

"Good. Give her my best regards."

"I'll do that. Good night Dad."

"Good night son."

I put down the telephone, went to the mantelpiece, picked up three letters in their opened envelopes, tore them across and flung them in the fire. I had never encountered my father when he was in an inferior position and I refused to do so. Was this cowardice? I think it was respect. I went down to see him on Saturday by bus (the railway line had been closed, uprooted by then) and enjoyed a really good day.

We walked by Uplaw farm on to a track over the moor. Dad, for once, talked cheerfully about the state of Britain. After years of Conservative rule we now had a Labour administration. Harold Wilson had to be cautious just now (said my father) and play the game with his cards very close to his chest, but when he finally recognised his true partners he would show his hand and British socialism might very well enter a new constructive phase. I don't know if Dad had picked up that metaphor from the *Daily Worker*, the *Tribune* or the *New Statesman* because he took all three. I made noncommittal grunting noises. My business acquaintances, some of them in the Labour Party, had told me that the new administration would be as conservative as it dared to be without provoking a trade union revolt. They were wrong. It became so conservative that it eventually provoked a trade union revolt. But although Dad had fought in the first and worst world war, and been through a general strike, a major lock-out and a depression, he had not faced the fact that it does not matter how the British manual worker votes at an election, because the leaders of the big parties only disagree about small things, things which do not disturb their investments. This perfectly frank and open conspiracy ensures whatever stability our Great and United Britannic Kingdom possesses and I approve of it – except when I get into my Scottish Nationalist phase and think, Fuck the lot of you. But I never argued with Dad about politics and he died without knowing I was a Tory. On this brisk afternoon with its cool breeze and alternating spells of rain and sunshine I heard his hopeful speculations with one ear and the skylarks with the other. We never spoke of the letters and this made me so happy that at last I said, with perfect honesty, words I had been rehearsing all the way

down in the bus: "Dad, we've a spare room in our house, why not come and live with us? Helen likes you."
He grinned with pleasure and said, "Thanks son but my affairs are not quite as desperate as that. I might even surprise you. What would you say if I got married again?"
"I'd say it was a very good thing. Have you someone in mind?"
He looked shy for a moment and murmured that, in a way, yes, he had, but in another way, no, he had not. Then his arm rose, he stabbed at the horizon with a finger crying, "Look! The peaks of Arran."
I saw a low dark smudge against a pale patch of clear sky but was not much impressed. On a clear day in central Scotland you can see Arran from any high place west of Tinto. I said, "Anyway, Helen likes you so come and stay with us whenever you want."
This was the closest we came to mentioning his nightmares and his loneliness after my mother left him. He never wrote to me about bad dreams again, so I like to think he stopped having them. And he never remarried and never came to live with us, though when Helen left me he suggested that, since he was now retired, I might "find it handy" if he "looked after the house" for me. It was a practical plan. At sixty-five he was healthy, brisk and a good housekeeper. He kept his rooms as clean and tidy as Mum had done, and cooked for himself exactly the meals she had made. We would have been comfortable together. But I ignored the suggestion. Sharing a house with him would have been too much like another marriage.

On this last walk together I started noticing the flowering turf edging the track. I saw daisies and buttercups, two colours of clover, and bright, delicate little flowers I felt I knew very well though I could not remember having seen them before. I plucked a few. The head of one, smaller than a small fingernail and with a very frail stalk, looked like a yellow and scarlet ladies' sandal made of impossibly fine silk. I said, "What is this one called? Is it a member of the orchid family?"
"I don't know," said Dad.
The head of another was the size and shape of a bumblebee

with brownish-purple fur and several purple-pink wings stuck on at random. I said, "What is this one called?"
"I don't know," said Dad.
I said, "That's strange. You used to be keen on botany."
"Me? Oh no. I like flowers but I don't give a damn for botany."
I reminded him of the book he kept bringing out when I was a child and we went walks together. He said, "I bought that book because you kept asking me the names of the flowers you saw and I didn't know them. My father discouraged me from asking questions when I was small, I'm sure it impaired my education."
So I had made Dad's walks dull by asking him questions, he made mine dull by answering them. Real people are inexplicable. Since I cannot understand myself, how can I understand others? We are mysteries, every one of us. No wonder we turn from ordinary facts of life to religions, philosophies, stories, films and fantasies. These can be completely understood because people have made them for people. I know exactly why Helga, face and breasts shiny with sweat, pauses waistdeep in weeds to tuck her open shirt into her jeans, rolls her jeans above her knees then, stooping low, steps carefully between two strands of wire and gradually gets her whole body inside this irregular cage of barbs with only one foot on the ground outside. Do strands of her blonde hair catch on the wires? Yes, I see her head tugged suddenly back, her face winces but she has time to free the hair with her hands until. The only noise is her sobs of effort until

Violent barking. A great Alsation dog springs through the undergrowth, white fangs in gaping mouth. Helga's appalled face. She drags her foot within the wire. The jeans bunched round her thigh catch on several barbs, so again does her hair. With loud snarls the jaws of the dog snap between the strands, just missing a buttock but ripping off a pocketflap, good. And now her struggle to get out of the wire on the far side becomes frenzied, with three results.
1 Shirt and most of the jeans are ripped off until she wears only short short short tattered shorts.
2 Squealing, moaning, tearwet, sweatwet, her face is jerked from side to side by many shocks and efforts.

3 Her lovely and increasingly naked body is displayed in stretched and quivering positions.

This lets me enjoy her in the postures of lovemaking without having to envy men or women sharing them. But the business must be imagined very carefully, for although the jaggy wire is stripping her, making her stretch and squeal etcetera I want no bloodshed. Metal must not touch or pierce her if I cannot. So although this episode will look realistic it must be cunningly contrived. Better imagine it happening in slow motion, ★★★★★★★★★★★★★★★★★★★
★★★★★★★★★★★★★★ good, ★★★★★★★★★★★★★★★★
★★★★★★★★★★★★★★★★ good, ★★★★★★★★★★★★★★
★★★★★★★★★★★★★★★★★★ good, ★★★★★★★★★★★★
★★★★★★★★★★★★★★★★★★★★ good, ★★★★★★★★★★
★★★★★★★★★★★★★★★★★★★★★★ good, ★★★★★★★★
★★★★★★★★★★★★★★★★★★★★ good, ★★★★★★★★★★
★★★★★★★★★★★★★★★★★ good, ★★★★★★★★★★★★★
★★★★★★★★★★★★★★ good, ★★★★★★★★★★★★★★★★
★★★★★★★★★★★ good, ★★★★★★★★★★★★★★★★★★★
★★★★★★★★ good, ★★★★★★★★★★★★★★★★★★★★★★
★★★★★ good, ★★★★★★★★★★★★★★★★★★★★★★★★★
★★★★★★ good, ★★★★★★★★★★★★★★★★★★★★★★★★
★★★★★★★★★★ and Helga is free and stumbling toward the motorway naked but for white boots, torn minikilt of thick seams, studs, rags around bum and cunt, blonde hair over eyes so that just before reaching the trees she pushes through a hedge and falls, rolls down the side of a deep ditch and sprawls weeping at the bottom. There, after a sob of utter misery (which gives me, personally, no satisfaction but I need it to make her convincing) she raises the upper part of her body on her arms and looks round.

She is on a track along the bottom of the ditch. A security fence on the far side shuts off the trees hiding the embankment. A few yards from her a parked truck with a locked cage at the back contains terriers, an Alsation and Janine, who crouches half-naked in a corner.

"You're a great runner, it's a pleasure to meet you," says Hugo affably. He sits on a fallen treetrunk with Cupid beside him, a half-empty bottle of cheap wine on the ground at their feet. Cupid says, "I've never enjoyed a nicer picnic."

Another voice says, "Could we have that last bit over again? From where she comes to the wire?"
Everything goes black.

Everything goes black, then white, then I see that the whiteness is a blank cinema screen, a small one in a private viewing theatre. The seats are upholstered in red velvet, four steeply banked rows with six seats to a row. In the front row sits Stroud, Charlie, Hollis (who I haven't introduced before) and Helga who leans back calmly smoking. She wears something expensive and fashionable, something suitable for a careerwoman in showbusiness, I don't care what it is. In the back row sits Max embracing and hungrily kissing the waitress who once served Janine. She is dressed as she was, his hand is inside her skirt.
"Congratulations," Stroud says to Helga, "it must have been very hard both acting and directing that."
Helga shrugs and says, "Easier than directing someone else."
"But that business with the wire – how did you make it look so convincing?"
"There's no secret. I did it slowly and took a lot of time."
Hollis speaks. He is a bright-eyed, eager young man in black slacks and sweater, his voice is disturbingly childish.
"By the way Helga, did you know we have your partner Janine with us now?"
"Janine Crystal?"
"Yes. You know she claims *she* directed your movie?"
Helga smiles and says, "Janine is an ambitious kid."

The theatre lights go dim. The screen flickers then we see again Helga the actress with weeds open shirt sweatshiny etcetera etcetera etcetera. I wish my fantasies did not depend upon so much machinery. There is too much of it in ordinary life.

7: CUPID AND HUGO ARE MY FAVOURITE VILLAINS.

7: CUPID AND HUGO ARE MY FAVOURITE VILLAINS. I am sorry they only appear in that short film. Sontag would have liked them, or liked analysing them. She would probably have discovered they were subconscious portraits of me and my Dad the timekeeper. She kept discovering that everyone under the surface was the opposite of how they looked on top, especially if the top was simple and obvious. So men who loved lots of women were suppressed homosexuals, and happily married couples were murdering each other, and babies and small children were monsters of destructive egoism. I believe that under the surface we are very like how we appear above it, which is why so many surfaces last a lifetime without cracking. My fantasy about a straightforward rapist like Hugo cannot last long because he is too much my opposite. I can only identify with middle-class rapists who fuck with the help of expensive machines and a corrupted police force and a worldwide financial network. This is not surprising. National Security thinks the sun shines out of my arsehole.

A firm is a team, of course, but at the level of practical

management I am the only essential man in the National team, all the others can be replaced. Reeves, the head of Scottish installations, is not an essential man although he draws a larger salary. He is an administrator, a glorified secretary. If they ever offer me his job I'll know the drink has made me prematurely senile. I am a supervisor, but a supervisor of supervisors. In every job the National undertakes in Scotland the team knows that one day, with no warning, I will suddenly arrive, run a few tests, ask a few questions, and any weakness in the system will be at once exposed. And repaired. And my report will affix the blame to the man responsible. I am the reason for National's high reputation in the Scottish business community, though not everyone knows that. Reeves knows it which is why he wants rid of me. He is a mixture of jealousy and ignorance. When my brain goes completely liquid the Scottish branch will be in serious trouble. There is nobody here who can replace me.

I am a liar. I know two young area supervisors who could do my job as well as I do. But does Reeves know them? I doubt it and I'm not going to tell him. He probed me recently in his sneakily English public-school way. He's jealous and ignorant but he's smart.

"I think you deserve an assistant, Jock. Someone who can drive."

"I can drive."

"O I realise that."

"Driving a car properly is a job of work. It consumes skill, intelligence, and nervous energy."

"O I realise that."

"The firm pays me to provide a precise kind of practical and psychological supervision. I prefer working with a clear, alert mind unblunted by two or three hours of sifting and responding to the signals and reflexes of inept, self-contradictory and frequently drunken drivers."

"O I realise that, so let the firm give you a chauffeur. One of the younger men. Pick him yourself. He can assist you by testing the less complex parts of the installation."

An assistant would discover I am alcoholic. Does Reeves suspect that? I doubt it. Before the incident with the whore last weekend the only folk with ground for suspicion were barmaids in quiet little hotels.

"What part of our installation do *you* regard as less complex, Reeves?"

"Perhaps the alarm circuits?"

"You are mistaken. Let me tell you something. An electrician can install and service the National system as though it is a collection of separate parts, but a supervisor must see and test it as a whole. He must *not* pass the responsibility for some details to someone else."

"O I realise that, but you know what I am trying to convey."

Yes Reeves, I know what you are trying to convey. You want me to help you replace myself with someone younger. Sorry old chap, no go. No can do. Until you persuade the firm to promote a supervisor from London over my head I will remain the Scottish National team's most essential man. Liar. I am not a man, I am an instrument.

I am the instrument of a firm which installs instruments to protect the instruments of firms which produce meat cloth machines and whisky, instruments to feed, dress, move and stupefy us. But the National installs most of its instruments around nuclear reactors – instruments powering the instruments which light, heat and entertain us – and banks – instruments to protect and increase the profits of the instrument owners – and military depots where the weapons are kept which protect the nation's instruments and profits from the protective instruments of the Russian instrument-makers. Mirrors reflecting mirrors are the whole show? No. Instruments serving instruments are the whole show. My father was an instrument regulating a coal-mine. This did not satisfy him so he became an instrument of his trade union and the Labour Party. He thought these were the instruments of a future of full employment, no warfare and the goods of life shared equally among those who make them. But the future does not exist. Most of us become instruments to get something NOW, what? Safety and pleasure. The safety and pleasure of big houses, rounds of golf and safaris in Kenya drive shareholders to operate the bank and Stock Exchange. The safety and pleasure of wee houses, the Saturday game and a fortnight in Portugal drive workers to operate the factory and office. Safety and pleasure drive me to drink and wank in a Peebles hotel but I am SICK of being an instrument joining instruments to instruments so that an imaginary Superb, handcuffed and nude, facedown and writhing screams NO NO PLEASE PLEASE DON'T DO IT AGAIN as Charlie, gripping her lovely buttocks, drives his stiff etcetera again and again through her etcetera etcetera. In my coat pocket is a bottle of barbiturate pills to be swallowed with the emergency whisky if the bombs drop before I reach the shelter. Why not swallow them and return to pre-birth nothingness now? "The coward's way out," they used to call it. But the coat is far away in the wardrobe.

I once knew a man who was not a coward, not an instrument. He died. Forget him.

I was once inside a woman's bum and was not cruel or selfish. I did not know where I was. She giggled and said, "Do you know where you are?"
"I think so."
"You're not in the usual place."
"O how does it feel?"
"Different. Not so exciting but nice. Don't come out yet."
"Are you not sore?"
"No."
"The books suggest it usually hurts the first time."
"I don't read books."
"Well either you've a great big arsehole or I've a wee toaty prick."
She squealed at that. Denny was easily shocked by frank language. Denny, I have been very lonely without you. Even with other women I have been very lonely without you . . . Strange. For a moment I thought I was going to cry.

Damn damn damn damn him for dying, that bastard should never have died, I will never forgive that bugger for dying, of course I forgive him for dying but till my dying day I will hate hate hate that he is dead. He was complete. Everyone else I have met emerged from childhood like myself with some talent or affection damaged or forced under the surface, but an inborn toughness, an accident of parentage had left this man intact, that is the only way I can account for him. As old people used to say of someone especially alert and intelligent, he *was all there*. Any woman he looked at felt beautiful, any man he talked to felt interesting, only the envious disliked him, his mere appearance gave confidence to the rest. He was, and seemed, magnificent. He was the least absentminded, the least mysterious man in the world. In the old Glasgow Technical College the head of department told our year, "There have been too many latecomers this term, too many of you have missed lectures and been absent without a doctor's line. All of this applies, of course, to one of you in particular."

Then the head looked straight at the middle of the back row where my friend sat, so everyone else looked at him too. He frowned, pursed his lips gravely and nodded as if saying, "Yes, I have been very bad, something must certainly be done about this."

But we all knew he was not depressed atall. How could he be? He was a natural engineer who learned as he breathed no matter how many lectures he missed, and had he been a poor engineer he was still incapable of caring what a mere boss, a mere professor said, unless he found it useful or entertaining. So his frown and nod of agreement struck us as stupendous irony, the best joke for a month. From the edges of the class smiles and nudges passed to the middle and suddenly people were laughing. The head of department tried not to. For a minute he fought to keep a straight face, and failed, and laughed, and became one of us. He had to. If he had not he would have proved himself a stuffed shirt, a fool who did not know that teachers are paid to serve their students, not the other way round. So when silence returned the head, with a gesture of comic despair, cleared his throat, started another lecture, and we rewarded him by paying close attention. We liked him now that he had proved himself a decent fellow, though he was a very ordinary decent fellow. The only folk who stayed calm during the uproar were my friend who raised his eyebrows a little, and perhaps myself, who was naturally impassive and tended to imitate him. At what seemed the height of the mirth he glanced at me with an apologetic shrug and spread of the hands as if saying, "Am I to blame if people behave like this?"

And of course people laughed even louder.

This brain of mine holds no irrational fears and only one superstition. If Alan had lived (he died in a fall which had as little to do with himself as a bottle has to do with an arm which accidentally knocks it to smash on a floor) I believe Scotland would now have an independent government. I do not mean that Alan would have become a political leader. A leader is a nose which the big owners and moneymen use to steer crowds by. Sometimes, not often, a leader is a hard nose which a determined crowd thrusts against the big owners. Who can always afford to retreat a little. Big money is clever, it does not need special people to lead it. When it cannot use clever cultured spokesmen like Macmillan and Heath it uses naive idiots like Hume and Thatcher and the newspapers praise their courage and sincerity. But Labour needs *special* leaders. Or thinks it does. Which is why it is continually defeated. Alan would not have changed Scotland by talking in front of a crowd, he would have set an irresistible example by doing exactly what he wanted in the middle of the back row. I imagine him inventing a cheap arrangement of mirrors, mercury rods and guitar strings which, installed up a chimney, would store enough energy to light and heat the room beneath with some left over to power a refrigerator, cassette-player or slow oven. A fantasy, of course, but given time Alan would have worked upon Scotland like a few ounces of yeast on many tons of malt, he would have fermented these arselickers and instruments, these stoical and hysterical losers into a sensible coherent people who would not *act as one* (healthy folk cannot do exactly that) but would hold together sufficiently to help themselves by helping each other. Whisky permitting, I will order my wits to find reasons for this faith of mine.

He did not fear any other people and did not fear the future. He loved and could use and mend anything the hand of man had made. He preferred working with cheap or discarded materials. He depended on his senses for vital information, especially his ear for rhythm. He could accurately describe the state of a car's inlet valve from the note of the exhaust. Once, lacking a spirit level, he made a horizontal surface true by placing a clock on it and adjusting the plane till the tick was identical with the tock. He could accurately tune any musical instrument although he did not care for music, a fact which hugely annoyed his father who played a cornet in the band of the Pavilion Theatre. The family home contained many well-tuned wind, string and percussion instruments which Alan had salvaged for a shilling or two from junkyards and practically reconstructed, but the only sounds he could be persuaded to produce on them were imitation birdcalls.

I can remember none of these things without his great head in its Harpo Marx cloud of curly hair, though black not blonde, and his Groucho Marx face but with a goatee beard improving the slightly weak chin. Nobody who saw him knew if he was strikingly handsome or strikingly ugly. He had a sallow-skinned Arabic-Italian-Jewish look. I think his father was Jewish. His mother was Irish. "Not Catholic Irish but tinker Irish," was how he described her and he certainly dressed like a tinker. On anyone else his clothes would have seemed accidental. On him they looked like the improvisations of a Grand Duke who had lost his fortune and valet in a revolution, like the casual wear of a more elegant, more easygoing, more practical civilisation. I remember various long woollen scarves, an army tunic with marks on the sleeves where the stripes of a sergeant had been unstitched, slim black evening-dress trousers with a black silk ribbon down the seam on each side. On damp days these trousers were tucked into Wellington boots, and had straps at the bottom which passed under the instep of canvas sandshoes on dry days. We must have been a strange contrast walking side by side, myself rather smaller than he in my conventionally creased trousers, waistcoat, collar, tie and jacket with the white triangle of a folded handkerchief peeping from the breastpocket. I walked with hands clasped behind my back. Alan usually had his arms folded on his chest but he did not strut or swagger. He placed his feet quietly and firmly, as if he only possessed – but possessed completely – the exact ground he trod upon. Sometimes I saw strangers in the distance laughing and pointing at us but if we drew near they grew quiet and respectful. Alan was four or five inches over six feet tall. No doubt this helped.

Why did he like me? He had my admiration of course but he got that from most folk. The only useful thing I gave him was help with mathematics. He cannot have attended a single mathematics class in his entire year. Had he done so the lecturer would have noticed him the first day then noticed he was absent afterwards. But mathematics was the only subject in which he had full attendance marks, because I always answered his name when the roll was called. A few days before the maths exam I visited his home and read him my lecture notes. He heard them lying in bed with a patient frown on his face like a Roman cardinal hearing the sermon of a very young priest. I never knew how much he understood of what I was saying though once, when I had recounted many calculations relating to the acceleration of falling bodies, strain pressure, spontaneous change and the tendency of systems to minimise their free energy, he yawned and said, "Very worthy. But it only tells us how things run down and spread out."
This was true, of course. All calculation involving time describes the heat-death of the universe, a stage between the big bang which made everything and the cold porridge it will amount to in the end. But Alan's description of the process was mechanical. Electricians seldom think of mathematics in these terms. Yet Alan always managed to pass the maths exam and was a first-class electrician. My failure to understand this comes from ignorance, not from something mysterious in Alan's mind. To him the forces of gravitation, and electricity, and whatever is generated in a centrifuge, or when we strike a match, were obviously the same thing. You need a big mind to see that, a mind as big as the mind of God, if God has a mind.

I must keep telling myself that I was not his best or his only friend, he had many friends. When we had free time we called at his house (where he was usually in bed) and

hung about gossiping together until he got up. I met a lot of different people by doing that. When he got up we usually went for long, slow, completely aimless walks on which everything we saw was interesting: the conduct of pigeons on a roof, the stitching of a shoe in a shop window, the expression of a girl waiting at a street corner, a phrase in an advertisement, crumbling mortar between the bricks of a new building, the tint of paintwork on a car. Alan never seemed to be leading the group (he walked in the middle) and he did not dominate the conversation, unless with an occasional question, glance or pointing finger. I think that while we talked he was learning from us. He seemed to know everything in the world but was completely unintellectual and had never read a book, unless perhaps *The Casebook of Sherlock Holmes*. He said "An educated man need know only one author thoroughly. Conan Doyle has given me all I require. I am not referring to his novels. A man like myself, with far-reaching responsibilities in the worlds of high finance and international power-politics, has no time for novels."
This remark led me to read all the Sherlock Holmes stories but when I referrred to them later Alan was strangely reticent. I suspect that the Holmes influence on him came through the old Basil Rathbone films he had enjoyed as a child.

He saw the true strength in a thing, that is where his own strength lay. He recognised at once tools and furniture which had been shaped to catch the eye by reducing their efficiency, or where the designer had tried for durability by using so much material that the structure was weakened. On a walk he stopped in midstride, stared at an office block and said, "If I was that building I would be aching all over, but especially here, here and here."
He slapped his neck, chest and knee. He could place his finger on the diagram of a slide coupling or electric circuit and say, "We don't need that bit."
I would patiently explain why that bit was essential then he would point out a simple adaptation which would totally abolish it. I believe that the hugest laugh in the world came from his mouth on hearing a radio interview with a carpenter who made reproductions of oldfashioned

spinning-wheels and sold them to tourists in a West Highland shop.
INTERVIEWER: This is a beautiful-looking piece. Expertly shaped. Exquisitely crafted.
CARPENTER: Thankyou.
INTERVIEWER: But does it work?
CARPENTER: Oh yes, it's perfectly functional. Plug it in, screw a bulb in the socket and it will make an excellent standard lamp.
For a week that exchange dominated our repartee.
ALAN (*Pointing to a new make of car/Glasgow's municipal building/the Principal of the Technical College*): That's a beautiful-looking piece. Expertly shaped. Exquisitely crafted.
MYSELF: Yes indeed, but does it work?
ALAN: Oh it's perfectly functional. Plug it in, screw a bulb in the socket and it will make an excellent standard lamp.
Later this was greatly shortened. If he got angry with someone he told them to screw a bulb in their socket.

Sexually he was as lucky as a man could be. He loved a girl who loved him, and they made each other miserable, and were sometimes very happy. In those days I was as lucky as he, but was eighteen and did not know this. I envied him (though without rancour) because his girlfriend was more glamorous than mine, and because he could have enjoyed many other women, especially young ones who recognised him as the tall dark irresistible stranger they had dreamed about. He was flattered by their attention and turned them away playfully and kindly. From his height they must have looked terribly fragile and he never took advantage of people weaker than himself. He never took advantage of anyone. He had only one defect.

I came home to my digs after midnight and found I had lost the key. There were no lights in the windows. Not wanting to wake the other lodgers by knocking I went into the backgreen and saw that a ronepipe was near my half-open window with some branches running sideways to kitchen sinks and bathrooms. I climbed up the wall by these and found the windowsill beyond my reach by a mere half-inch. I knew that Alan could easily reach it, that his home was near, that he would be up and doing because he preferred working when others were asleep. I visited him and asked for help. Without saying a word he accompanied me to the lodgings, quickly climbed the pipe and entered the window, which was on the fourth floor. I went upstairs expecting to find the front door opened for me, but some minutes passed before Alan opened it and his appearance was shocking. His face was white and staring, he seemed not to see or even hear me. I led him back to my room and made a mug of tea. He crouched in an armchair clutching the mug with both hands and staring into it as if he saw something dreadful there. Gradually his colour returned, he swallowed the tea, smiled and said, "Now you know that I'm afraid of heights."

That man was my friend and I have turned into *this* man. Oh never remember Alan again. Forget him and forget Denny who waits outside the door wanting to come in here and DESTROY me with her sad eyes which I was never able to face and have avoided for more than twenty years. Oh Denny, please leave me alone. Be a good girl and go away.

Helga will save me from her. Sip. Helga will lead my mind back into pleasant places. Sip.

What Alan saw in that mug was his own death. I can see mine in this glass, taste it on my tongue, feel it in the forgetfulness creeping across this brain. There are many things I used to remember, used to depend on remembering which I cannot remember now. Helen and I must have had many calm and pleasant times in ten or twelve years together but I cannot remember them. We must have had many holidays together. I cannot remember one. The braincells containing these memories have dissolved. There is now a black hole in my brain where light once shone, a hole which will get larger day by day until everything I know, everything I am has slid into it. Sip. Sip. Poor Alan, you were appalled by the sight of your death. You must have loved life. I loved life in those days but now I can take it or let it alone.

So in the private viewing theatre Helga sits watching for a second time a film of her tallslenderhandsomelonghaired blonde self having these tight jeans and blouse ripped off by the wire then stumbling through weeds all nude except for little kilt of rags around bum and cunt until she falls at the feet of Hugo and Cupid etcetera. But what is she wearing in the theatre itself? Verimportant that. In the absence of solid cuddleable women it is verimportant to rember to imagine desirable containers for them. Helga wears a crisp tight white blouse which emphasises small firm breasts, and very baggy jeans which I saw on a girl a few days or a few years ago. They were pale blue and gathered into the ankles like harem pants. Apart from the anklebands and waistband the only line which clung tight to the body was the seam between the legs so the anal cleft was quite distinct while the cloth rippled and flirted over her moving hips. Can women feel the pressure of jeans like an erotic caress? What was Helen wearing when I saw her enter the college canteen? I cannot remember, though the style clearly indicated a drama or art student. She looked wonderful. She was moving through a crowd of men so her face was a little disdainful as it floated above her tall, slender, handsome, longnecked body, turning slightly from side to side in search of someone she knew.

She was looking for Alan. When she saw him her face stopped being disdainful and became a little too bright and eager. As she came purposefully toward us he whispered, "Damn," under his breath but he greeted her with a pleasant, "Hullo Helen. What brings you here?"
She said, "Well, the show does. When can you come? We're rehearsing every night this week and it starts in a fortnight."
"Ah, the show. Naturally, the show. Yes of course, the show. Sit down and tell me exactly what you are talking about."
He pulled up a chair beside him and she sat down looking depressed and helpless. She said, "You've forgotten about it and you promised you wouldn't. I met you at a drama school party three weeks ago. You said you might help with the lighting of a show some friends and I are putting on at the festival."

"I remember perfectly," said Alan, "and of course I will help you with the lighting. Where is this show going on?"
"In Edinburgh of course. At the festival. We've got in with some people who have rented this fantastic place, an old condemned sweet-factory right in the centre. We can move in whenever we like. There's so much room we'll be able to sleep on the premises – all kinds of things will be happening there, jazz groups and folk groups and dancing and an all-night café with a cabaret. Art students are decorating the place. You *must* come. You'll enjoy it thoroughly and everyone will love to have you."
"I'm sorry," said Alan, "I can't visit Edinburgh in the near future. I am committed to solving the case of the nine Coptic prelates and the engineer's thumb. Luckily you don't need me. I'm brilliant, of course, but notoriously unreliable. The man you need is here, beside you."
Helen hardly glanced at me. In a distressed voice she said, "Are you sure you can't help us, Alan?"
He placed a fatherly hand on her shoulder and said, "You're a beautiful piece, Helen, but you ought to plug yourself in. The slightly undersized, perfectly formed unit I am offering you is a unique man. Many ignore him because he is obviously inoffensive. They are idiots. This man is magic. Describe anything you want done and he will do it quietly, expertly, and – if you arouse his blood a little – quickly. I am not suggesting that you seduce him. He gets all the real sex he needs. But he has been confused by the movies and the underwear advertisements. He wants some high life and glamour. In return for your company in a crowded room and a few sparkling glances (you know the sort I mean) he'll give you all the services of a first-rate workman. He operates with an astonishing lack of friction."
Helen had to glance at me then. I said firmly, "I know nothing about stage lighting."
"Good," cried Alan, "you will teach yourself to do it properly. You know my methods. Apply them, and soon lovely girls like Helen here will be flitting around you in all kinds of fascinating undress. They will all passionately want to be loved – by the public – but will be shadows in the dark, whispers in the void unless you press the right switches. Think of the power you will wield! You won't have time to

feel guilty about having so much beauty within touching distance because THE SHOW MUST GO ON."

In the cavelike rooms of that vast old factory in the shadow of the castle I saw Helen in jeans which exactly suited those lovely legs which stopped bleeding and we were married in six weeks so go away Denny the show MUST go on but only if Helga's jeans cuddle her cunt like an erotic caress. An idea. An orgasm race using hairdryers.

Helga, Big Momma, Superb and Janine stand in a row wearing very tight shrinkfit jeans which have not yet been shrunk. Ropes tie their wrists high above their heads but they do not hang from these although they would have to do so if someone pulled off their steep wedgesoled sandals with, ah, eight-inch high heels. These open-toed sandals allow me to imagine perfectly each lacquered scarlet toenail. The bucklestrap circling each ankle has a little bell fastened to the side of it, the sort pampered pussies have on their collars. Tinkle tinkle. A pleasant sound, yahooohay, a yawn. I am very tired. Where was I? Yes the high heels make my women stick out their bums while the ropes round their wrists stretch their limbs as taut as guitarstrings. But they are standing astride astride astride astride because each foot rests, not on the floor, but on an isolated block or brick which is twelve inches high and far apart from its neighbour. Singly each woman stands like an upsidedown capital Y and together they look like a short row of ⅄ ⅄ ⅄ ⅄ yes ⅄ ⅄ ⅄ ⅄ yes ⅄ ⅄ ⅄ ⅄ yes but try not to get carried away. They have been standing a long time like this, they are very tired, yahooohay. Their sweatdamp white silk shirts (no bras) are unbuttoned but in different states. Helga's white silk unbuttoned shirt is still tucked into her jeans. Big Momma's white silk yahooohay, I mean unbuttoned shirt is torn in two, each ragged half dangles from a sleeve which has sunk into a ragged wreath round the armpit. The white silk shirts of the other two hang wide open outside their jeans. This is a soft pillow. Yahoohay sleepy all my women wear the same kind of white silk shirt unbuttoned but in different states, my mummies share the shame mind of shite sick dirt, gunbuttered sluts in stiffening states ⅄ ⅄ ⅄ ⅄

hullo my dears ⅄ ⅄ ⅄ ⅄ ⅄ ⅄ ⅄ yes carry on ⅄ ⅄ ⅄ ⅄ ⅄
⅄ ⅄
⅄ ⅄
⅄ ⅄
⅄ ⅄
⅄ ⅄
⅄ ⅄
⅄ ⅄
⅄ ⅄
⅄ ⅄
⅄ ⅄
Y Y Y Y Y Y Y Y Y Y Y Y Y Y Y Y Y Y Y Y Y Y Y Y Y
Y Y Y Y Y Y Y Y Y Y Y Y Y Y Y Y Y Y Y Y Y Y Y Y Y
Y Y Y Y Y Y Y Y Y Y Y Y Y Y Y Y Y Y Y Y Y Y Y Y Y
Y Y Y Y Y Y Y Y Y Y Y Y Y Y Y Y Y Y Y Y Y Y Y Y Y
Y Y Y Y Y Y Y Y Y Y Y Y Y Y Y Y Y Y Y Y Y Y Y Y Y
Y Y Y Y Y Y Y Y Y Y Y Y Y Y Y Y Y Y Y Y Y Y Y Y Y
Y Y Y Y Y Y Y Y Y Y Y Y Y Y Y Y Y Y Y Y Y Y Y Y Y
Y Y Y Y Y Y Y Y Y Y Y Y Y Y Y Y Y Y Y Y Y Y Y Y Y
Y Y Y Y Y Y Y Y Y Y Y Y Y Y Y Y Y Y Y Y Y Y Y Y Y
Y Y Y Y Y Y Y Y Y Y Y Y Y Y Y Y Y Y Y Y Y Y Y Y Y
You bastard Y Y Y Y Y Y Yahoohay, another of those dreams. I have not dreamed that for twenty-five years. I used to dream it all the time.

It was a sunny summer in Glasgow, the streets quieter than usual. Perhaps it was the start of the fair fortnight. I walked along St George's Road and saw Alan strolling toward me round the curve of Charing Cross Mansions, arms folded on chest, great face surveying the white clouds. I was filled with delighted relief and laughter, I ran to him crying, "You're not dead! You're not dead!"
He smiled and said, "Of course not, that was all just a joke." And suddenly I grew terribly angry with him for making such a cruel joke. And then I awoke, unluckily.

8: I AM GLAD

I FELL ASLEEP BEFORE IMAGINING THE ORGASM RACE. If my four heroines are all ⅄ ⅄ ⅄ ⅄ together in it with the nasty Doctor, his drugs, the hosepipe, the hairdryers, Max, Stroud, Charlie, Hollis and a horde of waitresses in tight red satin slinky button-through dresses then clearly this race is an ultimate event to which every other plot inside my head tonight is converging. It must come before the last and biggest gangbang which will leave me completely exhausted and unconscious. Or so I hope. I have only once had enough self-control, enough insomnia to shepherd all my fantasies up to one point and it brought on a very bad attack of hay fever. But in those days my organisation was very small, just four poor little people and a shack in the hills.

Cupid, Hugo and Big Momma (God only knows what brought that mob together) pulled off a department store payroll heist and headed for the hills in a sharp red convertible meaning to lie low till the heat was off. Cupid was just a kid. Hugo was a wino, a liquorhead who had somehow kept his guts and his balls. Momma, a fat woman past fifty, was the brains of the outfit. In those days that sort of language came easily to me. In those days commercial television was just a gleam in John Logie Baird's eye. *No Orchids for Miss Blandish* topped the bestseller charts. But the trio were not readers so on their way to the shack they picked up Janine, a hitchhiker, to entertain them sexually. Since Big Momma was a lesbian there was not enough Janine for everybody. Cupid and Hugo ganged up on Big Momma and forced her to please them in a great many ways while Janine wandered about naked making cups of tea for people. I mean coffee. Americans don't drink tea.

But I was ambitious. Cupid and Hugo didn't know how to work with a big organisation so I dropped them. Last I heard they were working as extras in a blue movie. Big Momma and Janine I kept and I got me a good accountant, a smart lawyer, a doctor who pushed drugs and abortions to the highest levels of society, also a crooked police chief. That was Max. Together we kidnapped the wives and daughters of rich businessmen and had orgies with them which lasted for weeks. Ah, the stamina of youth. We raised money by sending the husbands and fathers photographs of their damsels in highly distressed states, with descriptions of what more would be done to them if we were not paid. We usually got the money and did what we liked anyway. The dames were eventually released with a slightly more knowing look in their eyes and no marks which a modest little dress did not hide. They could not identify us afterward because while in our hands we blindfolded them or wore masks, stopped their ears or spoke in whispers. I was now frequenting cocktail parties thrown by beautiful people and other celebrities. Sometimes the hostess, a film star or top fashion photographer's model whose lovely face seemed strangely remote and discontented, asked me listlessly, "Haven't we met somewhere before?"
This still happens. I always reply, "Not to my knowledge." Later, dancing with her, my hand caresses part of her back where I have branded my initials. She goes white and nearly swoons but I clasp her more tightly and sweep her body on through the intricacies of the tango. (You couldn't do that,

you can't even dance.) Shut up she recovers and whispers, "My God it was you!"

I smile and murmur, "Prove it."

Panting deeply she says, "Listen I . . . I must see you again soon, somewhere private, anywhere you like . . . please!"

"Why?"

"There is something I want to, *must* tell you, can you not guess what it is?"

"Unfortunately my work fully occupies me these days. You know what kind of work it is. Call me in a month or two, perhaps I can fit you in then."

In the forties and fifties this reply was more than an excuse because my organisation was expanding rapidly.

I had suddenly noticed that I was competing against my own kind. The academics/accountants/architects/advertising bosses/ bankers/ brokers/ businessmen/congressmen/doctors/ executives/factoryowners/government officials/heads of departments/impresarios/judges/journalists/key-operatives/ lawyers and media people whose women and wealth I abused all had the same tastes as myself, if they were not homosexual or crazy on art or some other screwball hobby. They had made their bucks by hard work and social conformity and what had it got them? A little prestige, a few creature comforts, an occasional weekend in Acapulco was all. Their children and wives were not especially grateful, their sex lives left a lot to be desired. They needed what I need, cunt, lots of it, served to me whenever I want in exactly the state I choose. These men were my brothers. If we co-operated we could all have us a ball. We had the capital and could push through the legislation to set up a worldwide chain of completely legal pleasure parlours. Jails and mental hospitals are full of sexually desirable women confined there because they have been too greedy, too active, too eccentric, too stupid to obey or cunningly twist the rules of conventional society. My organisation culls these women and uses them in ways which Stroud will shortly demonstrate to Helga in the viewing theatre, but what it comes down to is this: the male winners have a fucking good time with the female losers. Women's liberators accuse me of sexual chauvinism. I tell them that if women of the professional class will work along with the richer heiresses, divorcees and widows (there are more widows than widowers in this world, men die faster, even in peacetime) then they will have enough power to turn half the male jails into their very own studfarms with special lesbian annexes for those who don't want to muck in with us men. When we consider how the winners shaft the losers, the strong shaft the weak, the rich shaft the poor, accusations of sex-discrimination are irrelevant. Most men are poor weak losers. Many women are not.

If the foregoing words seem a little harsh let me tell you about those tastefully designed, blankwalled buildings with skylight windows which have appeared near all of the big and some of the smaller towns, each at the heart of a wooded estate with an electrified security fence round it. The women inside are not only happier and healthier than those in normal prisons and asylums (they could hardly be otherwise) they are happier and healthier than most women in the world outside. They sleep in comfortable, spacious, beautifully decorated boudoirs, they have extravagant wardrobes and access to soft drugs, sunbeds, sauna baths and as much as they want to eat. We don't mind them getting fat, or if we do mind we have exciting exercises which slim them down again. Since they outnumber their male visitors by ten to one, lesbian friendships are not discouraged. These friendships provoke tensions which combine with their class structure to provoke a plentiful fund of gossip. This structure is more complex than in my queen-slave Arabian harem. Here we have the favourites, the performers, the waitresses and the cyclists. The favourites wear anything they like, the performers wear what the favourites tell them to wear, the waitresses wear slinky tight red button-through satin, the cyclists wear tight coarse canvas jeans or overalls or short short shorts. The favourites draw a high weekly wage, the performers receive bonuses according to their quality of performance, the waitresses are paid in tips, the cyclists get nothing. But nobody is forced to be a cyclist for more than three weeks a year, the Doctor has forbidden it. Promotion and demotion are erratic. Some girls have been favourites for years, some frequently pass through all classes in a single month. The money earned is handed over in the form of crisp new notes. The wiser girls ask the management to bank it for them but a few get distinct reassurance from the sight and feel of firm little wads piling up through the years, so these have a safe in their boudoir whose combination-lock number is known only to themselves. The less wise girls sometimes get addicted to gambling which gives me an idea for an exciting strip-poker game shut up go back. The less wise girls sometimes get addicted to gambling, which has led to a certain amount of corruption. A secure favourite who dislikes a performer or waitress can make her life hell for a few weeks, and some unlucky women try to win favour by losing at cards to their tormentors. However, every room is constantly bugged, taped and monitored so the management always prevent glaring injustices from lasting very long. A little injustice stimulates conversation and communication, but too much makes a woman sloppy, despondent and unattractive. It is important for our women to know that when they reach retirement age they will have amassed enough to live upon comfortably for the rest of their lives.

Here is another fact for our critics to bear in mind. The sex life of our women is not only more varied than in the world outside, it lasts longer. Attractive performers of sixty are not unknown. No wonder that they depart from us with tears in their eyes. What, afterall, have they suffered? Some bondage and flagellation perhaps but in every life a little rain must fall. Anyway, an astonishing number of our clients are masochists, and I predict that if middle and upper-class women get the prison studfarm of their dreams the inmates will be ordered to put on some highly aggressive performances. There is a tendency for successful people who make it at the top to want a little ritualised humiliation in the bedroom. The fact that these people usually marry *each other* is one of the unsung tragedies of our time. However, it is now surely obvious that I have evolved from a smalltime crook to a public benefactor. Sontag would no doubt say that from being a small crook preying on small people I got a little bigger by preying on big people, then joined the big people to prey on small people in a big way. No doubt

Mister Karl Marx would agree with Sontag, but I am no Marxist. I say, so it goes.

Perhaps you are now in a position to appreciate me. As chairman of the vast multinational Forensic Research Punishment and Sexual Gratification Syndicate I am world-wide and irresistible. No government will ever oppose me because all governments are on my committee. The leaders of every successful movement acquire shares in my establishments. If it was widely known that the whole network has been spun like a web out of one brain – this brain – my life would be in danger from left-wing radical extremists, but my disguise is impenetrable. People know me as a modest and discreet Lowland Scottish electrical technician who is sometimes seen at small family hotels in Tillicoultry, Grangemouth and Nairn. My closest agents know even less than that. To them I am nothing but a voice along a wire.
TRING TRING.
That will be the Johannesburg call.
"Hello."
"Agent XPQR reporting from Johannesburg, sir."
"Proceed."
"I have a fresh cargo of *black molasses* in bond, sir."
"How much?"
"Twenty kilos."
"How fresh?"
"Four teens, four twenties, four thirties, four forties, four fifties."
"Four *fifties*, XPQR?"
"They're ripe, sir."
"O.K. Split the kilos five ways between Chicago, Sydney, Berlin, Paris and Glenrothes."
"*Glenrothes*, sir?"
"You heard me."
"How will I split it freshnesswise, sir?"
"Use your initiative. Check with the area supervisors."
"Certainly sir. Sir, where is Glenrothes?"
"Look it up in an atlas. The nearest docks are at Methil."
"Thankyou, sir. Good night, sir."
Click.
XPQR probably thinks I'm getting old, losing my grip.

Our Glenrothes centre does not need four fresh dames but it does need the extra colour, the extra sweetness of some soft black molasses. I am visiting Glenrothes next week, ostensibly to see what National are installing in a church there, even churches are getting security-minded these days. Hell, my mother's folk came from Glenrothes, I can afford to be lavish, afford to indulge myself. I made my bucks the hard way and the shareholders ain't grouching. (Stop fooling yourself.)
Better a happy fool than a suicidal supervisor of security installations. (You are not happy.)
Shut up you foul little still small voice.
Sip.
Take that, you stupid stinking turd of intelligent conscience.
Sip. Sip.
At this rate you will be completely washed out in less than a year.
Sip. Sip. Sip.

Yes sirree, as I glance backward over my early struggles, my triumphant career, my fulfilling decades of public service, I sometimes think my happiest moments were passed in that humble shack in the hills after Cupid and I ganged up on Big Momma. The place was not even wired for electricity but having some technical proficiency I turned an old bicycle frame into a simple generator. When it was ready Momma chuckled and told Janine, "Now you're going for a nice long ride. You'll sleep well tonight, honey."
I grinned and shook my head. I said, "You got it wrong, Momma. This little girl is insufficiently robust. It is you who are overweight. Get on to that saddle."
She gaped at me, trying to believe I was joking. I was joking, yes, but the joke was on her. I slowly removed my thick harnessleather belt then whopped her ass real good till she was begging to be allowed on to that saddle. When it got dark outside Big Momma was pedalling enough light for Janine, Cupid and I to play a long slow game of strip-poker. (Does poker not need four players?) Shut up, I make the rules around here. Janine lost heavily of course and we sure

made her feel it. Next day was hot and sunny, Big Momma was too weary to move so we gave her a rest and a suntan and sweated a few more ounces out of her. We pegged her starfishwise on the ground outside, flat on her back all naked and cursing until Cupid brownsugared no, buttered her tits to get the midges tickling. She sang a different tune then. (Are there midges in America?) You dope, there are midges EVERYWHERE, they are universal and ineradicable, they cannot be eliminated without unlinking that whole ecological chain which binds bird to beast, flower to fruit, herb and moss to tree and tundra and to those who wander thither and yonder upon the waste of the waters, midges CANNOT be destroyed without destroying MAN HIMSELF, why am I raving? Where did I pick up all this pseudoscientific biblical stuff? Did I hear it on the wireless? All I want is, yes,

Big Momma buttersoft and CLUTCHABLE, tearwet, sweatwet, quivering and moaning while Cupid tattoos her buttocks (we have turned her over) with as rich an arabesque of obscene words and indecent notions as is printed in the fabric of this brain. As Cupid I do that to her and as Hugo I turn her over again and stop her mouth with my kisses, her cunt with my cock. I fully occupy her for a while I am the only man in her world. I wish, I have always wished I could imagine her enjoying me too. However, I ejaculated three times, completely emptying my seminal vesicles into Durex sheaths inside a nylon sock inside a wollen sock. Neither pyjamas nor bedlinen were stained so Helen never knew. She was, thank goodness, a very sound sleeper. And then I had an attack of hay fever. The snorting and gasping awoke her and she went to the kitchen without being asked and made me a glass of hot tea with lemonjuice and brown sugar in it. This gave me time to flush away the Durexes and hide the slightly dank doublesock in the laundrybasket. Helen always behaved well in emergencies, doing the most sensible and helpful thing quietly and quickly. Only trivialities greatly frightened or annoyed her. I could never understand that. She was under strain, of course. Unless she too masturbated secretly she had even less real sex than I did, and I doubt if she masturbated. I once tried to talk to her about it and she covered her ears. I'm still sometimes sorry that we separated. Forget her.

Back to Momma pegged out etcetera but Momma is changing, the ropes fall from her wrists and ankles, she stands up looking much less massive but still pleasantly plump. She is wearing jeans that cuddle her bottom snugly but are wellworn and comfortable. Her shirt is simple and sexy, shortsleeved with thin redandwhite stripes, two big buttons. It is hard to see her face clearly although I seem to know it well. It is not a harsh or sour face, not a very hopeful face. Good. Very hopeful faces always seem on the edge of despair. It is an ordinary face. Millions of women in their fifties look like her. She watches me in a friendly way but I am sure I have never spoken to her in my life.

Denny would have looked like that nowadays if we had married. I hope you got pregnant, Denny.

O DENNY PLEASE PLEASE PLEASE HAVE BORNE OUR CHILD, GOD MAKE DENNY HAVE BORNE OUR CHILD, PLEASE *fucking* **GOD** *fucking* **EXIST** *and fucking well* **MAKE DENNY HAVE BORNE OUR CHILD, MAKE** *stop* **DENNY** *stop* **HAVE BORNE** *please stop* **A CHILD PLEASE. STOP. KNOCKING. THIS. HEAD. AGAINST. THIS. WALL.** Please Denny exist and have borne me a child.

Was I very noisy?

Listen.

No ringing echoes. No muttering from the next room. It is probably empty, these are quiet times for the Scottish hotel trade. No footsteps. Nobody coming, I cannot have been shouting or banging very hard. Head not very sore. Slight pink stain on wallpaper. Raw spot on brow, but no trickling blood. Small bruise or bump tomorrow perhaps. Lie down again. Drink? Better not in this state. Remember what happened in the pub last week after under the bridge. I *cannot* remember what happened in the pub last week after under the bridge but clearly I will do so soon. Tonight everything I want to forget is returning. I am cracking apart. Till a moment ago the thought of Denny bearing our child yes, in complete helpless loneliness was what I most feared to remember. Now the chance that a piece of Denny and me breathes and sees the light stops me fetching those pills and swallowing them with the last of the whisky, why? I do not know why. I will never know my son or daughter, though in a country as small as this a traveller like myself has almost certainly passed him/her in a street at least once. If I am a father. And I may be. Denny took no precautions. It was I who took the precautions, until the night before I went to stay in Edinburgh. I thought she was in a safe period or something. Liar. I was too drunk to think. A day or a week or a fortnight later I thought, 'Perhaps that little *bitch/whore/cheat* has trapped me, made me a father.' That became a reason for not seeing her again, a reason to forget her, until now. The possibilities were unthinkable.

(Abortion?)

Unlikely. Illegal then, and Denny was a coward about physical things, the slightest cut appalled her. She had nobody to suggest abortion to her, or make arrangements, or put up the money. But in other ways the Health Service was in good working order. In the normal course of things Denny would be hospitalised and the child delivered quite smoothly.

(Adoption?)

Probable. She had no parents, no friends, no helpers. I had deprived her of the one or two folk she knew in the hostel. She had a great deal of love in her and nobody to give it to, so she would want to keep the child. But a well-meaning socialworker could have persuaded her that this was an unkind thing to want, that she lacked the means to be a decent mother. Which was perhaps true. And Denny was one of those who are easily bullied by an educated voice. It was probably adopted.

(Suicide?)

I never thought of suicide before oh no no no no no no no no no crying, I have not cried, ha ha, since poor old Hislop and that daft crowd singing OH FLOOOERRA SCOAT-LAAAAAAN, WHEN WULL WEE SEE YOOER LIKA GEEEEEEN? when will we see your like again.

Denny was small but sturdy, not the suicidal type. I am the suicidal type and what pushes me to the whisky and the pills is not suffering but rage. Most suicide is a form of spite, I am sure of that, it is murder turned outside-in. Denny was incapable of rage. She never turned her suffering into defiance or into dramas which drew people's attention. Some childhood defeat had left her feeling that anger was useless so she swallowed suffering whole like a good wee girl, not spitting it back or biting the hand forcing it between her teeth. Those passive sorts never kill themselves. Liar. Even children can have more forced into them than they can bear. Dad only spoke once to me about the First World War but he mentioned Suicide Wood, a grove of leafless but not completely branchless trees in the mud of no-man's land, in the Somme I think he said, but there were probably several Suicide Woods, it was a very long line. Since nothing else stood up above ground soldiers went there to hang themselves. In the trenches they were confronted by an enemy as desperately unmoving as they were. On each side they had dour hardened men who had frozen into the nightmare life-in-death that thicks man's blood etcetera. Behind them was an organisation which shot them as deserters if they turned round and walked away, and behind that organisation stood their mothers/fathers/sisters/girlfriends/the newspapers/British Industry/Capital/Labour/The Church/The Law/The Government/ The King/ The Empire saying "Go forward lad! It's your duty! Only you can save us from being raped and plundered by those German boys in the trench before you." These were not toughguys. They lacked the guts to hold out their hands and mutter "Again!" to the mad teacher continually hitting them with his Lochgelly. So they hanged themselves. "They were mostly seventeen or eighteen," said my father,

"and sixteen-year-olds who had got in by lying about their age."
After a pause he said, "But we were all just children."
Denny was seventeen forget her. She was tough. She could take it. I bet she had my child adopted and is now happily married to someone of her own class background. She was quite an attractive lassie in her way.

And since I have at last admitted that I may be a father, a celebration! Fill the glass. A toast to, ourselves of course. Here's tae us, wha's like us? Damn few, and they're a' deid.

I am shit.

A piece of infromation about the Vietnam war stopped me watching/hearing/reading the news with more than a tenth part of my mind. I do not refer to the Mai Lai massacre. I had no sympathy with the far left-wing outcry at that little affair. Herding a lot of mothers and children out of their homes and killing them altogether and almost at once was an act of mercy compared to the killing of over five million Jews, and even more civilian Poles, Russians, homosexuals and gypsies in the Second World War. The population of Scotland is a bit over five million. To shepherd that Jewish Scotland out of its homes and into the suffocation ovens the police and civil services had to use many months of slow torturing degradation. The process would have been faster and more merciful if the army had been in charge, as at Mai Lai, but between 1939 and 1944 the armies were mostly busy with other sorts of work, so children travelled the last stages of that journey without the company of their parents. On the steps of the Palais de something in Paris, an exhibition hall near the Louvre, hundreds of suddenly unfathered and unmothered weans of a few months to a few years old stood/sat/sobbing/wailing/peeing their breeks with nobody to care for them but two or three frantic female bureaucrats frantically phoning the Prime Minister (or was it the President) to find out what they should do. But the Prime Minister/President was unobtainable. He refused to be informed. If Prime Ministers knew the effect of their decrees on all the people they govern their jobs would be impossible. They can only keep themselves sane and decent by protecting their ignorance. Mussolini, Hitler, Stalin could face the torture and death they dealt out because they enjoyed these things, but Pierre Levalle, Gerald Ford, Harold Wilson, Margaret Thatcher were not sadists, they had to ignore the terrified infants pishing the steps of an important public building, the young men and women shut in a football stadium having their etceteras twisted off by soldiers because they had defended their elected government, the deserted wife of an unemployed car-worker who, on a cold day, cannot choose between buying food and having her electricity cut off so spends the money on alcohol then silences her screaming baby by banging it against the wall. I am not being ironical. A government can only do public good by inflicting private injuries. I will go further. A government can only do public good by inflicting public injuries. These facts may be ironical but I am not being ironical.

(Give examples of public good obtained by public injury.)

I will. Lavalle, by obeying Hitler, made France more comfortable for more Frenchmen than any resistance did. Ford and Carter, by letting the Fruit Company and the C.I.A. do what they liked to South America, kept down the cost of food in North America. Our Harold and our Maggie, by playing along with the Stock Exchange and cutting taxation and the public healing, teaching and life-saving services, have given new power to the strong bits of Britain, the bits that keep it running.

(What bits are those?)

Who are you? Why do you quiz me like this? Don't answer because you are that still small voice which wants to get me guilty and raving, but several years ago a tiny little item of news in an obscure column of a Sunday newspaper showed me that, even though I am not a Prime Minister, even though I live at the social level where the world's main work is done, I had better ignore all politics, all facts not immediately under my nose. *In Vietnam*, the paper said, *observers in the zones defended by the United States military presence are disturbed by an increase in the number of deaths by suicide. Examples of teenagers committing suicide, though not frequent, occur in most cultures but the widespread phenomenon of children under the ages of twelve and ten committing suicide is something altogether new.* READ ALL ABOUT IT! OBSERVERS DISTURBED BY INCREASE OF WIDESPREAD PHENOMENON! Hahahahahahahahahahaha hahahahahahahahahahahahahahahahahahahahahahahahahaha hahahahahahahahahahahahahahysterically funny. Womb-shakingly funny. Earth-quakingly funny.

Suicide no no no not Denny small sturdy girl decent Health Service Vietnam war nothing to do with us yes we sold them weapons all in the way of business but that was another time another country and it stopped, it ended, the war ended, boat people yes some came to Britain and many Americans adopted Vietnam orphans, all forgotten now, over long ago, forgotten children. Forgotten children. Forgotten children. Have mercy God. Mercy God. Please please please have mercy on me.

Sweatwet, slightly bruised, pegged out starfishwise on this bed in this room in Peebles or Selkirk, what, apart from mercy, do I most need?

Sip?

No.

Sleep.

9:YAHOOHAY,

I AM LUCKY. Two naps within forty minutes, I do not often sleep so well. What was that dream? A lot happened in it but all I clearly recall is lying in a warm pool of seawater on a sunny beach. The pool was also a bathtub with flaking, cream-coloured paint on the bottom which I saw in an old house on Partickhill Road where Sontag lived with all those women and children. I lay in the water feeling very relaxed and watching the skin unwinding from around my chest in broad strips. As the strips floated up and flattened out on the surface I saw they were printed like newspapers with columns of words, dim photographs, an occasional headline. I was not interested in this old news, I wanted to see what was underneath. In a leisurely way I picked and peeled off the layers of skin-newsprint which still stuck to my chest until I had exposed the whole ribcage. I could see only blackness inside but I knew it contained a rare work of art, a white ivory figure of a girl, obscenely mutilated. I pushed my fingers between the ribs and almost managed to touch her.

Ugh. When I started remembering that dream I thought

it a happy one. It is utterly gruesome.

What can I think about now? I am sick of fantasies. O I will return to them but later, please God much later. I don't want to remember the past either. The past is a flowering minefield. All the goodness I have known grows there but grows among explosives which drive shrapnel into my brain whenever I disturb them. Try thinking about the future.

The future is nothing. Nada. I have reached the summit of my profession, the edge of the precipice. I can only be promoted sideways to a deskjob which would kill me in less than a year. My present job will do that too. Reeves wants me to retire and yes, I could do that with no great loss of earnings but retire to what? I have no garden to cultivate, no stamp collection to complete. I can be promoted into nothing, or wait for nothing, or retire into nothing. Hence my outcry a while ago, my hysterical prayer to have put someone in the world as a replacement. But it does not matter a damn who has fathered a child if he has not given it care and attention, and praying does more harm than good. Prayers work, they really do summon up God, but when the bastard arrives he does nothing but hang around my head telling me what a nasty boy I am. He's as bad as a woman. He detests my fantasy life. He has no respect for my ordinary, everyday life. I suspect he wants more gaiety and freedom. In spite of the vile publicity he has had from all his churches and most of his bibles I think that he dislikes stultification and cruelty, that the only pains he wants are birthpangs, the strains of making something good and new, the cares of mending something useful and old. BUT THE BUGGER OFFERS NO PRACTICAL SUGGESTIONS. "Love thy neighbour as thyself." The middle and upper classes are able to do that because they can choose neighbours of their own sort, but such advice is useless to the unemployed and though I am now middle-class it is no use to me. I could not love my wife, how can I love my neighbour? I do not even know his face, my neighbour is a noise in a room next door. Fuck off God and don't come back. I intend to forget you. My only hope for the future is a sudden change in my surroundings, a change I cannot initiate. A war would do the trick. Scotland is wired for it.

Scotland is wired for war, especially the bit north-west of Glasgow. The Nato nuclear bombers have come to the Isle of Skye. Apart from a handful of landowners and clergymen the local folk do not want them but no government need be moved by the wishes of the northern native, especially not the Gaelic native. Down waterlanes on the Firth of Clyde American and British missile submarines slip to and from their fuel bases. Between Loch Lomond and Gareloch one hill at least is honeycombed with galleries where the multi-megaton warheads are stockpiled. Some natural features of this wilderness are no longer marked on ordnance survey maps and new structures are certainly not marked there. This secrecy is not meant to baffle the Russians but adjacent Britons who feel uneasy about such things. In the event of a nuclear war (not the total sort big governments dread but the limited sort they hope for) it is important that the primary Russian weaponstrike is at Europe, not America, and at West Scotland, not South England. In the mid-seventies when the British government still pretended an interest in *devolution* (what a word!) there was a proposal to shift a big part of the Ministry of Defence from London to Glasgow. Sir William, the Lord Provost, thought this might bring employment to a city badly needing it. We were told later that civil servants refused to come to Glasgow because it had too few theatres, not enough nice houses and people. Whether true or false these reasons were irrelevant. Shifting the Defence Ministry to a city whose centre is twenty-five miles from the Gareloch would be a bit like General Haig shifting his staff headquarters to the edge of no-man's land. In the Home Counties civil defence instructors have been quietly telling concerned parties that if the war goes as expected the main English problem will be handling refugees from the north. But that problem is unlikely to be great. The army has plans to seal off badly radiated districts. Officers know they must order the shooting of people trying to leave. Our regiments have practised pushing back civilians in Aden and Ulster. If discipline holds – and for three hundred years the British soldier has been spectacularly obedient – the unhealthy bits of Britain will be sliced off to ensure that the healthy bits survive.

For three hundred years, in victory and defeat, against disciplined and undisciplined enemies the British soldier has been spectacularly obedient. At Hohenlinden, Quebec, Bunker Hill, Corunna, Waterloo, Peterloo, The March on Peking, The Charge of the Light Brigade, The Indian Mutiny, The Boer War, Passchendaele, Ypres, Gallipoli, forget Dunkirk but in Africa, Palestine, Egypt, Crete, Cyprus and Ulster our men did what they were told and sometimes a bit extra. Why should they not stand firm and ensure that the inhabitants of the Central Lowlands die in their own ditch and not somewhere else? They will be defending the biggest part of their country from the evil effects of Russian foreign policy, and I am sure the British High Command will be too tactful to use the Scottish regiments in Scotland. The Royal Anglians and Sherwood Foresters will seal off Strathclyde while the Argylls and the Black Watch deal with secondary targets like Tyneside, Merseyside or Birmingham. What matters nowadays is not where or why four or five million people die, but how fast. Whether we bake à la Hiroshima or spend a week spewing our rings up we will still have died faster than those Poles, Jews and Gypsies.

We?

Not we. I will live, if I choose. I know where the shelters are. I have supervised their security installations. I have tested their alarm circuits, surveillance circuits, defence circuits. I know too much to be locked outside in a state of national emergency. So I can look forward to several days, weeks perhaps, of canned soup and Scrabble games with the local administrators of national security. Unless the Third World War gets out of hand and we find it wiser to stay in hiding for months or years. I guess our average age will be around forty, the proportion of men to women three to one. If the electric generator fails or the food runs out an observer of human nature will find much to interest him.

But that is taking the pessimistic view. If the war is the sort that sensible people want – and surely in the high commands of Britain and America, Russia and China, sensible people predominate – then one morning before the century ends I will surface in a country which has suffered, what?

The main highland grousemoors and salmonrivers will be unpolluted, also the good beefproducing land and fishing villages and golf-courses of the north-east. Even Gleneagles and St Andrews are likely to escape. The borders and southern uplands, the milltowns of Tweedside, the Orkneys and oilrigs will be intact. Nothing will have perished but some crofting communities, seaside resorts and what was Britain's most productive industrial province when London was the commercial capital of the world. But the Clydeside has outlived its usefulness. During the Second World War it produced 90 per cent of British shipping but since the American polaris base arrived in the fifties capital has withdrawn and manufacture concentrated in the south. I am sure there is no connection between these two events, it is just a harmonious coincidence. Our big firms have been bought by bigger non-Scottish firms and then reduced in size or closed. Scottish investors prefer putting their money into business which operates in coolie nations where trade unions never had a chance. Glasgow now means nothing to the rest of Britain but unemployment, drunkenness and out-of-date radical militancy. Her nuclear destruction will logically conclude a steady peacetime process. It's a pity about Edinburgh. It has almost nothing to do with Glasgow but stands too near to go unscathed. Let us hope that only the people die and the buildings and monuments are undamaged, then in a few years the Festival can resume as merrily as ever. It is mostly the work of foreigners, anyway.

But if a country is not just a tract of land but a whole people then clearly Scotland has been fucked. I mean that word in the vulgar sense of *misused to give satisfaction or advantage to another*. Scotland has been fucked and I am one of the fuckers who fucked her and I REFUSE TO FEEL

BITTER OR GUILTY ABOUT THIS. I am not a gigantically horrible fucker, I'm an ordinary fucker. And no hypocrite. I refuse to deplore a process which has helped me become the sort of man I want to be: a selfish shit but a comfortable selfish shit, like everyone I meet nowadays. The militarisation and depression of Scotland has been good for the security business. Apart from the breweries my firm has been the only one to expand here in recent years. But the picture is bright in other areas. The worsened housing situation is enriching the building societies. The public health cuts and middle-class return to private medicine is enriching the insurance companies and the doctors. Greater unemployment and crime have brought new recruits to the army, powers to the police. Cuts in education have not benefited the teachers, but teaching has never been a highly regarded profession and rising illiteracy gets more people enjoying television, which has been made brighter and brisker by tax-cut boosts to big business and advertising. Meanwhile in England the wars and rumours of war have enlarged the military power and the arms industry. Sophisticated weapons are our main export, especially to the new countries of Africa, Asia and the southern hemisphere. We even sell missile systems to China, which shows we are not crudely anti-communist. And the banks are prospering. The more money a government borrows from its banks the richer the banks become. British banking has never been healthier where wealth accumulates and men decay getting and spending we lay waste our powers was it for this the clay grew tall shut up Hislop.

Shut up, Hislop, I bet you voted Tory like I do. A smart Tory does not believe this is, or can be, a pleasant world for most folk. He knows that anyone with five pounds in an account has inadvertently invested half of it in practices which would make him vomit if he could see them. He believes things would improve a little if the trade unions and Russians surrendered to him, but being a realist he does not expect surrender and works for what he and his associates can grab and enjoy now and in future. This is a natural Falstaffian approach to life and yes, recently Britain has become very Falstaffian.

We have become Falstaffian, our colourful past has returned, we display as rich a pageant of contrasts as in the days of Lizzie Tudor, Merry Charlie Stewart and The Queen Empress Victoria. Our own royal millionaire weds in Westminster Abbey and departs in a luxury cruiser to the cheers of the nation while unemployed children loot shops and battle with the police in the slums where ignorant armies clash by night. The Sunday papers bloom with technicolour adverts for expensive sexy clothes, luxury furniture, tropical holidays. Beggars have returned to the city streets, where were they for so many years? Gambling casinos and massage-parlour prostitution flourishes where wealth accumulates and men decay and every winter roofless vagrants die of exposure in greater numbers. Corruption is widespread and popular. Trainrobbers and hereditary tax evaders like the Vestey clan are applauded and excused, only social security cheats are scorned. The honest, kindly, thickwitted, slightly comic British policeman who everyone preferred to the gendarme and the yankee cop has vanished. The job got too tough for him. Nowadays the force must employ the sort of folk it once protected us from, and no wonder. The Great British Fictional Hero is a secret policeman licensed to kill and he is rewarded with all the sexual and social privileges the country can afford. I enjoyed the James Bond books when they first came out, I did not then believe that the British government employed secret killers. Now everyone knows that professional murderers make as honest a living in modern London as in Chicago or medieval Italy and I DON'T CARE. My father the socialist timekeeper would have hated all this. He only felt happy with the nation during the late forties and fifties, the austerity years of full employment, free school milk, food rationing and strict price control, the years when the motor car was a luxury and every town in Britain was linked by a nationalised steam railwayline. My father had no balls, he was worried and thoughtful all the time, no wonder I despised him. NO!

I did not despise him, he was a good man. I loved him.

I did not despise him, I loved him but he advised me only

once about sex. The day before I married Helen he made sure mother was out of earshot then said abruptly, "Jock. Regarding sex. Have you practised it more than once?"
I said I had. He said, "Good. Then I need say nothing on the matter, except that you should not neglect her breasts."
I said I would bear that in mind. He hesitated, blushed then said, "Another thing. Sex is more important for women than us, they get irritable if they don't have it once a week. In my experience Friday night is quite a good night."
I told him that I would bear that also in mind, then I went to the lavatory, locked myself in and sniggered heartily. I was eighteen and the idea of a married man making love only once a week struck me as absurd and even appalling. I did not know that already I had enjoyed more sex than I would ever have again, ever ever ever have again ever ever ever ever ever shut up ever shut up ever have again. All I need remember is that nowadays Britain is OF NECESSITY organized like a bad adolescent fantasy, hello Alan.

Alan. I see his head as big as the sky, the sardonic Arabic-Italian-Jewish face smiling out of the cloud of black hair. A small white sun gleams between two curls of it, this is an effect of perspective. Alan is actually standing against the window of his home in West Graham Street, on the top floor of the tenement knocked down in the sixties to let a motorway reach the Kingston Bridge. He holds the world carefully between his thumb and forefinger, it is a small blue globe marked with green and brown continents and islands, actually a child's pencil sharpener with a hole at the South Pole where the pencilpoint goes in. Alan enjoyed adjusting toys and ordinary tools until they were precision instruments. He would hone and realign the blades of a cheap sharpener until they could bring a pencil to needlesharpness with two delicate twists. But the globe-shaped sharpener belonged to me. I found it in the heel of my Christmas stocking when I was six, and loved it, and took it to school where it was stolen, so I am imagining, not remembering this. With a needlesharp pencilpoint Alan touches the spots on the globe where there is hunger, unemployment, riot, war and disease, spots not always identical but always connected. He says, "We don't need those bits."

I explain to him very patiently why these bits are essential and he points out a simple adaptation which will totally abolish them. But the adaptation is in the human mind and I cannot conceive it. The human mind after childhood is the most superdense rigid substance in God's universe, we will kill, we will die rather than change it. "Love your neighbour as yourself." "Do unto others as you would they should do unto you." Go away God. You cannot expect winners to take that advice, especially not winners who know they are ordinary people doing ordinary jobs. Alan never talked about politics. I don't know why I imagined him like that.

Alan never talked about politics except once when some of us sat yattering while he repaired a 1931 Mullard walnut-case wireless set. There was Isi the architect, and Wee Willie the anarchist alchemist, and Frazer Fairbairn, an unemployed gym teacher who said he had been forced out of education because of his progressive attitude toward the pupils. Frazer spend his days in public libraries getting very excited by every second or third book he read. He was telling us about Machiavelli's *The Prince*. "Listen," he said, "you have just conquered a neighbouring state, right?, and you want to conquer another. So what do you do to the defeated people to stop them revolting against you when you withdraw most of your army?"

We could not answer because we had not read Machiavelli.

"Easy!" cried Frazer, "You split the population into three, take most of the wealth away from one-third and divide it with the rest. The majority have now profited by being conquered. They accept your government in return for your help if the minority start a civil war to get their own back, a civil war which will *not* occur because the impoverished losers know they are bound to be defeated. The conqueror can now repeat his manoeuvre elsewhere. What I don't understand," said Frazer, "is why no governments have taken Machiavelli's advice? Surely the first to do it would conquer the world?"

Isi the architect said that Machiavelli's formula was far too arithmetical; human societies were natural growths which could not be divided and ruled along arithmetical lines. Wee

Willie disagreed. He said the nations were ruled by the power of gold, which had a numerical value the financiers juggled and bargained with; each morning and evening the Stock Exchange reports describe very precisely how the world is ruled by arithmetic. Frazer Fairbairn said, "Then why have governments not used Machiavelli's formula?" Alan, who seemed not to have been listening, said, "They do."

"Where?"

"Here."

After a pause I said, "You don't mean the British Empire."

"No. I mean Britain."

I did not understand him. This was in the fifties.

In those days I was calm, confident and very happy. Though not legally married I had someone more completely my wife than a signed oath could have made her and I suspected that I would soon have someone else. I was even complacent about the state of Britain. Winston Churchill was again prime minister but my politics were still shaped by my father's socialist rhetoric of the forties. "Thank Heavens Britain has stopped being *great*," he said, "for what is greatness in a country? As the word is commonly used it means simply the habit of interfering with other countries. Nobody today can doubt that the U.S.S.R. and U.S.A. are very great nations but Britain is giving back her Empire to the folk she stole it from. We have voted to be not *great* but *good*, and even at home we are an example to Russia and America. Without riot or arrest, without one single death or one broken law, our elected government has undertaken a truly socialist revolution."

"You are a very nice man, Peter, but also a terrible blether," said Old Red. "We are giving up an empire because we are too poor to hold on to it. And at home the Attlee government has done nothing but give a more lasting form to some measures introduced by a right-wing government in a state of funk. It was the coalition which froze profits, rents and prices, brought in rationing and took over big properties for the good of the nation. Our ruling classes are not idiots. They saw that Hitler would beat them if they continued feathering their nests at the expense of the worker, so they agreed to a temporary shareout."

"Which has been made permanent!" said Dad. "Nobody wants a return to the lockouts and strikes of the twenties, the depression of the thirties and a third bloody war. Everyone with a memory knows capitalism is a rotten system, so our lighting, heating and local housing, our main fuel, transport and healthcare are now public services belonging to the whole people. The whole people!"

"Peter," said Old Red very patiently, "the top men drawing the big wages in the newly nationalised industries are exactly the same sort of businessmen and landlords who used to own them. They are also being compensated by the British taxpayer for the loss of shares which before the war had become practically worthless. How do you think our managers and directors are using the new money they get from us? The banks have not been nationalised. They are investing in the oil and car industries, in building societies, in companies exploiting nations where socialism hasn't a chance. If the National Coal Board and British Rail were directed by miners and railwaymen, instead of former company directors and admirals of the fleet, they would cost the nation a lot less and keep the nationalised industries running far more securely."

"But working men can't run their own industries," cried Dad, then blushed and clearly wished he had used other words. After a pause Old Red said, "Spoken like a true member of the British Labour Party."

"I understand the point you're making," said Dad. "The Bar Association is run by lawyers and the Medical Association by doctors, why not have a railway system managed by enginedrivers and stationmasters? You must know the answer to that. Only people with university degrees have the training to direct large organisations. But in less than twenty years the new education grants will have produced a completely different breed of managers, folk whose fathers and mothers are working folk like ourselves. Can you seriously doubt that these will turn Britain into the nearly classless society we have in Australia and Scandinavia, with spacious homes for everyone and full enjoyment of the four freedoms Roosevelt spoke about: freedom from want, freedom from fear, freedom of belief and freedom of speech?"

Old Red sighed, whistled a line of *Over the Sea to Skye* and said, "It's your ostrich who talks the most perfect Utopian."

Did he really say that? It sounds the sort of thing Hislop said. I liked Old Red more than Mad Hislop but I didn't like him much. His arguments upset Dad and spoiled the quietness of our house, they distracted me from my schoolbooks and my fantasies.

Dad and Old Red completely agreed about one thing. Another Conservative government would ruin the country. The Macmillan administration disconcerted them terribly. There was an increase in upper-class luxury and even debauchery but the working class seemed cheerfuller too. However, by the end of the sixties it was clear that in the general scramble for the nation's pennies the investors, the professions and a few well-organised unions were still doing well but everyone else was beginning to lose. Harold Wilson became prime minister. "I just don't understand him!" cried Dad, "he seems to be telling us that he'll help Britain get a little more socialism when the Stock Exchange feels secure enough to allow it. Surely he knows that will never happen?"

"You must remember, Peter, that our Harold is a very clever and increasingly rich man who knows far more about the world of business than ignoramuses like ourselves," said Old Red. I chuckled heartily. Red and I now had something in common. We both thought Britain could only be helped by a political organisation which did not exist. He wanted a form of co-operative Ruskinite syndicalism, I wanted a strong government of decent Tory gentlemen who would prevent the worst sorts of poverty and social squalor, not because poverty and squalor are unjust, but because they are ugly and unsafe. So we were both amused by Dad's mixture of hope and shockability at the antics of the Labour Party.

One afternoon I came back from a very big job in the Shetlands and found a week-old letter from Old Red on the lobby floor. It said Dad had suffered a stroke and was in the intensive care unit of Kilmarnock Infirmary. I phoned and heard he had improved a little and tomorrow would be shifted to an ordinary ward. I went straight out to see him.

He lay in bed looking pink and feeble but also very tranquil and glad to see me. I explained the reason for the delay. He said, "I understand, Jock. A man's work must always come first."

I said my work did not come before him and in future he would always have an address where I could be contacted if he had another accident. And I would phone him at least twice a week. He smiled and said, "Not at all. A man's work must always come first."

I produced a book I had grabbed from my shelves before rushing out of the house and I said, "You'll have more time for reading now. I think you'll enjoy this, even though it's a novel. It shows the First World War from the Austro-Hungarian side. Listen."

I read out the beginning.

"And so they've killed our Ferdinand," said the charwoman to Mr Schweik, who had left military service years before after having been finally certified by an army medical board as an imbecile, and now lived by selling dogs – ugly mongrel monstrosities whose pedigrees he forged.

"Which Ferdinand, Mrs Muller?" he asked, rubbing his knee with Elliman's embrocation, for he suffered from rheumatism. "I know two Ferdinands. One is a chemist's messenger who once by mistake drank a bottle of hair oil. The other is Ferdinand Kokoska who collects dog manure. Neither is any great loss."

"O no sir, it's His Imperial Highness, the Archduke Ferdinand, the fat churchy one. They bumped him off at Sarajevo, sir, with a revolver, you know. He drove there in a car."

"Jesus Maria!" exclaimed Schweik. "What a grand job! And in a car too! Well, there you have it, Mrs Muller, in a car. A gentleman like him can afford a car and he never imagines a drive like that might finish badly. And I wouldn't mind betting, Mrs Muller, that the chap that did it put on smart togs for the occasion.

Potting an Imperial Highness is no easy job, you know. You've got to wear a topper, so the cops don't nab you beforehand."

Dad smiled and nodded but I was not sure he had been listening, though when I put the book on the bed he rested his hand on the cover. He spoke of the coming election. The Tories said they would *encourage enterprise* if they were returned, Labour said it would *show that it cared*. The small Scot Nat party had provoked a debate by referring to a fact: multinational companies were getting a lot of North Sea mineral very cheaply. Harold Wilson had announced that this was true, and only a Labour government had the power and will to tackle the big oil companies. Edward Heath had accused Wilson of planning to nationalise Britain's oil. Wilson had hotly denied this: he had only been trying to convey that a Labour government could combat tax-avoidance.

"Why is Labour afraid to nationalise?" said Dad plaintively. "A nationalised industry – the Gas Board – discovered North Sea Oil. If Britain kept its own oilfields and developed them very slowly and carefully, with British skill and capital, for the public good, we would not need to buy foreign fuel for most of the coming century and we would be a lot richer. The Electricity Board would not be turning to dangerous powersources like nuclear energy. But now most of our oil goes to Americans who pay less for it than we do, and they'll have exhausted the supply within twenty-five years."

He frowned as if examining an intricate knot then said shyly, "Son, I know your education was mainly electrical and that a technical college is not a university, but you meet more people than I do and are more a man of the world. Do you think things would have been different nowadays if the Attlee government had nationalised the banks?"

I said, "I'm sure it would have made a great deal of difference. And you are coming to live with me when you leave this place."

After a silence he said gruffly, "That won't be necessary."

I said, "It will be convenient. Don't think I want a housekeeper. A woman comes in to do the cleaning and laundering. But I'll enjoy reading an occasional book across the hearthrug from you. My place feels a bit lonely in the evenings."

I said this to make it easier for him to come to me, but as soon as the words left my mouth I realised they were true. The house with him in it would feel more genial, more like a home. He said, "Well, cleaning lady or not, I think there will be more for me to do around the house than you anticipate."

So the matter was settled.

It had been mid-evening when I entered the ward and now the nurses were tucking the patients in and dimming the lights. He composed himself for sleep with one hand resting on the book. We said good night. I got a phonecall next morning to say he had fallen asleep as soon as I left the ward and not wakened again.

A quiet death in the night without convulsion, choking or disarray. A suitable death for a man like that. A good death. I am glad we were friends before it happened and that we said goodbye properly.

Dad.

What is this ache inside me? It is pity, a slimy disgusting creature worming toward the surface of this face in order to split it open but by God it won't succeed. I hate pity. It does not work, it does no good, it is a device vicious people use to persuade themselves that underneath it all they are decent human beings. Why should I pity my father? He was a killer. At sixteen he joined the territorials who in peacetime, in their spare time, exercised under trained army officers in return for a small sum of money or else for none at all, just for love of it, I'm not sure which. The result was that when they killed our Ferdinand and Austria invaded Serbia and Russia mobilised and Germany told Russia to stop doing that and France mobilised and the British fleet went to Scotland and Germany occupied Luxembourg and Britain told Germany to keep out of Belgium and Germany said, "We can't, we're already there," and umpteen millions tramped into France in bloody big boots and started killing

each other – the result was, Dad joined like a shot. He wasn't a pithead man in those days, he was a miner and probably hated it. A hellish job, especially then. So out of the fryingpan of home-sweet-home into the fire of Flanders he went like a swimmer into cleanness leaping out of a world grown old and stale and weary, as someone wrote at the time. "You should not have gone, Peter," said Old Red, who had been a conscientious objector, "you should not have gone. Nobody should have gone to that war."
"We were just weans," said Dad, "we didnae know any better," but he survived till 1918 so it is statistically probable that he killed a German or two.

I must have met many killers in the ordinary way of business but only a couple I could identify. One was a town clerk in Fife, a neat brisk active chap like myself apart from a wife and a grown family doing very well in the world. I saw one of the sons a few years back and asked after his Dad. Dad had killed himself. Dad had been a sniper in the Great War as they called it in those days. He sat up a tree, neatly and methodically picking off any Germans who showed themselves. He was a good marksman, he killed a lot of them, he was praised and decorated for it. More than forty years later, after a second Great War with Belsen Dachau Warsaw Dresden Hiroshima etcetera, the thought of the men he had killed grew so burdensome that his life was unbearable. Of course there must have been more to his story than that. He was a kirk elder and religious people are always a bit insane and I wonder how he got on with his wife? The other killer was an exciseman attached to a distillery in Menstrie in the days when I installed the systems myself. A lot of peculiar people are in the excise, Burns was an exciseman but this bloke was not poetic, not peculiar at all as far as I could see. He had an air of calm self-contained dependability which I have found in a lot of ordinary people who have done military service. At quarter to five he would look into the warehouse where I was working and murmur, "I will be holding communion in fifteen minutes." I would clean up and go to his wee office and he, I and the distillery manager would have drams together till very late, three respectable Scotsmen quietly destroying their intelligence in a mood of relaxed reminiscence. We had one thing in common: each knew the others were alcoholics and trustworthy with it, so we ended knowing more about each other than our closest friends and families knew. The exciseman had been with the army in Israel when it was called Palestine. He had gone into a living-room with a machinegun and sprayed it from left to right killing *ratatatatatatata* three or four small children, mother, father and grandparents in less than half a minute. I said, "Were you under orders?"

He said, "No. I was simply told to search that house. It was a routine search. I'd searched plenty of houses without doing that."

I said, "How did you feel?"

He said, "Great. I felt I was shagging a woman. It was a good feeling."

I said, "Have you ever wanted to do it again?"

He shrugged and said, "Not particularly. I'm a quiet sort of fellow."

After a silence the distillery manager said that when he was a driver in the canal zone the sergeants told him that if he knocked down an Egyptian he should reverse over him because if he lived he would sue the army for compensation. I had no military stories. I was turned down for National Service because of bad eyesight. It must be a lot worse now. I'm the age Mum was when she left for New Zealand.

"We were just children," said Dad, "even General Haig was nothing but a jumped-up public schoolboy who didnae know any better."

"You should have been guided by your ain folk!" said Old Red sternly. "You should have listened to the Scottish Socialists, Keir Hardie, John Maclean, Maxton and Gallagher. They wanted the working class to stop the war by a general strike – as had been agreed with the German socialists beforehand. But no. When the flags started waving the crowds started cheering and the German socialists joined ranks with the Kaiser and English Labour joined the Liberals and Toe-rags. And the Clydesiders, the only folk who wanted to *change* the rotten set-up were decried as cowards and imprisoned for telling the working

class that it was being led into the mire."
"Well," said Dad with a sigh, "in the circumstances it could not have been otherwise."
"You are WRONG, Peter!" said Old Red. "You should be ashamed of saying such a thing. A child is listening –" I was trying not to listen – "and could be influenced for life. Those who think the past could not have been different come to feel the present cannot be changed or the future either. God knows I am a dedicated atheist but even Christianity is better than spineless oriental fatalism. The common folk *did* stop the war by going on strike. You were involved, weren't you? In 1914."
"Oh that," said my father, "yes."
"Have you told your boy about it?"
"No."
"Tell him! Tell him now!"
"The boy is trying to do his homework," said my mother.
"This will only take two minutes, Mrs MacLeish," said Old Red. "Jock, listen to your father and you'll hear something so important that nobody has printed it in schoolbooks in case children learn from it. Carry on, Peter."
"Well," said Dad awkwardly, "on the morning of Christmas day 1914 the firing did not start as punctually as usual, in fact didn't start at all. We all heaved a sigh of relief – it looked as if Jerry was going to be sensible. Then we saw a few men walking about between the lines in German uniforms and in full view of our trenches. Madmen! I stared at them. Suddenly Tommy Govan beside me started laughing and climbing the parapet. I thought he had gone mad too.
I grabbed him. He said, 'Don't worry Peter, this is a holiday!' So I followed him. This happened right across France the whole length of the line. We couldnae say much to them because of the language but we shook hands, swapped fags, exchanged a slug of rum for a slug of schnapps. It turned out to be a very pleasant day."
Old Red said, "How did the officers take it?"
"O some got very angry and brandished their revolvers: 'Back to your trenches you traitors!' sort of thing."
"And what did you say to that?"
"Nothing. We turned our backs on them. In the circumstances they couldnae do a thing. However, next morning

the big guns woke us up again and everything was back to normal. The big guns never stopped after that. It was them that called the tune."

"And now could we have a bit less about war in my kitchen?" said Mum quietly. She was knitting. She despised the gossip of women, she hated the arguments of men. She was as silent as I am nowadays.

"We were just children."

Before President Reagan announced his ten-year multi-megabuck missile modernisation programme the B.B.C. broadcast a film of American armed-forces chiefs who explained why it was necessary. I liked these men. They had none of the drawling condescension of the English officer class. They were middle-aged but pink and healthy, enthusiastic about their work and keen to explain its problems to the general public. A communist or pacifist might have thought them EVIL but they were obviously innocent, boyish men with straight, competitive one-track minds. Their only problem was this. Any improved weapon which they or their technicians could devise had been devised, or would soon be devised, by their opposites in Russia, so they had to have it first. They were not warmongers. No doubt a few were like my friend the exciseman, normally dependable men who sometimes, with their finger on a trigger, would enjoy going *Ratatatatata* and exterminating three generations, but that sort are always a minority. The majority definitely hope, and the minority usually hope, that the weapon race lasts for ever. A continual weapon race with continual weapon exercises is their only notion of peace. Without such a peace they would be useless men, mere timeservers. And this is true of all technicians, scientists, bureaucrats, industrialists, computermen and machinists who profit by the defence business in America, Russia or anywhere. Today everyone who profits is profiting partly from the defence business. If there was a revolution in Russia tomorrow, if a liberal regime came to power as in Greece or Spain, we would have to treat it as a potential enemy or form an alliance with it against China, which also has a great many soldiers. But the race must continue. We must all hope, all pray that it never ends because we can only imagine one ending. Boomboomboom. Our defence systems run like my fantasies which can only continue by getting much bigger and nastier than were first intended. Nobody can keep control of a processs like that for ever. In 1914 and 1939 the big industrial nations, having fucked the rest of the planet (in the vulgar sense of the word) started wanking all over each other. None of them enjoyed it but they could not stop. This will soon happen again. I am ready for it. Sip.

A year or several years ago I sat near some young men, idiot Tories and idiot socialists who were having the usual heated discussion in which each side contradicted itself far more than its opponents. The Tories said that the Shah of Persia was a good ruler because he had dragged his nation into the twentieth century, Stalin a bad ruler because he destroyed the rule of law. The socialists said Stalin was a good ruler because the U.S.S.R. was too backward to be governed democratically, the Shah a bad ruler because he had destroyed primitive forms of tribal communism. I was tempted to tell them that any govenment which arrests, imprisons, tortures people without a proper public trial by jury is a bad government, but that would have raised the question of Ulster so I was silent. Among these men sat a fat Buddha-like fellow who was paying for the drinks. Because he was listening quietly, and because the youngsters sometimes referred their arguments to him, and because he always responded with a slight smile or shake of the head, I thought, 'One of my kind. He knows they're talking nonsense.' Our eyes met and he nodded to me, then one of the younger men asked my opinion. I said I was only interested in things I was able to change so did not give a damn what any foreign government did unless it threatened us with war, a remark which of course swung the discussion on to the topic of THE BOMB. I suppose this was the middle seventies because not many people call nuclear weapons The Bomb nowadays, just as people stopped calling the First World War the Great War in 1939. Anyway, the idiot Tories said the world was a safer place because of the bomb, and if it was not they would rather die than live on a planet ruled by Russia; the idiot socialists said Russia was only an imperialist state because she feared America, and if Britain dismissed nuclear weapons from her shores America would ensure the Russians did not invade us. I said that if I owned a small bottle of strong barbiturate pills I would not care a damn which was more likely, a nuclear war or a Russian invasion. At this the fat older man quivered and snuffled (it was his way of laughing) and the younger men left the hotel. I bought the older man a large Glenlivet. I learned he was a chemist, a widower who lived in rooms behind his shop on the main street. Near midnight, when we were both well oiled, he said, "I'll give you what you want. Come home with me."

But I am sorry Dad did not live long enough to read about Schweik because his book is the funniest and wisest ever written. Schweik is an old soldier who pretends to obey his commanders but twists everything to suit himself and can talk his way out of any situation. His stories are as pithy as the parables of Jesus and nobody has spoiled them by explaining what they mean. In one of them Schweik crosses a public square in Prague or maybe Budapest, it is very dark, he passes a monument in the middle. A drunk man is feeling his way round and round this muttering, "I managed to get inside so there *must* be a way out." He has been doing it all night.

I am not a true Conservative. A true Conservative has faith in some established institution which he thinks will save him: the Stock Exchange, the employers' federation, the army, the monarchy. In essence I don't give a tuppenny damn for that lot either. I suppose I am a nihilist now. Realising this, a great weight falls from my mind. Where have I left my four women and what is happening to them? Since everyone except the poor and helpless gain by increasing danger, poverty, and helplessness – and since the poor and helpless would do as we do if they had the chance – it can be no very bad thing to extract a little fun from imaginary victims.

10: TO STOP A MASS DANGEROUSLY OVERHEATING, DIVIDE IT.

10: TO STOP A MASS DANGEROUSLY OVERHEATING, DIVIDE IT. So here comes a cool catalogue of caged beauties for me to divide, rule, tattoo, massage and variously goad into ecstasies of shameless wantonness if I manage to keep the head.

1 JANINE

In her early twenties. Abundant dark dishevelled hair, dark accusing eyes, sulky red mouth like Jane Russell in *The Outlaw*. Slightly smaller than most women were she not wearing high-heeled white platform-sole shoes. Slender ankles, knees, waist but plump hips in white suede mini-skirt, full thighs and calves in black net stockings, plump shoulders and I will not neglect her breasts in a white silk blouse. Stroud ushers her along a softly lit brown-carpeted corridor. Opening a door he stands aside to let her through and at once she is dazzled by low lights shining straight into her face. A voice cries, "Come on in Miss Crystal, show us how you can walk!"

She feels Stroud's hand between her shoulderblades press her firmly forward. She hears the door close behind her

with a double click. She senses a great dark space on each side, and two or three figures in a pool of light in front of her, and a continuous purring noise, can it be a film projector? And she shows them how she can walk. Her heart is thudding but she would feel a completely passive victim if she stood still so with a pang of excitement the actress in her takes control. Though every muscle is tense with terror she gives a splendid performance of a woman strolling casually forward. The performance is helped by realising that the surrounding space has people in it, a seated audience which she cannot see clearly for the dazzle. She concentrates on the sound of two unfastened studs in her skirt clicking with each step she takes. "That's a sexy noise," a childish voice says, and giggles.
'Act calm,' thinks Janine. 'Pretend this is just an ordinary audition.'
Splendid.

2 SUPERB
A ripe housewife in her early forties. A thickish body slightly flabby in some places (stomach, forearms, thighs) but practical and sensual with dark shoulderlength hair which is straight, not curly like Janine's. The breasts I will not neglect are nude under the bib of yes, her whole body is naked under the white sweatsoiled denim of yes, *dung*arees which tightly cuddle her fulfilled cunt but are otherwise very loose and baggy and rolled up to the knees as she sprawls dozing on the fleecy flattened carseat. Charlie leans down to kiss her. He says, "We've arrived, honey."
"I don't want to move."
"Lie on your front."
"Why?"
"I've a surprise for you – a present."
She turns over. She feels him grip her right arm. Something cold clicks round it above the elbow, her left arm is wrenched painfully back and with another click she finds her elbows locked together behind her. She cries, "Hey that *hurts* Charlie!" and starts struggling on to her knees but his arm forces her down, he lies with his face close to hers and whispers, "Honey, you've got to listen or you won't understand a thing. *Will* you listen?" – and his hard hands squeeze

her soft forearms cruelly tight – "*Will* you listen to me?"
She stares at him, mouth and eyes wide open. He says softly, "Remember the night we met and I told you I could make you an actress? Remember I said on the phone this afternoon that I'd have you giving performances sooner than you expected? Well I meant every word. And your first performance will be tonight."

He kisses her violently then says, "I'm going to tell you something that won't make much sense till you're a few weeks older. I love you, you bitch, and I'm giving you to people who will teach you tricks you never dreamed existed. But I'll keep returning to you again and again and in the end you won't want to live without me and we'll have had more fun together than you thought possible in your whole goddamned selfish little life. Understand?"

And grabbing her head in both hands he kisses her again, then sits up and touches a switch. The hood of the car rolls down. He sounds the horn loudly, twice, then gets out of the car, comes round to her side and opens the door. In one hand he holds a thick leather collar. Too stupefied to understand anything she lies staring at him as he reaches in and buckles it round her throat, then takes a chain leash from his pocket and slips it to a ring on the collar, then stands back from the car and tugs the chain hard. He says, "Walk, bitch."

(Control yourself) trembling and aghast she obeys the pressure of the collar and struggles to her knees, extends a leg and again feels the chilling grittiness of concrete under her bare foot. The buckle of the collar is huge and sharp-edged so she must stand with her chin held very high. She is facing a closed door. He comes behind her, a hand unfastens the buttons over her right hip then slips inside the dungarees and caresses her belly while the other hand slips under the bib to caress her breasts. He presses her back against him, she feels between her buttocks his penis blunted by two layers of cloth, feels his lips kissing her between the shoulderblades. In her state of strangeness and dread these pressures are comforting. The door suddenly opens and that is enough for now. Except that this happens in a windowless garage with twelve cars parked in it and room for several more.

3 BIG MOMMA

I don't know her age. She has a small girlish head with closecropped ash blonde hair and you have to look very close to see the fine little wrinkles of age. The head rises from the body of one of those hippo-like whores who keep surfacing in Fellini films. In my teens and twenties I found them repulsive. But what is she wearing and where is she? Since I abolished the police station sequence I have left her nowhere. I will compensate by putting her in two places at once.

(A) In the pool of light toward which Janine walks Big Momma is standing astride astride astride with her hands on her hips and a smile like the smile of a greedy little girl looking at a plate of cream cakes. But she is looking at Janine. She wears one of those conspicuously openable dresses I am far too fond of: tight creamcoloured linen with great big buttons many of them unfastened. Her flirtatiously scanty black panties and bra are obvious through it. No stockings, sensible sandals.

(B) The door before Superb suddenly opens and Big Momma walks toward her grinning like a greedy little girl looking at a plate of etcetera. She is dressed as in (A) and walks straight up to Superb who is clasped by Charlie against his body. Momma says in a coarse throaty whisper, "Gimme a taste," and standing on tiptoe she kisses Superb quite gently. Then she says, "The leash please, Charlie. It's my turn to take her a walk. I've a pack of hot dogs back there who can't wait for her."

Ooooh nasty.

4 HELGA

In her mid-thirties. Of all my women she is the most athletically lovely with no sagging lines at all. She has the tall spare slender figure which unobservant idiots call "boy-ish". She is not at all boyish, though her breasts are small and far apart. The nipples cover half of them and as I consider her I am disturbed by a strange feeling which has nothing to do with the story she is in, a feeling of . . . friendliness. Why? Friendliness is irrelevant here. I feel like a gangster play on the radio which is being interrupted by an opera on another wavelength. Dad liked opera though he pretended not to. Sometimes mum or myself came into the kitchen unexpectedly and found him playing the Third Programme very quietly with his ear close to the set. He always switched at once to the Light Programme or Scottish Home Service and turned up the volume. I believe he sang in some sort of choir before I was born. He would have detested the nasty sexual world I have devised. I am sure he felt in his bones that sexuality was wicked. Which is why I feel in my bones that wickedness is sexy. Get back to Helga in the viewing theatre.

4 HELGA

In her mid-thirties. She wears **********************
She is wearing *********************************
Why can't I make her ****************************
****
************************* something inside my head is resisting the story of Helga. God, probably. I should never have asked him here. Helga is crucial, she brings all the other girls together. Forget what she looks like, what she wears. Imagine what she sees, hears, says. It may be possible to slip her past him that way. Here we go again.

4 HELGA

watches the film of Janine's audition right to the end, then presses her cigarette carefully into the ashtray. She says, "The editing was crap but the material is real hot stuff. She wasn't exactly acting, was she?"

"The word *act* is employed in two ways," says Dr von Stroud whose first name had better be Wilhelm or something even more Germanic, "The proverb, *It is actions, not sentiments which count* suggests that value is mainly in deeds. The phrase, *She did not mean it – she was just acting* suggests that deeds are worthless unless caused by a sincere, immediate feeling or desire. The actions of Janine in your own beautiful film indicated lust and terror but were caused by a desire for money and to flaunt herself." (This Doctor is a bore.) "In our film her declared feelings and acts were directly caused by what her fellow actors did to her. Yet our film did not succeed! We who helped create the performance were greatly entertained by it at the time, but the art by which we recorded it was inadequate. Editing, camera-work, lighting, the setting could have been improved. Which is why we are paying you to direct our future productions."

"Who has directed them so far?" asks Helga.

"Mummy," says Hollis and giggles, but Helga looks at Dr Wilhelm no but Adolf is too trite, Siegfried too operatic, Ludwig, no I like the Pastoral Symphony just call him the Doctor, Helga looks at the Doctor who says, "You will meet her shortly. But first let me show you some other people you will be working with."

The Doctor climbs up to a slide-projector behind the back row of seats which are as deep as oriental divans. Max and the waitress sprawl here embracing but apparently asleep, though his right hand, inside her dress and between her thighs, sometimes moves a little. The cinema darkens. With a click the screen suddenly shows ******************* damn *************************************** ** ** ** damn, damn ********************************** ** ** ** damn ***************************** no satisfaction. (You'll have to skip this bit.)

I'll have to skip this bit. Helga says, "Who's the big woman? The cropped blonde."

"She is the member who has so far directed our productions," says the Doctor, "we no longer find her satisfying. She knows nothing of filmwork and has become such a prima donna that she insists on acting in everything and always the same role."

"Oh I can't wait to see her face when she realises she is no longer in charge," squeals Hollis.

"We will allow the truth to dawn upon her in easy stages," says von Strudel. "She knows you are being employed as a film-maker but does not yet know this will affect her position. So you will watch one of her productions, one of her rehearsals. If you suggest an improvement she will at once reject it, she only likes her own ideas. But we will support you and make her do what you suggest, and thus establish your authority."

"Have you fixed a date for this rehearsal?" asks Helga.

"It will take place here, and very soon. Momma is bringing us a completely new girl – a girl new, I mean, to the disciplines of our organisation."

"And what is the piece called?"

"It is called *The New Girl's First Day* and is my friend Maximilian's favourite production. You have chosen the actress for it, have you not, Maxie?"

"That's right," says Max, and bringing his lips close to the waitress's ear he murmurs (but the acoustics of the place are so good that every word is audible), "And if you don't make with the sex exactly when I want it I'll have you acting in it too."

"But honey," the waitress quietly wails, squirming against him, "you know I always give you what you want."

"In that case," says von Strudel, "since we have a few minutes to while away before the production team arrives, I suggest *** *** ************ postures ******************************* *** ***************************** drench *************** *** *** *** ************ sobs "Please don't make me," but ************ *** *** *** *** ******** drenching ********************************* *** *** *** *** **but

but ★★★ ★★ ★★ ★★★ and ★★★★★★★★★★★★★ and ★★★★★ and ★★★ it's no use. The resistance is too strong. I'll have to think about something else until it vanishes. Think about real sex. How often have I had it? Start at the beginning.

DENNY 1953
Two months of sex three times a night. Is that possible? Is memory exaggerating? Perhaps, but I often went to bed with her thinking, 'Not tonight, I'm too tired.' I would embrace her cosily and slowly come awake all over. Nearly every night I am sure we loved on getting into bed, then once when waking in the smaller hours, and once just after or before the dawn. What delicious deep sleep she gave me in between. But *surely* it cannot have been three times a night? Let's say twice a night which is 2 months × 4 weeks = 8 weeks × 7 days = 56 nights × 2 per night = 112 times, let's say 140 no no no 150 times at least with Denny I'm certain.

HELEN 1953–4
In the six weeks before marriage we did it fully only twice, or perhaps only once. Nothing happened during the honeymoon, then twice a week for not more than ten months is 10 × 4 × 2 = 80 but some weeks we didn't so more like 60 plus twice before marriage and once just before she left me in 1967 is 63 times with Helen.

SONTAG 1971
Six or seven weeks but so erratically that three times a week on average is probably on the generous side so 18 times with Sontag.

THE EDITOR 1974
Once one night and twice one night is 3 times with the editor.

THE CHEMIST 197?
No times. Nothing really happened.

THE WHORE 1982
No times either but for a moment I felt alive again. For years I had lived in great deadness of spirit, a deadness I still inhabit but last week was unusually painful. Spring is always the worst time for me and we had three or four days of sunny weather which affected the women as usual. It looked as if all of them between fifteen and fifty had come out dressed to provoke my lust. The sight gave me such pain that I had to walk about staring at the pavement a yard before my feet. I also grasped the pillbottle in my pocket like a talisman though I was in no danger of suicide. I will only be in danger if I sit down, empty the pills on to a tabletop or bedspread like this one and count them. There should be more than fifty. If I count them it will occur to me that only cowardice stops me swallowing them with a big tumbler of Glenlivet, and that if I do not swallow them I will detest and despise myself till my dying day. But I am in no danger of counting them if I walk about, keep staring at the pavement and visit crowded pubs. When I'm at home at the weekend I make a practice of pubcrawling. I spread my drinking between about twenty pubs, visiting six or seven in a single night but never the same pubs two nights running. In this way nobody gets to know me thoroughly or notices how much I drink. There is a lane which rises from the bank of the Kelvin and is so little used that it is still cobbled with stones of the horse and cart days. After dark I approached the arch of a high bridge where the lane begins and saw a shapeless dark figure descending the slope on the far side. I do not know how I knew the figure was female or how I sensed that it had sensed me. We slowed down as we neared each other and when the width of the arch separated us we were standing still and I had an erection. This was a novelty to me. I can induce erections by fantasising but I must cuddle real women for a very long time before I go stiff down there. I was astounded by what this woman was doing to me. She was squat and old with a bloated discoloured face but I felt hopeful and grateful, I crossed over

and put my hands on her shoulders. This is hard to remember.

Remember it.

She said, "Yes all right but I've got to be careful, I want to see what I'm getting, ken?"
I thought she was talking about my prick and that she was worried in case it was diseased. I led her into a dark space behind a cast-iron pillar of the bridge, unzipped my flies and took the penis out. She felt it. I said, "It's all right, you see. Come home with me," and I zipped it in again and led her back the way I had come. I was so excited that I babbled to her, I can't remember what. I wanted to make her excited and hopeful and compliant also, I put a twenty-pound note into her hand and told her she would get more tomorrow if we spent a good night together. She suddenly stood still and said, "But will ye marry me?"
I said, "No, I've been married already."
She said, "Then I'll never content ye. No no no no I'll never content ye, I cannae dae it."
We were beside the entrance to the underground railway. She walked away into it with my twenty-pound note. I stared after her and shouted feebly, "Please come back," but she disappeared round a corner wailing, "No no no I cannae content ye, I cannae content ye."
I grew angry and bellowed, "YOU ARE UNJUST!"
I turned and ran up that lane and in a minute was in a crowded pub ordering a large gin and tonic. Gin has a foul taste but I take nothing else at the weekends because it is not noticeable on the breath. The penis was lying down again but I still felt like babbling though I do not often talk because people who talk give themselves away all the time. I saw a man I knew slightly and said to him, "A funny thing just happened to me."
I told him about it. His face took on a vague, absentminded look, he said, "Excuse me," and went away.
'Not very social,' I thought. I saw a girl who attracted me, a student possibly, she stood in a group of other girls. I said to her, "Hullo."
She answered, "Hullo!" with a surprised but pleasant smile.

I think she thought we had met before and that she had forgotten where, I am obviously a respectable man who does not chat up young strangers just because they are attractive. I said, "There are a lot of funny people around here, you know. I've just met one."
I told her about the whore under the bridge. To make the girl laugh I used an astonished, half-glaikit Glasgow voice like Billy Connolly's. I spoke loud enough for a lot of people to hear me. *Oh God let me not remember.* I don't remember much else. Except getting very angry when they turned their backs, and hurling my glass over their heads at the gantry and grabbing another glass from a table and hurling that too then running out. I ran and ran a long way. Later I saw a Pakistani grocery which was still open. I remembered I had no eggs and bacon for breakfast and went inside. A boy of perhaps twelve, thirteen, fourteen was serving behind the counter, a handsome self-contained little boy. The shop was otherwise empty, I

Do not make me remember more. I do not deserve mercy but I need it. Give me peace God. Stop me remembering that I went to the back of the shop where a cold cabinet full of dairy produce stood. Stop me remembering that I thought I could not be seen from the counter and started stealing eggs bacon butter, dropping them into my broad coat pockets and it is not far to the wardrobe.

Wardrobe doorcreak. Coat pocket. Cool small bottle fits hand snugly. Back to bed. Unscrew cap. Slight rattle of little white blunt torpedoes spilling on to coverlet. Will you stop remembering that you went to the counter with only a carton of 1, 2, 3, 4, 5, milk in your hand 6, 7, 8, 9, 10, 11, 12, 13, 14, 15 and stop remembering that the boy marked the price on the till and said, "Is that all?" and I said, "Yes" and 16, 17, 18, 19, 20, 21, 22, 23, 24, 25, 26, 27, 28, 29, 30 stop remembering that he came round the counter and quietly put his hand in my pockets and took out all I had stolen and laid it on the counter and 31, 32, 33, 34, 35, 36, 37, 38, 39, 40, 41, 42, 43, 44, 45, 46, 47, 48, 49, 50 will do the trick but I still have 51, 52, 53, 54, 55 and 56 if I *cannot stop* remembering that he said

Stopped. Good! You nearly drove me too far, God. I am leaving the pills on the coverlet in case you make me remember what the boy said.

That whore showed I am not yet completely dead. I am grateful to her. The aftermath is unimportant. Let me remember other good lively times with real women.

THE EDITOR
had a lovely cunt, why do I remember it so clearly? A chamber upholstered in slick wet warm smooth satin like a royal Victorian railway compartment with little unexpected buttons and chandeliers in the walls. I must have had my hand in there a lot. She loved being entered, perhaps loved it too much. Even when we had both been dry for a long time her cunt still clung to my prick demanding to be rubbed, and when at last the friction hurt me so much that I had to withdraw she felt she had completely lost me so she told me to leave. She valued prick too desperately much, as I over-value cunt. That is why we both had so little of what we fancied. I was once with some journalists in the Glasgow Press Club and they started gossiping about women and someone said my editor was frigid: nobody had ever managed to get into her but soandso who was a fair judge HAHAHA and he said she wasn't much good. I could have told them that she had been tender and pleasant to me, except afterward. But that would have sounded like boasting and perhaps started a rumour that she was a secret nymphomaniac. Men who gossip spitefully about women are not the arrogant bastards they want to seem. They are humble people trying to show their importance, like servants boasting about their aristocratic connections by describing intimate details of aristocratic life. They talk nastily about sex because they resent being unable to enter this world, or feel much ecstasy, or replace themselves, or respect themselves, without help from a woman. What sex does not sometimes hate the other for threatening its independence? But I am not humble so I did not say, "She was not frigid with me," I said, "There may be more to her than you have noticed."

And these journalists went on boasting and moaning about their sweethearts and wives until a young one said, "I wish I could be sexless and self-contained like Jock here."
I smiled slightly. An older one said, "Nobody is sexless. Jock must have a source of satisfaction somewhere, he couldnae stay sane if he didn't."
I stood up and said to the older man, "What would you like to drink?"
He was right. My source of satisfaction is Helga sitting with Stroud in the viewing theatre watching Big Momma in her tight white cotton dress leading by a leash collared Superb who is barefoot and nude under her dungarees down a ramp to a circle of light where the Doctor stands stop. Remember realities.

SONTAG
visited me for the second time bringing pans full of messy mixtures. Her taste in food, I found later, was like her sexual tastes, she got a lot of ideas from fashionably eccentric books on the subject. These usually combined an oriental religion with recent chemical discoveries in order to advertise cheaply exotic recipes, but Sontag was too adventurous and impatient to read any single recipe from start to finish. She never completely formed an image of what she was going to make but started with a pile of ingredients, two or three vague ideas and a grimly determined expression on her face. The result depended on intuitive improvisation, and if this failed she blamed the shop where she had bought the ingredients. But I always praised her cooking as I praised her lovemaking, because both were better than I could do for myself. She was a woman, we comforted each other, we did not live in the same house so her irritating habits were bearable. She would have liked us to live together but I was afraid of coming to love her four-year-old son. In a few months I might have felt like a father to that boy and then I suspected Sontag would start treating me as selfishly as she liked and I would be unable to leave her.

After we had eaten our first meal together (I had provided a lot of wine but she drank sparingly) she made very muddy bitter coffee in a peculiar ladle she had brought. As we sipped it she told me about her husband and why the marriage had failed, I cannot remember the details. She asked me why my marriage had failed and I told her I was bad at sex. I knew this was not the complete truth but the complete truth is an exhausting tangle, it saved time and breath to sum it up in the commonplace phrase Sontag's mind would eventually reduce it to. We talked some more about love and sex and agreed that our feelings had been too recently hurt for us to want a love-affair, and that sex without love was dangerous because always one of a couple came to feel more deeply than the other etcetera. Then she yawned and said, "I have an idea. It is too late for me to walk home and a taxi is expensive. My son is being looked after by one of the girls I live with, he will not need me till tomorrow. Since there is no risk of sex between us why should we not sleep together? Because yahooohay, I am suddenly very very tired."

I said that was a sensible idea, would she like to use the bathroom first? I gave her a clean towel and as I did not want to use the bathroom at all I undressed and slipped into bed. I did not know what would happen. I had almost lost interest in her, being slightly bored, but hopeful too. She came to bed and lay naked in my arms for an hour and then whispered, "You devil!"

I said, "Why?"

"You said you were incapable of sexual response and you are trembling with lust."

I was not trembling with lust. My prick was completely flaccid. I felt nothing but wonder at being home again.

I once started the Proust novel about *Time Redeemed* but soon gave up. I dislike books with heroes who do not work for their living. However, something in the first few pages made a distinct impression. When the hero is an old man he chews a sweet cake of the sort his auntie gave him when he was a wee boy, and because the taste of the cake is exactly the same as in the past he enjoys it just as much. And the million things which happened to him since he first tasted that cake – the aunt's death, a world war which destroyed his home and killed his friends – these are suddenly a slight detour away from and back to a moment which is exactly the same. Eating that cake abolished time for him. Women's bodies do that for me when I am allowed to hold them and I stop being nervous. I am not referring to fucking, I am referring to THE LANDSCAPE OF HOME. Every woman has her own unique scale of proportions but the order of these warm soft slopes and declivities is the same, and whenever I am allowed to explore one of these landscapes I feel I have never been away from it. I felt this the first night I slept with Denny, I thought, 'I have never been away from here,' yet I had never before slept with anyone in my life. Unless with my mother, as a baby. Which was no explanation, as a baby is too small to feel its mother's body all over, so the familiarity of Denny's thighs, buttocks, stomach, glens, glades, banks and braes must have been mine when I was born. But this has nothing to do with lust so I said, "Let's just go to sleep, Sontag," and did fall asleep. So did she, perhaps. I awoke stiff and inside her, it was very comfortable. She said, "Well?"

"What's wrong dear?"

"Do you not intend to do something?"

"Is there a hurry?"

She withdrew from me, put on the light and sat crosslegged on the bed and frowned, right hand cupping and supporting left elbow, left hand cupping and supporting chin. She said, "You are worse than I thought. I expected premature ejaculation, that is the usual British problem, but this is worse. There must be a medical name for it. I will investigate."

I realised that I appealed to Sontag as a problem to be solved. It was then she asked about my fantasies. I wish she had kept them for later. Perverse pantomiming is fun but should be played on a platform of something calm and ordinary. However, Sontag wanted to be a thinker, a teacher, and could not relax in ordinary states. She did teach me one glorious lesson, though not in words.

After four or five weeks we had never been together in company so she gave a party in the old house on Partickhill Road. I think the women she shared with gave it too, for certainly Sontag had no air of being a hostess. It struck me as a wild kind of party but perhaps I only thought that because of loud rock music on the record-player and because nobody was introduced to anybody. Certainly I saw no unpleasantness apart from the unpleasantness I made for myself. The average age of the women was thirty though many of them had younger sisters. The men were mostly much younger, longhaired students in their teens and early twenties, but I noticed five or six men of my own age. Like myself they seemed slightly outside the party but showed no interest in each other. Sontag and I sat on a sofa watching the dancing and I grew very depressed. The other women seemed more attractive and interesting than Sontag, their partners seemed more attractive and interesting than me. When Sontag asked me why I was silent I told the truth. I said I felt we were stuck with each other because we were unable to attract anyone else. She looked at me thoughtfully for a while, nodded, got up and went to a slightly older man who leaned smoking against the mantelpiece. She spoke to him and they started dancing. They were still dancing an hour later when I left. I could not ask another woman to dance with me because I cannot dance. Next day I phoned Sontag but she was either out or pretending to be out. A week passed before I could get her on the phone. She said, "Well?"

"Could I see you tonight?"

"No, we are finished with each other. I thought I had made that clear."

After a pause I said, "I realise why you finished with me."

She said, "Good. Then no more need be said."

But she did not at once put down the phone. After a pause and with an effort I said, "Thank you for being so nice to me. I hope you are happy."

She said, "Goodbye Jock," which was the last I heard from her.

Did I deserve that? Yes I deserved that. I deserved that. I deserved that.

A long time after I met someone who had known Sontag in those days. I learned that the man beside the mantelpiece had been an almost total stranger to her, a post-office engineer who was being divorced by his wife. Sontag and he spent the night together and two days later he moved in to live with her, though the other women did not like him much. After two months he got a job in England and Sontag and her son moved down with him to London. I hope she is happy there. She deserved happiness. She was brave.

My mother was brave, she deserved happiness too, I see that clearly now. At the time I was so choked with anger that I burned her letter. But I had read it twenty or thirty times so I have the words by heart, though memory may have twisted or rearranged them.

Dear Son,

This letter will come as a Shock and Annoyance anyway because I have not wrote you more than a postcard or Xmas card before now, anyway you and me were never Great Writers it was your Dad who was the Writer among us. You will have had my card from New Zealand. My cousin was not right in his head before the End but I think he recognised me so may be by being there I soothed his last moments so the journey was worthwhile. Or so I hope. He was past 80 anyway and went away from Scotland before you were Born or intended so this is not Matter to you. But Son on the boat coming back this man got very Keen on me God knows why because I am no Chicken and defnatly not the Come Hither type. I did not like him Atall, he is much older than me who am no Chicken but he does not look it, he dresses far too young by our Standards, patterned socks and shorts and shirts, loud voice too, the pushy sort I never fancied. I do not mean he is not Polite. Son he was perfectly Polite but defnatly Not My Type what he sees in me I just cannot fathom especially as he has made his Pile as they say and retired and is a Widower. But his money is not matter to me if that is what you are thinking. Son he makes me laugh sometimes though I am not the humorous type neither are you or your father so you will think I made myself Cheap, I did not. He ate at my table on the voyage and kept asking me to dances on board and I kept saying No until the last night on board when he danced with me for the first time I have danced since Months before I met and married your Father. Then he proposed to me though he knew I am a married woman and made me very angry. I said "Certainly Not" but he did not care. He said he would be touring Scotland before Europe and in a week would come to the long town and must see me again. I told him I would see him in a month, not sooner, if he was really Keen, but even then I might say no. "That was all right by him," he said and I won't go into any more details because your father now knows all this but I told your Father you should first hear All from me because I am leaving with Frank to go Back with him to New Zealand on Saturday next from Glasgow Central Station at 3 p.m. I would like to see you before I go if you will not just be mad at me for being a bad woman. If you have only Hard words it will be best to keep away. Son I don't know what you will think of me when I tell you this but I do not like Frank more than I like your Father how can I? Your father is a good man, I have lived with him for 23 years, he was always a decent husband as far as that goes but I need a change. Your father likes everything steady, I was never the steady type but of course a woman with a Son has to behave a lot better than she feels but you are on your own now, married, you don't need me. I don't think you ever did, after you were 10 or 11 you started living in a world of your own sitting over your books frowning and smiling to yourself like a little old man. You were always much closer to your Father than to me. That bit still bewilders me. I never felt close to my father before she left him. I thought my closest connection was with her but that she and Dad were completely one. I suppose the truth is that we were all three equally lonely and separate from each other. *You like having everything steady too so I know you will be angry when you read this. I just hope you have made the right Choice in Helen. And try to be kind to your father.*

Love from

Your Bad Old Mother

P.S. At Central Station on Saturday next I will stand alone just inside the barrier for a while before the train leaves with Frank in the carriage so you need not see him if you don't want to. The train leaves at 3 p.m.

Yes I was choked with anger. Each minute that I thought of the matter I alternated between a frigid determination not to visit the station and a redhot determination to go and yell and scream at her. Then I thought of a compromise. I would go and talk to her in a restrained way until the porter started slamming the doors for the train to leave, then I would embrace her, lock my hands behind her and refuse to let go. Even if Frank charged up and tried to free her I would not let go. I imagined him fat and bald like a caricature American in sandals, bermuda shorts, dark glasses and a ten-gallon hat. He might punch my face till it was bloody but I would not let go and then Mum would recognise what a brute he was and tell him to leave and would go back to Dad. Perhaps. I am now astounded at the violence of these feelings. I have never been aware of loving my mother much. Since leaving home I had seen her on few occasions, and mainly from a sense of duty.

I arrived in the station at twenty to three, and as I approached the barrier I walked slower and slower. She was not inside it. I bought a magazine from a nearby bookstall and stood partly screened by it, pretending to read but looking toward the train. Either they had not yet arrived or they were on it. Shortly after quarter to three I saw her come along the platform, a taller woman than most with a strikingly straight back and grey hair. I recognised the plain black coat she wore but not the hat, which was purple and unsuitable, I thought, and matched the frames of new spectacles with outer corners curving up like wingtips which were also unsuitable for a respectable woman of nearly fifty. But at the first glimpse of her my plan became quite impossible. I knew I could never raise a hand against her. She stood still beside the barrier for a long time. I could see her face but her poor eyesight ensured I would be part of a blurred background until I took a few steps nearer her. I could not move because I could think of nothing to say. I was not angry now. I tried to think, but all the words I knew seemed tangled in a tight ball, I could think and feel nothing which would stop me standing half-hidden by the magazine and staring and staring, Her usual expression had always been a brooding frown, she smiled by pulling her mouth further down at the corners as if to stop them going up, I could not read her present expression which was vague, perhaps a little lost. Sometimes she looked at her wristwatch or removed or pulled on a glove. At last a man in a respectable black suit came up to her from behind and my heart jumped because for a moment I thought it was Hislop, but no. His face was plump and boyish. He spoke to her, took her arm and led her back along the train and into a carriage as the porters started slamming the doors. I was drawn to the barrier by them moving away and I must admit that from behind they looked a well-suited couple in spite of her extra inch. After the train left it struck me that just before they reached the carriage I should have yelled, "Goodbye Mum! Goodbye Mum!" and frantically waved. It would not have made her miss the train but she would have known I cared enough to say Goodbye.

For a few years Helen and I received a greetings card from her each Christmas with a Dunedin postmark but no address which would have let us answer it. Did Dad get a card also? If he did he never spoke of it. The cards stopped after five or six years. If she is still alive she is over seventy. I never remember her birthday. We did not celebrate birthdays in our family. Wait a minute, Dad did keep her cards. I found them in the little bureau drawer after he died along with his birth certificate for 14 January 1896 (*father, Archibald MacLeish, Coalminer/mother, Jeanie Stevenson, Power Loom Weaver*) and his First World War medals, and wedding photo, and a little magnifying glass which came with some stamps he once bought me. I threw all these things out. No good comes from brooding upon the past.

O I have just realised that the whore under the bridge was Denny. That is why my body recognised her at a distance after all these years. But the face old bloated discoloured someone had hit her, yes that was Denny's face but I was thinking too much about my prick to recognise it until now. God damn my fucking prick, ha! My hair is trying to stand on end. Did she recognise me? We were both drunk. She asked me to marry her, it must have been Denny. No it must not have been Denny. It was not Denny please.

The boy took the stolen groceries from my pocket, laid them on the counter and said quietly, "Out of respect for your age and pity for your condition I am taking no steps in this matter. But if I find you doing this again I will inform the police."
I looked at him lovingly. I patted his shoulder and said, "You are a good man."
I left the shop feeling sober and proud to be one of a species which had produced a boy of such dignity and decency. And now I am a coward if I do not eat these and drink that. Divide into three piles of roughly twenty, no need to count, and fill tumbler.

Gulp swallow. Gulp swallow. Gulp (rotten taste) swallow, swallow. Pills, whisky all gone tata.

And now?

11:THIS IS VERY NICE.

No sweat, no hassle, no bother at all. Quickened heartbeat like strong wee galloping horses *dradadum dradadum* but I lie like a duke in a speeding carriage, jocose and easy-oasy, relaxed and okey-dokey, in love with easeful death and ceasing upon the midnight with no pain. Actual time 5.52 but thank you Hislop, your account of present state is otherwise accurate and melodious. It cannot last, of course. How long till coma and zero? Fifteen minutes? An hour? Must I completely digest these pills? Full digestion takes at least two hours. I should have asked the chemist about this but do not worry. Jolly Jimmy Body has been slipped a Mickey Finn by his aristocratic jockey Melancholy Montague Mind and before sunrise both will drop out of the human race damn. Damn, I am starting to feel randy. How inappropriate. How annoying. Temporary side-effect of? Last assertion of expiring? Prick's Last Stand as in (so they say) hanging? Why not? Mine not to reason why, mine not to make reply, mine but to backward lie as in rape, enjoying, what?

Red velvet divans, oriental luxury, the Ruby Divans in Green's Playhouse, biggest cinema in Europe so they said.

The fog on frosty Novembers made it hard to see the screen from the highest circles but in one of the Rubyred Divans, snug little alcove for two, Denny and I saw *Sudan* in which Pharaoh's daughter, sultry 1940s Hollywood brunette, is captured by Arab slavers and branded but falls in love with barbarian leading to happy ending with total abolition of slavery in ancient Egypt. Denny asked wonderingly, "Did it really happen like that?"
I laughed and cuddled her for wondering if it could have happened like that. She said mournfully, "You shouldnae laugh. I cannae help being ignorant. My education was rubbish."

Gone soft, I have. She who first made me stiff now makes me weak. Good Denny, sturdy wee compliant pony, a lovely ride. Be glad she loved you. Melt. Wait softly for your end, wail softly for your end. I WILL NOT. Prick knows there is still a spark of delight under this dying ash, poke for it. Stiffen poker how? Let heart beat me harder, *dradadum*. My kingdom for a horse. Help me, Hislop. It fell about the Lammas tide
When the muir-men win their hay,
The doughty Douglas went forth to ride
Into England, to drive him a prey.
AND HE HAS BURNED THE DALES OF TYNE
AND PART OF BAMBROUGHSHIRE, AND
THREE STRONG TOWERS ON ROXBURGH FELLS
HE LEFT THEM ALL ON FIRE.
Young Lochinvar is come out of the West,
The Assyrian came down like the wolf on the fold,
I galloped, Dirck galloped, we galloped all three,
Bring me my bow of burning gold!
The battle closes thick and bloody,
Forth flash'd the red artillery,
Storm'd at with shot and shell,
Boldly they rode and well,
Into the jaws of Death,
Into the mouth of Hell
Rode the six hundred.
Steady, boys, steady. Sweating, hard are we?
Preclimactically tense? Excellent.

Sound the clarion, fill the fife!
To all the sensual world proclaim,
One crowded hour of glorious life
Is worth an age without a name

BUT please also always to remember that beneath the hammerblows of fate (*dradadum*) in the very storm, tempest, and, as I may say, whirlwind of your passion (*dradadum*) you must acquire and beget a temperance that may give it smoothness. So cool it, man.

Bravo Hislop. Maybe you knew your job. Perhaps all teachers should pour fine stuff into children's ears and leave their memories to resurrect it when they find their own thoughts inadequate. I stand again tense in the chariot of bed, controlling hands on the reins of a foul imagination which, properly controlled, will pull me to a little glowing core of delight in the valley of the shadow of death (perhaps you are not dying) SHUT UP SHUT UP oh what can I do tomorrow if I do not die tonight? I cannot face another superintendent of bonded warehouses, another bank manager, another security officer with acting rank of colonel. I can no longer hide from them the Hislop in me, the mean snigger at a world ruled by shameless greed and cowardice and which thinks these insanities are serious essential traditional straightforward commonsense business. They are that, indeed they are, but the knowledge now stamps my face with a smug little rigid grin. Just before I took the pills something happened (what?) which makes me incapable of my job although I cannot live without the movement it gives, the rides and blissful naps in planes trains taxis, the cosy anonymity of a different loungebar and bedroom every second or third evening. But I need the rides most, hurling warm through all weathers and seasons with a paperback thriller on my lap and always Scotland outside the window with more changes of nature in ten miles than England has in fifteen or Europe in twenty or India, America, Russia in a hundred. If I stop travelling and stay in one place I will become a recognisable, pitiable ("Out of pity for your condition I will take no action") despicable drunkard. I can only keep my dignity and stay mysterious by ceasing upon the midnight with no pain etcetera. The chemist was a heavy man with a face like a glum cherub's. "These will do the trick," he said putting the little bottle in my hand. A soft hiss and a foosty smell came from the gas chandelier, yes a gas chandelier dimly lighting that queer little parlour. Can pills lose their potency? These have not. They are working.

They are working. My heart aches and a drowsy numbness pains my sense as though etcetera and the ache, the pains are rhythmical, *dradadumba dradadumba*, a change from our old friend dradadum. Shakes me, it does. Cold sweat now, too. Splendid, I like this. At school I envied the sickly types who went down with flu, broke a leg, had tonsils or appendix out; it freed them for a while from the common rut. I have never been ill. Even hangovers, in the days when I noticed my hangovers, did not unnerve this hand which delicately, firmly manipulated the tiniest and most intricate connections. Now the raised forefinger vibrates violently, I feel the pulse ache in it. The stiff indicator under the belly also coldly vibrates. Queer feelings queer words are abroad in me, words like Chimborazo Cotopaxi Kilimanjaro Kanchenjunga Fujiyama Nagasaki Mount Vesuvius Lake Lugano Portobello Ballachulish Corrievrechan Ecclefechan Armageddon Marsellaise Guillotine Leningrad Stalingrad Ragnarok Skagerrak Sur le pont d'Avignon Agincourt Bannockburn Cavalry Calvary Calgary Wounded Knee Easterhouse Drumchapel Maryhill West Kilbride Castlemilk Motherwell Hunterston terminal megawatt kilowatt dungaree overall kilowatt equals one-point-three-four horsepower I'm back to dradadum, I am in chaos, I am sick, my head is full of rubber bullets, my head is full of snow and it's melting, my head is full of wee boats and they're all sunk, my head is full of Reichstags and they're all burning, my head is crammed with engines doing different things at different speeds (you can't control them) I CAN'T CONTROL THEM QUICK GRAB JUMP ASTRIDE ASTRIDE ASTRIDE THE NEAREST CLING LIKE GRIM DEATH TO BIGGEST FASTEST LOUDEST GOING DUNGDUNGDUNGDUNGDUNGDUNGD UNGDUNGDUNGDUNGDUNGDUNGDUNGDU NGDUNGDUNGDUNGDUNGDUNGDUNGDUN GDUNGDUNGDUNGDUNGDUNGDUNGDUNG

DUNG DUNG DUNG DUNG DUNG OVER
DUNG ALL DUNG OVERDUNG ALLDUNG
UNDERDUNG DAFFYDOWN DILLYDUNG DING
THE DUN DEAR DOWN AMONG THE LEAVES SO
GREEN O O O O O O O O O O O O O O O O O O OO
l i Not much time left folks so let's cut the cackle OO
s and ignore the couple signalling from the wings OO
t e everyone wants into the act but I am the boss OO
n around here I am the director I may not have OO
l had a university education but I know where OO
i the power lies my hand is on the switches so the OO
s t little ladies have to obey ME Janine folks you OO
e have already seen folks she as you know gives OO
n her name to the show she is the titbit I will keep OO
listen till last when she will pop up and tickle your OO
i fancy when you least expect it just like she did at OO
came because the start meanwhile I proudly present the last act OO
you we've all been waiting for **The New Girl's First** OO
called **Day** as performed before the Selkirk Branch of OO
and now the Multinational Playboy, Punishment and OO
your Sexual Gratification Syndicate to a select audience OO
hot in the tiny viewing theatre where Gayboy Hollis OO
and cold (did you know he is Big Momma's son? No is he OO
floods wonders will never cease how could a dyke like OO
of her produce a poof like him) Gayboy Hollis slides OO
speech hardly back a panel in the wall and wheels out a trolley OO
allow loaded with beguiling properties while the door OO
me opens and here comes our very own Big Momma OO
a word leading leashed tethered barefoot nude-under- OO
in white-denim-dungarees Superb while Dr Sieg- OO
edgeways fried von Strudel tells the company "Feast your OO
fallen! *vile eyes vile eyes vile eyes vile eyes vile eyes* HOT
mighty are the *vile vile vile vile vile vile vile vile vile stop seeing,* HOT
How *stop thinking such things I am not a very bad man* HOT
yourself? *parents were good folk were noble folk in a quiet way* HOT
Is it Jehovah! *what condemns me to this filth filth filth filth filth* HOT
Jumping *filth filth filth filth filth filth filth filth filth filth filth* HOT
listen sorry about that intrusion folks our patron COLD
i am feels obliged to advertise his higher nature COLD
not whenever the room temperature hits a certain COLD
what level otherwise he depends on lowbrows like COLD

us to keep him hopping and interested so say COLD
your piece von Strudel: "Feast your eyes. COLD
This woman has not come to us through our COLD
usual legal processes so she brings to her COLD
situation refreshing amounts of indignation, COLD
outrage and sheer astonishment. She perhaps COLD
suspects she is dreaming! Let us assure her COLD
that in less than a fortnight the life she has COLD
been plucked from will seem the dream and COLD
a surprisingly dull dream too." Superb COLD
screams, "Max!" and laughs hysterically COLD
because in the dimness outside her circle of COLD
light she can now see Max sprawling on the COLD
divan caressing the nearly naked waitress COLD
who clings to him with convincing ardour, COLD
Max says, "I thought you were visiting COLD
your mother tonight Terry, what made you COLD
change your mind?" "Help me Max!" COLD
whispers Superb. He says, "Yes, sure, if COLD
you've something for me. Have you any- COLD
thing for me Terry?" The answer he wants of COLD
course is "Yes, everything I've got," but COLD
Superb can only stare at him. "She is too COLD
new to understand that question," says von COLD
Strudel, "you must repeat it in a week or COLD
two. Gag her." "This is just a rehearsal," COLD
whispers Momma to Terry taking from COLD
Hollis a small rubber ball and a nylon COLD
stocking. "Today you learn the movements. COLD
Next week we'll give you the words." She COLD
gags Superb, unfastens, removes her dunga- COLD
rees and I must not imagine her nakedness COLD
the nakedness of women does not excite me COLD
it stuns dazzles light pours from their naked- COLD
ness I have never been able to face it since I COLD
got rid of Denny so **ECLIPSE** Superb in COLD
black thighlength leather boots with seven- COLD
inch stiletto heels linked by a slender chain, COLD
Hollis and Big Momma lace them up tight COLD
tight tight as high as her bum tugging the COLD
laces hard till she winces, whimpers then COLD

you
were
told
not
an
owner
true
makers
never
own
what
they
make
i
have no
authority
that
tool
of
high
rabbles
who
live
well
by
serving
the real
makers
badly
i
am not
mys-
terious
am no
king
judge
director
inspector
supervisor
landlord
general
manager
or
any kind
of master
no
expert
computer
planner
lawyer
accountant
clergyman
policeman
teacher
doctor
father

who	removing handcuffs they bind her arms	COLD
is cruel	behind in one long blackleather sleeve which	COLD
to be	must also be laced up far too tight and last	COLD
kind i	the blackleather corset, "Breathe out as far	COLD
do	as you can honey," advises Momma and as	COLD
not rule	Superb takes a deep breath instead they	COLD
thunder	fasten the corset round her and tug the laces	COLD
threaten you	tight in hard little jerks each time she *has*	COLD
will	to breathe out and at last her hips and ex-	COLD
not leave	posed breasts swell full and round from a	COLD
you	waist more slender than dieting could achieve	COLD
atall? atall,	*"These will do the trick," he said putting the*	OO NO
to you	*little bottle in my hand, heavy man with face*	OO NO
nothing Is there	*like glum cherub dusty parlour stuffed salmon*	OO NO
hold on?	*in glass case soft hiss and foosty smell from gas*	OO NO
to catch something	*chandelier he blinked and closed eyes tight*	OO NO
concrete a little	*mouth gaping and pursing like dying fish he*	OO NO
man	*leaned down and embraced me, our spectacles*	OO NO
our poor not give	*clicked, I felt fishy wetness on nose and cheek,*	OO NO
Could you	*I felt suffocated, kept still. He stood back, tears*	OO NO
non being! articulated	*trickling mouth gulping beseeching. I shook*	OO NO
barely of	*his hand enthusiastically saying far too loudly,*	OO NO
declaration	*"Thankyou" – pocketing bottle – "You are a*	OO NO
annihilating	*real friend, a real friend, nothing need worry*	OO NO
a truly of nullity;	*me now." He knew what I meant, bit lip, let*	OO NO
parade ascending	*me out but. In the moment of embrace I felt a*	OO NO
is an	*sweet voluptuous helplessness like nothing I*	OO NO
so, that saying	*have ever known and suffocation was part of*	OO NO
mind me	*it, melting helpless sweetness desire to be used*	OO NO
don't If yez	*anyhow, anyway, absurd, two ageing bespec-*	OO NO
Madam!	*tacled professional men he ten fifteen years*	OO NO
or Sir	*older than me who am no chicken but his pills*	OO NO
Begob	*are doing the trick trick trick trick trick trick*	OO NO
listen i am light	well how about that folks our exalted	COLDER
air	patron is queer as a coot but why let	COLDER
daily bread	that spoil our games with the dames?	COLDER
common	Superb stands tall now trimmed and	COLDER
human	slender strained pained svelte in chic	COLDER
warmth ordinary	leather exposed aghast what says von	COLDER
ground	Strudel? "The tight enclosing pressure	COLDER
that	on limbs, waist, throat confirms our	COLDER

drinks Superb of her bodily presence making COLDER
every stain her intensely of the *here* and the *now*. COLDER
takes This pressure is experienced as a COLDER
back painful insult but the sensitive flesh COLDER
all who and muscles will soon feel the con- COLDER
fall striction as a form of support, which, COLDER
renews emphasising the naked exposure of COLDER
all who the parts with clefts and openings in COLDER
have not them will soon incite a high degree of COLDER
poisoned sexual anticipation and even appetite. COLDER
their seed By the expression of our Superb's COLDER
my superb features we can see she fears as COLDER
one much. But not at once. Has the new COLDER
power is film director any suggestions to COLDER
letting offer?" "First I would like to know COLDER
nothing the exact role of the big lady in the COLDER
rest which linen button-down. Is she an actress COLDER
is not or a director?" "If you knew anything COLDER
well at all about the establishment which COLDER
balanced my only is supposed to be employing you," COLDER
intelligence snarls Big Momma, "you would COLDER
is what know I am both." "In that case I COLDER
you lend when you suggest that from the audience's point COLDER
forget of view the show will look a lot sexier COLDER
yourself if you too change your costume at COLDER
i endure for this point." "That's a great idea!" COLDER
you shrieks Hollis. "Shut up you runt," COLDER
endure hisses Big Momma, "this new lady COLDER
you why always has clearly not been informed that COLDER
run away I am special! I am the one member COLDER
tear apart of the staff who is also on the com- COLDER
climbing higher mittee, and my money pays for this COLDER
by show! Yes ma'am, you are looking COLDER
kicking at a millionaire when you look at COLDER
me down o me. These doctors lawyers police- COLDER
i men and agents are only here to help COLDER
bear it me spend my cash in ways I, person- COLDER
you ally, find enjoyable, and I will find no COLDER
no longer pleasure at all in stripping off and COLDER
can dressing up to make the show sexier COLDER

NOOOOOOOOOOOOOOOOOOOOOOOOOOOO

“What are foot-
balls made of?”
“I don't know,
what are foot-
balls made of?”
“Hide, man!
Hide! Hide!”
“Why? Why?
Who's coming?
Who's coming?”
“No! No! No! I
mean the pig's
outside! The
pig's outside!”
“Well, bring
her in –
any friend of
yours is a
friend of mine.”

hate sex hate sex hate my sex I *SCORCHING*
can play no good games in this *SCORCHING*
tight suit which does not fit I *SCORCHING*
cannot move I shit it sticks stif- *SCORCHING*
fens stinks I hate to sit in this *SCORCHING*
stiff state it does not suit man *SCORCHING*
woman brute bird turd word *SCORCHING*
name echoes fact act same noun *SCORCHING*
as verb like my shit and I shit I *SCORCHING*
ache and my ache my scream and *SCORCHING*
I scream I dream and my dream *SCORCHING*
is an echo echo echo echolalia *SCORCHING*
lovely word echolalia brain dis- *SCORCHING*
ease echolalilalilalilalilalilalila *SCORCHING*
lilalilalilalilalilalilalilalilalilalilalilalilalilalilalilalilalilalilali

listen i am the mercy you asked for the child and future you prayed for a new past lis ten look back the past is that foun tain where all streams spring listen streams you damned flow under my ground. dig here for the needed water.

“Euphony! O euphony!” *Shhhhhhhhhh*
screamed Hislop (you funny *Shhhhhhhhh*
little man). “Who will give me *Shhhhhhhh*
back a single euphonious line! *Shhhhhhh*
You are a gang of barbarians but *Shhhhhh*
God knows I have toiled honestly to *Shhhhh*
improve you, I have persistently dinned *Shhhh*
into your ears the purest verbal melodies *Shhh*
in English literature has *no* good come of *Shh*
that? The lowland Scots have a native incapacity *Sh*
for euphony but need they detest and reject what *S*
they are powerless to produce? I will give a pound note” – he pulled one out and waved it about – “I will give this pound note to the boy or girl who can repeat a single euphonious phrase. Come! Two hundred and forty pence, an eighth part of your father's weekly wage for three or four words which will flow into the ear and give peace to the heart. You know the kind of thing I want. Now folds the lily all her sweetness up. Blue, glossy green and velvet black. Like swimmers into cleanness leaping. Or Mesopotamia! Or incarnadine! Or porpentine! A single splendid word will put this money in your pocket, surely, surely one of you has learned something from me that strikes them as beautiful?” and he twisted his face into a horrible parody of pathetic appeal and we were petrified because behind the parody we heard a real note of pathetic appeal. One of the

braver girls raised her hand. He nodded. She said in a small voice, "Bird thou never wert sir."
"Good!" he said in a delighted voice. "Bird I never wert. Who else finds that euphonious?"
Heather Sinclair, a friend of the brave girl and our best speller, put up her hand then all the girls did and most of the boys. The only ones who still sat with folded arms were myself and the other toughguys who no longer feared the belt and did not give a damn for Hislop and his stupid games. He paced up the passage between the boys and the girls muttering, "Wert. Wert. Wert. Wert" with every footfall. He stopped by an empty desk, produced a cigarette lighter and said, "Hands down. Agnes, doubtless, remembers me saying that Percy Bysshe Shelley pinnacled dim in the intense inane is one of our most mellifluous poets, but to my ear *bird thou never wert* sounds damnably ugly and a downright lie when we consider that wee Percy is talking to a skylark. But vox populi, vox dei. I must give Agnes something for trying."
He set fire to a corner of the pound note, dropped it on the desktop, quenched the flame after a minute with the flat of his hand, placed the charred fragment of paper ceremoniously in front of Agnes then went back to his own desk shivering and making an ach-ach-ach sound like a parked lorry in bad condition with the engine running. I feel fine. These pills are definitely harmless, there is nothing at all wrong with me. All the changes of heartbeat and temperture, the cold and hotsweatcetera were causeby nothnbut funkan, but funkanan (you gibber) THE SWEATS WERE CAUSED BY NOTHING BUT FUNK AND (GOD HELP ME) FUNKANANANANANANANANANANAN *HYSSSSSSSSSSSSSSSSSSSSSSSSSSSSSSSSTERIA* ***good to see you again folks thought we had lost you back there just as things were getting interesting. "But Momma," says the Doctor, "the committee feels that a change of role may do you good. Of course at first you will not enjoy it, nobody ever does. But that phase is temporary. You have helped many girls through it. Do what our new director suggests!" "You are out of your mind if you think I'm taking that crap from you," says Momma shakily and walks to the door, it jerks open, she squeals for who comes in but coalblack naked sixfootsix ME with this huge erect dong and I***

uncoil a thick black whip and say, "Momma I am gonna help you
strip oh my oh my oh my oh my oh my oh my oh my oh my oh my oh my
HONEYMOOOOOOOOOOOOOOOOOOOONMUM

A genetic ist fella told me we humans differ from other brutes by drinking when not thirsty, eating when not hungry, fucking all round the calendar regardless of climate and torturing and killing helpless creatures of our own kind. In plain language, we have an inborn capability for intoxication, greed, lust, cruelty and murder: a fact which your thinking moralist will always find more significant than our ingenuity in constructing such bizarre containers of ourselves as the Polaris submarine, Sistine Chapel, and suspenderbelt.

*silky milky silky milky silky milky silky milky silky*CH
*milky silky milky silky milky silky milky silky milky*CH
*silky milky silky milky silky milky silky milky silky*ACH
round full cheeks chin soft smooth shoulders breasts ACH
bellyfolds thighs labia and buttocks overlapping AACH
caressing cuddling completing each other how AACH
else but by vile force can I get back into and AAACH
among warm soft mild eternal you? I want AAACH
to fill up and enclose you becoming your AAAACH
tampon and your corset your core and AAAACH
your rind your furniture your walls AAAAACH
the youshaped basket with the big AAAAACH
spike holding and piercing you AAAAAACH
the boa constrictor entwining AAAAAACH
you whose head pushes right AAAAAAACH
through your cunt filling AAAAAAACH
you up inside I want to AAAAAAAACH
be much too much for AAAAAAAACH
you whole absolute AAAAAAAAACH
overwhelming and AAAAAAAAACH
inescapable o o AAAAAAAAAACH
o this is hell AAAAAAAAAACH
hell o please AAAAAAAAAAACH

let me in let me in let me in listen i split myself in two making you from a careful man and brave woman and now my fine blend and strong make my good maker makes him self nobody nothing a tool blunted by deliberate stupidity listen not bad nature i am nature but the dull habits of a bad job make you nothing nobody a tool blunted by deliberate stupidity not bad nature i am nature but the dull habits of a bad job make you nobody nothing a tool blunted by deliberate stupidity not bad nature

WHO IS THIS DAPPER CHAP APPROACHING *help o God* WITH MODEST ARCHANGELIC SMIRK?

I am o I
am I
am

Be tween extr emes of vic ious mock ery and virt uous plea there is a mid dle way. All like nice times. Only a sick few seek them in mur der or mar tyr dom

SUFFUFFUFFUFFUFFUFUCKUCKUCKUCKATING

When at last our mid dle gro und is found I am nine ty per cent cer tain no body will be very far from it; least of all my self. I Here stand. Join me.

let
me be
free as

THE SOCIAL DEMOCRAT FINANCING *a sinking* A POOR GOD WITH COMMON DEVIL'S WORK!

let me be let me be let me be you are of me for me making light by opening your eyes building space with each movement reforming the world with each thought for better or worse you cannot stop being god by splitting into a roman circus where sense feeling memory hope dreams and reason fight bind torment each other to amuse this forlornly plotting almost amputated head your weak

stone going OOOOOOOOOOCH
down through OOOOOOOOOCH
your soft Pacif OOOOOOOOOCH
ic deeper than the OOOOOOOOCH
air is high the one OOOOOOOOCH
eagle lost and lonely OOOOOOOOCH

Do you
see how li
ttle I am?
Our man,
by arrogati
ng the given
make cruelty
of Hell has shr
unk Mr Satan
O'Firefly the Fir
st to the pathetic
scope of his lower
case deity. I make
Mann's claptrap cr
itic. Goethe's pimp
ing Mephisto look
like bloody giants! Is
this the melancholy
end of the protestant
tradition?

ness cowardice indifference create
history as much as your strength
courage intelligence but too muc
h is made by default sliding dow
n into depression pain warping
war poisoning seed you can m
ake mend things no need to di
e so come alive aloud remak
e repair becoming me again
st this waste of my whole
well made lovely complet
e world

floating in your endless OOOOOOCH
blue blue blue blue blue OOOOOOCH
the morning star shining in OOOOOCH
your black vacuum a solitary OOOOOCH
baton rapping order order order OOOOCH
into your roaring symphonic chaos OOOOCH
God folks that is not how it is or FUCKEAS
ever can be when these highbrows get EFULDEA
sexy they go right over the top you're THFUCK
a lot safer with me lady my demands are CEASIN
all external and ritualistic so shake those GONMI
tits those hips Momma as you turn to run you DNIGH
know it is no good because out snakes my cruel TWIT
big black whip with stinging crack splits creamy HNO
linen across your plump hip and at last oh at last PAIN
you feel the trap bite trap bite trap bite trap biteTHIS

Listen
come alive
for gods sake
work as if you were
in the early days of
a better nation i can't
take more from you are
infecting me not by your vices
but by your harsh wee virtues i
the way the truth the life rave like
a damned scots moralist listen theres
a hell of a good universe next door lets
go quick to sink bend down hold on tight
fingers in gullet let it come let it come let it
come let it come let it come let it come let it come

whipstattoosleatherLochgellytawsprickscuntsjeans ISF
bikinisfishnetstockingsblousesthreepiece UCKIN
suitscollarstiesdungareesoverallsex GMURDE
surveillancealarmdefencetrap RHELPPOLI
securefamilysalarytrap CEMUMMYDA
lovesecuritysex DDYMUMMYDA
happiness DDYMUMMYDADD
trap YMUMMYDADDYMUM

BOAK BOAK BOAK o BOAK BOAK BOAK
BOAK BOAK BO y AK BOAK BOAK
BOAK BOAK BOAK e BOAK BOAK BOAK
BOAK BOAK BO a AK BOAK BOAK
BOAK BOAK BOAK y BOAK BOAK BOAK
BOAK BOAK BO e AK BOAK BOAK
BOAK BOAK BOAK a BOAK BOAK BOAK
BOAK BOAK BO a AK BOAK BOAK
BOAK BOAK BOAK y BOAK BOAK BOAK
BOAK BOAK BO e AK BOAK BOAK
BOAK BOAK BOAK a BOAK BOAK BOAK
BOAK BOAK BO a AK BOAK BOAK
BOAK BOAK BOAK a BOAK BOAK BOAK
BOAK BOAK BO a AK BOAK BOAK
BOAK BOAK BOAK · BOAK BOAK BOAK
BOA... BOA.. :
BOA . BOA . ·

boa?

All over
equally aching
in what feels like every nerve muscle bone
every part of me except the teeth.

But I will live,

And I'm not sorry either.

And I am completely clean! Not a drop missed the basin.
A miracle.
Thank you mother.
Thank you father.
Early training counts.

Turn on taps, flush down mess.
Complex mess.
White pills, green peas, diced carrot.
Rest of dinner indistinguishable but all there.
My stomach must have gone on strike quite early tonight.
It knew something bad was on the way before I did.
Wise old stomach.
I won't be so nasty to you again.

But what a typical piece of human daftness, to poison myself in a fit of despair because I could no longer stand work that I hate, work that was killing me!
Idiocy.
Typically human.

Some scum still sticks, scrape loose with fingers.
Swirl away, whirl away down plughole.
Wash fingers – dry fingers.
All clean. Good. Stop tap.
To bed. Lie down. Slip under sheet.
Good.

Ache. Ache. Ache. Ache. Yahoohay. Ache.
Slip asleep?

Yes.

Slip,
    slip aslee

burning? No heat, no smoke, no burning here. Another dream then.

I sat in an open sportscar speeding over the small wooded hills east of Glasgow between Twechar and Kilsyth. It was a clear cold sunlit autumn day, the colours inexplicably bright. The sky was pure cold cold blue blue blue, the leaves on the trees a yellow like none I have known, leaves like steady flames undimmed by the sunlight, too yellow to be golden but dusted a little with gold in the distance. The best yellow. And under the yellowleaved branches grew mild green pure dewy turf between orangebrown clumps of bracken, crimsonbrown and purplebrown drifts of fallen leaves, khaki carpets of withered grass. The car, veering and twisting between the treetrunks, followed no track but went smoothly by going very fast. It skimmed through bracken-clumps and crossed ditches and hedges without the slightest jolt. I felt recklessly happy, recklessly sure of the driver's skill. She was driving dangerously but well, I knew I would laugh aloud and still love her if the car crashed. Which happened. Bang! we struck a tree. I was flung through many screens of yellow leaves and came down flat on my back in an open field. I lay looking at a small high white cloud in the huge skyblueness and suddenly a voice near my elbow, speaking so distinctly that it woke me up, said, "His room is burning." It is *not* burning yet these words seemed, still seem very hopeful. I don't know why.

Awake again with less than an hour till daylight, more than two hours till breakfast. What shall I do with my mind? What story is left for me to tell?

It behoves a man every so often, from time to time, now and again, to speak out and inform the world (that is to say, himself) just what his game is; and if (having been carried by the prevailing current up shit creek after mislaying the paddle) he has no game of his own and finds life pointless, it even more behoves him to tell truthfully how he reached this pointless place in order to say Goodbye to it and go elsewhere. If he wants a change. Which I do.

The story of *how I went wrong* is called From the Cage to the Trap and describes events which took place in my eighteenth year of life during certain months of 1953, particularly those three months and three weeks when I was richer and happier than kings presidents millionaires etcetera, for my talent and personality were recognised – I had a good friend – I enjoyed the only true wife of my body – became one of a noble community which depended upon and honoured my genius – and at last captured the bride of my fancy, a glamorous and enchanting actress. Unluckily these months also contain my meanest and most cowardly actions, actions I have been trying to forget ever since. But as a radical friend once said to me in a voice shrill with conviction, "Those who forget their own history are condemned to repeat it – as farce." She was quoting Marx but I don't care who I get helpful hints from. Only socialists refuse to learn from their opponents. I don't mean the ordinary corrupt socialist politicians, I mean faithful hopeful innocents like my father. The pureinheart socialist believes he can learn nothing from his opponents because these will shortly vanish since they are WRONG and therefore somehow, even now, a thing of the past. Why am I into politics again?

Funk, of course. I am postponing the moment when I start telling my story in the difficult oldfashioned way, placing events in the order they befell so that I recall the purchase of my new suit before, and not after, I seduce Denny in it. This had better be done, though it will be hard. When we cannot see our way in the world of course we circle circle circle until we stumble on a straight stretch of it, but then, even though that stretch was left behind years ago, let us use it to go *forward* for a change. Straight movement leads to pain, of course. As a leader of the Scottish Educational Authority once said to me as I moved toward his desk on trembling knees, wondering if he was going to belt me, and how much, and why, "To travel hopefully, Jock, is better than to arrive." But if we prolong hope by circling round and round the spot which was once our destination hope dies of its own uselessness. We have avoided the disappointment which comes from finding out about a place, but also the regret, the delight, the renewal of departure. I once said a very witty thing to a man who asked what I got from work which made life worth living. After thinking for a while I said, "The travelling expenses."
He laughed and said, "Well, I suppose you see more of the country than the rest of us, but is that all you get out of life?"
I said, "It's the main thing, but it also gives me security. I

am heavily insured against several very nasty possibilities." And being a bit of a Bolshie this man said slyly, "Are you insured against the collapse of the insurance system?"
I said, "Of course! I vote conservative, like most of us."
I am travelling in circles again. But it *should* be possible for me to tell a straightforward story. I have been practising since the age of twelve and perhaps earlier.

Perhaps earlier. When I was thirteen or fourteen or fifteen Mum suddenly said, "Why do you never talk to me now?"
"What about?"
"What you're thinking."
I did not say, "I can't do that because half of it's obscene," I said, "I'm sure I talk to you as much as I ever did."
She sewed a few more stitches then said quietly, "You've forgotten."
"Forgotten what?"
"The stories you told me. You imagined that queer little people lived behind the grate and inside the furniture. The ones inside the cooker were the chefs and made the food turn out properly, and the ones inside the lavatory pan were the dirty ones and you had fits of the giggles when you told me about those. I didn't always know what you were saying. The ones inside the wireless set made up the news and played the music, and the one inside the clock made the hands go round. He was called Obby Pobbly and he told the others what to do. You were very keen on that clock –" she nodded to the electric clock on the mantelpiece – "because it didn't go ticktock like the one in the parlour but made a grumbling noise which is a bit like Obby Pobbly. But you've forgotten all that, it seems."
I could not disagree. If I had not completely forgotten Obby Pobbly I wanted to forget him for I had started telling myself stories about a very free attractive greedy woman who, confident in her powers, begins an exciting adventure and finds she is not free at all but completely at the disposal of others. As I aged that story grew very elaborate. The woman is corrupted into enjoying her bondage and trapping others into it. I did not notice that this was the story of my own life. I avoided doing so by insisting on the *femaleness* of the main character. The parts of the story which came to

excite me most were not the physical humiliations but the moment when the trap starts closing and the victim feels the torture of being in two minds: wanting to believe, struggling to believe, that what is happening cannot be happening, can only happen to someone else. And I was right to be excited by that moment because it is the moment when, with courage, we change things. Why *should* Janine feel helpless when she realises Max has lied to her and is abducting her? He is driving a fast car along a motorway, his hands are occupied, if she removes one of her ridiculous shoes and threatens his eye with the heel he will certainly stop or change direction if he sees she is serious. But she is not used to acting boldly, she finds it easier to pretend Max is honest and decent, hoping her act will make him more so, and thus he drives her into the mire. My fancies keep reliving that moment of torture for Janine because I have never fully faced it in my own life and I am travelling in a circle again.

Telling a straightforward story is like cooking a meal, hard to do thoroughly if you are doing it for yourself alone. I must use my imagination again, deliberately this time, to conjure up a suitable audience.

God?

You've gone very quiet. You were raving away goodstyle back there, I was too excited about other things to hear the words before you told me to put three fingers down the gullet but I recognised the wee voice. You've been here for a long time, sabotaging my exotic sexdreams with old memories of the homely facts, upsetting my arguments with awkward questions slipped in among them (so to speak) between brackets. You sounded more like Groucho Marx or a critical housewife than the Universal Frame-maker. Which is all right by me. I hate Big Daddies. What I need just now is what we all need, the unprejudiced ear of someone too wise to be chilled by wickedness or softened by suffering. My wickedness and suffering are average for a middle-aged man in these parts, so if you curse, forgive or bless me you will be committing a serious irrelevancy. I need to see myself clearly. Guilt, self-pity, self-satisfaction will equally prevent this. Your old book says you are the source of light – help me become less mysterious to myself.

It is ignorance of my own nature which has made me an easy tool in the hand of others. (What others?) My employers, I suppose. Another thing: one solitary god is too few for me. I need more of you. (The Holy Trinity?) Too abstract and episcopalian. (JesusMaryandJoseph?) Too catholic and familiar. Nor do I want you splitting into Jupiter, Mars, Venus etcetera, those Mediterranean aristos make me feel cheap and inhibited. Why should you be less to me than all mankind? Now *there* is an audience which deserves my full attention. I'll burst my braces to tell a straightforward history if you can appear to me as that. (I'll try.) Good, then I'll begin. (Clear throat.)

Chrm.

Your Majesty, Your Royal Highnesses, My Lords, Ladies, Officers, Non-commissioned Officers and Men and Women of the World, and also, and especially, those who lay claim to none of these titles, particularly the punters north of the Tweed:

Pray silence for the one and only Jock MacLeish, Lord Lyon King of Shocks, Sparks, Currents, Alarms and Others of that Ilk, Baron Magnum of Banks, Braes, Bonded warehouses, Faslane, Dounreay, Hunterston, the Shetland Radar Defence Net, Edinburgh Zoo Lionhouse and the Burrel Collection Basement, Various Distilleries but Smith's Glenlivet Malt for preference and London Gin when pubcrawling in Glasgow, where was I? Oh yes. **LIST, LIST, O LIST! I will a tale unfold whose lightest word will harrow up thy soul, freeze thy young blood, make thy two eyes, like stars, start from their spheres, thy knotted and combined locks to part and each contiguous hair to stand on end like quills upon the fretful porpentine!**

Thankyou and good night, Mr Shakehips Slopspeare. Don't call us, we'll call you.

(Excuse me Sir, you have just imbibed the last of the whisky. If you seriously intend to regale us with a sober and consecutive narrative before the advent of the sun I suggest that you go first to the basin and force down your thrapple not less than ten tumblerfuls of cold tapwater.)

Thankyou G. The flesh is weak but will try to take that advice.

12: LIFE WAS COMFORTABLE BUT DEPRESSED IN THE HOUSE WHERE I WAS BORN.

12:LIFE WAS COMFORTABLE BUT DEPRESSED IN THE HOUSE WHERE I WAS BORN. The depression was equally shared so we did not notice it. I only once heard my parents laugh and never heard them raise their voices in anger, or complain, or weep. The only one to raise his voice in our house was Old Red when he denounced the capitalist class or talked Utopian, which was why Mum and I disliked him. We knew that most families were noisier than us, but also felt that noise was abnormal and unhealthy. We believed very few people were as normal and healthy as us.

This is how I came to make them laugh.

I was seventeen and had sat an entrance exam for the Glasgow Royal Technical College. I still went to school, though the teaching would only have value if I failed that exam and had to try another. Leaving home in the morning I sometimes met the postman in the street and said, "Anything for me?" and one day, from the bundle in his hand, he extracted a buff official envelope with my name on it, the first letter addressed to me in my life. I placed it carefully in my pocket. Instead of going to school I took the colliery road which led down through the skirts of the town to a bridge over the river, and then I turned along a track through the wood on the further bank. My heart was thudding very slow and hard. I was sure I had passed the exam, but how well had I done? The day was close and warm, the sky a ceiling of smooth grey cloud with no hint of rain. I left the track and climbed a steep path through bracken and bluebells and came to a flat place surrounded by birks and rowans under an overhanging rock. William Wallace was supposed to have hidden here from the English but most Scottish towns have an obscure corner where that is supposed to have happened. The place was better known because on Sunday nights some miners called the Boghead crowd used it for illegal games of pitch-and-toss. I sat on a low boulder, read my letter and sighed with relief. I had done well in the exam. Excitement gripped my legs. I left the boulder and waded uphill through the bracken by no path at all, delighting to feel my body break and tread underfoot the resistance of the fronds. Fifteen minutes later I paused, slightly breathless, and looked back. This part of the country was a sort of fertile plateau through which the river carved a steep valley, so the high land was good pasture and cornfield, the low ground was wooded and shaggy. Facing me, on a ridge across the valley, lay the whole length of the long town: a quarter-mile terrace of but-and-ben cottages in the east, a centre of two-storey houses where the shops, pubs and cinema were, a row of mansions and bungalows standing in their own gardens, and a council estate of semi-detached villas in the west. All this, with the railway station, four schools, four churches, cast-iron swings and roundabout in the park should have seemed familiar because I knew it thoroughly, but it did not look familiar. It looked queer and lonely, because I was going to leave it.

I wandered about the town all morning, mostly in the outskirts, sometimes in the main street, and every ordinary friendly thing from the monkeypuzzle tree on the Church of Scotland manse lawn to a fat old cat basking on a sill had that queer foreign look. I stared a long time at an advert in a chemist's shop. It showed tall white identical castles receding to a horizon. Before them a knight in white armour held a shield labelled **GIBBS TOOTHPASTE** and waved a triumphant sword over a batwinged reptile labelled *Dragon Decay*. A slogan somewhere said

GIBBS IN THE MORNING,
GIBBS IN THE NIGHT,
KEEPS EVERY CASTLE
SHINING AND BRIGHT.
(Your teeth are every castle.)

I had known that advert for years, why? Nowadays companies change their displays, slogans, packets and products continually, they spend millions on advertising to stop the government taking it in taxation. My seventeenth year was closer to the time of thrift and rationing when only the government spent money on adverts, adverts which told us to buy as little as possible. MAKE DO AND MEND they said, above a picture of a cheerful housewife sewing a patch on her husband's jacket, DIG FOR VICTORY, above the husband planting cabbages on his suburban lawn, HOLIDAY AT HOME! IS YOUR JOURNEY REALLY NECESSARY? That daft toothpaste advert had been in the window since 1940 and had entered my daydreams. I still sometimes wore the armour, rescued Jane Russell from the dragon and, finding her ungrateful and treacherous, chained her up in those castles. But I was not daydreaming now. I was asking the advert, 'Will I remember you when I'm gone? Will you remember me when I'm gone?' and the answer, 'Probably not', confused and puzzled me though I was too excited to feel depressed. I stared an equally long time at a three-foot-high marble soldier in puttees, cape and round puddingbasin helmet, his hands clasped and head bowed over a grounded rifle. He stood on a pillar carved with the names of over two hundred men from the town and its surroundings who had died in the First World War. A recent bronze plate listed an additional forty killed in the Second World War. *Their Name Liveth for Evermore*, was inscribed above the lists, and *Lest We Forget* underneath, and

I could not connect the inscriptions, which seemed to deny each other. The two wars did not interest me but I suddenly wished that the soldiers who had fought and survived them were also listed, for then I could have read my father's name.

I arrived home for dinner at twelve-thirty as if I had just come from school and said nothing about the letter. I kept my mouth shut till later that evening when we were all gathered round the table for tea. This was usually a meat or fish course with bread, biscuits, cakes and (of course) a big pot of tea. Dad received, in addition, the remains of the soup or pudding Mum and I ate at dinnertime. Half-way through the meal tonight Dad said, as I expected he would, "I wonder when we'll hear from the Technical College."
I said casually, "I got the letter this morning."
A fork with a bit of potato on the prongs stopped still for five whole seconds in front of Dad's open mouth and was then laid down carefully on his plate. He said, "Well?"
"I've passed," said I, calmly continuing to eat.
He said, "Passed have you? Good! But what's wrong? What are you trying to hide?"
"Nothing," said I, and handed him the letter. He read it with a face wrinkled and concentrated in a great worried frown while Mum turned her startled stare from me to him. He laid down the letter, tilted his head back and made a dry, hacking noise like this: "AKHA! AKHA! AKHA! AKHA!"
My mother cried out, "*What's wrong*?"
He said, "Wrong? He's sixth best out of two hundred and eighty-two applicants! He's sixth best in the whole West of Scotland!"
My mother chuckled, left her seat and cuddled me and I cuddled her back. Then she got embarrassed and pulled away. If I had not surprised her with my news she would never have cuddled me. Dad was grinning and shaking his fist at me and saying again and again, "Ye bugger! Ye bugger! Ye bugger!" – so I allowed myself a small smile. If I had proudly told him the news when he came in from work he would have given that small smile, and said something like, "Fine! You arenae the best, but you certainly are not the worst." Like most parents he did not want his child to

openly display pride and happiness, because these states make other people envious, and often go before a fall. By hiding my feelings I had tricked him into showing his, and had risen above him.

My parents had been paying a weekly sum into a Scottish Co-operative insurance scheme which could be realised after my sixteenth birthday. It was devised to help working-class children across the gap between their schooling and their employment, and as I now needed new clothes for the Technical College, and as I had stopped growing, my parents decided to spend the whole sum on clothes which would last till I was fully self-supporting. At the time I thought this decision perfectly natural though now it astonishes me. Since setting up house together they had lived carefully on less than twelve pounds a week, where did they get the courage to dispose of two or three hundred pounds in less than ten days? They must have been mad, as mad as a woman I overheard in a London bank. She wore a smart leather trousersuit and in a loud hooting voice said to a friend, "It cost me nine hundred pounds. I couldn't possibly afford it of course but we must be extravagant sometimes, just to cheer ourselves up." She could afford it all right. Part of her knew that the price of that suit was the weekly take-home wage of six railwaymen working overtime or twenty families on the dole, so her delight in extravagance came from feeling superior to the rest of the world, superior to fate. I hope my parents felt some of that delight as they discussed spending the equivalent of half their yearly income on my wardrobe. If so they excused the feeling by pretending they were completing a job of work. They had produced a brain which the Scottish Education Department had stamped "First Class". Now they would post it to the world in a suitable packet. Hitherto my mother had chosen all my clothes, so we were surprised when suddenly Dad uttered forceful opinions.

"A made-to-measure singlebreasted suit of the best quality Harris tweed is a . . . a . . . a . . . timeless garment. The style of it has remained virtually unchanged for well over half a century. American businessmen wear it to conferences. Highland crofters wear it to church. A British workingman can wear it anywhere without appearing a traitor to his class."

"Made-to-measure suits are very dear," said my mother, "and not at all necessary. An off-the-peg suit may not fit Jock perfectly but I'm a good enough needlewoman to adjust it, as you well know."

"I will prove to you," said my father, taking such care to speak slowly and quietly that we knew he was greatly excited, "I will prove to you that a made-to-measure suit of the sort I am imagining will be the best possible economy. In off-the-peg suits the trousers wear out long before the jackets do. They must! If a man is not crawling on his knees like a collier or humping weights on his back like a dustman then the part of his anatomy which suffers most wear is the seat. I am certain that – other things being equal – the life-expectancy of the jacket of an off-the-peg suit is more than twice that of the trousers. But those who bespeak a suit from a good tailor can order all the trousers they want, which is another instance of the rich spending less money in the long run through their ability to be lavish in the first place."

"So you want us to buy the lad a jacket and two pair of trousers in the same cloth."

"No!" said Dad, "I want us to buy him three jackets and three waistcoats and seven pairs of trousers and two overcoats of the same cloth! Let him change his trousers every day of the week. The fabric will suffer so little strain that with ordinary care it will look continually smart and last him a lifetime."

Mum said firmly, "I have never heard a more ridiculous suggestion. Why buy the lad a lot of nice clothes if we don't give him some variety? Jock needs a couple of ordinary suits for everyday wear, one in a medium grey check and one in brown. And he needs a dark suit for formal occasions and a blazer and flannels for sunny weather and holidays. I can see the sense in two trousers to a jacket, yes, fine, but seven identical trousers and three identical jackets are utterly daft."

Dad replied in the cautious, downcast but obstinate tone he used when speaking of sexual matters.

"I do recognise that a variety of clothing is biologically

essential to women, especially to the young ones, because they use clothes to draw attention to themselves, and men (younger men) like them for that. But what an employer values in a man – what a man values in his workmates – what a man values in himself – is consistency. If Jock goes to Glasgow equipped as I suggest he will impress his teachers and workmates and prospective bosses with a neat, simple, consistent appearance bordering upon the miraculous. The material of the suit I have in mind is dark enough to wear at a funeral but not dark enough to suggest one, so with the right colour of necktie it can be worn on any occasion. In rough working situations, of course, it will be protected by overalls. But I agree that he requires a blazer and flannels for especially sunny days. We don't get many of these."

Mum said firmly, "The idea is ridiculous. People will laugh at the boy."

Dad said, "I doubt that."

They could not agree so I was in a position to adjudicate. Like most seventeen-year-olds I had very little sense of my own identity, so the idea of striking a mysteriously consistent note in the turmoil of Glasgow appealed to me. I opted for six pairs of trousers, three jackets, two waistcoats and an overcoat of the same cloth, and a black dinner-jacket with matching trousers, and the blazer and the flannels.

The suit was ordered from a tailor in Kilmarnock and after the second fitting we visited a haberdasher to get socks, shirts and underwear. Since Dad had gained most of his own way in the matter of the suit he agreed completely with my mother's choice of the other things, so my wishes were not consulted before we came to the necktie counter. The salesman displayed ties of silk and cotton and wool in a great many patterns and colours. My mother fingered them, held them up and laid several aside before it occurred to her to ask, "Have you any idea of what *you* would like, Jock?"

I pointed to a rack of bow ties and said, "I would like those."

Mum and Dad stared hard at me and then at each other. They were alarmed. Bow ties in those days – perhaps even nowadays – were worn by professional people in risky businesses like horseracing, the arts and journalism. Uni-

versity lecturers who courted publicity often wore bow ties. My mother said, "Are you sure you want one of those?"
"I want them all like that."
"But is it *important* to you?"
I shrugged and said, "The money you are spending is not mine so I'll wear whatever you buy. But you asked what sort of tie I would like, and now you know."
There was a look of helpless worry on her face which cut me to the heart. She said faintly, "What colour?"
I said, "I leave that entirely to you."
The only bow ties without vivid patterns were wine red or dark blue, so she bought half a dozen of the dark blue, then returned to the shirt counter and changed my white shirts for pale blue ones, so that they would match. My father, for political reasons, would have preferred a red tie, but a red tie on a white shirt was too strikingly radical even for him, and a pink shirt for a man was unthinkable. It hinted at homosexual tastes which in those days were downright criminal.

I cannot remember what weather lay over the streets and houses of the town when the train took me away from it. Mum and Dad saw me to the station and we said very little before the train pulled out. Beyond the station the line curved across the valley on a high viaduct, and a minute later I could look back and see two tiny figures on the end of the station platform, one with a flickering white speck attached to it. Either Mum or Dad was waving a handkerchief. By the time I had pulled out my own hanky and lowered the carriage window some trees had come between us. I shut the window, crossed my legs carefully to avoid injuring the trousercrease, folded my arms across the neat new waistcoat, sunk my chin on to the tie and was perplexed by a total absence of feelings. I knew I would be revisiting the long town, but in an essential way I had left it for ever and I did not care. I thought that perhaps, in Glasgow, when I was a lonely unit among a million others, a toothpaste advert or a face in the street might bring back childhood memories on a big warm wave of nostalgia. But this never happened. Yes, at first I was very lonely in Glasgow but I enjoyed that. Loneliness felt like freedom. I was sure it would lead to something exciting, something with sex in it. With a pang of guilt I decided that my childhood, apart from a few infantile memories, had been a depressing business and I was better away from it.

My parents had found me lodgings on Paisley Road West in the home of a dependable motherly woman who would tell them if anything went wrong with me. I soon shifted to the flat of a young law student in Hillhead who did not care what went wrong with his lodgers, as long as they paid the rent and did not fight each other. At college I had difficulty at first with the purely mathematical functions, but after six weeks I suddenly realised the almost complete congruency between these and the practical work, and had no trouble with my exams after that. In the Tech refectory I sometimes ate at the same table as Alan. One day, when that table was full up Alan said, "Make room for Jock," and tilting his chair on its back legs he stretched an arm across and grabbed an empty chair from a table near by. So I knew we were friends. And then I met Denny.

The woman behind the serving hatch in the refectory had always been pleasantly chatty, but one day I noticed a new girl who seemed to actively hate me. She was small and chubby with a moony petulant face which she turned away while serving me, and when I handed her the money she took it with a disdain which suggested I was the filthiest man in the world. I found this upsetting because I had been perfectly polite. Next day when I approached the hatch one of the other women called out, "Denny! Here's Jock."

She served me in exactly the same way, except that this time she refused to take my money at all but scurried sideways and started serving someone else. I laid the coins on the counter and went away feeling puzzled. She served me the third day with the same averted face, placing the food on my plate more slowly. Before passing it to me, with the fearful look of someone forcing herself to jump across a dangerous gap, she bit her lip, hesitated and whispered, "Rotten weather."

I said, "Yes it is," and held out the money. She gave an

obstinate little shake of the head and hurried to the next customer. The other serving ladies smiled at each other and I left the hatch feeling I had been made to look foolish. I now knew that I attracted her, but she did not attract me. My notions of female attraction were based on Jane Russell and various fashion photographs. I was ignorant.

Walking back to Hillhead that evening I began to feel different. It occurred to me that Denny might let me do anything I wanted with her and the thought made me dizzy. I had never, never, never believed that a woman could desire a man. The universal habit of marriage showed that they needed men, but folk often need what they don't want and want what they don't need. My sexual daydreams were full of capture and bondage because I could imagine no other way of keeping a woman I wanted. Denny had no place in the world of my imagination yet I found myself walking faster till I was almost running, and when I reached the lodgings I had decided that next day I would ask her out. But a fortnight passed before I asked her out. In the evenings I walked the streets past couples standing in cinema queues and troops of girls hurrying to the dancehalls, and now the only fact which fed my strong feeling of a great good time coming was the fact of Denny. But next day the sight of her in the refectory completely chilled me. She looked too small and ordinary to associate with enormous desires and satisfactions – she was exactly the same height as myself. Not that she was an ugly girl. When she did not notice I was near she joked brightly with the other students, who were fond of her, and she looked pretty on these occasions. But whenever I came near she lost all confidence and behaved like a young schoolgirl in front of a ferocious headmaster. This did not please me at all. I desperately wished I knew some other women. Alan said, "You ought to be nicer to Denny. She's a beautiful piece. If you made her happy she would operate with an astonishing absence of friction. And you need a woman."

I said, "I don't like her voice. It sounds cheap and tinny."

He sighed and said, "Then think of her from the economic standpoint. She not only refuses to let you pay for your meals, she now refuses to let your friends pay for theirs.

This won't last for ever if you don't encourage her a bit. She loves you."

But only the coldest sort of sexual frustration drove me to Denny in the end. I lay at night in bed haunted by imaginings which seemed thin and futile. I could no longer take Jane Russell seriously. So when one day Denny whispered, in her fearful jumping-over-a-precipice voice, "What do you do in the evenings?", I said, "Will you meet me tonight?"
She nodded and said, "Mhm."
I said, "What about seven o'clock at the front entrance?"
She said, "Aye, all right."
She did not look happier, she looked slightly more worried and resigned than usual. I left the serving hatch thinking, 'The bitch! She doesn't like me but she certainly wants it. All right, I'll give it to her.' I had the shallowest notion of what "it" was – a minute of naked grappling and kissing followed by a minute of slotting together and pumping was all I could conceive. And I was completely wrong about Denny. She wanted me, not "it", but accepted that "it" was the price she must pay for my company.

My heart sank when I saw her that evening. The cheaply fashionable dress she wore was wrong for her kind of shape, and though she had taken a deal of trouble with her hair and lipstick the result was not successful. But she looked cheerful and hopeful for a change, and when we started walking she slipped an arm through mine, and the part of my arm and body which touched her felt warm and secure. Only my head was irritable with her appearance beside me, so I took her into the dark of a picturehouse and we kissed and cuddled in the back row of the stalls among several similar couples. This was not satisfying. My furtive squeezing and fumbling brought none of the quick passionate excitement I sometimes saw enacted on the screen before us, so when we came out at nine-thirty I said, "Are you coming home with me?"
She said miserably, "I'd like to, but I don't want to get into trouble."
I said, "I'm not a fool, Denny. I know what precautions to take."

She said, "It's not that. You see I live in a hostel where they lock the doors at ten. If I'm not back before then I get into trouble."
I said grimly, "So this is the end of our evening, is it?"
I stared at her accusingly until she whispered, "Mibby I could say I missed the tram and spent the night with a girlfriend."
I said, "Fine!" and steered her firmly by the arm to Cowcaddens Underground, but when I got her into my room off Hyndland Road I was nearly paralysed by embarrassment and worry, because I had never before been all alone with a woman. I coped by behaving almost as if I was completely alone. I made a supper of toasted cheese and cocoa (for two instead of one), ate and drank mine, then brushed my teeth, and wound up the clock, and carefully undressed, folding each article of clothing into its proper place. She sat watching all this with an empty cocoa mug clutched on her lap. I did not put on my pyjamas. I took a contraceptive from a packet, showed it to her and climbed into bed saying, "Come on, Denny, we arenae doing anything unusual."
She said in a wobbly voice, "Can I put the light out?"
I said, "Please yourself."
She switched the light out and undressed. Meanwhile I managed, with much fumbling, to fit the sheath on to my wholly flaccid penis. Then I felt her cold body slip in beside mine and we lay together for a long time. I was waiting to be possessed by a demon of desire which would inspire me to seize and pierce her. This did not happen, though the chill gradually left her skin. I wondered if I was impotent, then remembered how often I masturbated. I wondered if Denny was getting impatient, and if I was perhaps a suppressed homosexual. Would she tell the other refectory women next morning how useless I was in bed? She sighed and snuggled more deeply into my side, and a moment later I noticed she was asleep. I thankfully pulled off the sheath and fell asleep also.

I woke before dawn to find our bodies intimately twined although Denny was still sleeping. For half an hour I lay wholly comfortable and at peace, though I regretted that this was not a sexual feeling. I could not help being ignorant. My sexual ideas came from films and books and jokes which all showed love as quick climaxes, because they had to describe it faster than people did it. The alarm clock rang and we got up and dressed on opposite sides of the bed without looking at each other. I heard her say thoughtfully, "No harm done, anyway." I said nothing. I did not know what to think or feel about what had or had not been done. She said, "Mind you, I'll be crying my eyes out before tonight."

"Why?"

"The matron of the hostel where I stay takes herself very seriously. A girl who isnae in on time can say she's sorry till she's blue in the face, but matron is never satisfied till she sees the tears."

I thought of Hislop who was never satisfied until he had dammed the tears up. The world seemed a terribly queer place. I made a breakfast of bacon, eggs, toast and tea and we talked while eating it.

"My Daddy was not very nice to my Mammy but I think he's dead now. We havenae seen him for years. Goodriddance to bad rubbish, I say. My Mammy's all right, but she sometimes takes funny turns. And when she takes one of her funny turns she has to go into hospital and I have to go to the hostel."

"Have you no relations you could live with?"

"Hundreds, but I wouldnae live with scruff like thon."

It turned out that our birthdays were in the same week, a coincidence which struck her as miraculous. I learned she was sixteen years old. I had thought she was older than me and much more experienced. I was glad I had not seduced her for she had enough trouble in her life. I avoided travelling into college with her that morning by telling her my first lecture was at eleven, which was a lie. We separated without making plans.

But in the following days her manner when we met at the serving hatch was relaxed and cheerful. She seemed now to think we were connected. I did not tell Alan I had taken her out, but in the dinner queue he once glanced from her to me and murmured, "Excellent."

We were connected. I could not forget the smooth comforting warmth of her body when I had wakened with her. I lay awake at night, wanting it again. I became very angry with myself. I said, "You idiot! You don't need comfort, what you need is – " here I hesitated, rejecting "extasy" as too romantic – "What you need is fun," and I masturbated, but that did not help. Masturbation was a substitute for extasy but no substitute for the comfort of a smooth warm body that liked me. So on Friday I said, "I'll see you tomorrow at one o'clock."

She nodded and said "Mhm."

Her appearance in the street was as disappointing as the first time. I took her home with me at once and when we got inside the room I said, "Please come to bed with me, Denny," and was surprised to notice my voice was humble and pleading. It surprised Denny too. She said wonderingly, "Don't worry, Jock."

We undressed and got into bed and cuddled for an hour or two. Nobody ever had a skin which was smoother and sleeker than Denny's so it was easy for us to slide and swim all over and around and under each other, though we had sometimes to stop and disentangle the bedclothes. The palm of my hand still remembers the exact shape of her foot, a small soft globe blending into a larger squarer globe (there cannot be a square globe, yes there was) a soft globe blending into larger squarer globe with five little crisp globes along an edge. Her body was all smooth tight soft globes (how can tight be soft? It was) soft smooth tight globes like silken dumplings blending into each other at the wrist ankle knee elbow breast thigh waist blending in lovely curving creases which a fingertip exactly fitted. Sometimes I said, "Are you tired of this yet?" and she said, "No, not yet."

I took her out for a meal and no longer cared if her dress looked poor and her lipstick wrong. I was so dazzled by my knowledge of her body that I could not face her and kept blushing and keeking sideways at the floor. I had meant to take her to a cinema after the meal, but when I whispered, "Can we go back and do more of that?" she said, "Don't worry, Jock, it does no harm."

I wondered if I had invented a completely new and harmless sort of lovemaking that could go on for ever because it was never satisfied. And when, later that evening, I saw her on to the tram which would take her to the south side where her hostel was, I felt very pleasantly exhausted. "See you on Monday," I called, waving cheerfully, and the tram moved off and I turned to walk home and

and I was embarrassed by the first continuous erection I ever experienced. It happened suddenly and would not go away. It made walking difficult and I could not stop it. I was not thinking lustfully of Denny or anyone else when this happened, I was not thinking at all, I was stupefied to find that my body had a memory and will of which my mind knew nothing. With a few respites this erection lasted till the following Monday. It was a pain, but a pain I was pleased to suffer, and if I had known the address of Denny's hostel I would have phoned her at once and asked her over to share it. When I saw her on Monday morning and said, "We must meet tonight," she said, "Sure," with something of her old, worried look, so my manner must have changed a little. When we got to bed I slipped on a sheath and we cuddled and I entered her quickly and easily. I was so glad to be inside that I lay perfectly still. It was she who started moving, so I moved too, to be companionable. I kept stopping whenever the excitement became very great. I feared that if I ejaculated I would go small and feeble and she would put me out. I had ejaculated several times a week since I was twelve and felt there was no future in it. But I did ejaculate at last, and we slept, then woke and made more love, and slept, and woke and made more love, and slept. Then I heard the alarm ringing, and Denny was sitting up and saying dolefully, "It'll be the tears again for me tonight."
I said, "Why don't you get a room of your own?"
She said, "How could I?"
I thought hard for a while. I asked what her wages were. She got not quite three pounds a week, which is about twenty-four pounds in modern money, enough to buy food and rent a cheap room if she shared it, but with almost nothing left for entertainment, clothing or transport. In the catering and cleaning businesses employers could and still do pay

such money to women of all ages, because these women live with a parent or husband or in a hostel, like Denny, and of course they have little or no union. She said, "The hostel isnae a bad place, I mean, it's clean and there's quite a good crowd of girls there. Most of them are dead ignorant, like me, but we have some great laughs together."

I said, "You've got relations."

"Well?"

"If you said you were going to live with them, would they take you?"

"Sure, but I'm not going to live with thon scruff."

"You could pretend to go and live with them but come and stay here."

"Could I?"

"My landlord spends the weekends at his parents' house. If you don't swagger about the place as if you own it, and if you keep out of the kitchen and stay in this room as much as possible he won't bother us. And then we can be together as much as we like."

Denny looked worried, then smiled, then looked worried again, and I noticed I was in danger of proposing marriage. We went together to the college, sitting side by side in the underground and holding hands. When we went our separate ways my penis stiffened again and I felt a ring of tightness throb around the top of it as if Denny was still moving there. This invisible wedding ring was with me all that day. I have never felt it since.

Was Denny a virgin before she met me? I entered her very easily and do not think I gave her pain, but breaking a hymen cannot always be a dramatic event. Was there blood on the sheets afterward? Perhaps. My sheets were often bloodstained because Denny did not mind making love when menstruating and her blood was not a kind of dirt which disgusted me. I did not notice if the sheets were stained the first time, I was too occupied to care. I was unusually lucky. I could easily have met a girl whose notion of lovemaking was as muddled and impatient as my own, a girl who felt obliged to hurry herself and hurry me into some sort of climax. She would probably have succeeded, and that pleasant but inadequate experience would have been the pattern of my future lovemaking. Maybe Denny's sexual wisdom came from some lucky earlier experiences, but perhaps she was able to give and take delight easily because she did not think enough about sex to turn it into a problem. There are such women. They are seldom glamorous or clever, they are not promiscuous, being usually married to self-satisfied chaps who do not notice why they are well-off, but though few men enjoy the favours of these women we are always glad to see them. They prove that the pain of love is not inevitable, but merely the frequentest sort of bad luck.

Not long after this Denny spent a night with me again, then came to live with me under the conditions I had suggested. She had her own key to the flat, but hid this from the landlord and his other lodger by ringing the doorbell before using it. If one of them opened to her she said, "Is Jock in?" and if they said, "No", she scurried past them into my room saying, "I'll just wait for him, then."
They found this amusing because she spent more time in that room than I did. I got more pleasure with her than with anyone else but I was afraid people would notice this and think I depended on her. I was afraid she would think that, so when I went out in the evening saying, "I'll be back by nine", I would usually be back by nine, but sometimes stay out till ten, and on these occasions she greeted my return with as much heartfelt relief as if she had feared I would never return. She must have been lonely in that room with only the wireless for company, but I did not like being with her in the streets. The faces of people walking toward us often had a soft, amused, wondering expression which I found annoyingly condescending. Once, coming out of the cinema, a gang of adolescent boys followed us almost the whole way home, laughing and chanting, "Hairy pie! Hairy pie! Who's got his hairy pie?"
Denny clutched my arm tight and kept hissing, "Pay no attention! Pay no attention!" as if she feared I would turn round and attack them.

We sometimes quarrelled, of course. I was neat and she was messy. She could not be an hour in a place without

disarranging something and shedding wisps of hair, a kirbygrip, a safety-pin or a lipstick-case. Though she worked in a refectory she was not a good cook, so I made the meals and expected her to clean up afterward. There were never many dirty dishes, but she would bustle about in a busy, unsystematic way for half an hour, and when she sat down there would always be something like an egg-stained plate with a jam-stained knife on the floor under a chair. This sometimes made me angry and silent with her. She feared my silences. One evening, when I had been perfectly quiet for fifteen minutes, she shouted "All right! If you really hate me so much why don't you hit me?"
"I never hit people!" said I indignantly, really shocked by the idea.
"But you want to! So do it! Do it!"
She rushed at me. I found myself shrinking back into a corner of the sofa, blushing and wriggling and giggling, "I don't *want* to hit you!" as she frantically slapped and nipped me. One of her slaps struck my testicles, not hard enough to disable me because I grabbed her and spanked her and undressed her etcetera so it all ended tenderly with us both gloriously exhausted. Thereafter she brought most of my bad moods to that conclusion, but I had very few bad moods. She was messy and I was neat but she loved my neatness. We were making love one day when she started weeping, I hope tears of joy, and she cried out, "Oh you're so neat and clean! So neat and clean!"
She liked my clothes, especially the six identical trousers, and learned to iron and press them with great care. Perhaps she saw me as the sort of expensive doll she had longed for when she was wee.

I used to think Denny was foolish because she had no definite ideas about the world. I had very definite ideas: the world was a mess, but its problems could be solved by modern technology, and when Alan and I left college we would begin to improve things. I was an ignorant git. If intelligence asks searching questions and does not relax on a pile of glib answers Denny was the intelligent half of us. I once saw her frown and move her lips as if talking to herself. I touched her brow and said, "What's happening in there?"

She said, "Jock, what is the most important thing to know?"

"What do you mean?"

"I mean, my education was rubbish, the school taught me nothing. What should it have taught me?"

"It should have taught you to earn a decent wage."

"No, I don't mean that, I think I mean geography. Surely geography is the most important thing?"

"Why?"

"Because if you don't know geography you don't know where you are, so everything you think is wrong. I used to think England was a different island from Scotland, like America is. Well, I know now it isn't a different island, but when I hear about all these other countries in the news, Korea and Berlin and Germany and Hungary, I don't know how far away they are so I don't know how much I should bother about them. Well-educated people stop me in the street with collecting cans, and they ask for money for the starving weans in Korea, and I give them a tanner if I have it because weans ought not to starve, that is definitely not right. And then I wonder, where is Korea? Won't it cost a lot of money to send my money to Korea? Would I do more good if I gave my tanner to my wee cousin in Shettleston who stays in a room where the floor is wet all the time?"

I could not answer these questions so I thought them naive, but I can answer some of them now. I could tell Denny now, "Geography no longer matters because there is no near or far, the monetary sheath enclosing the globe has destroyed the geography of distances. A company like Lonrho mines platinum in South Africa, insures lives in Bermuda, publishes half the Scottish newspapers and owns property everywhere. The Polish communist party crushes trade unions and keeps wages down to pay back money borrowed from the capitalist west. All the powers that be are in some sort of disreputable alliance, and they continue to be by allowing people like you, Denny, as little as possible in the way of knowledge and wages and living-room. You were born in a trap, Denny, and will live and die in that trap, and if you bear a child the trap will pinch both of you harder and harder because the trap is getting fuller all the time. I was born in the long town, a trap for colliers. When the pit is shut down next year it will be a trap for the unemployed. My mother, by a skilful use of clothing and emotional blackmail, trapped me into doing my homework so as to free me from the long town and she succeeded. I became a free man who could choose his own job and I chose to work for the trapmakers. Modern technology cannot solve the world's problems because in all societies technology is used to accumulate wealth, not spread it. The banking nations approve of revolts in the communist block, the communists want revolution in the capitalist block, but eastern communists grasp and increase their social privileges as much as our own Sunday-supplement-swallowing middle class who, if they ever notice you, Denny, will find your wish to understand the trap you are in amusingly naive, quite charmingly pathetic and touching, really. But if you go on strike and demonstrate for better wages (you won't, you have no union, but if you do) then cabinet ministers drawing salaries of twenty-nine-thousand-nine-hundred-and-fifty-a-year (on top of interest on private investments) will appear on television to explain in brave, loud, haw-haw voices that there is not enough money to help you, that your selfish greed is the thing which has reduced Britain to its present deplorable plight. And if you are asked to say something in your own defence, Denny, your voice over the wireless waves will sound stupid and funny because you don't know how to address the public. Your school did not teach you to speak or think, it taught you to sit in rows and be quiet under strong teachers or rowdy under weak ones. The people who manage you, Denny, have been taught to make brazen speeches in firm clear voices, THAT is FAR more important than geography or technology, because RHETORIC RULES, O.K.?" (keep off politics) Thankyou for reminding me, God. I will keep off politics.

I did not want to leave Denny all alone in that house. I asked her to come with me when I visited Alan, who admired her, but she said, "I'm never going to visit him."
"Why not?"
"I hate that big Alan."
"Why?"
"He thinks he can do anything he likes."

She was right. In Alan's company I always felt that anything we imagined was possible. After a pause I said, "That is no reason for hating him. He never wants to do nasty things."
She said, "Mibby he can do anything he likes but people like us cannae do anything we like."
I saw then that Denny, who lacked proper parents and education and could not even dress properly, thought she and I were the same sort of person and Alan and I were not. This put me in a bad mood which I did not allow her to turn into a friendly sexy squabble. I became perfectly quiet and sat with my arms tightly folded on my knees and let her slap and nip me until she was exhausted and weeping and pleading; then I stood up and walked out of the house without saying a word.

It was a mild sunny summer evening so when Alan opened the door I suggested we go a walk and enjoy a pint somewhere. He was wearing pinstriped trousers tucked into wellington boots and a dirty collarless shirt with the sleeves rolled up. He said, "Good idea, Jock, but let me finish this small job first."
I followed him into the front room. He was stripping paint from a table he had found in a midden.
"A valuable antique?" I asked ironically, for it looked nothing special to me. He said, "Not yet, but if I stain and polish and keep it for sixty-eight years it will become a valuable antique."
The circular top was two feet across with a single, tapering leg ending in a tripod base. The tripod was certainly elegant. Alan showed me that the sections had been so dovetailed and angled that the joints would be strengthened, not weakened, by ordinary wear. He said, "It won't last for ever, of course. One day an unusually heavy weight will be placed off-centre on it here, and it will crack here."
He touched a line in the grain of the wood. I said, "Could you prolong its life by reinforcing that part?"
He said, "No. It's too well made. Additional material would weaken the rest of the structure."
He worked on the table for two hours, delicately scraping and sandpapering. I did not mind. We chatted, or I leafed through his piles of old technical magazines, or listened to

the pigeons croodle-crooing in the chimney. At last he said, "It's a bit late for a walk and a pint, Jock, and anyway I have no money. How much have you?"

I showed him a halfcrown, a florin and sixpence. He said, "My table has a Parisian look, let's have a continental evening at home. For less than that money you can buy a bottle of Old Tron, a unique full-blooded Scottish wine greatly favoured by the afficionados, the cognoscenti and connoisseurs. Use the change to purchase two cigars of the best quality. I will provide glasses, a match and, of course, the table."

When I returned he had gained formal dignity by donning his army officer tunic and knotting a white cotton scarf round his throat. The newly cleaned table now stood before the open window and had three upright chairs round it and three glasses on top, besides a shining brass candlestick holding three inches of candle, and a clean saucer containing matches and a cigar cutter. Alan unwrapped the cigars and laid them across the saucer saying, "It is not yet lighting-up time."

He poured some of the red syrupy wine into two of the glasses then carefully emptied the rest into a cut-glass decanter which he placed in the exact centre of the table. Like an experienced waiter he pulled out a chair and pushed it forward under my thighs as I settled into it, then sat opposite me. We touched glasses and sipped. I said, "You are expecting more company."

He said "Carole may drop in."

Carole was his girlfriend, an artist. He said, "Why do you never bring Denny to see me?"

I told him what Denny had said. He sighed and said, "She understands me. She really is very sharp. You ought to marry her."

I said, "I have just turned eighteen. Denny is the first and only woman I ever slept with, and she chose me, I did not choose her. And I will not marry till I earn a wage that will support two of us, without debt, in my own house."

He said, "Yes. A pity."

I said, "Will you marry Carole?"

"No no no. Have you seen how she handles her belongings? She likes books on art, she really does study the pictures and read the text, and because she is expertly shaped and exquisitely crafted plenty of infatuated dolts give her these books. And as soon as she owns one she gets it smeared with paint and bends the spine back till it cracks. She would treat me like that if I married her, so I never will. But I'm afraid we'll continue to see each other, probably even love each other, till death-do-us-part. Carole has a grip like an iron vice. I envy you with Denny."

I said mildly, "I don't believe a word of that."

"A pity."

The street was getting a ruddy tint from the descending sun. We watched it and sipped the wine, commenting on the passers-by and whatever we could see of life through the windows of the tenement opposite. Carole arrived, a slim girl with a lost lonely fascinating look. I think she was sorry to see me there but I don't know how she conveyed that. She was pleasant and friendly. She wore flat sandals, jeans, a paintstained sweater and her hair in a pony-tail. Alan said briskly, "Carole, you are improperly dressed for a continental evening. Please go to the bedroom, take off all your clothes and put on this. And remove that rubber band from your hair, I am sure Parisiennes don't wear rubber in that particular place."

He gave her a black dress which had belonged to his mother who must have been a big woman, for when Carole came from the bedroom it hung to her ankles and would not lie on both shoulders. She looked splendid. She could look splendid in any garment. Alan lifted her hair, laid the mass of it carefully on her naked shoulder, then placed behind her ear a convincing white blossom he had made a moment before by cutting and folding a sheet of paper. He handed her ceremonially to the chair between us and filled the three glasses with the last of the wine. The street lamps came on. He lit the candle, clipped the cigars and bade me set fire to mine first. For half an hour we sat sipping and smoking and watching the slow summer gloaming darken the street, and colour the sky above the opposite tenement, and bring electric lights on in the rooms facing us. I knew that the window framing this subtly altering picture was framing a picture for the street outside: a picture of a young candlelit woman seated between her lover, a fine tall man, and his friend, a refined smaller one. I felt, I'm sure we all felt, as good-looking, as interesting, as comfortable, as civilised, as everlasting, as contented as folk in a good painting by Renoir. Alan had contrived this, but the foundation of my contentment was the knowledge that Denny was waiting for me a mile to the west. My body was already anticipating the peaceful satisfaction she and I would know after we had delighted each other.

I returned later than I intended and was very glad to find Denny sitting in the kitchen chattering cheerfully to the landlord, who was appreciating her company. I had advised her to avoid him because I had feared he could not do that. He was a solemn young fledgling lawyer whom I greatly respected, perhaps because he was rather like me. He dressed in good suits, chose his words carefully and hardly ever smiled. But now he was chuckling. Denny was telling stories about her relations – the ones she disliked – and though the information shocked him he enjoyed being shocked, and kept asking questions. She was exhilarated to find she could entertain a man of his sort. We all had a cup of tea together and when at last I said briskly, "Bedtime, Denny," he detained me for a moment as I was leaving the kitchen and whispered, "You have a great wee woman there."

When I embraced her that night I knew how very lucky I was. That was the happiest day of my life.

So when Alan introduced me in the refectory to a woman he did not want and who did not want me, why did I follow her to the drama college? Greed. I wanted to discover how much more enjoyment I could have. From the serving hatch Denny saw me talking to Helen, and later that day she said glumly, "I bet you fancy that big woman."

I said, "She's a snooty bitch and I'll have nothing to do with her, I'll be working for a group, a team. The experience will be useful. I may even make some money."

But when I met the team I abandoned hope of money. They were too disorganised to make any of that.

I found them in the Athenaeum, whose pillared front and

marble entrancehall did not prepare me for the small corridors and dusty rooms I first had to search through. Two women and three men stood on a square of brown linoleum staring with their mouths ajar at the door I had opened. Another man sat on a line of chairs against a wall. One of the women was Helen. She quickly introduced me to the director who said something like this: "It's terrific that you've turned up, er, Jack, Jake, Jock is it? Good good good. We're all of us absolutely delighted to see you, we'll be totally dependent on what you're going to do for us *but* I'm going to ask you to be angelically patient because you've interrupted us in the middle of something important. Would you mind parking your botty on one of those chairs and just . . . observing us? Soak in the atmosphere. Don't judge us harshly, we're at the amorphous stage. Here's a copy of the script. Don't take it too seriously. We've made a lot of changes that are not marked in, and there's bound to be more. Later on you and I will have a tête-à-tête and hammer something solid together. Now darlings, back to where you were."

This speech annoyed me in so many ways that as I walked to one of the chairs against the wall I was imagining walking out of the building, but I sat down and divided my attention between the script on my knee and the continuing rehearsal, which kept quarrelsomely interrupting itself.

The play was a modern version of *Aladdin and His Wonderful Lamp*. Apart from the hero, who was a Scottish working-class simpleton, the characters were upper-class English types of the sort who are continually caricaturing themselves on radio and film. The production called itself *A Political Pantomime*, and had no doubt been written with satirical intent, but I saw nothing funny in it. Only Helen made it worth watching. She played a selfish, sexy, calculating bitch with so much vigour that her lines sounded witty. When not performing she sat hugging her shoulders as if she was cold, and her face above the long elegant neck looking as dreamy and remote as Carole's; or else she lay flat along four seats with closed eyes, her hair and one arm hanging to the floor. I thought it remarkable that she could put on three different versions of herself – aggressive, thoughtful or utterly abandoned – within three adjacent minutes. The director, who also played the hero, struck me as a silly man and a bad actor. I can still picture him distinctly: effeminately handsome with narrow, pale-blue eyes and well-groomed wavy blond hair. He wore sandals, black slacks and sweater, also an earring and many silver necklaces. But in the fifties men who wanted to look gorgeous never wore jewellery, so I have imposed these on him from a later decade. When not acting he spoke a drawling Oxford accent which became very distinct when he pretended to lose his temper, which was once every five minutes or so. He called people "darling", or "blossom", or (when pretending to be angry) "tooty-fruity", and he waved his arms a lot, so I knew at once he was homosexual. I was wrong. He was the lover of Helen and also of Diana, a less glamorous girl who acted all the other female parts in the play. Diana knew he was also Helen's lover. Helen was only beginning to suspect he was also Diana's lover, and Diana was her best friend. This was why Helen was so thoughtful between her performances and did not hear what folk said to her unless they spoke louder than usual. The others present were Roddy and Rory, straightforward manly young actors with no extravagance of dress, speech or manner, and a middle-aged man with the truculent, querulous voice of someone who knows he is insignificant and resents it. He sat in a hunched position and passed remarks that nobody else seemed to hear. I assumed he was a janitor attached to the rehearsal rooms. Wrong again.

As the rehearsal continued the truculent man hunched further and further into himself, then covered his face with his hands and started saying in a monotonous voice, "Oh no . . . Oh no . . . Oh no . . . Oh no . . . Oh no . . ." until the director stopped in mid-declamation and said wearily, "What is it this time?"

"Overacting."

"You are telling me that I cannot act?"

"I am telling you that your Glaswegian dialect is the corniest sort of ham."

"Tooty-fruity, you are insane!" cried the director in a clear, shrill Oxford-accented, phoney, fury, "I was born and bred in the Calton. My father works in Parkhead forge. Until I was twelve years old I thought that only the monarchy and Hollywood film stars had lavatories in their own houses. And now a schoolteacher from Carntyne tells me I can't speak the dialect of my own family!"

The querulous man said, "Yes, Brian, I agree that you are, essentially, a dirty wee Glasgow tyke from an even slummier background than my own. You are also quite a good actor. You can act *anything* except what you essentially are."

The director, with an indefinite expression on his face, walked round the room in a slow circle. We were all watching closely so he must have felt that his present performance was more interesting than the scripted one. When he got back where he had started he said mildly, "There is a simple solution. Let me play McGrotty as a cockney. I'm a master of the jellied-eels-on-the-Old-Kent-Road dialect. We're putting this thing on at an international festival, remember, with many more English than Scots in the audience, so there's no need for us to be narrowly provincial – is there?"

The truculent man covered his face with his hands and said in a muffled voice, "I will not let you turn my play into a vehicle for your national inferiority complex and your London West End ambitions. Give the part to Rory. He knows how to act it."

The director smiled and said brightly, "I wish you were dead. Do you know why I wish you were dead? If you were dead I could turn this script into a great piece of theatre. It has a good plot, meaty parts, some very funny lines and only one defect – an author who has no practical theatrical experience and is hideously alive. Do me a favour. Go away and die."

The author, his face very white, left the room with no dignity at all for he stumbled going through the door and made two efforts before slamming it behind him. I had never heard adult people being so deliberately nasty to each other before. The two girls stared at the director with something like awe. Diana said hopefully, "Perhaps he won't come back."

"We need him," said the director wearily, "we need his

name on the programme. Roddy. Rory. He's gone to drown his sorrows in the Red Lion. Follow him there and buy him pints and tell him what a great writer he is and what a bastard I am and how everybody else is on his side. He makes these scenes because he wants to be flattered, so lay it on thick. Take Jock with you. The girls and I will get down to some real work together and join you in the pub in forty minutes."

When Roddy and Rory and I got to the nearest pub the playwright was not there but we bought pints all the same.
Roddy said, "What do you think of us, Jock?"
I said, "You are interesting people."
Rory said, "What do you think of our director?"
I said, "Is he queer?"
"Oh no. Roddy and I are the queers in this company."
My insides turned to nearly total panic. I could not have been more embarrassed if they had told me they were Catholics. They were watching me closely so I managed not to react. Roddy said, "You haven't batted an eyelid. Do you think Rory is joking, Jock?"
After a silence I said, "Not necessarily."
They chuckled as if this was a joke and my insides started to relax. Roddy said, "A friend of poor Helen, are you?"
I said, "I'm a friend of Alan who is a friend of Helen."
Roddy said, "Ah! Alan! I could go for him."
Rory said, "I couldn't. Mind you, if he asked me nicely I would probably submit."
I said, "Why did you say 'poor' Helen?"
They told me about Helen and the director and Diana. I then asked if the production had any chance of doing well. Rory said, "There is a chance, yes, there is a slim chance."
Roddy said, "It would have a very good chance if Brian gave the lead part to Rory."
I said, "Then you are in agreement with what the author said?"
"Oh yes. Even Helen and Diana say privately that Brian is hopeless in the lead."
"Why don't all of you tell him that?"
"If we all tell him that he's perfectly capable of cracking up, then the whole production will fall apart. We're hanging on

in the hope that he sees the light for himself. He might. He's not a fool."

I wanted no part in a company which depended on the whims of a raving egoist. I decided that when Helen arrived I would take her aside, quietly tell her this, then apologise and leave.

The director arrived arm-in-arm with his women. All three were as hectically elated as if they had been drinking and I had no chance to talk quietly with Helen. Her gaiety had a wild, defiant note, she almost reminded me of Jane Russell. I don't often notice the inside feelings of people but I sensed that Helen would soon be wanting an alternative to that director, an alternative who was completely unlike him. Suddenly I was also elated, so elated that I disguised it by consulting my watch and saying abruptly, "I must go."

"Listen, I'm sorry this evening has been such a shambles," said the director escorting me to the pub door. "Next week we'll have that tête-à-tête I promised you, we'll hammer out a lighting script and arrange to get what you need. The thing to remember is, we're performing on a bare platform with no curtains or backdrops or any kind of scenery, just desks and chairs and things, so all the transitions and the mood of the setting depend on you. I know you won't let us down."

When making love later that night I was also caressing and entering an image of the desperately elated Helen, so I kept being surprised by the shortness of Denny's legs.

Some time in the following week I visited the warehouse of a theatrical hiring agency and after half an hour's discussion of the available equipment I had identified the main sorts of stage lighting and learned that it came in floods (which can be faded in or out more or less rapidly) and spots (which can be widened into quite big pools). I never had a tête-à-tête with the director, who was always too busy to attend to practical details, but I worked out a lighting script in discussions with Roddy, who was in charge of properties, and Diana, who was the production manager. When I asked them the colour of the clothes and the furniture they did not think it was my business. I explained that some colours would look vivid or dull, depending on the colour of the light. Roddy said, "I think you're being too subtle, Jock. A production like ours doesn't need coloured lighting."

Diana said, "Wait a minute! Could you make a telephone glow in the dark?"

I said, "Given an ultra-violet bulb and a telephone coated with the right enamel, certainly I could. Or I could mould a telephone in acetate and put a small bulb inside. But if total darkness is not essential I can make the right colour of phone glow bright in a dimly lit area by putting the right spot on it."

Diana said to Roddy, "You see, that might solve the main problem."

The play had scenes in which people who were supposed to be in different buildings telephoned each other from opposite sides of the stage. Everyone but the author thought these would be hard to dramatise. Roddy turned quickly to a page in the script and said, "Of course! End of scene five. Harbinger starts his final monologue extreme right, then the lights start to fade, then he shoots himself, slumps over the desk and we cut the floods to a small spot on him which also lights the telephone. Miss Soames enters, picks up the phone, speaks the number, then at the very moment when the other phone starts ringing we see it shining in the dark extreme left! You're a genius, Jock."

They seemed to believe I had given them an idea, though I had only asked what they wanted and told them what could be done. Diana said, "I'll break it to Brian."

Roddy said, "Would it not be easier if we treated it as a technical matter and let Jock just go ahead and do it?"

Diana said, "No, I'll break it to Brian. Since the idea comes from Jock he won't feel threatened."

Diana was a very thin girl with irregular features and a lot of common sense. Though not pretty she was attractive, and I could not understand why she and Helen let themselves be loved and bullied by a pretentious idiot like Brian. They treated his rottenest behaviour with motherly protectiveness. Now I come to think of it, so did Roddy and Rory. Brian was very mean with money. He would lead us into the Red Lion after a rehearsal, fling himself dramatically on to a bench, lean back with closed eyes and softly whine, "Get me a drink, somebody."

Whoever was nearest the bar, Helen or Diana or Roddy or Rory or me (why me?) would buy and bring him a pint, he would swallow a quarter of it in one dramatic gulp, then lie back again with the closed eyes and murmur, "Thanks. I deserved that."

Around him the company would nudge and grin at each other, taking care that he did not see them do it. Then I noticed that when he lay back like that his narrow eyes were not always completely shut, and he was actually watching the others nudging and grinning. I understood nobody in that company except the author, a simple soul. The others did not speak to him so I felt obliged to explain the script and the lighting cues. He attended closely then said in a relieved voice, "Yes, that won't interfere with it."

He believed his play would be a success if only the actors followed all his instructions and distinctly pronounced his words. He had no interest apart from that in the direction and lighting of the play, and mainly attended the rehearsals to prevent, as far as he could, the director altering his words.

The author was not the only one to flee from the rehearsal rooms after an exchange of cruel language. Everyone but myself did it some time. Even the director did it, after Helen disagreed with him over a point, and appealed to the rest of the cast, and they agreed with her. The wounded parties usually rushed to the pub and since I was often free at this stage in the production I was usually asked to follow them and soothe them. This was easily done. I listened to their complaints with great attention and said as little as possible. I allowed myself to show a certain amount of surprise, for the causes of the quarrel were usually different from the argument which expressed it. Helen told me her suspicions about Diana; Diana told me how guilty she felt about Helen; the director told me never to get entangled with women because it was HELL, Jock, sheer sheer sheer bloody unmitigated Hell; Roddy told me how afraid he was of losing Rory; Rory told me how stiflingly possessive Roddy had become. When they had taught themselves cheerful or tranquil again they would pay me a wee compliment, like "We're all less tense since you joined us, Jock," or "You're very sympathetic toward people who are different from you."

I was not sympathetic, I was just interested in them. Only Helen seemed ashamed of talking without restraint. She said afterward, "I was silly to go on like that. I'm sorry, I find it hard to be reasonable."

Only Diana was interested in me. She once interrupted her babble about Brian and Helen to say, "How is your own love life? You have one, haven't you?"

I told her I did not like talking about it. She said, "No wonder I feel safe with you."

I stared thoughtfully into my glass to avoid looking at her speculatively. I did not know if her remark was an insult or a compliment but it excited me. I wondered if she would tire of the director at the same time as Helen did. I wanted Helen, I had no intention of giving up Denny, and if a selfish noisy childish man like Brian could enjoy two women simultaneously why should not a kindly discreet intelligent man like myself enjoy three?

For I did not neglect Denny in those days, I did not, I did not. I liked her more than ever. The actors fascinated me but it was good to go home to supper with someone who did not feel that all the world was a stage and everyone else a good or bad audience. I became nicer to Denny because I was plotting to be unfaithful to her. I stopped being unpunctual. I bought her presents of chocolate, and cartoon-strip love-stories which she read with great concentration. So when I remarked casually one Friday night that I was going to Edinburgh next day and might have to stay till Sunday she looked worried, but not more worried than if I had told her I was going to visit Alan. That was before we went to bed. I was woken later on by a queer muffled squeaking noise. We were not entwined as usual. She had slid down under the bedclothes as far as she could and pressed her face into the mattress to hide her sobbing from me. Her head was beside my hip. I stroked it and said, "What's wrong?"

I could not hear her words till I had crawled down beside her. She was saying, "You're goantae leave me you're goantae leave me and you won't come back, won't ever come back."

I tried to cuddle her. I said, "Don't worry, I love you! You're all right because I love you!"

I had never spoken the word *love* seriously before and have never used it since, but when I heard it leave my lips I knew I meant it. Yet she still said, "No no no never, you'll never you'll never come back", and I noticed that apart from me she had nothing much to hold on to, nothing but a wage which could not support her, relations she distrusted and a forbidding public charity. Beside such weakness I felt gigantically strong, as strong as the whole world put together and I was delighted to discover my strength, because now that I loved her she had no cause to weep. No matter how many other women I loved (a man as big as the world cannot be confined to one woman) she would always be perfectly safe because I loved her first and best. I said, "Listen, Denny, you've nothing to worry about because one day I'll probably marry you, Denny, yes, I'll probably marry you because I like, no, I really love you, Denny!"

Words meant nothing to Denny when she got depressed. Eventually she let me cuddle her but the sobs shook her body like incurable hiccoughs till they no longer distressed but bored me, then I got sick and tired of them and fell asleep.

She was very quiet over breakfast next morning though I had made scrambled eggs on toast, which she greatly liked. I said to her, almost pleadingly, "Don't worry, Denny! I'm not angry with you."

She said nothing. I said, "No couple should expect to sleep together every single night of their lives. And Edinburgh isnae at the other end of Scotland, it's less than an hour away by train. And you're perfectly safe here, the landlord likes you."

"Well I don't like him."

"Why not?"

"He looks at me in a funny way when you're no' here."

"What do you mean?"

She said nothing. I said, "As if he fancies you?"

"Mhm."

"I'm not surprised. I fancy you myself."

She looked at me with an expression I could not read. I said patiently, "That was meant to be a *joke*, Denny."

"Oh. Sorry."

She was silent, then said violently, "I've no right to be here when you're no' here! People think I'm your hoor."

I prickled with lust at the word but said sternly, "I am shocked to hear you employ the language of the gutter, Denny. And I'm appalled to hear what a low opinion you have of yourself. If that's what you think of yourself, no wonder other folk think it too."

She looked astounded and said, "Did I say that? I'm sorry, I didnae mean to say that."

She really believed, because I had told her so, that she had called herself a whore. Yes, people with a confident tongue can tie up people like Denny in all kinds of knots. This is supposed to show our superior intelligence, but since it has nothing to do with truth or decency it merely demonstrates a special sort of skill, the skill of the jujitzu fighter who can knock someone down with a simple handshake. Having knocked Denny down I tried to pick her up. I said patiently, "The thing to remember is, that our landlord is a law-abiding, sober, respectable citizen. And a generous one. He let this room to me as a single man, you and I both use it now and he hasnae raised the rent. Which is a good thing. If he did that we could hardly afford to pay him. And a funny look won't hurt you. He can't help being attracted by someone as, as, as nice as you are, Denny. But he is not a danger. He's a mother's boy. He's five or six years older than us, he's never had a girlfriend in his life, and he still spends Sunday in Helensburgh with his mother. But I see my words are having no influence on you, Denny. All right. I will not go to Edinburgh today. Here and now – at this present moment in time – I cut all connection with that stupid company. They will fall apart without an electrician. They will detest me, and rightly so, for I detest myself, I am clearly a man whose word cannot be trusted. My reputation, my career will be damaged by this, but don't worry, Denny. You and I will live happily ever after. Mibby."

So I got her begging and weeping and pleading with me to go to Edinburgh until at last I gave in to her and went. Are you still listening to me, God? This is terrible stuff. Very ordinary and very terrible.

So that morning Roddy, Rory and I packed the lighting equipment into the back of a Ford van, then Roddy and Rory drove to Edinburgh and I went to Queen Street station to meet the others. Why? I had charge of that equipment, I had borrowed the van from a friend of Alan, why did I not drive it? Because I could not drive. I could draw blueprints of internal combustion engines but had no driving licence. This was common in forties-fifties Britain. Few lecturers had cars and even fewer students. In the recent war, because of fuel shortage, the only civilians allowed to drive cars had been doctors, and most professional people found this no hardship because they used public transport anyway. So the growth of the British car industry, the coming of the motorways, the dismantling of the rail system, the ringroads slicing up the cities, the spaghetti junctions, the multi-storey car parks, the streets subdivided by yellow lines and rented for parking to the people living there, the euphoria of the North Sea oil boom, the depression of the British coal industry, the depression of the British car industry, the depression of the British steel industry, the discovery that North Sea oil benefited hardly anyone in Britain but the shareholders – all this, though partly conceivable, had not been conceived. So because Roddy could drive and Rory was his closest friend and the van had only room for two I met the director and the girls and the writer at Queen Street station and we travelled to Edinburgh by steam railwaytrain. I am not telling you lies, children. Piston-driven steam locomotives did not disappear with Queen Victoria; until the sixties of this century they were built in Springburn and shipped to Europe, Africa, Asia and the Americas, they were built with parts forged in local foundries like Parkhead, Blochairn, Dixons, the Saracen, all gone now like the shipyards they also served. Yes, Glasgow was still the centre of British shipbuilding. In the recent war Clydeside had built and repaired more ships than the whole of the U.S.A. Attlee had recently signed a treaty with Truman (or was it Eisenhower?) leasing parts of Britain to America for use as missile bases, but the Polaris submarine was still a design on a drawingboard and a few years would pass before it entered the Holy Loch. A few years would pass before the big men in the employers' federations pulled their industries out of Scotland so the future looked bright when we left the train at Waverley station and I was astonished to see the Edinburgh tramcars were all a funereal chocolate colour. In Glasgow each tramcar had a 2½-feet-wide band of colour going round it between the upper and lower decks, blue or yellow or red or white or green according to the route it ran, and the rest was painted orange and green with cream and gold borders, and the city coat-of-arms on the sides in green, white, gold and silver. And there were no advertisements on these trams or on the buses either, why? Did the city fathers believe that adverts would spoil the appearance of a public carriage? Perhaps. The Glaswegians were proud of their tramcars, God knows why. Why should folk be proud of anything in a place which exists just to make money for those who can get it and make poverty for those who can't? Perhaps there were no adverts on the trams because advertising was not then an industry employing most of the country's artists, entertainers and newsmen. We had no commercial radio or television, no shopping centres, leisure centres, arts centres; nothing but the B.B.C. and shops and public baths and theatres. Oh, Britain was a primitive country in those days, primitive but in working order. We had come through a war, built a welfare state, had full employment and were still the richest country in the world after the U.S.A., the U.S.S.R. and Switzerland. We did not feel smug about this. The loud haw-haw voices kept telling us how drab and colourless we had become. The Tories had just won, or were about to win, an election in which they said that the British working man deserved more good red meat on his table. A team of British trade unionists had devised a democratic constitution for the unions of West Germany, a constitution which ensured that the German workers were not divided against each other and could bargain realistically for a share in the bosses' spoils; but the part this would play in making Germany the industrial capital of Europe had still to be demonstrated. I am very sorry God, I would like to ignore politics but POLITICS WILL NOT LET ME

ALONE. Everything I know, everything I am has been permitted or buggered up by some sort of political arrangement. So we left Waverley station and climbed one of the steep closes which tunnel through the high buildings of the old town, and found our premises were locked because Roddy had the key and had not yet arrived. So the director seized Helen's hand, Diana seized mine, and we went to see the sights with the writer trudging glumly behind.

The day was fresh and bright, windy and sunny. We went up to the castle, then down past the cathedral to the palace, then round and on to the Calton hill. The director climbed upon the pedestal of the national monument and strode senatorially between the big pillars declaiming verses from *Julius Caesar*. He was in an exalted state and so, I think, were the girls and myself, for we climbed up beside him. Newcomers to most cities feel buried in them because the nearest buildings hide all the others, which hide the surrounding country. Edinburgh is different. The director said to me, "One day, my boy, all this shall be yours," and swung an arm round the whole horizon indicating: the queer lunar-looking mountain of Arthur's Seat then the rock with the old town on it linked by bridges to the squares and crescents of the new town which sloped downhill through several parks to smoky ports around the broad firth with ships on the glittering surface and the railway bridge crawling across like a steel Loch Ness monster into the distinctly hedged and wooded fields and hills of Fife with the dim Ochils and dimmer Grampians on the left and on the right a long grey line of North Sea supporting more ships with the Bass Rock like an ornament on a shelf close to the cliff and cone of Arthur's Seat again. The director shook his fist at the urban part of this scenery and told it loudly, "At last we come to grips, you and I."

"A sham: An empty, pretentious sham," said the writer just as loudly. He was leaning against the pedestal with folded arms, his head a yard beneath the soles of our shoes.

"How can this splendid capital be a sham?" said the director.

"Easily," said the writer. "If you ignore the natural geo-

graphy all that catches your eye here are ruins and remains and monuments – nostalgia made solid."
"Beautifully solid!" cried the director. "This is a truly beautiful setting."
"A setting for an opera nobody performs nowadays," said the writer, "an opera called *Scottish History*. You love it because your approach to life is just amateur theatrical. I hate it because the only parts of the scenery that really work here are the factories and shops, which might as well be in Glasgow. Look at that litter bin!" – the writer pointed to an ugly metal container on four short legs – "A label on the side says THE AMENITY OF THIS CITY IS RECOMMENDED TO YOUR CARE. The signs on the bins where we live say KEEP GLASGOW TIDY. That demonstrates the only essential difference between the two cities."
"Envy!" shouted the director triumphantly. "This man hates Edinburgh because it is grander than Glasgow. Forget about him, darlings. He'll warm to the place when our production makes him famous here."
We returned to the performance place and found it open.

It was a set of rooms near the castle which had been taken by radical Glaswegians who originally wanted to put on a political cabaret. They got the place cheap, partly because it was going to be replaced by a police station, partly because the lawyer acting for the landlords did not realise money could be made in the fringe of the festival, which hardly existed at that time. The rent was paid in advance by a practical radical who could cook and who had agreed to run the restaurant to which the cabaret would perform. After ordering an oven, fridge, cups, plates, cutlery, chairs, tables etcetera he discovered that his friends disagreed violently about what a political cabaret was. None of them had seen one, though they all believed it flourished on the continent, particularly in 1930s Berlin. He also discovered that several hundred people could be housed and entertained in the space he had rented. A dusty Victorian office was entered from a pavement on top of the shops on the north side of the West Bow. Irregular stairs went down to a vaulted cellar with two levels of floor and many alcoves. The stairs had an arch on one landing which was sealed by a partition of rough planks. When the partition was pushed down it uncovered a windowless hall from which other stairways, some stone and some wooden, went up to more rooms and to rooms above those. Most rooms had dusty windows and fireplaces, one with a carved stone chimney-piece showing a coat-of-arms and a sixteenth-century date. Doors were painted with names indicating forgotten functions: *molasses room*, *sugar room*, *candy room*, *accounts*. A chamber sealed by another inadequate partition contained a long ornate table, two wooden thrones carved with trowels and compasses, and two tall gloomy portraits of tall gloomy men, much larger than lifesize, who seemed to be clan chieftains wearing a mixture of highland and masonic regalia. This district of rooms, beside the door to the walkway above the shops, had double doors from the cellar into the West Bow, a door which opened through Deacon Brodie's close into the High Street, and an emergency exit through a public house facing the Scottish National Library on George IV Bridge. So the practical radical applied for a licence to run the place as a nightclub and sublet other areas to dancebands, folksingers and our theatre company. He promised these groups (hardly any of whom were radical) a proportion of the nightly takings which would yield him a big profit if the venture succeeded, and he offered free food and bed room for the duration of the festival to whoever would help decorate and run the place. A couple of his friends denounced him as an exploiter, while refusing to share his expenses or the work of management. Since their only practical proposal was that he abandon the place and leave to the landlords the rent he had paid, he thanked them but preferred his own practical proposal.

Practical. The foregoing story may not be practically true. I pieced it together from bits of gossip overheard in the practical days which followed us all standing in a cold bare dirty draughty windowless hall lit by a feeble but practical light bulb. Why is *practical* running in my head? Because the director said, "You see the problem, darlings. We have five days to convert this into a pleasant little theatre with a stage and auditorium etcetera. I wish they had given us at least a platform. I'm sure we were promised a platform, but you just can't trust these radicals. Jock. Roddy. You are our practical men. Work out what we need, will you? It's quarter to eleven. Give me a list of what we need in thirty minutes at the most, because we have to move fast. Yes, and give me a list of the local firms who can supply what we need. Now come away with me, petals, let us leave the practical people to their deliberations. I feel that I deserve a very strong black coffee."

The girls and Rory and the writer went off with the director leaving Roddy and me staring aghast at each other. We spent five minutes denouncing the director and lamenting the impossibility of the task he had set, we spent ten minutes considering the problem in order to demonstrate to him how insoluble it was, and we discovered that we needed scaffolding, planks, more lighting equipment and many gallons of paint. We spent ten more minutes measuring the place to find just how much we needed, then went over to the Scottish National Library to get the addresses of suppliers from a local trades directory. The Scottish National Library did not have a local trades directory, so we consulted one which belonged to the public house facing it, and handed the director his list in not much more than thirty minutes. He read it and said, "Are you sure this is all you need? Should you not add a little extra to allow for a margin of error? It's a mistake to stint yourself at the formative stage."

I told him that we had, indeed, listed extra to cover the margin of error. He said, "Excellent. Our problem now is, that we have no money to hire or buy any of this, so we'll have to borrow or beg it. Jock, you are obviously a trustworthy fellow in that perpetually neat suit of yours. If Roddy drives you to these firms, will you ask to see the manager and explain the urgency of our problem to him? Don't – before you see him – breathe a word about your business to his underlings. Underlings always say no to borrowers and beggars. Go straight to the man at the top and tell him that if he supplies what we need we will mention his firm on our programme. Don't – unless he asks – tell him we are not part of the official festival. If he assumes we are, so much the better."

I said firmly, "I refuse to borrow, I refuse to beg, and I refuse to tell a lie, even by implication."

"Jock! What a very queer attitude! Borrowing is no more a crime than lending is and our whole society is based upon lending. However, the girls will probably be better at this job. Helen. Diana. My loved ones. Would you mind dreadfully doing a little bit of whoring for me? I am not asking you to surrender all of your sweet bodies. Just burst in upon these repressed Conservative Edinburgh businessmen looking dishevelled and sexy and helpless. Explain to them the urgency and enormity of our problem and tell them how poor we are. And don't waste time. As soon as you notice you're going to be refused rush to the next address on the list."

Diana said to Helen, "We'll have more impact if we dress the same. Borrow Rory's jeans."

Diana was wearing bluejeans, Helen a tartan skirt which, to the ignorant eye, looked very like a kilt. So Helen swapped with Rory and oh oh oh oh oh oh oh whoring . . .

Whoring. I have this delicious vision of all the women I ever liked. Jane Russell Denny Helen Diana Sontag the editor the whore under the bridge all all all stand in a row before me for inspection with their arms behind their backs to present their breasts in white cotton blouses and hips in tough baggy bluejeans but so tight round the crotch that the seam rubs their clitoris if that is practical (stop me God) their bodies, like sturdy tulips, tall lilies, slender daffodils, sprout from the thick plantpots of jeans whose legs are rolled up to midcalf showing red and white striped anklesocks and sannies, I mean sandshoes, I mean sneakers is what the Americans called canvas shoes in the fifties yes yes yes (stop me God) and I am a glorious pimp beloved by all my seven women, I am very cruel and hard with them (stop me) I rent them out to a wide variety of customers and reward them by sleeping with each one once a week, unless she has failed to give a customer perfect satisfaction in which case I punish her by NOT sleeping with her or by fucking her up the bum (STOP) but probably none of this is practical.

Not practical. But Helen and Diana, excitingly similar yet excitingly different in white blouses, bluejeans, anklesocks and sannies, went whoring for the necessary materials and without surrendering their sweet bodies they borrowed and begged all we needed, yes, and got planks and scaffolding delivered to us by lorry without one penny being paid. Then we started building a stage for the actors, a tower and gantry for the lighting equipment, and platforms to seat the audience. I was in charge of this part of the operation.

I was in charge and I discovered (or pretended to discover, I cannot now remember which) that the girls were better builder's labourers than the men. They and Roddy and I did the building. Rory and the writer put coats of white paint on almost everything which did not move. The director drank coffee in other parts of the building or drifted around us passing remarks which were seldom helpful. "It's terribly bleak," he said plaintively, "terribly stark. You're all working wonderfully hard, I'm not complaining about that, and the result is undeniably impressive. If we were putting on a performance of Orwell's *1984* in a Siberian labour camp I would feel perfectly happy. But this play is a comedy, in a festival."

"You said at the very start," said Diana, "that the changes of set and mood would be indicated solely by the lighting."

"Yes yes yes, petal, but this is more extreme than anything I had imagined possible. Look at that!" – he pointed to the lighting tower – "Could you not swathe the hideous structure in something colourful and symbolic?"

"Like what?" said Diana.

"I don't know, but we can't just leave it. I mean, Jock will be fully visible to the audience. All the time."

"He'll wear black overalls," said Roddy, "he won't be conspicuous. He'll be up there before the house starts to fill, reading a newspaper perhaps. Why not? The audience will notice him but ignore him, just as they ignored the properties men in Chinese classical drama. Anyway, we've no time to do anything else. Swathing of any sort will interfere with the lights, and the final rehearsals *must* start tomorrow."

The director grunted and wandered away. He came back later carrying a bucket of black paint and with a smug little smile on his face. He was followed by a hairy art student in a paintstained dressing-gown. We had seen this man working in the cellar downstairs on a frieze of fabulous monsters round the restaurant wall. He now set a ladder against our own glaring white walls and without apparent premeditation he covered them in a couple of hours with big silhouettes of Westminster Abbey, the House of Commons, Tower Bridge, the Tower of London, Marble Arch, the Eros fountain, Nelson's monument, Broadcasting House and Saint Paul's Cathedral. He finished by adding a few details in lines of gold enamel. Various people came from other parts of the building to stare at the result. The director gave them a small lecture.

"You see the idea, perhaps. The audience occupies the same simple setting which the actors do. The properties we will use are all exposed in their places on the uncurtained stage. Nothing is disguised, nothing hidden. Even our electrician will be a visible part of the drama, in fact he will be the first character on the stage. As soon as the audience is seated and it's time to begin, Jock will check the fire-exits, close the house doors, walk down through the audience, mount the stage and pick up his overalls, which will be on that desk just left of centre. He will pull these on over his splendidly dapper suit then climb into that tower thing, sit on that plank, and gradually extinguish all the lights until we are in total blackness, apart from the little red bulb high up which shows Jock where his switches are. He puts on a recording of Big Ben chiming the hour, and as the notes fade away he turns a spotlight upon Arthur Shotts and Charlie Gold who enter through the main door at the back. He keeps the spot on them while they stroll, chatting, down toward the stage, and just before they reach it I – sorry, no, Eustace McGrotty, our hero – he blunders into them out of the darkness. From then on Jock, though visible, will be completely ignored, like the properties men in the classical Chinese dramas."

I said loudly, "This opening is news to me."

"News?" said the director wonderingly, "News? Surely I told you all this yesterday. I thought of it yesterday."

I said emphatically, "It is news to me."

"But you will do it, I hope. Why be a power behind the scenes when you can be a performer also? Listen!" – he appealed to the writer – "You like the idea, don't you?"

"It can do no harm," said the writer.

"You hear that?" cried the director triumphantly. "Even he is enthusiastic. Helen. Diana. My loved ones. Woo Jock for me. Seduce him. Persuade him."
I said, "I will think the matter over," and went out for a walk.

I was excited by the notion of starting the play like that, for I had come to envy the actors who would perform in the pools of light I cast. But I had spoken privately to one of the other helpers around the place, an apprentice electrician who struck me as reliable. He had agreed to take over my job on the opening night if I taught it to him before the final rehearsal. I had three reasons for arranging this.
FIRST
I knew the play would flop because the director insisted on playing the hero, a part for which he was unfit.
SECOND
Even so, I now respected and even liked the director, a little. He was a raving egoist, yes, but not an idiot, and he really did hold the company together. I no longer believed I could take one of his women away from him. The idea of doing so seemed dirty and shabby.
THIRD
Denny was taking my visits to Edinburgh very badly. I slept with her most nights of the week, hitchhiking back to Glasgow to save fares and leaving again very early next morning; but our lovemaking, especially when we awoke around dawn, which had been our best time, was now stale and hurried and desperate. Her hands clutched me like little claws. That very morning, in a fit of weakness or strength (tell me which it was, God, because I don't know) I had told her, "You ought not to worry, Denny. After tomorrow I'm coming back to you for good."
She had sighed with relief. Her claws had become gentle hands again.

Thinking of these things I walked gloomily down the Mound. The day was sunny and windy again. I seem to remember flags of all nations flapping on their poles along Princes Street. I noticed that Helen was walking on one side of me and Diana on the other. Diana said, "We've been sent after you to woo and seduce you. Do you really hate the idea of starting the play like that? I think it's a glorious idea."

Helen said, "If he doesn't want to do it I don't see why he should."

I said, "I'm leaving the company tomorrow."

"Oh you can't do that!" they cried out simultaneously. I said, "I will certainly do it if Brian doesnae give his part to Rory."

We were standing still now, staring at each other. Helen looked horrified. Diana looked delighted. Diana said, "Good! You must tell Brian that."

Helen said, "If Jock tells Brian that, Brian will have a nervous breakdown."

Diana said, "No. Brian is a lot tougher than he pretends. Come on Jock."

She seized my arm and led me back to the West Bow. She was very excited. Helen became excited too and seized my other arm. I swept in on the company with a woman on each arm and feeling important. The director said, "Good good good, darlings. I see you have persuaded him."

Diana said, "In a way, yes, we have, but in another way, no, not at all. Tell him, Jock."

I said, "I will do anything you ask me to do in this play: provided that you switch parts with Rory. If you don't I am leaving the company tomorrow, though of course I will provide you with an adequate substitute."

The director said, "You fucking wee bastard."

He said it in an ordinary Glasgow voice which was perhaps his natural speech. He looked round at the others, who gazed back at him hopefully. He said to Rory, "What do you think of that?"

Rory shrugged and said, "It might be worth trying."

Roddy said quickly, "Rory doesn't *really* want your part, Brian, he just feels – we both feel – in fact everybody feels he is not right in the part of Sir Arthur. You would be a much much better Sir Arthur."

"Thankyou, Roddy," said the director, "you are very tactful. My electrician has just booted me in the groin. My entire female cast is applauding him. My second male lead shrugs his shoulders and you provide the magic words which will save my self-respect: I will be a much much better Sir Arthur."

"Nobody listens to me, of course," said the writer, "but I told you that weeks ago."

"Dear pretty splendid beautiful Brian," said Diana, "we all love and admire you, we can do nothing without you, without you our entire world will fall apart, but could you not just once, for the company's sake, let us read through the play in the way Jock has suggested? If it doesn't work we'll all know what complete fools we have been and we'll never dare to question anything you say ever again."

The director looked at her blankly for a while then said in his ordinary voice, "All right."

They sat round a table and read the play with Rory in the main part. After a shaky start it went well. Rory was a convincing Glaswegian simpleton and the director a convincing upper-class English bully. Before they reached the end of the third scene the director said, "Stop. I was wrong and you are right, I was wrong and you are right, I WAS WRONG AND YOU ARE RIGHT."

He banged the table very hard with his brow and went on doing so until we prevented him, then he violently embraced Helen, pushing his face into her hair, cried out in a muffled voice, "Please be kind to me Diana, I mean Helen", and burst into tears. It was a disgusting performance. He was overacting, but overacting something he felt, so we could not laugh.

I was worried when I went back to Glasgow that night. I regarded myself as an honest, consistent, dependable man and in the space of a few hours I had told Denny I was finishing with the company and told the company I was appearing in their late-night show for the next three weeks. I had other reasons to worry. Denny was unemployed because the holidays had begun and nearly two months would pass before she returned to work. She was too young and badly paid to draw national insurance, and if she applied for national assistance she would be visited by an inspector who would ask to see her rent book. If the inspector learned she was living with me he would refuse assistance on grounds that she was *cohabiting*, which means, being given food and houseroom in return for being fucked. The assumption that a woman living with a man is a self-employed whore is good practical Conservative economics. It saves the nation money, which is why in 1982 the cohabitation rule is still in force and will be in force until the Third World War. I accept the inevitability of this but thirty-odd years ago I was less bland, because my grant looked like being used up some while before it was renewed. I wished Denny would find a temporary job – her labour exchange had not offered one. Labour exchanges. We don't have these nowadays. When there were jobs the exchanges used to offer them, and when there were none they paid out insurance money and assistance money from adjacent counters, sometimes the same counter. On adjacent benches sat unemployed navvies, unemployed clerks, bankrupt businessmen and husbandless mothers. Very primitive. Now we have Job Centres and the Professional Register and the Social Security Office under different ministries. The bureaucracy has divided and increased in order to divide the hugely increased body of unemployed. Very practical. (Get back to Denny.) All right.

All right, Denny was my whore since the authorities would define her as that and a whore was a luxury I could hardly afford. Of course if she declared herself homeless and destitute she would be sent to some institution like the one I had persuaded her to leave, but I did not want to lose her. I loved her dearly for loving me so dearly, but I also disliked her for being such a fucking problem. I hated the glad light in her face as I entered the room, as if there were now no problems in the world because I had returned to her. I looked hard at her and the glad light died in her. Compared with Helen or Diana she seemed very very ordinary. She said quickly, "What's wrong Jock?"
I said, "Nothing. Let's go to the pictures."
I grudged spending money on cinema seats but it was better than sitting at home. The film had Bette Davis in it and was about smart New York theatre folk who kept reminding me of the company in Edinburgh. I disliked that film but it incited me to compose in my head a speech of explanation to

Denny, a speech I did not deliver till the following morning. Before the film ended I got up and said, "Come on, let's go for a drink."

She said, "We cannae *afford* that, Jock."

"All right, you stay here, but I'm going for a drink."

We entered Launders' Bar on Sauchiehall Street with fifteen minutes till closing time, because in those days the Glasgow pubs shut at nine p.m. I ordered and drank several whiskies very rapidly. I had never done such a thing before. Perhaps I suspected I was going to kill part of her and wanted to anaesthetise myself first. My victim refused to touch anaesthetic so I drank hers too.

Our lovemaking that night was the worst I have known. She scratched my back bloody while I mentally whipped and raped her between Jane Russell and Helen and Diana and Bette Davis in a dungeon in a castle in a hollow tooth because WHY WERE THESE FUCKING WHORES MAKING MY LIFE PRACTICALLY IMPOSSIBLE? I could feel her cunt gripping me like a beak, trying not to let me go from that place where I had once loved to lie feeling her softly cosily cuddling my prick, but that would never happen again, never again, no no no no never again.

"You can be hard down there? I can be harder, my dear."

Did I say these words or only think them? I had her weeping, but I doubt if they were tears of joy. If they were tears of joy then what followed must have been even worse for her. Some time after dawn broke I said firmly, "This has got to stop."

I arose and shaved and washed and dressed. I had a hangover, of course, and remembered with a shudder that I had used no contraceptive. I gave Denny a cup of tea in bed, then paced up and down the room delivering a speech which went like this.

"Denny, I want you to listen to me carefully. I am going to tell you something you will not like to hear, but there is a practical reason for it which I am sure even you will understand, I mean money. We need more money because you have no job and my grant was not intended to support two people. So I must get more money somewhere, and I will. This daft play in Edinburgh – this company – has a chance of doing well, I think. All the omens point that way, so I am going back to Edinburgh this morning, and you will not see me for perhaps more than a fortnight, though I will of course write to you, yes indeed, you will get a postcard from me every morning because I love you, I think. I am placing the rentbook here, upon the mantelpiece. It contains two weeks' rent and five extra pounds for food etcetera because I have no wish to be mean and I know you are not extravagant, Denny. So now, what about a nice wee good-bye kiss?"

Was a more practical, reasonable, considerate farewell speech ever spoken?

It was a lie. It was an anti-Denny demolition job. The speech meant this: "You are not coming to Edinburgh with me. You will never see me at work, or meet or mix with my interesting new friends or have an exciting life, because you are not in my class. You are just the wee hoor I keep at home. You are a luxury I can no longer afford, but I am maintaining you for sentimental reasons because I am better than you, although I am also tired of you."

I did not know I was saying this, but Denny was sharper than me and she knew it. When I handed her the cup of tea her face had the exhausted but newly-born look of someone who has come out of a bad storm or a bad illness. She maybe thought our desperate lovemaking had brought us together again and was wholly unprepared. In a moment her face went sharp and ugly, became the face of a nasty little terrified girl, then not even the face of a girl or a child but the face of something presexual and preanimal, something that was nothing but agonised helpless lostness and complaint, petty, nagging complaint because out of a mouth wide enough to emit the most deafening yell in the world came only a thin, eerie, continuous whine. Only horror-films and fairy-stories tell the truth about the worst things in life, the moments when hands turns into claws and a familiar face becomes a living skull. My words turned a woman into a thing and I could not face the thing I had made because the thing saw in my face the disgust it caused me. I turned my back upon the thing with the whine, I speedily packed my suits and underwear into a couple of cases. I was

afraid that the thing with the whine would jump up and grab me. I rushed out saying, "This is not the end of the world Denny, I'll drop you a postcard. See you in three weeks, that's a promise."
I fear I cannot go on with this story, God. It is too dismal.

Needlessly dismal. I could easily have taken her to Edinburgh. We had plenty of room there. One of the upper chambers had been turned into a dormitory for the performers and helpers, it had been scrubbed clean and rows of mattresses laid on the floor. The mattresses were called cowlays. The practical radical had rented them from a farm-supply-warehouse, they were of green plastic but perfectly comfortable when covered by a blanket. Being too shy for communal sleeping I took my cowlay into a closet beside a fire-exit at the top of a small wooden stair. Denny could have slept with me there, the strangeness of the place would have refreshed our lovemaking. She would have worked in the restaurant, which needed helpers after the first two nights. Later on I saw opera singers washing plates behind the counter, not for money but just to be helpful. When the club started succeeding all sorts of surprising mixing and joining happened between the members and the performers and those who ran the place. The cast of a famous Oxford or Cambridge drama group ate and drank beside the Gorbals Young Communist Party: plumbers, electricians and folksingers who had split with the official party after Khrushchev's anti-Stalin speech. Both lots were delighted to be rubbing shoulders with such dangerously far-out people. Had Denny been there she would have been welcomed as a useful, practical, good-natured attractive lassie, not well-educated, perhaps, but who is? If a good education is reading and remembering a lot of good books then most lawyers, doctors, business-men, members of parliament and royalty don't have it. If good education means a wider experience of people and possibilities then that nightclub would have been the best possible school for Denny because she was only sixteen or seventeen and, as Alan said, very sharp. But I wanted to be A FREE SPIRIT, someone posh who could flirt with posh girls like Helen and Diana who (I learned later) were not very posh, but seemed posh to me because they dressed well and had the confident speech-style they had learned at drama college; while they (I learned later) thought I was an eccentric scion of the landed gentry because of my Harris tweed three-piece suits and blue bow ties and the confident speech-style I had learned from my father and Old Red and a lunatic English teacher and a gifted descendent of some Irish tinkers. But I am sure they mainly suspected me of exalted origins because of the relaxed bodily assurance I had gained with Denny, who I did not want them to meet. Our system of class prejudice is the cleverest piece of self-frustrating daftness since the Tower of Babel, it benefits nobody but a few at the top. We fool ourselves into fooling others into fooling ourselves even more. Get through this dismal story as fast as possible. (You exaggerate.)

Correct, I exaggerate. The rest of the story is not all dismal. I will tell it a night at a time.

FIRST NIGHT

The club opened its doors at five o'clock and thirty or so helpers and performers sat round the great cellar feeling excited and uneasy and foolish. We had spent so much time getting premises and productions ready that we had failed to advertise them, taking it for granted that "word would get around". By nine o'clock four customers had joined us and were drinking coffee and being serenaded by a glum guitarist. Our director suddenly used up nervous energy by ordering us to carry down the big masonic portraits from the upstairs room and place them on each side of the stairs to the hall where we would perform. He also ordered the art student to paint top hats on the chieftains' heads. The art student said, "I don't think I should. They've been ruined by what looks like two centuries of mastic varnishing, but for all I know they could be Raeburns or Ramsays."

The director said, "They are ugly objects nobody gives a damn for. I'll give you a couple of quid to turn them into something amusing within the next forty minutes."

The artist complied. Our show opened at eleven o'clock to

an audience of three. The director said beforehand, "Regard this as a rehearsal."

SECOND NIGHT

We played to an audience of ten or twelve, half of this being smart young people wearing (is this true or has my memory imposed it on them?) black dinner suits with white starched linen shirtfronts and collars with black bow ties. Our company was greatly excited because this was the cast of the Oxford or Cambridge group performing in the official part of the festival. At the end of the show they applauded politely. We cleared everything up and went downstairs and occupied a table in the cellar, where helpers and performers still outnumbered the customers. The club had no liquor licence but members could buy it outside and bring it in. The director produced bottles of wine and invited us to get drunk with him. The girls refused and so did I. After that sordid night with Denny I had decided never to drink alcohol again. The writer seemed to be drunk already. At this moment one of the Oxford or Cambridge cast, who were all drinking at a nearby table, said, "May I join you for a moment?"

Our director said, "Please do."

The English actor, who became well known later on, although I cannot now remember if his name was Frost or Miller or Bennett or Moore, sat down with us and said, "Congratulations. Your show is very good."

"We don't think so," said the director.

"Don't worry about the thinness of the house, that could improve quite rapidly," said the actor, "but would you consider it an impertinence if we gave you one or two notes on your characters and timing? You see the play mocks the kind of people *we* are, and mocks us very cleverly, but the impact will be even greater, we feel, if you slightly modify one or two details. For instance, you – " he pointed at Rory – "you were splendid up to your final speech, the speech that ends the show, but you should *not* play that speech for laughs. You are no longer a sympathetic moron, you have become *it*, *the thing*, *the establishment*, *old corruption*, there are hundreds of names for the power you have become. It is time to reveal to the audience that this play, after all, is no laughing matter, so expand. Terrify them."

Rory nodded thoughtfully then said, "Should I hector them like an angry trade union official?"

"Certainly not. Bluster has no effect on the British public when uttered with a regional accent. You've got to be damned hard and dry and incisive. Use an Anglo-Scots accent. The Scotch do change their accents when they get into positions of power."

"Thomas Carlyle didn't!" said the writer loudly.

"As far as I know Thomas Carlyle was never in a position of power," said the actor, "fortunately for Britain."

"You English are cunning bastards," said the writer, and walked out. The director apologised. The actor said, "Think nothing of it. Writers are notoriously temperamental. Now, you, in the part of Sir Arthur – "

He spoke, we listened, and were gradually joined by the rest of the English company. We tried to hide how pleased and flattered we were beneath a certain stiffness, and failed, I think. The English mixed their practical suggestions with so much friendly appreciation that they seemed not to condescend at all. A feeling of festivity resulted. Our director said, "Have you a suggestion about the lighting?"

The English actor started to laugh. He said, "None! None at all! The lighting is perfect."

I said, "So what's the big joke?"

He said, "You're the electrician aren't you? Congratulations on a splendid performance. I loved the way you appeared to be doing a difficult job which you thoroughly despised but were determined to do properly, no matter what anyone else thought. You were in silhouette most of the time, but when your effects were most theatrically stunning your whole body registered a sort of glum resignation and perseverance which nearly had me falling out of my seat. Who designed that amazing structure you occupy?"

"I did."

He looked solemn for a moment. He said, "I apologise, but it's hard not to laugh at the wholly unexpected. You see, what you've built works wonderfully, but it could only work with this particular play, in this particular acting space, with you operating it. You are either an undiscovered genius or an uninstructed amateur."

"Our Jock is both," said Diana, putting her arm around my shoulders. Helen looked at me closely, I think for the first time. With an effort I met her eyes and smiled slightly, then I told the English actor, "You are wrong, my lighting is not perfect. Your advice to Rory about the final speech has given me a better idea. Good night."

I went back up to the acting area hoping Diana or Helen would follow me out of curiosity. They did not, so I went to bed.

THIRD NIGHT

A lot more people came to the front office in the earlier part of the day and signed on as members, so when the premises opened for the evening the public outnumbered the staff by two to one, and later by three to one. Our audience filled over half the available seats because the English company returned bringing actors and musicians and singers from other festival productions, and these applauded so generously that we felt as famous as they were. Downstairs afterward there was a lot of dancing, starting with jive which I disliked because it made the partners hold each other in harsh, spasmodic ways. Then there was Scottish country dance, which Old Red once said would be the ballroom dancing of the future after the Great British Revolution. In each group every dancer comes to handle all of the other sex equally, and when groups split and reform with adjacent groups the dance is supposed to go on until everybody has held, twirled or embraced all of the other sex on the floor. When we had exhausted ourselves with democratic revolutions we had some slow private-enterprise waltzing. I waltzed once with Diana and once with Helen. Diana told me she was afraid that Brian was becoming far too keen on her, which was a pity because she was becoming keen on someone else, someone in the same line of business. I said, "Oh?"

After a pause she said sadly, "Directors seem to be the only men I can fall for."

With a pang of jealousy I realised that the new man was our

friend in the English company, who directed it. However, I wished her luck. Helen told me very little. She and I never had much to say to each other. I realised I enjoyed her conversation less than I enjoyed watching her on the stage, and that she knew this.

By four in the morning everyone had left except the artists and helpers. The practical radical gave everyone free toasted cheese and coffee, then the party became a ceilidh. Roddy, Rory, the director and I sang *The Ball of Kirriemuir* in a quartet, which led to each of us delivering a short solo, because in early adolescence we had all learned or invented a verse which the others did not know. The English theatre people sang the libellous and bawdy versions of songs they did differently on stage, and the folksingers sang the then unpublishable versions of Burns' songs, which have since been published, but fairly recently. The opera people were too shy to sing when not rehearsing privately or on stage so they performed some comic charades. The concert musicians were more daring. They borrowed instruments from the jazz and folksong people and joined with these in duets, trios, quartets etcetera which mostly sounded tuneful to me, though people who knew about music kept laughing because of the eccentric combinations. I drank none of the booze which was freely passed around yet felt as drunk as those who did. This was our happiest night.

FOURTH NIGHT

The club received such an influx of new members that the practical radical recruited kitchen-staff from among his folksingers, and our company washed and dried plates in the earlier part of the evening before playing to a full house with a lot of people standing at the back. From the top of my tower, high above the familiar silhouettes of London, I conducted our actors on to the stage in travelling spots of light. I cast pools of it for them to plot and pontificate and die in, and floods of it for them to quarrel and make love in. I struck the chimes of Big Ben and made telephones glow in the dark. I was monarch of all I surveyed, my right there was none to dispute. In the final scene, when the whole

auditorium was used to represent the House of Commons and all the cast but Rory rose out of it to ask querulous questions, I bounced so much unexpected light into the audience from a reflector on the stage behind McGrotty that he became a shadow with a voice in the middle of a dazzling radiance. I struck the final notes of Big Ben, put on all the house lights and there was loud applause. The actors went forward and bowed to it and some audience voices shouted, "The electrician! The electrician!" The director beckoned to me. I climbed down to a very loud storm of applause. I removed my overalls, hung them neatly on the scaffolding and then (none of this had been rehearsed) Diana and Helen seized a hand on each side and led me to the front of the stage. I could not find it in me to acknowledge the applause by bowing, but I gave the audience a nod of approval. For some reason this provoked so much laughter that Diana and Helen, without changing their dresses or removing their make-up, led me out through the audience and down to the cellar where a table with food and wine was reserved for us. Diana kissed me enthusiastically (but chastely). Helen squeezed my arm and said, "You really are perfect, Jock."
Bliss was it in that dawn to be alive, and to be young was very heaven. The director arrived and said, "What has he got that I haven't got?"
The girls coldly ignored him. Something was happening among these three which I did not understand, though I knew it had nothing to do with me. I suddenly thought how much Denny would have enjoyed the show and my success in it. I had not sent her a postcard yet, but promised myself I would send one next morning.

FIFTH NIGHT

This was like the fourth night. The girls and I walked out through the audience again but since this was not a spontaneous act it felt phoney and we never repeated it.

SIXTH NIGHT

Half the folk who queued for the show had to be turned away and were angry because they could not book for subsequent performances. (Having no clerical staff we had simplified our book-keeping by not having tickets and admitting people when they paid cash at the door.) At the very end, without being beckoned, I climbed down, stood in line and bowed as gratefully to the audience as the rest of the company.

SEVENTH NIGHT

The *Daily Record* or the *Bulletin* or the *Scottish Daily Express* printed a double-page article about our club, three-quarters of it filled with photographs. One showed myself in silhouette at the top of the tower while Helen and Rory, fully clothed, simulated sexual intercourse on a carpet of light at the bottom. One showed the most glamorous girl in the university review drinking and laughing with the hairiest man in the Gorbals Young Communist Party. One showed Rae and Archie Fisher being applauded by Felix Stokowski and Albert Finney, or perhaps it was Robin Hall and Josh Macrae being applauded by Yehudi Menuhin and Tom Courtenay. The text said that the organisers of the Edinburgh Festival were seriously worried because our "friendly, informal Glaswegian atmosphere" was "attracting worldwide celebrities of the stage and concerthall away from the mausoleum-like solemnity of the official festival club".

An article by Cordelia Oliver or Martin Baillie or someone else in the *Manchester Guardian* or the *Glasgow Herald* or the *Scotsman* said that our club provided the only truly Scottish contributions to the festival. After mentioning the folk-singers and dancebands the critics said that the political pantomime *McGrotty and Ludmilla*, "although clearly an amateur production", was performed with so much zest and technical ingenuity that it communicated more pleasure than the official festival production of a play by Bernard Shaw or Brendan Behan or John Osborne or John Whiting. Diana was especially commended in the part of Miss Panther and I as the electrician.

This publicity caused high spirits and hilarity among all the club performers except Helen, Diana and me. Helen

became very quiet. Diana said, "I feel like a traitor. Helen is a far, far better actress than I am. That critic has no judgment whatsoever."
Helen said, "I don't give a damn for the critic, I'm worried about that photograph. What will my father do when he sees it? He's terribly square. He didn't want me to go to drama college."
Diana said, "Maybe he won't see it."
"Oh yes, he'll see it. The neighbours will show it to him."
I realised that Helen's people were less posh than I had thought. Very posh people don't have neighbours, or none they care about. And I was sure we were all becoming too lucky too fast. I felt as my mother possibly felt one morning when the postman, delivering a parcel, told her it was going to be a fine warm summer day. She said grimly, "We'll pay for it."

I went to the director and said, "Brian, the show is now making money. For reasons I will not explain to you I need money. I know that half our take goes to the club and the rest will be divided among us equally. Please pay what you owe me now, and hereafter I want my cut of each night's take on the following morning, or better still, after the show."
He said, "Oh you are an impossible man. Frankly, I would prefer to give everyone their cut when the show ends and we've had time to add up the expenses."
I said, "No. So far the expenses have been equally shared between us. The actors have provided their own costumes, I have bought petrol for the van, everything else has been borrowed."
"But I've provided my own costume AND bought booze for the company."
"None of which I have drunk. If you do not give me what is due to me today, or at the very latest tomorrow morning, I promise I will return to Glasgow and register as an unemployed student."
The director groaned and said, "All right Jock, all right. But I wish you wouldnae clap a loaded gun to my skull every time you ask me for something."
The Oxford accent and the mannerisms I had once hated in

him had almost vanished, he sounded like an ordinary man with ordinary worries and I was sorry for the change. As an ordinary man I respected him more but enjoyed him less. I was sure his worries came from his lovelife, and was glad my lovelife had no complications. I was lusting to return to Denny though I had been too busy to send her a postcard yet.

He gave me the money. I hurried over the bridge to the central post office and put it in my savings account. The show went on as usual.

EIGHTH NIGHT

More newspapers reviewed us favourably and so did the Scottish Home Service. I thought of asking my parents to come and see the show, but if I asked them to do that why should I not ask Denny? So I asked nobody.

At twenty to eleven Brian and I, who were on the door, had just told the end of the queue that the house was full when our friend the English director arrived with someone who wore very good clothes and had a well-groomed but strange head. The top half looked old and the bottom half young. The English director said, "Listen, could you possibly squash in just two more of us?"
Our director said, "Sorry, but if we let in one more body suffocation will ensue. We're almost a fire-hazard."
The actor said, "But you see this is . . ."
His companion said, "No no no. I can surely come back tomorrow night, if your friend will be kind enough to keep us a couple of seats and not make a fire-hazard of his theatre."
His English accent was so smooth and grave that it made the smoothly accented English director sound unstable.

After the show we all cleared the place up then went downstairs and found, as usual, the English company and its friends at the table reserved for our company and its friends. The stranger was sitting beside the English director who told us, "Meet Binkie."

This struck our company almost totally silent, though our director said, "O."
Diana and Helen stiffened while the joints of Roddy and Rory seemed to slacken and their manly faces began to smile vacantly. We hesitated until the stranger, with a slight nod and turn of a hand, indicated that he expected us to sit at our own table. I sat as far from him as possible beside an English actress who was straining to hear the conversation. I asked her who he was. She whispered, "Binkie used to own the whole of the West End but he still has quite a slice of it. Shh."
This sounded like a line in a highly improbable novel so I asked Helen the same question. She whispered, "He's a great producer. We get lectures on him at the drama college. Shh."
In the bright light of the restaurant Binkie no longer looked strange, he looked like a plump, elegant, ageing but not yet old man. He sometimes smiled or nodded but said almost nothing. It seemed that he neither wanted nor was expected to speak. The other English kept entertaining and informing him by talking loudly to each other in a strangely ritualistic way. Nobody spoke about themselves, except indirectly, but all praised each other while pretending to tell stories against each other. The English director looked modestly embarrassed while his cast gave different versions of a tale which demonstrated how, under stress, he became forgetful and rude in ways which strengthened, almost by accident, his superb qualities as a director. The subject of this tale suddenly interrupted it by crying, "I've had enough of this! I may be pretty bad but what about you, Judy?"
He pointed at his leading lady and told a story about how comically prone to sexual misadventure she was in ways which somehow enhanced, or showed up by contrast, her qualities as an actress. As he came to the titillating details of the story Judy hid her face in her hands and cried, "Oh no! Please stop! Don't let Binkie hear about that!" and afterward her friends emitted a burst of laughter which the director bridged by shouting, "And then! And then! And then she . . ."
Binkie was being steadily told that they were all eccentric, silly, lovable, efficient, talented, and related to important people.

And now the English tried to widen the game. Their director told an obliquely flattering story about our company, and appealed to our director for confirmation, and our director answered with a monosyllable. The English director hesitated, but Judy took the story from him and continued it with great energy for a minute, then tried to pass it to Rory, who grinned and nodded, then to Roddy, who grinned and nodded, then to Diana, who seized it and brought it to an end with one bright hysterical sentence. The English laughed appreciatively and then there was silence. The Scots could not play this game. It was not a game in which we could be beaten, like football, it was a game in which we displayed ourselves, like beachball, and we had been taught *not* to display ourselves, taught that it was wrong to talk in class, unless the teacher asked a question and we knew exactly the answer he wanted. So the Scots were silent until Binkie, who should have been silent too because the game was being played for his benefit, decided to join in. He asked our director a question, and our director answered with three monosyllables. I was ashamed for him, ashamed of the Scottish. I wished he would turn into the old glib garrulous Brian with the phoney accent and the sickening catch-phrases. The English would despise him for these but they would also notice an energy they could not despise, an energy which could be useful to them or useful to someone. But he spoke three short words. Binkie nodded as if he had received weighty information, then asked another question and our director pointed at me. The English director jumped up and shouted, "Jock! You're being very quiet at that end of the table. Come up and join us."
He placed a chair between Binkie and himself and I sat down in it determined to be as dour as the rest of my company. On my right hand was a man people treated like God. I did not think he was God yet my heart beat as hard as if I was on holy ground. I despised the illogical action of my heart, so I wanted to despise him.

Binkie gave me no chance to do that. He smiled and murmured something polite. The English director said, "We've all been telling Binkie about the strikingly original lighting effects you produced for the show."

I said, "I tried to produce suitable effects."
The English director said, "Could you adapt these to a more traditional theatre space?"
"Certainly not. I would devise different effects for another theatre."
"How would you go about doing that?"
"First I would examine the acting space, because I have never visited the stage of an ordinary theatre. Here we had to build our own. Then I would familiarise myself with the lighting resources, and find how much money was available to extend them."
The English director said, "Extend them?"
I said nothing. Then Binkie spoke in a remote, rather sleepy voice: "The lighting resources of a well-equipped modern theatre are pretty extensive already, and I gather you have done something quite stunning with a few ordinary floods and spots."
I shrugged and said, "If you want the best from a creative electrician you must expect him to enlarge his scope."
"Creative electrician!" said Binkie, and somehow conveyed, without smiling, that he was amused. I said sternly, "What is the nature of *your* connection with the theatre?"
After a pause Binkie said, "I make money by it. I find it an interesting way of making money. I meet such very charming people."
He gave me a small charming smile then transferred it to Rory who sat across the table from him. Rory no longer looked manly. His head lolled so far to one shoulder that the neck seemed broken. He had the face of a wistfully dreaming girl. The English director said loudly, "Creative electrician, yes, an interesting idea. You see in the professional theatre only the artists – the directors and actors and designers – are expected to be creative. The technicians do what they're told, though they're well-protected by their unions, and very adequately paid."
I shrugged and said, "Most folk who train for a trade or profession become mindless tools of it, even in engineering. Even in architecture. Even in banking, I believe. But in Glasgow – Glasgow Tech – we have a different approach."
This was a lie. I had no reason to think our Glasgow lecturers were more inspiring than in other technical colleges. It was

Alan and his friends who had made me feel that great new things could come from us, but I enjoyed suggesting that I had a city and an institution behind me.

"Of course," said Binkie thoughtfully, "some people have to be mindless tools. If our hammers refused to hit our nails because they were sorry for nails then nobody would have a decent roof over their head."

I said, "Men and women are not hammers and nails."

Binkie nodded and pursed his lips in a way which indicated perfect tolerance of my opinion and perfect understanding of why I held it. And I saw a world where most folk were ignorant wee nails, like Denny, being struck again and again by cleverly forged hammers, like me, in the hands of directors and designers and artists who were encouraged to be charming human beings by a few people, like Binkie, who found this an interesting way of making money. And these few folk thought they were producers! They really believed that without them roofs would not be built, crops planted, cloth woven or plays performed. And people agreed with them. All the actors, Scottish and English, knew that Binkie could not build a stage, or write a play, or light one, or act in one, but they reverenced him as A GREAT PRODUCER because he had once owned the whole of the West End and still had quite a slice of it. No doubt he also had theatrical judgment, but probably no more than the young English actor-director who was now acting as his adjutant-in-the-field, or Secretary-of-State-for-Scotland, or highly intelligent flunkey. What made Binkie a power was his wealth and the intelligence he used to keep it, and this intelligence was not necessarily his own. As Old Red once said, "Capital can always buy brains. Brains swarm to it like flies to a dungheap." Yes, intelligences go whoring after money more than bodies do, because we are not taught that it is whoredom to sell a small vital bit of our intelligence to people we don't like and who don't like us. The worst crime in the world is murder, but selling your intelligence comes close behind because murder follows it, gaschambers, Dresden, arms manufacture, napalm, body dumps and every sort of massacre. I now know that that sort of selling is exactly the great whoredom and mystery and manyheaded creature of the Apocalypse which the rulers and nations of the world worship to this day. Except in Poland. Recently some Poles refused to bow the knee, but I cannot possibly have seen that the world was like this in the early fifties.

In the year which followed The Conquest of Everest and The Coronation of the First Royal Great British Elizabeth I cannot possibly have seen that the world was like this. I did not know if Binkie's power was inherited like money or rented by money but I did recognise it. I recognised and admired and desired the power of this elegant, plump old man. I felt my mouth soften into the effeminate smirk which disfigured Rory's face, and when I noticed that, my small spark of dislike became hatred and my mouth hardened again. He turned and faced me with a courteous glance of mild inquiry and I wanted to lean forward and bite his nose off without in any way touching the rest of his body. This impulse was so astonishing that I could not move, I merely gaped and perhaps bared my teeth a little. I felt the English director's hand on my arm. He said urgently, "How would you go about expanding the resources of modern theatrical lighting?"

"Eh?"

"Modern theatre lighting. You spoke about expanding its resources. Were you talking randomly or had you something in mind?"

It was plain that if I did not suggest something interesting (in the theatrical sense of the word) the English company would feel they had patronised a gang of inarticulate, truculent louts. I said, "Stage-lighting today should be more positive in its use of shadow. Darkness could be as distinct a dramatic element as light is. With a little more invention we could use blocks and beams of it."

The English director said, "What exactly are you referring to?"

I said, "Imagine a big stage sticking quite far out into the audience from the . . . the . . . that square arch the curtains hang from."

"The proscenium."

"Thanks. On this stage we have people doing things in front of what is supposed to be a house, but the house is represented by a block of darkness. I will call it negative light instead of darkness, because the eye can always pierce the darkest shadow a little when there is light near by, but it couldnae pierce this black block. The block can contain whatever furniture you like, and actors who step into it become invisible. Yes, and we could surround the blocks with pillars of negative light which people could come out of or vanish into on cue. Then at the touch of a switch the negative and positive light zones are reversed. We see a well lit room surrounded by spotlights with people in them."

"Is this practical?" said Binkie.

"Certainly not. The concept of negative light is a recent one. But a team of people I know will make it possible in ten years, if you give us the money."

"And you are a lecturer in a Glasgow polytechnic?"

"No. I'm a second-year student in the Glasgow Royal Technical College founded by Professor John Anderson, author of *The Institutes of Physics*, in 1796."

"It sounds enchanting," said Binkie in his sleepy voice. I thought he had decided that the Scots, when not inarticulate and truculent, were a race of boastful fantasisers, but I felt friendly toward him now. My sudden conception of negative light had restored my confidence. I even had a notion of how to achieve it. I believed that after a few discussions of the problem with Alan I would be able to map out a research programme. I relaxed and became voluble, remembering a speculative article in one of Alan's old technical magazines, probably *The Scientific American*. I said, "If you are interested in more immediate practicalities I offer you the hologram. It is possible to project a small solid-looking image into an open space, an image people can view from every side but not touch, because nothing is there but reflection. With adequate funding my team, two years from now, will project on to a stage the solid-looking image of a big tree in the Amazonian rainforest. The branches will sweep down over the audience until they appear to touch the back row of the stalls. We could even project a pro, what did you call it? a proscenium with all those daft plaster cherubs and gilded twiddly bits, and a curtain that looks like scarlet velvet and seems to open, and private boxes on each side with posh people in them who lean out and even applaud at certain

moments. I am not talking about an image projected on a screen, don't think that, I refer to an image projected upon a space. Looked at from any angle in the auditorium it will appear three-dimensional. Looked at from the stage it need not appear at all, if we do not want it to. The actors would know the position of the illusion by marks on the floor. If one of them placed a kitchen stepladder a few inches behind the trunk of my big tree, and climbed up and stuck his head forward, the audience would see a living bodiless head stuck to the trunk of a tree twelve feet above ground."
"Stupid conjuring tricks!" shouted the writer, "Good theatre gives us men and women acting as if they are loving and governing and tricking each other and dying, yes dying! Aristophanes, Shakespeare and Ibsen didnae need these daft pyrotechnics and neither do we."
The success of his play had not changed the writer. He was as gloomy and critical as he had always been, so we ignored him as usual, though I thought Binkie gave him a sympathetic nod. I said to the English director, "These devices would be especially helpful to you. Think of the freedom you would have. You could enter any big hall which had a platform and in two or three hours, with the help of a single skilled electrician and his projectors, you could make it look like the inside of La Scala Milano. You wouldn't need the London West End then to put on a play in an expensive-looking setting."
The English director stared hard at the tip of his cigarette. The Scottish director suddenly guffawed. Binkie said, almost loudly, "Your device would certainly enable us to dispense with a lot of scene-shifters. But you have forgotten the seats. The audience like a lot of comfortable seats. Experimental theatre people always forget the audience."
I nodded at him approvingly. I said, "Correct. I forgot the seats, and my team, which does not yet exist, will take at least sixty years to project an image people can sit upon. Your profits are safe till the end of the century."

It is queer to think that I was perfectly sober when I said all this, or else said something very like it. I was only partly joking. I laughed at Binkie in a knowing way, daring him to take me seriously. He was old enough to have been wooed by several people using this gambit, but he looked slightly pained, I thought. He said vaguely, "It all sounds enchanting."

Judy stood up and spoke out decisively.

"Jock, I had better dance with you, because you are clearly a man with an important future. May I have the pleasure?"

As we edged between the tables toward the dancing floor I told her, "You Oxbridge lot are great wee managers."

She said, "Well, the conversation was becoming rather fraught."

"Did I annoy your friend?"

"O Binkie is too grand to be my friend. I suspect he's too grand to be anybody's friend. And he's far too grand ever to be annoyed, he knows it's a waste of time. Still, it would be a mistake to get on the wrong side of him."

The dance was the spasmodic jive sort so I tried to lift her off the floor and nearly succeeded. She said, "Better not. I believe Binkie has gone now so we can go back to the table and get deliciously sloshed."

At the table everyone was now chattering as excitedly as a class let out of school. The English director cried, "Jock, these solid mirage projectors and solid shadow projectors, are they possible or were you just imagining them?"

I said icily, "Since I imagined them of course they are possible."

He said, "That makes no sense to me. Can anyone here tell me what Jock means? Geoffrey, you keep in touch with science and dreary things like that, can you tell me what Jock means?"

He was looking at a friend who studied architecture. The friend said, "He means that science can solve any purely technical problem it recognizes. By the end of the century, for example, we may have men on the moon. Any adequately qualified, sufficiently funded research team which tackles the problem of projecting big holograms with portable equipment will eventually do so. But not in two years. Ten or twenty years, perhaps. Confess that when you said two years you were romancing."

I said stolidly, "I will not confess that. My team could do it in two years. My team will contain a genius."

They started laughing. I shouted, "Not me! Not me! I have a friend who is going to astonish you all!"
"Yes, genius can speed a team up," admitted the architect, "but genius is terribly lacking in team spirit. That's why we discourage it."
"You two are saying things which I have no wish to know. They terrify me," said the director, who seemed not terrified but very cheerful. He poured me a glass of wine. It occurred to me that I would not get very drunk if I drank only wine so I began drinking a lot of it quickly. We were all cheerful in an overstrained way which was soothed by alcohol. Binkie had been among us so we felt ourselves on the edge of a dangerously exciting future.

From the edge of a dangerously exciting future I looked forward to myself standing on a gantry over a space as vast as London, though it was also a stage and a television studio. My skills had enabled my friend Binkie to regain the whole of the West End, so we had gone on to take the North, South and East Ends, then the Centre, then the Provinces.
(Were you drunk again?)
And happy, because my projectors were equally effective outside the theatre. Our hologram navy was the most visually terrifying in the world, being based on a film of the British Spithead review in 1910. At the speed of light I could make it appear anywhere at any altitude, but we preferred moving it slowly at ground level. The steady advance of these huge dreadnaughts through the streets of Prague, or was it Budapest, had driven the Russian tanks out of Hungary, or was it Czechoslovakia, or both. In the same year they had mysteriously appeared in the South Pacific, sailed north through Chile, crossed the Andes and driven the hirelings of the American fruit company out of South America. Bombs and guns had no effect upon these ships, nor could they themselves do damage, but armed forces which tried to ignore them were isolated in vast negative light fields which blinded them long enough for the local patriots to win bloodless but practical victories.
(What happened next evening when Binkie saw the show?)
You ought to be more interested in world peace because I finally established it. Populations basked, undressed and

danced in the warm floods of light and music I poured upon them, Hollywood actresses parked their rocketplanes on the Thames embankment having crossed the Atlantic through a tunnel of rainbows cast by my projectors, Jane Russell, Jayne Mansfield, Marilyn Monroe yearned to meet me. Whoever was touched by my spotlight became famous, but I did not light only lucky people. My searchlights and cameras showed the bad schooling and housing of folk whose work was essential and the arrogance of public servants who behaved as if they were overlords. Social reform always followed these revelations, but like Binkie I preferred to stay out of the limelight. Even so I was a legendary figure. When the sun shone brightly the Londoners told their children, "The Scotch electrician is smiling again."

(What happened on the next night when Helen came to you?)

That is unimportant because actresses were not the only women who loved me. In order not to seem inhumanly grand I let myself be seduced by all of them just once, while never failing to fly up north for weekends and holidays, for that was where my wife and children lived. Yes, Denny and I had married at last. Our home was a six-room-and-kitchen Hillhead flat with oriel windows; also coalburning fires and quaint art-nouveau mantelpieces and beaten copper fenders, even in the lobby; also a wally-tiled close with carved bannisters on the stairs and the landings inlaid with four colours of geometrical mosaic. The whole world was astonished by my devotion to a plain wee woman in a Glasgow tenement, but the Scots understood me. They knew I was still one of them, even though my spotlight on corporal punishment had abolished the use of the belt in schools (chew on *that*, Hislop) even though I had refused to make Glasgow the capital of the British Commonwealth. "The centre of a properly lit land is everywhere," I had declared. "The exact spot in which our public servants confabulate is unimportant."

The truth was I did not want to be involved in politics. While working hard in every field of energy and communications I was helping my friend Alan establish the proper place and destination of man in the universe.

(What did you do when Brian was arrested by the police?)

Bear with me a while longer, God. It is true that I felt above and beyond myself when I imagined such things and here I am imagining them again. Yes, I feel almost your equal again as I survey the universe from my imaginary future, and of course this will lead to a fall again, but in this exalted state I glimpse an insight which, properly worded, will clear you for ever of those Stalinist crimes imputed to you by your most ardent admirers and which the intelligently decent have NEVER been able to thole. Allow me a few more overweening minutes then let me fall gently. With a parachute, please.

Alan was principal of the Glasgow Royal Technical College, originally founded by Professor John Anderson, author of *The Institutes of Physics*, in 1796. In his early days Alan had given the world the Caledonian sunmill, a delicate toylike structure of shaving-mirrors, coloured steel cubes, guitar-strings and a simple beam balance which, mounted on a chimney head, could supply a room below with all the domestic heat and light it needed at no cost. He now perfected the negative light probe, a delicate toylike structure of shaving-mirrors, coloured glass balls and copper wire which, attached to a common television aerial, allowed the owner of the set below to view any part of the universe above his house at any degree of magnification whatsoever. Mankind could now make an up-to-date map showing the position and features of every galaxy, star and planet which existed.
(What did the company think of you when Brian was released?)
Why have you no interest in physics? Negative light costs nothing to produce and has no rate of travel because its single infinite wavelength is identical with the span of the universal continuum, thus enabling it to operate simultaneously everywhere. Professional astronomers were too few for the survey we had planned. We needed amateurs, all the amateurs the world contained, so in every language we broadcast an appeal for helpers which was also a course of instruction in astronomy and in how to build the probe, use it, and record the findings. The only payment we offered was the satisfaction of discovering stars and planets never

before seen by the human eye and helping to complete the greatest work of scientific art conceived by the human mind: THE MAP OF EVERYWHERE. "Remember, the universe is boundless but continuous," said Alan at the end of the broadcast, "so don't stop discovering and recording until you see your own bum on the screen."

The people of the earth, most of whom had television sets by this date, responded a million-billionfold, especially children, housewives, invalids and the elderly. A crippled ten-year-old girl in a Cambodian brothel discovered the first completely negative constellation in which the void between the various bodies is the source of its light, heat and gravity. A team of Derry charwomen mapped a galaxy where energy operates in parallelograms, making cubical suns whose cubical planets skip from corner to corner of rectangular orbits. An anonymous member of the U.S.S.R. Supreme Praesidium sent word of The Cuckoo Cluster, a collection of dully smouldering orbs which revolve in the same path until one overtakes and absorbs the others, getting hotter and faster as it grows bigger until it explodes and breaks down into the same number of spheres trundling round the same dull track. As the blank spaces in THE MAP OF EVERYWHERE steadily filled up the worldwide enthusiasm for astronomy grew until it seemed that all humanity was stretching its neck and straining its eyes outward in search of something it longed for but was unable to find. At last each viewer, having pierced the continuum, saw upon the screen the bluewhite cloudmarbled globe of their own home and knew:

The world is the lonely living centre of the universe. The universe is a rich whirlpool of energy which coheres again and again into every conceivable body of gas and mineral, but only one of these bodies grows living fruit. The rest are not only devoid of thought, they collectively lack the resources to nourish one primrose, one blade of grass. The only life we will find on other worlds is the life we take there. And this is good news because,

MODERN SCIENCE CAN SOLVE ANY TECHNICAL PROBLEM IT RECOGNISES

therefore

WE CAN DOME THE CRATERS OF THE MOON AND GROW FORESTS IN THEM
and then
STRIP FROM VENUS HALF THE CLOUDS WHICH MAKE HER SURFACE A FACSIMILE OF ANCIENT HELL AND GIVE HER MOIST AIR RAINING AN OCEAN WHICH, STOCKED WITH PLANKTON AND WHALES, WILL COMPOSE A WARM PACIFIC PLANET WITH VOLCANIC ISLANDS WHERE SLOWLY NEW LIFE WILL TAKE ROOT
and then
HOLLOW THE LARGEST ASTEROIDS, LIGHT ARTIFICIAL SUNS IN THEM, ACCELERATE THEIR AXIAL ROTATION TO PRODUCE CENTRIFUGAL INTERIOR GRAVITY, BUILD HORIZONLESS GARDEN CITIES ROUND THE WALLS AND LET ADVENTUROUS GENERATIONS SAIL TO THE STARS IN THEM
because
WITHOUT FIGHTING OTHERWORLDLY HUNS, PLUNDERING OTHERWORLDLY AZTECS, KOWTOWING TO OTHERWORLDLY SUPERMEN, WE CAN CREATE ALL THE GOOD WORLDS WE EVER IMAGINED
and thus
LOVE, SEX, BIRTH, CHILDREN NEED NO LONGER LEAD TO POVERTY, FAMINE, WAR, DEBT, SLAVERY, REVOLUTION, THEY WILL BECOME OUR GREATEST GIFT TO THE UNIVERSE WHICH ENGENDERED US!
However
THE COST OF FERTILISING THE WASTE OF THE UNIVERSE, STARTING WITH THE MOON, IS SO GREAT THAT ONLY A RICH PLANET CAN AFFORD IT
so we must
EMPLOY EVERY LIVING SOUL TO FERTILISE OUR OWN DESERTS, RESTOCK OUR OWN SEAS, USE UP OUR OWN WASTE, IMPROVE ALL GROUND, NOURISH EDUCATE DELIGHT ALL CHILDREN UNTIL ALL ARE STRONG, UNAFRAID, CREATIVE,

PRACTICAL ADULTS WHO LOVE AND UNDERSTAND THE WORLD THEY LIVE IN AND THE MANY WORLDS THEY COULD LIVE IN
for it is technically possible to
CREATE A WORLD WHERE EVERYONE IS A PARTNER IN THE HUMAN ENTERPRISE AND NOBODY A MERE TOOL OF IT
yes God we can
BECOME GARDENERS AND LOVERS OF THE UNIVERSE BY FIRST TREATING OTHERS AS WE WISH THEY WOULD TREAT US AND LOVING OUR NEIGHBOURS AS OURSELVES
(What happened three nights later when you went home to Denny?)
FUCK OFF YA FUCKIN BASTARDING BAMPOT YE! LEA ME ALANE YE BLEEDN CUNTYE! YE ROTTN PRICKYE! Yes I'll tell you about that but not right now. Give me a bit more time. Please.

God.
I.
Think.
I.
Am.
Going.
To.
Weep.

Of course I will not weep. To our tale. Kings may be blessed but Jock was glorious, o'er all the ills of life victorious.

All were glorious round that table. We were leading lights who would soon dazzle the world. We were not jealous of each other. In a crowd as happy as ours those who shine brightest do so because the rest want them to, have fuelled them to. Radiance belongs to everybody. This struck me as an important discovery but when I tried to explain it everybody started laughing. The English director cried, "Admit it, Jock. You want the theatre to belong to the electricians." I said, "Naturally. How can I give my best to an organisation which is not mine? The writer thinks the theatre his because he writes the plays, the actors think it theirs because they perform them, Binkie thinks it his because he owns it, the audience think it theirs because they pay for it, and since your job is to join all the other people together you probably think the directors are the bosses of the show. Why can't the electricians be raving egoists too? Everyone who is essential to an organisation should be bosses of it. That is democracy."

"You technical people are far too bossy already," said the architect. "You've made my profession almost impossible. Architecture is the most essential of the arts and used to be the most splendid. The world's greatest buildings were once magnificent hollow sculptures which whole communities were proud to enter. Not now. Nowadays our designs are so restricted by plumbing regulations, lighting regulations, heating, ventilation and fire regulations that not even our geniuses, not even Lloyd Wright, Gropius or Corbusier have been able to make modern buildings look as good as they are useful."

"The fault is yours," I said, "you refuse to recognise that plumbing and wiring are as much architecture as walls and windows. It is ignorant snobbery for arty architects to think that technicians are not their equals and partners. The greatest social achievement of the last eighty years is in sanitary engineering. The U-bend, which seals our houses from the germs in the sewers, was invented eighty years ago and has saved more lives than penicillin, but who knows the inventor of the U-bend? Every city and town in Britain has a man-made river-delta under it which sends streams of pure water right to the top of every building, high and low, while shorterballs, I'm shorry, waterfalls, handy wee waterfalls gush out on every floor at the turn of a tap or pull of a plug. And instead of displaying these great clean systems proudly, like the roof-supports of the old Greek temples, you bury them like dirty secrets in walls and obscure closets. No wonder your art has become a matter of phoney façades."

"A lovely notion!" said the English director. "Imagine a wedding reception with the buffet spread between the crystal pillars of a plumbing system. We watch the turds of guests upstairs descending these shining columns in a welter of brown bubbles and amber pee, while we sip champagne and nibble small triangles of toast spread with gleaming globes of caviare."

All sorts of mixing and joining occurred in the club but that night I felt most of it was happening in my head. There seemed nothing in the universe I did not understand because my mother's cryptic silences, my father and Old Red's conversations, Hislop's poetry, the lectures at the Technical College, Alan's middenraking, the arguments of Alan's friends, even Denny's wish to understand geography, amounted to a complete and satisfying explanation of the whole. I was eager to pass this understanding on to my friends. I was sure it would do them great good. My idea was simple and single but even the women kept laughing at the words I used, and they, I felt, had more to gain from them than anyone else. "If universe cone or globe," I told Heldianjud, "which same thing really then dictorship, hiarchy because of topbottom, insideout, but no! Allcontinuum! Democracy!"

"Jock," shouted the English director, "you are becoming a bore."

"Must make clear then," I said, bathing in and clutching Judianhels hair which kept flowing away from me. "Shoot up far fast enough head crashes into own bum, fall fast enough down bum crashes on own head so why travel, no centre except where *we* are no matter *who* we are therefore need for infinite respect, infinite love or all makes no sense ken? Bodies × sympathy + a lot of space = democracy, I love ye, ken? Because we can all do what we like."

I noticed that the English director was standing up and bawling in the voice of an English sergeant-major.

"JOCK! SLAVE OF THE LAMP! LISTEN TO ME YOU ORRIBLE LITTLE MAN! I COMMAND YOU TO TRANSPORT THIS CELLAR WITH ALL ITS REVELLERS, AND SUPERSTRUCTURE, AND ROCK, AND CATHEDRAL, AND CRUDE OLD CASTLE, TO THE GARDEN OF THE EMPEROR OF THE DEMOCRATIC CHINESE PEOPLE'S REPUBLIC! SET US SAFELY DOWN THERE BEFORE DAWN BREAKS, GENIUS OF THE LAMP,

LEAVING NOTHING BEHIND BUT THE SMALL HAIRY MOLE ON THE INNER SURFACE OF JUDY'S LEFT THIGH."
He was taller than me so I stood on my chair and said, "This cannot be done because I have left my screwdriver upstairs, but anyone who keeps hold of their screwdriver can do anything, moreover"

At this point the chord of recollection snaps and I remember nothing more

NINTH NIGHT

before waking in bed with a feeling I became familiar with in later years. All my muscles ached but it was a refreshing ache, like the ache of having been born or of having done good exercise, yet my brain was uneasy. It suspected that I did not deserve to be born. My mattress was on a plank platform, scrubbed very clean, which bridged the well of the stair from the room below. I was wearing pyjamas and my clothes lay folded beside me as neatly as usual, though the socks were under the pile instead of on top. Beside the clothes was another small sign of derangement, my watch, which had stopped at half-past-eleven. I had failed to wind it up. Through a small high-up window I saw that the sky was the colour of late afternoon. The evidence was that, however intoxicated, I had left the company and gone to bed in decent order.

I got up, put on dressing-gown and slippers, took my toilet things and went to the least visited lavatory on the premises by the most roundabout route. Having carefully washed and shaved without being seen by anyone I returned to the closet and put on clean socks, underwear and shirt along with a jacket, waistcoat and trousers unworn since the last pressing. I knotted on a necktie, polished my shoes, then went downstairs with what I hoped was my usual air of alert self-possession. Though less than half full the restaurant was doing brisk business. I went behind the counter and poured myself a bowl of cereal and a mug of coffee. I carried them to our table where nobody paid me any attention.

They were discussing a newspaper article. Everyone seemed depressed or angry. Helen looked white and ill. She said, "Oh how could he write that? How *could* he write that?"
I asked what was wrong and they passed me the paper.

Under the headline **WOULD YOU LET YOUR DAUGHTER? MINISTER DENOUNCES COWLAY COMMUNE IN THE FESTIVAL FRINGE** was a photograph of the room which the helpers and performers used as a dormitory. It had been taken in poor light with an exposure that made it look shabby, dark and dirty. The story beneath began with the words, "How would you feel if you learned that your daughter was sleeping for nights on end in this huge barn-like chamber with thirty or forty men, most of them total strangers to her? Long-haired, bearded strangers with so-called *advanced* opinions about sexual morality and how society should be organised?"
This was written by a journalist who had recently spent a lot of time in our company. He was a cheerful, friendly soul and his paper had printed one of the first articles which had said that the club was an exciting, glamorous place. This was no longer news, so having learned of our sleeping arrangements (which nobody had thought to hide) he discussed them with a popular and easily shocked Church of Scotland clergyman who liked having his words broadcast through the press. The clergyman said, "This sort of example is leading thousands of young people down the slippery slope to perdition. I know my views are old-fashioned, but that cannot be helped. I got them from Jesus."
The journalist had then referred the matter to a more liberal clergyman who said that Christ taught that forgiveness of sin was a higher virtue than strict sexual continence. Having thus obtained a balanced religious view of the matter, the journalist had discovered the home addresses of the girls who used the dormitory and had phoned their parents to ask what *they* thought. Under the subheading A TERRIBLE SHOCK, Helen's mother was quoted as saying, "This comes as a terrible shock to us. Her father and I knew nothing about it. Perhaps Helen has been a little bit unwise, but I'm sure my daughter is doing nothing very wrong, really."

Under these words was printed the bottom part of the big photograph which had greatly upset Helen two days earlier. The caption said, "Nineteen-year-old Helen Hume as she appears with Rory McBride in the Cowlay Communists' political pantomime."

I reread the article carefully. It was cleverly written. It described a place in which fornication was conceivable, then quoted the words of one who, without knowing the place or people, assumed that multiple fornication was actual, then the words of someone who thought fornications were forgiveable, then the words of some anxious people who had also never seen the premises but were almost – but not wholly – convinced that *their* child was not fornicating. Yet not one libellous word stated that anyone was fornicating. Of course there must have been some lovemaking in the upper chamber, because a lot of mixing and joining happened in that club, but I am sure there would have been more if we had been using the North British Hotel. Communal sex is even less probable among the Scots than the private kind, which is why I had shifted my mattress into a closet.

After a long silence Helen said again, "How *could* he write that? I gave him my age and my address because I thought he would write nice things about us. I told him my parents had been upset by that photograph, and he said he would do his best to redress the balance. How *could* he write these things?"

"He makes his living by it," said the English director.

"That is the excuse German businessmen gave for manufacturing Zyklon B gas," said the Scottish director.

"Exactly," said the English director. "Exactly. Exactly. But this stuff isn't lethal gas, it's nothing but a cloud of foul language and in our business we learn to shrug that off. Three-quarters of what appears in the press is just a silly game. The pressmen know it's a game, they laugh at it themselves. So should the readers."

Helen said, "My parents have no sense of humour, I'm afraid, and neither have I. I don't think I can go on tonight. Cowlay Communist! My dad will murder me."

Her voice suddenly sounded like Denny's. She wept. Our

director laid an arm round her shoulders. She shrugged it off but allowed Diana to dry her tears with a handkerchief. Judy said in a matter-of-fact voice, "You must go on tonight. Because of Binkie, you know."

"Damn Binkie."

Judy turned to me and spoke as if opening a more cheerful topic.

"Did you sleep well, Jock?"

"Yes thanks."

"Who undressed you, by the way?"

I stared at her.

"Do you remember who put you into your pyjamas?"

I had to shake my head.

"Surely you remember the anal entry?"

"You're joking."

"The flagellation."

"Certainly not."

"The fellatio."

"What is fellatio?"

"Sisters!" Judy said to Diana and Helen in a tragic voice, "Our charms were wasted on this man. He doesn't remember a single thing."

I was confused. I said, "Do you mean that you er – ?"

She said, "Yes we put you to bed. You were amazingly articulate for a bit then you suddenly collapsed and went infantile. Men don't know how to handle a baby so we had to do it. By the way, who exactly is Denny?"

I stared at her again. She said, "You kept calling for Denny in the most heartrending tones while clutching as much of us as you could get your hands upon. Then you said angrily, 'I don't love you! You aren't Denny', and wept passionate tears."

Diana said, "I don't remember that. I remember him saying he was cold all the time. Even when we were tucking him in he kept whining about how cold he was, then he stopped and said in a perfectly sober voice, 'I am going to marry Denny.' Then you passed out, Jock."

This was disturbing news. Helen said, "You behaved disgustingly, Jock. We all behaved disgustingly. Especially *him*."

She nodded grimly at the English director who frowned

then said, "Careful, Helen. You'll end up believing that hypocritical reporter was telling the truth about this place."
"I think he was," said Helen, and started sobbing again.
Judy and the English director stood up. He said in a tired voice, "Who wants a hair of the dog?"
I went with them to the Deacon Brodie tavern where we met Brendan or perhaps it was Dominic Behan and I had several hairs of the dog that had bitten me so badly.

Helen did not withdraw from the show that night. Her performance at the start of it was shaky and nervous but by the interval she had picked up confidence and we felt everything was going to be all right. Shortly after the interval a bad thing happened. In order to keep a travelling but vertical spotlight on Helen I was moving stealthily along the gantry over her head when my foot slipped, the light crashed and burst against a girder, for a second or two I was dangling by my hands. The audience gasped then laughed and applauded as I swung myself up, screwed in a new bulb and continued as if I was perfectly resigned to accidents like these. But the laughter and applause were the wrong kind. Helen started speaking faster and faster, clearly wanting the play to end as soon as possible. She hardly let the other actors finish their lines before gabbling her own. Her vowels changed from posh English ows and aws to very flat ehs of a sort then common in the Glasgow Kelvinside district. Before the end of the play she stopped acting altogether and became nothing but a brave Scotswoman performing a distasteful duty. The audience no longer laughed. Only Rory's final speech gave it an opportunity to applaud.

Helen did not come forward to bow at the end. I remained up the scaffolding with my back to the audience even after I had put the house lights on, even after the public had filtered out. I hated myself. I did not want to be seen or heard by anyone, especially not by those in the company. I had ruined the show and did not know how to apologise. I fiddled with a junction box while Roddy, Rory and the director cleared up below in almost total silence. At one point one of them said, "I take it Diana is looking after Helen?"

"Yes."
A bit later someone muttered, "I doubt if Binkie found that very impressive."
"To hell with Binkie!" said our director too loudly and too cheerfully. "We don't need him. Before he turned up last night I thought he had died centuries ago. We can't expect to do equally well every night of the week, and we've been performing steadily for nine nights running – even a professional company would find that hard to sustain. Stop brooding up there, Jock. Come downstairs for a drink."
I said, "No drink for me tonight thankyou and I am not brooding. I'm checking connections. Some wires were wrenched."
"See to it tomorrow. Come for a coffee."
"No thanks. When I've finished working here I'm going straight to my bed."

When everyone had gone I went quickly to my closet, opened the fire-exit into Deacon Brodie's close, made a quick visit to the tavern and returned from it with a quarter-bottle of whisky. I got into bed, switched the light off, downed the whisky fast. I was an alcoholic novice in those days because that small quantity made me unconscious almost at once. I had several whirling and uncomfortable dreams. In one of them I was crossing a wet street which I suddenly noticed was covered by thousands of worms, so many that I had to stand perfectly still to avoid crushing them. They were the usual thickness but their length varied enormously. One, which was travelling very fast, was twenty or thirty feet long. I heard a stumbling noise and when I opened my eyes the wormy street vanished and I saw darkness. Someone was gasping for breath beside me. A hand, I think, brushed my leg. I switched on the light and saw Helen glaring at me wildly. I was so sure she had come to attack me for ruining her performance in the play that I raised my hands to protect my face. I took several seconds to notice she was not heaping insults on me. Her voice was loud and accusing as she said, "Jock, you keep looking at me all the time, you don't think I'm completely ugly and stupid and untalented and dreary do you? Do you? Do you?"
I said, "Er no, not at all. No."

She said, "Then show it", and sat on the edge of my mattress. She was acting as if she was drunk but it was a poor performance. I could see that she was perfectly sober. I realised what she wanted me to do and felt terribly depressed. I started explaining that I was not good at sex, that I needed to sleep a long time with a woman before I could make love, but she interrupted me by saying, "All right, you're throwing me out, but can I wait here for just five or ten minutes please? I know I'm imposing on you but will five minutes take too much of your time?"

I said, "Please stay here as long as you like."

She turned and embraced me, pushing her tongue deep into my mouth, and I was astonished to notice I had an erection. She withdrew a little and said, "Well?"

I gazed at her openmouthed. I nodded a couple of times. She quickly took off her blouse, jeans etcetera, got in beside me and lay perfectly flat. She said, "Right. Go ahead."

I cried out wildly, "This is impossible!"

She said, "Are you impotent or something?"

That angered me and I knew how to turn anger into lust. I mounted her and after some stiff shoving I got inside. Everything was over in two minutes. I rolled off her and lay feeling as destroyed under the waist as a bee which has lost both sting and abdomen. I put an arm round her, hoping for some warmth and gentleness, but she sat up and said, "I need a cigarette."

She sat crosslegged on the bed, draped her blouse round her shoulders, took a packet from her jeans pocket. The underblanket had slid partly aside exposing the shiny cold green plastic of the mattress. She said, "Cowlay Communist."

Her face looked stone hard and completely miserable. I wanted to tell her how wrong all this was but she obviously knew. She said, "Now, of course, you'll go about telling people I'm a whore."

"Certainly not."

"Then you'll go about thinking it."

"I certainly will not."

Whores give quick sexual relief to those who don't want affection or cannot obtain it, so I had been the whore. I started telling her this but she said, "Damn. I've left my lighter downstairs and damn, I need a smoke. Really *need* it."

She glared at me. I said drearily, "Where did you leave your lighter?"

"On the table, in my handbag. You know what my handbag looks like?"

I realised that some man, probably Brian, had made her feel a helpless outcast so she was consoling herself by using me as a servant. I got out of bed feeling glad she did not love me. I would only need to console her for a short period of time. I sighed and said, "I suppose I had better get properly dressed."

She said, "Don't be so stupidly Victorian. It doesn't matter what people do or think in this hellhole."

So in my pyjamas, slippers and dressing-gown I went looking for her lighter.

The hour was some time between two and five in the morning. As I crossed bare floors and descended stone steps I heard a harsh repetitive roaring which grew louder and louder. At the end of the great cellar Albert Finney and a friend, or else Tom Courtenay and a friend, were slowly riding a motorbike round and round in a circle. The only other people were the Scottish director, Diana and the English director. They were sitting together in a row but seemed to have big spaces between them. The Scottish director looked furtive, Diana looked lost but strangely smug, the English director looked stunned. I walked across to them and shouted over the racket, "I'm ashamed of myself. I ruined the show tonight. I am very sorry."

They stared at me blankly. The Scottish director shouted, "What?"

I repeated my apology. The English director shouted, "The show. Yes, but a lot has happened since then. Never mind about the show."

After a pause I shouted, "Has anyone seen Helen's handbag?"

They found it on a chair. I bade them good night and went upstairs. I learned later that after the show Binkie had told Diana, through the agency of the English director, that he would like her to audition for a small part in a London show, a show in which the English director had been promised a larger part. Diana was so delighted that she told

Brian, and Brian suddenly realised she and the English director were lovers. His grief at this discovery was so huge that Helen was forced to realise that he and Diana had also been lovers. It is possible too that Helen envied Diana's success with Binkie. Certainly Rory envied Diana's success with Binkie, because his grief at Binkie's neglect of him was so spectacular that Roddy decided that Rory and Binkie had been lovers, and threatened suicide. At this point Judy, who was also the English director's lover, suddenly slapped his face, said something astonishingly obscene about him and his Scottish connections, and walked out followed by the rest of the English company and their friends. Then Helen set off upstairs with an ominously deliberate tread, I suppose to seduce me, while Rory and Roddy unexpectedly went to a party together leaving the three doublecrossers to commiserate.

Helen was not in the closet when I got back upstairs. I was relieved but also worried, so I visited the well-publicised dormitory. The wall facing the door had a row of uncurtained windows admitting some light from the night sky and the streetlamps of the West Bow. I saw a bare expanse of floor with, to right and left of it, a row of mattresses supporting quiet bodies in sleeping bags. I saw Helen's mattress was occupied so I tiptoed over to it. On a large suitcase placed flat like a tray lay her folded clothing, a toothbrush, a book and the packet of cigarettes. I respected her for laying out her things, in a distraught hour, as neatly as I would have done. I was placing the handbag very cautiously beside the suitcase when I noticed she was not asleep. From deep inside her sleepingbag came muffled but unmistakable sobbing. I felt a pang of affection for her, because she was not really a stony woman. I stooped and gently patted the contour of her shoulder and murmured, "Don't worry, Helen."

The sobs stopped and her tearwet face surfaced among folds of the bag like the face of a nearly drowned woman emerging from black water. I had never seen her so beautiful. She whispered, "I'm sorry, Jock."

I smiled at her and whispered, "See you tomorrow."

I returned to my bed and fell asleep at once. Helen's apology had restored my confidence. I was now sure that the worst possible things had happened to the company, and that the company would survive them.

TENTH NIGHT

I woke very fresh and early next morning and saw that the sky through the little window was clean pale blue. It struck me that since the start of the show I had seen nothing of Edinburgh except the inside of the Deacon Brodie, which explained my recent unhealthy frame of mind. I arose, washed, shaved and dressed, feeling glad I had at least maintained clean habits in a place where they could easily have slackened. Then I went a walk. It was yet another sunny windy day, the weather that August cannot always have been as windy and sunny as I remember it. I walked again down that High Street which has half of Scotland's ancientest buildings on it, or seems to have. In those days there were fewer galleries, souvenir shops and gift shops, and the middle classes had not reoccupied the old tenements. Projecting pulleys from fifth, sixth and seventh-floor windows held out washinglines across the courts and closes, and I seem to recall skirts and pants flapping like flags over the High Street itself, but surely that was illegal? Opposite the main gate of Holyrood I saw a wee general-goods store of the sort that sold liquorice straps, the *Sunday Post* and Will's Wild Woodbine cigarettes in green and gold paper packets of five. A very old man sat on the shop windowledge, hands crossed upon a stick planted between his legs. He wore a hookerdoon bunnet, smoked a short clay pipe and looked thoroughly at home. I was sure that when the queen was in residence she often saw him from the palace windows, for nowhere else in Britain did the royal and the ordinary come so close. For no sensible reason this thought greatly cheered me.

I crossed the palace yard to the south gate and followed the road through a meadow to a small loch with swans. I climbed up past a bit of ruin to the end of the Salisbury Crags and walked along the top of these. I descended through grassy dells to the steep side of Arthur's Seat, then toiled straight up until I reached, and leaned breathless against, an indicator table beside the tip of the cone. Great spaciousness again. A few white mammal-bellied clouds dandered like plutocrats across the blue floor of the sky, and the reeky old city and many sorts of town and village and farmland were below me, and bleak hills edging the borders behind me, and the blue mountains edging the highlands in front, and the firth between them widening with islands and ships to the sea. Was Ben Nevis and Ben Lomond and Tinto Hill visible that day? Not likely, but I think the indicator pointed to them as if they were. Glasgow was hidden by the moors beyond Bathgate and I regretted this, because it was only forty or fifty miles away. I realised that Scotland was shaped like a fat messy woman with a surprisingly slender waist. A threestranded belt of road, canal and railway crossed that waist joining Edinburgh and the ports facing Europe to Glasgow and the ports facing Ireland and America. And the woman was rich! She had enough land to feed us all if we used her properly, and sealochs and pure rivers for fish-farming, and hills to grow timber on. Her native iron was exhausted, but we had coalbeds which would last another two centuries, and a skilled industrial population who could make anything in the heavy-engineering line. All we needed were new ideas and the confidence to make them work, and Scotland had Alan and I and many like us who could make practical realities out of any number of new ideas. The dramatic disaster of the previous evening came to mind and I grinned because drama is unimportant. But I was glad to have learned about theatrical lighting. If I ever got interested in television (television could easily become an important industry) then the experience would be useful. I was also glad to have met Binkie, for in trying to impress him I had become inventive and voluble in an unexpected way. The negative light concept now seemed improbable but the hologram was not. It would require the development of narrow but intricately structured lightbeams. Electromagnetics held the solution to that problem and such beams would be useful in many more fields than entertainment. I was young, I was learning, I belonged to a splendid country, I was on the edge of an unforeseeable future but I knew it would be a great one. I ran downhill by the easy gradient, taking great leaps to work off my exhilaration.

I walked round a lot of Edinburgh that morning, avoiding places where I would meet people I knew. I saw some splendid early engines in the university museum, climbed the Scott monument, then lunched on a pie and pint in a basement in Hanover Street. The bar was crowded except where three men stood in a small open space created by the attention of the other customers. One had a sombre pouchy face and upstanding hair which seemed too like thistledown to be natural, one looked like a tall sarcastic lizard, one like a small sly shy bear. "Our three best since Burns," a bystander informed me, "barring Sorley of course."

I nodded as if I knew what he meant then went out and bought a picturecard view of the castle. I dispatched it to Denny from the central post-office with a message saying that I loved her and missed her and would be home in four days. I may even have mentioned marriage. I hope not, but it's possible. My experience with Helen the night before had put me off the idea of casual sex. I felt friendlier toward Helen since her seduction and apology. I even admired her for it, but I never wanted to lie with her in bed again.

The club was quieter than usual when I returned. I sat drinking coffee beside Roddy, Rory and the writer who were also quieter than usual. I said, "Where are the girls?"

Roddy said, "Helen's gone home to her parents. I expect Diana's at the police station again but that won't do any good."

I said, "Helen home? Diana police station? Why?"

The three stared at me as if I had asked what country we were in. Roddy said, "Surely you know that Brian's been arrested?"

My imagination took a flying leap. I said, "Do you mean these paintings were valuable after all?"

"Yes, they're worth thousands. But that's only part of it."

In the early forenoon the police had come to the club, probably because a newspaper had hinted that it was a bad place, and because policemen are paid to arrest badness.

After questioning some members of the staff, and looking into every room, and finding nothing criminal (for there was nothing criminal to find) they asked to see the club books, in order to take them away and have them examined by experts. They said the process might take two or three days. The practical radical reminded them that he could not legally open his club without his books, and since it was only operating through the festival, a closure of two or three days would either bankrupt him or make him unable to pay all his helpers. The police said this was unfortunate, but that if his books were in order he would certainly get them back in two or three days. This was before the days of the cheap photocopier. The practical radical asked permission to accompany his books to the station so that, if experts had no immediate use for them, he could copy out entries with the help of a friend. The police said yes, so Brian and a portable typewriter accompanied the practical radical to the police station, because Brian knew how to type and was equally keen for the club to open that night. Shortly after they left, one of the landlords of the club premises arrived with his lawyer – their curiosity had also been stimulated by the newspaper article. They were surprised to find the club occupying twice or thrice the area agreed upon, and appalled at the additions to the portraits, which were indeed by Raeburn. They demanded to see the individuals who had authorised all this. Rather than direct them to the police station everyone denied knowledge of their whereabouts, but said they would be back before evening, and would contact them at the first opportunity. The landlord and lawyer went away in very bad tempers. Diana ran to the police station for instructions and was told that Brian and the practical radical were now locked in the cells for assaulting the police, resisting arrest, and wilfully destroying public property. She was not allowed to speak to them because she was not a lawyer, and because they were receiving medical treatment for injuries sustained while committing the second and third of the crimes charged to them. Diana returned to the club with this news, whereupon Helen announced that she was sick and tired of all this; she could not take any more; she was going home to her mother and they need only phone her if they wanted her for something really important. And she packed her things and left.

The rest of us were also greatly disturbed, though when Brian came to tell the whole story we learned that nothing queer had happened. On reaching the police station the radical and he were given a table in the corner of a busy office. He typed, the radical dictated, and after an hour they stopped to calculate. They found that if they worked continuously until the club was due to open they would copy fewer than half the entries, so their work was useless. They explained this to the sergeant in charge of the main desk, and pled to be allowed the loan of their books during the late hours when the club was busiest, since no professional expert would want them at such times. The sergeant explained that he had no authority to allow this, and neither had anyone else in the station. This news made Brian and the radical talk faster and louder. They repeated what they had already said but larded it with irony, sarcasm and threats of legal action. Brian said that not even the police were superior to the laws that protected the freedom of Scottish citizens. He and the radical were excited by a powerful sense of injustice. They thought that because they had done nothing wrong they were perfectly safe, which was itself a wrong assumption. They waved pointed fingers at the sergeant, which was a technical assault, so he charged them with assault. On the way to the cells they moved slightly faster or slower than the policemen escorting them wished, so they fell down and badly bent the metal frame of a wastepaper basket. But no bones were broken, and the bruises needed only superficial doctoring. The chain of events which dragged them into the cells was inexorably commonplace.

So that night we put a sign on the main entrance announcing that through unforeseen circumstances the club would be closed until further notice, then we barricaded ourselves inside and sat in glum little groups listening, as the evening wore on, to the hammering on the door of angry members demanding the return of their fees. I felt a huge frustration, a great desire to be doing something positive and practical.

The frustration was partly sexual. Helen had aroused but not satisfied me and I was desperate to enter Denny again. Around me were many dour people becoming stolidly drunk with no prospect of wit or exuberance. I said to the remnant of the company, "I tell you what I will do tomorrow. I have been paid for the work I've done here – I don't suppose you have?"

They had not. I said, "Right. If Brian and Helen don't come back tomorrow afternoon I will dismantle the theatre and return the scaffolding to the firm which lent it. I will also pay rental on a van so that Roddy and Rory can return the lights and properties to Glasgow."

After a silence someone said, "Why the hurry?"

I said, "I see no hurry in that action. I dislike waste, that's why I'll do it. Between bad publicity, police harassment, angry lawyers, angry landlords, angry customers, destroyed masterpieces, an injured director and a missing leading lady the show has now no chance at all. Hanging on here is a waste of time, energy and money. The police are going to keep those books for at least another couple of days, so even if the club does manage to open again, and even if Helen and Brian do come back to us, we will only have one other performance, a performance in which the cast will again outnumber the audience. Let's not descend to that."

Diana said, "You are not the director, Jock, you are our electrician. Nothing may be as definite as you think. We should do nothing until Brian gets back."

ELEVENTH NIGHT

But by three o'clock next afternoon Brian had not returned and I was prepared to wait no longer. I phoned the firm which had lent us the scaffolding. It had some spare men who could pick it up within the hour. They were even prepared to help dismantle it. I said, "Come on over."

With the help of the Gorbals Young Communists, who were also sick of doing nothing, we unscrewed and unclamped and lowered and stacked while watched in perfect silence by Roddy, Rory, the writer and Diana. My work-team was efficient. By five o'clock all poles, clamps and planks had left the premises. I removed my overalls. I washed. I joined the silent company at the cellar table. My body was pleasantly relaxed from the afternoon's exertion. I knew people were displeased with me, but knew that feeling would pass because I had acted sensibly.

Ten minutes later we were roused by a cheer from people at the end of the cellar near the door. The practical radical and Brian were entering with sticking plaster on their faces and bright determined grins. Brian came straight over to us.
"All right, darlings!" he said with all his old swagger. "Sorry for the hiatus but now we're ready to roll again. Business as usual tonight."
Diana said, "You mean the club can open?"
"Yes. They gave us the books back when they let us out two hours ago. The desk sergeant said, 'Here, do you want these things? They're no use to us,' and handed them over."
"What about the charges?"
"Our lawyer says that if we plead guilty to police assault they'll drop the bit about resisting arrest and damaging the wastepaper basket. It seems that the most we're liable to is a five-pound fine, but we may be let off with an admonition if we act apologetic enough."
"What about the paintings? And the landlords?"
"We've just come from the landlords. They've been very reasonable. I told them that the Raeburns had been vandalised with poster paint, which washes off very easily. And the club is going to pay rent for the extra space we've grabbed, so everything's fine. Would someone get me a very strong coffee? I feel I deserve it. Where's Helen by the way?"
"She's gone home to her parents."
"Well for Heaven's sake phone her! We need her for the show tonight. In fact don't just phone her, tell her we're coming to collect her and do it. Jock, she trusts you, you go and get her. Her folk stay in Cambuslang, it's only an hour away by train. Why is everybody looking so glum?"
I told him what I had done. He sat down at the table and said, "All of it?"
"Yes."
"Stage *and* auditorium?"
"Yes."

"Oh my God. What time is it?"
"Too late to get the scaffolding back. Everything's shut, you see. I'm sorry, Brian. I'm sorry, everyone."

Brian sat still for a long time. His only signs of pain were a few deep sighs. It occurred to me that he was the only one among us who had loved the whole show. The actors, the writer and I loved the show for what we gave to it, but he had loved the whole thing, and now he just sat sighing and shaking his head slightly. Diana sat beside him and laid her arm on his shoulder as tenderly as a fine doctor laying a bandage on a wound. He smiled slightly and said, "I'm all right, Diana. I'm all right."
I wanted to tell him that first thing tomorrow I would get back all the scaffolding, renting it myself if need be, but that would have been a phoney suggestion. Stage and auditorium had taken four days to erect. It just might be put up in one day if everybody co-operated, but who would have the energy to act after that? Certainly Helen would not. I said firmly to nobody in particular, "I have acted hastily and foolishly."
"Yes," said Brian, "yes I think so too. But thanks for the help you've given us. I hope the pay was sufficient. You've done rather better out of the show, financially speaking, than the artists, but that's usual, isn't it, for technicians? I'm sorry you ended by dropping us in the shit – "
"He's a mediocrity, that's his problem!" shouted the writer.
"Not always," said Brian, "not to start with. But he's probably tired by now. So am I. So are we all. Come to think of it, I dropped us in the shit too, by losing my temper in a police station. Most unwise. Let's go back to Glasgow."
"This is stupid!" shouted the writer. "You don't need a lot of poles and planks to put on a play, you don't need him – " he pointed at me in a way which demonstrated why pointing is a technical assault – "He ruined our last performance by his stupid tricks with a handheld spotlight. All a good play needs is a room, an audience, your talent and my words. We have these. The talent and the words are inside your heads. Draw a space for the action with chalk lines in the middle of the floor. Place mattresses round for the audience to lie, kneel or sit on. Get them settled and act! Act! This is an

opportunity for my play to be performed as it should be performed, without a lot of contraptions and paraphernalia and stupid bastarding glamorous magic machinery."

"A very daring concept," said Brian, "but I doubt if the public is ready for it. I know I'm not."

That evening Brian and the writer and I went back to Glasgow by train. Roddy and Rory had decided to stay at the club till the festival ended. I had given them vanhire money to return the remaining equipment to Glasgow whenever they liked. I now felt that, financially at least, I was now no luckier than the rest of the company, excepting Brian. Brian had legal expenses and perhaps a fine to pay, but he recognised that the fault was his own. Diana also remained in Edinburgh, I suppose to see the English director again. She accompanied us to Waverley station and at the barrier kissed Brian, and even the writer, with very great warmth, but she wholly ignored me. I was sorry, because before today I had felt that Diana was my best friend in that company.

On the train the only person who said much was the writer, who would sometimes stare out of the window and make a cryptic remark for no apparent reason, though it was always aimed at me.

"Wee hard men!" he muttered as the train pulled out of Falkirk. "The curse of Scotland is these wee hard men. I used to blame the English for our mediocrity. I thought they had colonised us by sheer cunning. They aren't very cunning. They've got more confidence and money than we have, so they can afford to lean back and smile while our own wee hard men hammer Scotland down to the same dull level as themselves."

Brian said wearily, "Leave Jock alone will you? He was one of us before the journalists and the police put their boots in."

I said, "Thanks Brian."

His defence disturbed me though the writer's remark had not. Criticism always fails when it tries to upset someone by linking them to a national group.

I said goodbye to Brian (not the writer) at Queen Street

station, and did not see him again for ten or fifteen years or could it be twenty (yes it could be twenty) years. I decided to be extravagant and take a taxi, yes a whole taxi for myself, though there would have been plenty of room for my two big suitcases on a tramcar. O, I yearned for Denny. I was glad now that the Edinburgh business had ended so soon and we could be together again. I felt in my bones how delighted she would be to see me three days sooner than expected. In spite of my burdens I raced upstairs, opened the flat's front door, dropped the cases and twisted the handle of my room shouting, "I'M BACK DENNY!"

The door stayed shut. I knew it was not locked, because only an inner bolt ensured privacy when someone inside wanted that. I was perplexed by the door's resistance. I seemed to hear movement yet nobody opened it for me. I panicked without knowing why. I certainly did not imagine what I eventually discovered, I probably imagined Denny on the floor in some sort of fit. I stood back, then ran and struck my right heel against the spot with the bolt behind. The door sprung in. I entered and saw my landlord standing on the hearthrug.

His appearance puzzled me for he had very large testicles and no apparent penis. This was an optical misreading. His penis was not evident because it was erect and pointing at me, not because I had aroused it. Someone nude and female crouched on the rug behind him. He looked foolish because he wore neatly polished shoes and anklesocks with a pin-striped shirt, collar and waistcoat. The woman behind him, Denny of course, was not completely nude either. She wore a skirt I recognised with unfamiliar net stockings and high-heeled shoes. I think I said in a vague way, "Aye of course. This is it. Yes indeed."

Denny started making the same intolerable whining sound she had made when I last saw her. What should I have said?

I should have politely allowed the landlord to leave us alone, because he was eager to do that. I should then have made us both a cup of tea, and sat beside her, and talked kindly and reasonably. "Denny," I should have said, "I hope you do not love that man, because he is not able to love you like I do. He needs sex but he does not need you, and it is you who I need – and sex too of course. So from now on we had better stick together. This should be easy because I don't think you love that man, I think you were just doing a bit of whoring because you felt lonely. You probably are a wee hoor, sometimes. So am I. I've been whoring too, but it isn't as much fun as the publicity suggests, so I'll stick with you if you don't walk out on me.

"But there must be changes, Denny!" (I should have said). "You've got to stop hiding from the world in this wee room of ours. We must visit people. Take me to see your relations – they can't be all as nasty as you say – and you can come and meet my father and mother. Social shocks will be experienced by one and all, because like nearly everyone in these fucking islands you and I and our nearest and dearest are snobs, Denny. But true decency and intellience are not destroyed by social shocks, Denny, they are exercised and strengthened by them. And you must come and meet Alan and his friends, who are not snobs because they are interested in learning about the world, and real learners find snobbery a waste of time.

"Moreover, Denny" (I should have said), "let me teach you to cook a decent meal. If you learn to do that I will clean up afterwards because I like a tidy room. Careful cooking takes time but it's fun when you do it properly, and if you get it wrong I will only spank you if you ask nicely for it. And now can we go to bed please? I have been very lonely without you."

I said none of that. It did not occur to me. My head had a dull humming inside which made speaking and thinking difficult. I looked absentmindedly round the room at my most essential possessions: books, drawing instruments, an alarm clock. They were not much. My clothes and toilet things were packed in the two cases outside. There was also a radio and dishes and cooking utensils, but Denny was welcome to those. My third suitcase, an empty one, lay on top of a wardrobe. I took it down and put the books,

instruments and clock inside. I doubt if Denny saw what I was doing. Her hands covered her face, she rocked her body to and fro making this continual irritating keening sound, yes it was her keening which made clear thought impossible, made it absolutely necessary for me to get away. Our landlord hopped about on one foot and then the other, pulling on first his underpants and then his trousers and gabbling this sort of thing: "looks bad but not what you think not serious at all she doesn't care for me really you don't know how lucky you are crumbs from a rich man's table yes crumbs from a rich man's table I've been picking up I mean you didn't even write to her not one postcard till today what do you think you're doing? What do you want that for? That's mine."
My problem was to carry three suitcases with two hands. I saw a striped necktie on the bed. I picked it up and tugged it to test its strength. The landlord thought I meant to strangle him because he retreated behind Denny who uncovered her face and went quiet. That was a relief. I knotted the tie in a loop round the handle of the suitcase and slung it from my shoulder. I said, "Don't worry, Denny. You still have a man to look after you."
She screamed like a steam whistle. I bolted. I charged across the lobby, flung the front door open, swung the two other cases and myself on to the landing and slammed the door behind me. I leapt downstairs with the third suitcase banging against my hip. The screaming did not seem to diminish with distance. It was a sequence of screams, each short and identical, each divided from the next by the same short space of frantic breath. The screams sounded louder when I got into the street. A couple stopped and stared openmouthed from the opposite pavement. As I ran towards the underground I realised that each scream was a word, my name, repeated again and again. 'She must faint if she keeps that up,' I thought, 'Oh God let her faint now please.'
But she had not fainted when I turned the corner and for a time I heard a distant *Jeek! Jeek! Jeek!* behind the footsteps and clanging trams on Byres Road.

Goodbye Denny. I never learned what became of you. When the Technical College reopened I did not revisit the refectory in case you were there, for I was about to become a married man. When friends told me you were not there I still did not go to the refectory in case the women you had worked beside gave me painful news of you, or worse still, asked me what you were doing. A lot later I met someone who lived in our lodgings a year after I left. He had never heard of you but he told me something surprising about the landlord. He became a skydiver. In the sixties he joined a club whose members leapt from aeroplanes and fell great distances before opening their parachutes. He died in the highlands when his parachute did not open in time, a strange death for such a neat, orderly, legal young man. My informant was an officer in the Royal Air Force and a very posh type indeed – or he pretended to be. He said, "It wasn't his class of sport, you see. His social background was, well, not quite top drawer. His father was a chartered accountant of lowly origins so the son joined the club to prove he could be one of us. It was a very very sad business. That type always makes a mess of things."

So the landlord was the second man I knew who died by falling from a height, and I will never discover what you did when you stopped crying my name, Denny.

I arrived on Alan's doorstep and asked if I could stay with him until I found another room. He said, "Of course, come in", but when I told him what had happened he nodded thoughtfully and placed an ancient typewriter on the kitchen table. He started reducing it to its components so methodically that I began to feel I did not exist for him. I said, "You are not very sympathetic."

He said, "I thought you and Denny loved each other. You looked as if you did."

I said, "I thought so too, till an hour ago."

He said nothing. I said, "What would you do if you found Carole in bed with . . . with me, for instance?"

He said, "I'm not sure. I would probably thump her and kick you out. But I doubt if I would cut communications with either of you. I have no real pride you see."

I said, "I have no taste for physical violence."

He shrugged. I felt exhausted. The sun had not yet left the sky but too much had happened since I had wakened that morning in Edinburgh. I unpacked and spread my sleeping-things on a sofa, got between them and slept.

I dreamed I was a redhot demon raping Denny among the flames of Hell. She screamed and beat my face with her fists, and I awoke and found I was beating my face with my fists. I lay till dawn in a state of petrified longing for her, yet it never occurred to me to return to her. The thought of her half-nude and doing enjoyable things with that half-nude lawyer made me groan aloud. I was rotten with rotten pride. When I got up next morning I was still exhausted but determined to find a place of my own. Instead of seeking a new place I returned to the flat kept by the respectable lady on Paisley Road West. I asked if she had a room to let. She asked why I needed one, and why I had left her premises ten months earlier. In a low, monotonous voice I said that I had gone to live with friends who were not as I had thought. I had the previous evening discovered them engaged in an activity which, though not criminal, was of a sort I would not insult her ears by describing. While saying this I almost believed I was an innocent country lad appalled by the corruption of the big city. The respectable lady softened at once. She said that since I had at last learned the value of a respectable home she would not bar me from one: she had a spare room, and it would be mine.

A dull time began. I still visited Alan's house but was no longer at ease there. Alan certainly had great natural talents but why did he surround himself with charlatans and eccentrics and bores? I think now that I was disappointed with myself and therefore disliked folk who were still hopeful. My disappointment was partly sexual. Once again I had no woman acquaintances and did not know how to make any. So when Alan said, "A friend was looking for you the other day", and handed me a note from Helen, I felt a spurt of hope. The note gave me her phone number and suggested we meet for a chat. I phoned at once and thought she answered. I said, "Hullo Helen. Jock here."
The voice said, "Exactly who is speaking?"
"Jock McLeish. Could I speak to Helen Hume please?"
"Just wait there please."

I realised I had been talking to her mother. Then Helen spoke and suggested that she come to my lodgings. I said, "That would be awkward. My landlady doesn't approve of female visitors. Let's meet in a pub."
"No thankyou Jock, I saw enough of you in pubs during the festival. Let's meet in a tearoom. Where do you live, by the way?"
I told her my address and she suggested we meet in Miss Rombach's at the foot of Hope Street. Her tone was businesslike. I asked if she had heard from the other members of the company. She said she would tell me what she knew when she met me and hung up. I felt chilled. She had not used the tone of a friendly girl talking to a former lover.

The sight of her at the tearoom table also chilled me. She was well dressed, elegant and handsome as ever but in a "please don't touch me" way I had not noticed before. While the waitress was bringing tea she said almost nothing at all. I said, "Have you heard from Diana recently?"
"Yes. She's in London. She's pregnant."
"O."
"So am I."
"O?"
"And I don't know what to do."
I thought about it. The only possibilities were abortion, marriage or adoption. I feel, "It must be very difficult for you. How does the er, father feel?"
"The father?"
"Brian."
"You are the father."
"But Brian and you were . . . Surely it was Brian and you who were . . . ?"
"Yesyes Brian and I were lovers, but not lovers in any way you would understand. If you must know the truth, I was a virgin before you did what you did."
I felt inclined to laugh. Helen not only sounded as if she was acting, she sounded like a poor actress in a very poor play. I was sure she was telling the truth because nobody lies about such important things, but when she said, "So what can I do?" I wanted to tilt my chair on to its two back legs, hook

my thumbs into the armholes of my waistcoat and say with an American accent, "Any damn thing you like, honey. Any damn thing you like."

But she stretched a hand to me across the tablecloth, I saw tears in her eyes, I took her hand in mine and thought hard. Abortion was illegal and dangerous. Marriage, no no no. She did not love me, I did not love her. I said, "The child should be adopted. I hear there are waiting lists of childless people who want to adopt unborn children."

"Yes I've heard that too. But who will pay for it? You see the neighbours and my relations must never find out. Father and mother are absolutely firm about that. They will die, they will kill me if anyone else finds out. So I must go away to a hotel in the south of England before I become noticeable, and then go into a nursinghome, and that will cost a lot of money."

"Your parents have decided this?"

"Yes but dad, I mean my father, has had a very difficult life. He's always been careful with money so he doesn't see why he should pay for anything. And if you look at the business from his viewpoint, why should he?"

She was staring straight at me. Without moving her head she slid the pupils of her eyes sideways for a moment, and without moving my head I realised that three men at a nearby table were watching us. Could the oldest of them be her father? I stared a question. She nodded slightly and whispered, "Yes, I'm sorry Jock. I'm sorry."

There were tears in her eyes and of course if they spilled out the men would think I was being brutal to her. But they were out of earshot so although my knees trembled I tried to be reasonable. I whispered, "I can't pay for hotels and nursinghomes, I have only my grant to live on."

"What about *your* father?"

"He isn't a rich man, he's a collier. A miner."

"Miners are rich aren't they? The newspapers keep telling us that. Jock, hold my hand again, just to stop me screaming. I hate the way I'm talking to you, it's not my way, it's dad's way."

I also was on the verge of screaming. I felt that my life was sinking from one level of nightmare to another. I held her hand in silence and even got some comfort from this. At last I said, "Do you feel any better?"

"A bit."

"Listen, I must go away and think. You must let me go away and think about things very carefully for a while."

"How long?"

"A week."

"Oh God a whole week!"

"I need a week to find out about money and . . . and . . . other possibilities."

"What possibilities?"

"Not abortion. Not abortion, I promise you Helen."

Abortion must have been her worst fear. Some years later she told me that her father had discovered a safe but expensive abortionist he would have sent her to if I had been willing to pay. She now sighed with relief, dabbed her eyes with a hanky and managed a sad smile. She said on a conversational note, "Actually Jock, if you decide on marriage it might not work out too badly. You're quite kind and dependable. I'm neither of these, but if I try hard I may not upset you too much."

I wanted to escape from this woman. I said, "How can I get away? I don't want to talk to your father."

She said, "I don't want him to talk to you. He can be astonishingly antisocial when he's roused. I think that if I sit here while you take the payslip to the cashdesk he won't follow you. And when you've paid you can walk right out through the door. But we'd better act like friends before we separate."

She gave me her hand again and I shook it wildly. I walked as straight to the cashdesk as my trembling knees would allow, and paid, and left.

Outside I stopped myself from running across Hope Street against the traffic lights and jumping into the first taxi in front of Central Station. I walked back to my lodgings telling myself that in this world men never chased other men along city streets, knocked them down and kicked them until they agreed to marry their daughters. I looked behind only once while going over King George V Bridge, and nobody seemed to be following.

I walked the floor of my room in huge agitation. Nothing I had just been told made reasonable sense so my reason could make nothing of it. How could one or two not very enjoyable minutes make a whole new human being? Helen's pregnancy had nothing to do with me, except that I had caused it. But how could I tell an angry father that his daughter had used me like a whore, discarded me and then proposed marriage? That was no foundation for a happy family life, adoption was the answer. Only money, my parents' money could save me from a hideous loveless marriage. Tomorrow, no, tonight I would return to the long town and tell them the whole story. But how could I? We had never talked about sex, never mentioned our emotions to each other. Would they believe I had been used like a whore? If they did, why should they think that a reason for giving me money? But if I simply said I had got a girl pregnant they would surely expect me to marry her. Perhaps I should run away to London and get a job as a bus-conductor. Perhaps I should emigrate to Canada. Perhaps I should kill myself. But first of all, this very night, I would go home to the long town and stay there till the term started. The important thing was to make no promises I would live to regret. The important thing was not to let strangers push me around. Then the doorbell rang.

The front doorbell rang. I heard my landlady open it, and then a dull but insistent male voice, then some footsteps, then a tap at my door and the landlady was saying, "Mr McLeish! Visitors for you!"

I opened the door and three men walked straight in through it without looking at me till they were all inside, then the last of them shut the door firmly and stood with his back to it. My nightmare sank to a newer and lower level because I could see these men hated me. They all thought I was utterly wicked. They had come to claim compensation for the damage I had done their daughter and sister, and they would seriously injure me if they did not get it. The father was the spokesman. He was an ordinary height but righteous indignation made him look as solid as granite. He said, "Right. What are you playing at?"

"I'm not playing."

"Oh yes you're playing. You arty student types think life is a game, but with respectable people like the Humes life is NOT a game. You upper-class arty types think you can do anything you want to a decent girl because your powerful connections will protect you from the consequences. Well you've made a bad mistake, son. We're here to teach you that your powerful connections will not protect you from ME."
For the second time within the hour I said, "My father's a collier – a miner."
He said, "Then why are you wearing a bow tie?"
I said, "Why not? You are wearing a bow tie."
His was also blue but had a pattern of little white wheels. He said, "Impertinence won't help you. If you're a miner's son why are you at drama college?"
I said, "I'm not. I'm studying to be an electrical engineer."
He said, "Then there is no possible excuse for you."
But my words had disconcerted him. He was forced to notice that his daughter had told him almost nothing about me.

Mr Hume was a tobacconist employing two assistants. He was also an agent of the Scottish Co-operative Insurance Society, which was originally founded to give ordinary working people one of the benefits of capitalism. He was a staunch Conservative but when he wanted to bully wealthier people he automatically spoke like a morally superior working man addressing the idle rich. On learning that I did not belong to wealthy people he did not at once speak like the morally superior middle class confronting the lazy worker. He did that a week later, when he met my father. His accent now became more like his daughter's accent, more the accent of an employer, but he spoke as if he was my social equal, though a much wiser, honester, more virtuous equal. Five or six years ago I read a novel in which the main character made a speech so like Mr Hume's that I have never since been able to remember them apart. It was a novel which gave an impression of curt masculine authority by having a single surname for the title. *Gillespie* by Hay? No. *McIlvannie* by Docherty? No. *Docherty* by McIlvannie.

Docherty is a stern honest collier who lives in a place like the long town. His son gets a girl with child, the girl's mother tells Docherty, and Docherty becomes that horridest of commonplaces, a Scotsman pretending to be God. He pretends very well. He tells a truth or two. He says that the rich can evade the consequences of their misdeeds because money can buy immunity, privacy and special considerations, but the only wealth of ordinary people is their decency – their readiness to help and defend each other in time of trouble. If an ordinary man illtreats and abandons the woman who has trusted him he is openly announcing his isolation from the human race. He is crossing that barrier which divides humanity from – I forget exactly what. One or two phrases kept recurring in the diatribes of both Docherty and Mr Hume: "that poor girl", "that poor lassie", "that poor woman". Applied to Helen these phrases had not much force. Helen was not very poor. Her education was good, she had social confidence, she feared nobody in the world except her father. But as Mr Hume stonily raved and thundered like Moses on Mount Sinai he was talking about Denny, although he did not know it. My blood ran cold. I chilled all over at the truth of his words where Denny was concerned. She had loved and trusted me and given me everything I wanted, everything my own parents and education had not given, and I had responded by three times deserting her, twice out of greed and vanity because I wanted other women, finally out of spite because in her loneliness she had given comfort to someone as lonely as herself. I must have already suspected I was shit for Mr Hume's words completely crushed me. I saw that I was a dirty bit of stupid wickedness and it was right that three men were flexing their muscles to punch me. One with his back to the door, though grotesquely tall and skinny, looked very like Helen. Only Denny had ever beaten me, for fun, and Hislop of course, to make a man of me, and Hislop had failed. He had made nothing but another Hislop. Mr Hume suddenly stopped thundering and said in a shocked voice, "This is no laughing matter!"

I was shuddering with silent laughter and had a grin that hurt my face. I no longer feared anything because perfect self-hatred casteth out fear. I sat down, folded my arms and crossed one leg over the other. This made me safer. Standing men cannot with dignity punch a seated one, and these belligerent men stood very much upon their dignity. I said softly, "Please inform your daughter that I love her dearly and will marry her whenever she feels it best that I do so."

He gaped at me. If (as I suspect, but maybe I wrong him) if his moral bullying had been aimed at making me buy Helen an abortion this outcome was a defeat for him. The abortion was to have been at my expense. A wedding would be at his. He did not shrink, but his mass lost some of its righteous density. I was still grinning but he did not mention that. Maybe the grin indicated pain. He said plaintively, "Would she not prefer to hear these words from *your* mouth?"

I said, "Perhaps. She and I have arranged to meet a week from now when we will discuss the matter in detail, but if you feel before then that she requires reassurance, tell her what I have just said. Tomorrow I am visiting my parents. The news will be as much a shock for them as for the rest of us – "

"No miner need regret seeing his son marry my daughter!" cried Mr Hume.

"Good," I said. "I will phone Helen when I return."

I stood up and pointed at the table where my books were spread. I said, "And now I would like to resume my studies. The college will reopen shortly and I had better do well there, I will soon have a wife and family to feed."

I walked to the door and said to the tall, staring youth who stood against it, "Excuse me please."

He stood aside. I learned later he was only fifteen. He said uncertainly, "I'm called Kevin."

I opened the door and said, "Goodbye Kevin."

He walked through after the briefest of inquiring glances at his father. His older brother followed him without a word though on the way past he gave me a straight hard stare. I answered with a nod and another "Goodbye".

Mr Hume left with slower steps, sighing and shaking his head. He stopped in front of me and said, "You're a cold fish."

I shrugged. I felt that what I was no longer greatly interested me. He went out and I shut the door.

The room was calm again. It contained a queerly familiar feeling, a slight but steady pinching pressure on the brain and heart. My parents' house had felt like this in the years before I escaped from it to Glasgow. After the nightmare of the last hour and a half this well-known sensation was a comfort, and it was deserved, which was also a comfort. For more than six months I had lived in a free vast universe with no limit to the things I might do, the love and comradeship I might enjoy. I was now starting to pay for that freedom. From now onward Glasgow and the universe would feel like my parents' house, and in some centre of myself a voice whispered, "Quite right too", and sniggered meanly.

Back in the long town my parents received the news with regret but no acrimony. Dad said with a sigh, "Well, Jock, it is not the first time that has happened."
Mum glanced at him expressionlessly. He seemed not to notice and explained that he was referring to history – the unlooked-for pregnancy was a very frequently recorded historical fact. Their resignation must have depressed me if I had hoped they would ask if I really loved the girl? (No.) Did she love me? (No.) Had we not considered adoption? (Yes.) What prevented that? (Money.) How much was needed? (Between two or three hundred pounds.) Well son, your mother and I are by no means rich, but we've a little laid by, so if it's any use to you etcetera. But they only asked if she was a nice girl, and the news that she was receiving a college education, and that her father owned his own shop, reassured them on that point.

So all the McLeishes visited the Humes in Cambuslang. Mum was probably sincere when she told Mrs Hume that it must be wonderful to have a house with your own garden round it but her tone conveyed more politeness than admiration. Mr Hume asked Dad about the state of the British coal industry in the tones of a successful industrialist querying an employee of a less fortunate rival, but Dad's quiet answers discouraged condescension and both sides got down to business. There was not much to be decided. Everyone wanted a quiet wedding. Mr and Mrs Hume wanted a quiet wedding in a local church followed by a reception for a few family friends at a nearby hotel. I said I would prefer a wedding in a Glasgow registry office followed by a meal in a restaurant for the families alone. Mrs Hume said, "But that will suggest we have something to be ashamed of. Something to hide."

I said, "We have."

"*You* have!" Mr Hume said fiercely. "My daughter has not."

To my astonishment Helen said quietly, "I agree with Jock."

At this the elder Humes ignored their daughter and future son-in-law and appealed to the elder McLeishes: "Surely *you* see the importance of a respectable start in life for a young married couple?"

My mother said, "I know what you mean, but should not the wishes of the bride and groom come first?"

"Certainly not," said Mrs Hume.

"Remember who will be paying for all this," said Mr Hume. "Me."

This caused a silence. Mr Hume broke it by saying, "Helen! Do you really detest the notion of a decent wedding, or are you trying to curry favour with your future husband?"

She shrugged her shoulders.

"Well then," said Mr Hume cunningly to me, "since both my daughter and your parents are prepared to be guided by your preference, the only real difference is between you on one side and myself and Mrs Hume on the other, and we outnumber you two to one."

I arose, seized the shaft of the standard lamp and, swinging it like a scythe, knocked the cut glass vases off the sideboard, the framed views of Clyde coastal resorts from the walls, and Mr Hume's spectacles from his heavy selfish dour practical face. Then I peed on the hearthrug. No I didn't. I said, "Do what you like, Mr Hume."

If there was contempt in my tone he did not notice it.

During this visit I sometimes saw my mother direct upon Helen, when Helen did not notice, a glance of puzzled curiosity. She was clearly wondering, 'Is this the woman who so exercised my son that he lost half a stone in six weeks and had to have the waistbands of his trousers narrowed?' She could not understand it. She recognised that Helen was not a sensual woman, or not a woman whose senses could be much roused by me. Denny and I had always slept in each other's arms but even when we were married Helen turned away from me after lovemaking. I saw Mum give up the question with a slight shrug and headshake. Maybe she decided I was a secret footballer. My path to matrimony was punctuated by cryptic shrugs.

So everything was settled to Mr and Mrs Hume's satisfaction, but I planned a small, satisfying revenge on them. I would ask Alan to be my best man. If I rented him an evening dress with starched shirt front etcetera, his friendly but impeccable lordliness would make it impossible for the Humes and their relatives to feel anything but inferior to this peculiar person. And at the reception I would have Isi with his thick German-Jewish accent and absentminded air varied by intense moments of intellectual curiosity, and wee Willie with his Glasgow shipworker's accent, and ancient boyish face, and shining enthusiasm for a future based upon alchemy and anarchy. These three would be perfectly polite but would strike everyone except my father (who would enjoy conversing with them) as indefinably and totally wrong. But I did not at once visit Alan to discuss the matter, because everything concerning my marriage made me lethargic.

Then one day on a billboard outside a newsagent's I read the words GLASGOW TECH STUDENT PLUNGES TO DOOM. One of Glasgow's ornate Victorian buildings near the city centre was awaiting demolition. Alan's fractured body was found shortly after dawn in a lane at the foot of the back wall. The report hinted that he had fallen from the roof while attempting to strip lead from it. Which is possible. He hated waste and was always short of money. But why should a man who feared heights force himself on to a great height to make a few pounds, at most, when many would have felt privileged to lend him a fiver? But he hated borrowing. O, I was enraged with him, but not surprised. With his death the ceiling and walls of my shrunk universe narrowed even further. I asked Dad to be my best man, and the wedding was as dull as the Humes wanted it to be.

But before the wedding came THE SHOW OF PRESENTS. I had not realised how many folk in the long town respected my parents until I saw in their house the swelling heap of domestic utensils and ornaments which was later carted to Cambuslang and added to THE SHOW OF PRESENTS in the Hume's bungalow. Do other countries than Scotland practise this natural, obscene ritual? Married couples naturally want all the gifts they can get, their families naturally want to display the extent of their friendships, friends and relations naturally want their generosity to be widely recognised. So in the bride's parents' best room the tables and sideboards are loaded with presents all ticketed with givers' names so that everyone's generosity can be priced and compared to whoever is interested in the matter. Well, the fucking royal family do it, why should not the fucking Humes and McLeishes? And this socially competitive incitement to generosity does more than satisfy our greed for gifts and ostentation, it makes the young folk less likely to escape each other.

Shortly before the wedding I got a letter from Helen asking me to phone her at the house of a friend. I did. She said tensely, "Jock, please come and see me tonight. I need to tell you something."

I said, "Helen, three days from now I will promise before witnesses to see you practically every day of my life. Do we need to start sooner than that?"

I heard her draw breath and moan as if I had punched her so I apologised and went to the home of the friend. Helen opened the door and led me into a room with floral wallpaper, thick Persian carpet, Chinese display cabinet and a fat 1930s three-piece suite. A shadowy brothel atmosphere was imparted by wall-lights in orange parchment shades with scarlet fringes. We sat on the sofa with two feet of space between us. Helen told me that she was not pregnant after all. That morning her bleeding had started again. She said, "It was all psychological – hysterical, if you'd rather call it that."

I thought hard for a while then said, "Good. You can go back to college and finish your education as you planned. Yes, a baby would have been an economic disaster for us at this stage. Thanks for the news, but you could have told me over the phone."
She said, "You still want to marry me?"
"No, but I must. Because of the presents. Do you still want to marry me?"
"No, but I will. Because of the presents."
We both laughed hysterically until Helen, at last, started crying, then I think we cuddled each other. There was no love between us but there was sympathy. Each knew how miserably lonely the other was. I could not ask my parents to return the thirty-odd presents to acquaintances all over the long town, still less could Helen ask her parents to return fifty-odd presents to theirs. No explanation, no excuse, no apology could justify a mistake which had made so many folk spend such a lot of money.

I now think my mother would have had no difficulty in returning these presents. I seem to hear her saying in her driest voice, "Our Jock is a soft mark where the lassies are concerned. One of them persuaded him she was in a state which she turned out not to be in, and her hoity-toity parents took her seriously. However, the mistake was discovered before any real harm was done, and Jock has learned to be more careful in future. I'm sorry to have to return this – I hope you soon find another use for it."
Mrs Hume could easily have found a similar formula to win sympathy for Helen by discrediting me: "I'm afraid my daughter's fiancé misled her as to his social origins. We discovered that for all his fancy ways he was nothing but a miner's son and an inveterate liar. The poor girl is very cast down, of course, but she'll recover. Please forgive me for having to return this but I'm sure you understand."
Why did Helen and I not see that returning the presents would hurt our parents a lot less than a marriage would hurt us?

Cowardice. Cowards cannot look straight at the world. I proved a coward when I let Mr Hume bully me into marrying his daughter. Helen proved a coward when she decided she was pregnant, or when she realised she was not. Stop. Do I believe that? Helen never looked like a coward to me, not even when she was near to screaming in the middle of Miss Rombach's restaurant with her father and brothers ready to attack me from a nearby table. When she seduced me, when she told me she was pregnant, when she told me she was not pregnant, she struck me as a self-willed woman just managing to keep hold of an unbearable situation. That is not cowardice. But if she was not a coward then she married me because she wanted to. What a queer idea. Can it be true?

The marriage was not a bad one at first. There was no excitement or discovery in it but our life together felt more like freedom than life with our parents had felt, and we never quarrelled. We occupied two rooms in a shared flat at a corner of Elmbank Street, and we worked hard to qualify for dependable, well-paid jobs because Helen had now no interest in acting as a profession, and without Alan I saw that my dreams of becoming some sort of inventive pioneer were just fantasies. We became friendly with another young student couple whose names, faces and natures I cannot remember, except that they were more outgoing than ourselves, and took us on a camping holiday to a highland glen where we experienced alternations of heavy rain and hideous midge-clouds. Helen and I preferred sinking into domesticity in the evening and at weekends. We played a lot of Scrabble – no it was cribbage, Scrabble had not been invented. Helen concentrated harder on being a housewife than I did on being a househusband, though I was never unfaithful to her, except with bondage magazines. She became a primary teacher, I joined National Security Ltd. We bought the flat which is still my home.

I enjoyed my work in those days. I had complete charge of the installations from start to finish, only one assistant, and had to use my hands as well as my head. But the head came first. When I visited a really large plant some underling would show me round the entries, stores, safes and power points, give me plans of the wiring, ventilation etcetera, and think he could leave the rest to me; but to secure a place against acts of God, and human carelessness, and criminal intent, I must know the work schedules, work routines (which differ from schedules) and work habits (which are outside schedules and routines and can contradict them). I needed information which many employees preferred keeping to themselves, and I seldom left a big job without a close talk to the production manager in which I told him some facts about his own internal organisation which he would have to take account of, if he had any loyalty to his firm. I installed our systems (yes, I'm boasting) with love and understanding, and this was recognised and noted, which is why I have sat on committees responsible for the actual design of new factories, banks and museums. That came later. In those days all my work was in the Glasgow area so I could be home by six-fifteen and find Helen ready with the dinner – her teaching job stopped at four. What a good time that was! I had every domestic comfort and a job which used all my faculties and brought me money and a sensation of power. I would have liked some passionate sex too, but only a fool expects to enjoy every good thing in the world.

One day in the office of the old Cosmo Cinema the manager told me he was having a preview at which Tom Courtenay or Albert Finney would be making a personal appearance. I told him that my wife and I had once known the great actor socially, so he invited us along. Helen refused to come so I stood sipping a sherry at the edge of a small crowd in the foyer. Tom or Albert suddenly saw me and said with very pleasing warmth, "Jock! The genius of the lamp! How are you getting on? What are you doing?"

I said, "Fine thanks. I'm with the National Security company."

He said, "A professional company I hope?"

I smiled and said, "It's not a theatrical company if that's what you mean. And though it has a local base it's pretty big. We install fire alarms, burglar alarms, every sort of alarm you can imagine."

He said, "Oh!" and after a pause, "I don't suppose you'll last long at that."

I said, "Why not? The pay's excellent."
He looked at me as if his earlier recognition had been the result of an accident. He said, "Yes, why not? Good luck Jock."
He moved away leaving me slightly annoyed with him. Theatrical folk think everybody who is not one of them dwells in outer darkness, but Albert or Tom had a broader experience than most theatricals. I thought he would have known that modern technology is far greater than a theatrical device. It maintains our prosperity and security. It guarantees a future of increasing peace, prosperity and quack quack quack quack quack.

In the sixties I still believed such quackery. A lot of folk did. On a station bookstall one day I saw that the *New Scientist* or *New Society* or *New Statesman and Nation* was advertising an article by C. P. Snow, the only modern English novelist (apart from the thriller writers) I had been able to read. None of his characters was memorable but the research and administration they engaged in was described with a fair degree of accuracy. This article was called "The Two Cultures", and pointed out that most middle-class people either had arty or scientific educations. The scientific lot often read books and saw plays, so they knew something about art, but most arty folk knew nothing and cared less about science – the laws of thermodynamics aroused no enthusiasm in them whatsoever. C. P. Snow thought this a pity, because it condemned writers and artists to a hopeless view of the world. They saw life as a matter of individuals being born, copulating and dying, which *were* pretty hopeless pastimes, being only half of what we actually did. Viewed socially, however, we were immortal because we kept adding to the amount of human knowledge and technical skill. Scientifically and politically the most advanced nations had abolished hunger and poverty among themselves and were now preparing to help the backward nations up to the same level. This heroic task would be tackled by the scientific part of our culture, and the arty lot would feel more cheerful if they learned to celebrate the achievement. Heech! On reading that I squared my shoulders, smiled smugly and thought how true, how true. In those days I was as politically naive as Lord Snow.

When did my job start to sour? When did my marriage start to stale? When did I start drinking too much? When did capital leave Scotland in a big way? When did the depression come to Britain? When did we start accepting a world without improvement for the unlucky? When did we start accepting a future guaranteed *only* by the police, the armies, and an expanding weapons race? There was no one point after which things got worse but my last spasm of scientific, social delight was in 1969.

I was delighted when Armstrong stepped on to the moon in 1969. As a Scot I was envious but as a skilled technician I was jubilant. The backing for the enterprise was military, yes, but the scientific and technical skill which did the job was not working to kill men but to lift them safely across a 225,000-mile vacuum to another world and back. We did it! Scientific technical men did it. So what?

I was depressed when the first photographs of the far side of the moon showed it very like this side, but more monotonous. And when the Viking probe landed on Mars and showed it more like the moon than we expected. And when we pierced the icy clouds of Venus and found no steaming jungle or bubbling mineral-water sea but just a blasted redhot dust desert. There was some excitement when radio telescopes picked up the first pulsar waves and a Cambridge team thought it might be the "Hullo there, folks!" of an extraterrestrial superintelligent civilisation. But there is no evidence of intelligent, or commercial, or even downright stupid broadcasting from the stars, and of the forty-odd planets (counting moons) which spin round our own star, only the earth and her useful wee moon are worth a docken to a living soul. Why does this make me feel trapped? Why do I feel trapped upon the most intricately varied, richly vital world I will ever discover? The only world which can bear me? A world where technically minded men like myself (and I include the political, business, army and arty folk who batten on us) are undoubted masters?

Self-disgust. We have committed horrible crimes which do no practical good. We make deserts.

We can do splendid things. In Holland we laboured to grow food and flowers on the bed of a turbulent sea. Green fields in the Scottish lowlands cover what was bleak moor two centuries back. The great dams authorised by Roosevelt put thousands of unemployed men to work and laid the dustbowl caused by the destruction of the prairie. But we made deserts and still make them, deliberately and accidentally. By legal process, by fraud and by force highlanders were cleared from glens and islands because they profited only themselves, the lazy sods, and it was technically practical for big landowners to profit more by sheep instead. When sheep stopped being profitable the owners made wilderness which rich southerners rent for bird and beast-killing holidays. That wilderness now has a technically sophisticated fringe of weapontesting ranges, megaton warhead dumps, nuclear submarine bases, nuclear bomber bases, nuclear power stations, dumps for nuclear waste (from England) and in Gruinard Bay, sparkling bluegreen water over white sunlit sand when I saw it last, an island poisoned for at least a century with anthrax to show what we could do to central Europe if Germany invaded Britain. Practical economics, you see, plus the defence of freedom by advanced technology, as in Dresden, Nagasaki, Hiroshima and Vietnam where military technologists also saved thousands of families from evil political regimes by burning them in their homes and poisoning their ground. But most of the deserts we make are accidental because in the race for quick profit accident MUST occur. Hence cancerous seafouling lakeshitting industry, rainpoisoning riverpoisoning forestwithering factories, soilkilling cattle-crippling mencrippling fertiliser, nerverotting medicines, bonewarping babyfood, THALIDOMIDE THALIDOMIDE THALIDOMIDE *Here is the nine-o'clock news. Today the Prime Poisoner declared in parliament that recent falls in the poison rate had had an adverse effect upon Britain's already unhealthy balance of poisons. She said that if the national union of poisonworkers persisted in its demand for a 15 per cent poison increase for its members it would poison the country right out of the*

European poison market. However, shortly before closing today the poison exchange index showed a point 4 per cent increase in response to the poison survey which indicates a clear victory of President Poison in the forthcoming American poison campaign. President Poison has promised to tighten his embargo on Russian poison exports along with a massive increase in public poisoning in order to give the free poisoners everywhere a clear lead in the nuclear poison race. Today's fine weather caused a brisk flow of poison to the seaside resulting in a twenty-two-mile poison jam on the London to Brighton road and a multiple poison pileup on the M1 in which eighty-three were injured and seventeen lost their lives (stop this) *I can't because technology has magnified to world-destruction point the common smash-and-grab business tactics and bullyboy politics which everyone* (not everyone) *which too many seize as golden opportunities or take for granted* (stop this) *how stop when books say we are selfish competitive beasts and all the true bonny good things we discover or make/solar system/Sistine ceiling/penicillin/are got by overcoming and humiliating each other* (crap) *yes crap but in Scotland 1982 that shitty thought looks like Your Own Great Gospel, O Lord, for here is no dream or plan to make or share good things or set an example and honestly, God, I no longer think Scotland worse than elsewhere and I can only stop raving by retreating into fantasy* (retreat).

Janine is worried and trying not to show it but she cannot see clearly for the dazzle. She concentrates on the sound of the two unfastened studs in her skirt clicking with each step she takes. A childish voice says, "That's a sexy noise", and giggles.
'Act calm,' thinks Janine. 'Pretend this is just an ordinary audition', and this is NOT the fantasy I intended.

One of the earliest aims of the United States space programme was to create a self-supporting human colony on the moon, and since the cost was astronomical, in 1960 they offered the problem of making and shielding a lunar atmosphere, along with the water and vegetation which would keep it pure while nourishing the inhabitants, to research teams in other countries. Nations helping the project would be represented in the colony by a proportion of settlers commensurate with the money they spent, and Russia was not excluded, because a lunar colony has no military value. Meanwhile America concentrated on the launching and carrier crafts which had military applications, but her best scientists and the best part of her public were guided by a nobler vision, so in 1982 everyone can see, on cloudless nights, a silvergreen glint in the globe of the full moon, a glint which casts a shadow. This is the garden village where young healthy skilled folk of several races co-operatively farm, construct, research, play and go out to explore. How does it look when the moon is crescent? Hislop once told me how it looked. In the months which followed him making a man of me I seldom listened to his mellifluous chanting, but I once heard him describe a becalmed ship in a seafog at night. The stars were very dim. Dew dripped from the sails. The only clear light shone upon the face of the steersman, "till arose", no, "till climbed above", no, "till clomb above the eastern bar the hornéd moon, with one bright star within the nether tip". I sneered because I knew that was scientifically impossible, but yes the lunar colony does shine like a small green star in the elipse of black sky between the horns of the crescent moon, a star where men and women make love, make children under a sky of stars surrounding the huge crescent of the earth. The lunar colony has only one disadvantage. It has no military value so it was never created.

Everyone wanted the moon until one day a great nation became wealthy enough to woo her. So scientists and technicians went pimping to this great nation and got rich by selling a quick moonfuck. A slow moonfuck would have been more satisfying but would have got the pimps fewer fast bucks, so the pimps hyped up their pay by inventing THE MOONRACE, they pretended Russian rapists might bang the moon first, which was impossible. By the late sixties the Russian lead in space technology was far away in the past. In space technology, oil technology, military technology she is a decade behind her opponents because compared with us she is too few and too poor. Sure, she can poison our planet several times over in a few hours, but for a quarter-century The Free West has been able to do that

much faster and more frequently. So we summoned the energy to jump to the moon by deliberately scaring ourselves with our own shadow, and we said, "Hiya moon! This is a proud moment. Have a flag. Have some recording equipment. And now I must get back home to the dear old arms race. So long!" and the peoples of the earth said, "So what?" and now nobody wants the moon. She holds nothing human but shattered rockets and rundown machines that litter her crust like used contraceptives proving that Kilroy was here. The moon is still a dead world and nightly reminder that technological men are uncreative liars, mad gardeners who poison while planting and profit by damaging their own seed, lunatics who fuck and neglect everything in reach which has given them strength and confidence, like . . . like . . .
(Like Jock McLeish fucking and neglecting Denny for a woman he could not fertilise?)

Yes.
Yes.
Yes.

We fear responsibility, you see, so inaccessible bodies attract us most. We neglect the ground below our feet and gaze at the stars hoping they are peopled with nasties so horrible that we will look decent beside them, by goodies so wise that they will take us by the hand and guide us on to The True Way. Aliens must be our inferiors or superiors, you see, because we do not believe in equal partnership, in equally shared goods and responsibilities. Small communities live by such equalities but only the French and Russians tried to create them on a big scale and they FAILED hahaha FAILED hahaha FAILED and we are glad: we are sure that only the poor and hungry will benefit from a free and equal society. *Free and equal society*. These words stink of the vilest votecatching rhetoric, they mean as much as *love* and *peace* do in the prayers of an army chaplain. *Freedom equality love peace* are now nothing but embarrassing words, so if the scientists of the world learned today that microbes live in the dust of the Crab Nebula they would feel a completely unselfish delight. Life has a chance in the universe if it exists where we cannot reach it.

We confess to thee we have done that which we ought not to have done, and have not done that which we ought to have done, and there is no health in us.
(Where did you learn that, Jock?)
Lighten our darkness we beseech thee o Lord, and by thy great mercy protect us and save us from all the terrors and dangers of this NIGHT we are making. I don't know where I learned these things. Perhaps I heard them on the wireless when I was wee, for I know there was a time when you were worshipped as an extraterrestrial Big Daddy who would one day screw up the earth like bumpaper and flush it down the stank because too many bad boys and girls used it: after which you would make a nice clean earth for the nice clean boys and girls you had allowed to survive the old dirty one. But it is practical, scientific, technically-minded business and military and political folk who are treating the earth like bumpaper and if we flush it down the stank there will be nobody to replant the desert we make. For you are not extraterrestrial. You are the small glimmer of farseeing, intelligent kindliness which, properly strengthened and shared, will light us to a better outcome. Lead kindly light amid the encircling gloom.
(Sentimental rot.)
How dare you adopt that negative tone? It is I who am the cynic, the external judge and condemner of everything. I only believe in an opposite like you to keep a sane balance in my head. If you cross into my corner of the ring you will drive me into yours, and honestly, G, I lack the strength to be useful, farseeing, kindly.
(Strength comes with practice, sir.)
Don't try to teach me anything, G. Only arrogant people try to improve themselves morally. Moral self-improvement is antisocial. It disturbs those who are improving themselves financially.
(How remarkably witty, sir! You really are in sparkling form this morning.)
Morning?

Morning. Switch light off. Between bluebell window-curtains, a vertical crack of cold grey dawn. Selkirk? Peebles? Get up. Step to window. Gently pull curtains.

Dawngrey sky, dawngrey sea, grey mountains between them. Where am I? High window this. Grey motorway below, then docks, sea etcetera. This is Greenock, why? O God, now I remember. Meeting last night at I.B.M. plant. Bad.

Shortly after start I went absentminded. Later on I tried to concentrate and could not understand what they said to me. I could hear each syllable with great distinctness but it might have been Chinese for all the sense it made. I was being asked questions. I tried nodding intelligently then nearly blacked out. Recovered and, "Glass of water please?"
"Cretinly, cretinly," they said (must have been "certainly", actually).
"Cretinly? Wery vitty," said I, grinning Hisloply, and I could no longer remember why I had come there. I told them so. Apologised. Recent overwork. Understanding smiles. "Don't worry, Jock, we'll get a car to take you to the station."
They did. Why am I not in my own bedroom? Glasgow only forty minutes from Greenock. Ah of course. Car got me to station twenty minutes early for train. Nipped into pub while waiting. Missed train, missed next train, missed last train, hence here. Seems decent hotel. Saw I was gent in spite of state. But I have lost my last illusion, the illusion that nobody knows I am an alcie. By ten or eleven o'clock Reeves will have been told, but ninety minutes till breakfast call at 8.15. I can always grab his ear first if . . .

I feel sincerely tired now, tired and clean and sad, why clean? Lie down again. Lie down (I do) sincerely sad and clean, why sad? What a lot I have lost: a little pencil sharpener shaped like the world, Denny, Alan, mother, father, wife, many familiar streets and buildings, whole districts and industries suddenly not there any more. Listen. A bird is cheeping.

> A bird used to visit this shore (warbled Hislop)
> It isn't going to come any more.
> I've come a very long way to prove
> No land, no water, and no love.

Not sensible. A shore is the edge of the land so there must be land. A shore is the edge of a sea so there must be water. And if someone goes a long way to prove something then they must like it a lot, even if they never discover it. But the verse seems to mean more than the words, it keeps running in my head. Warble on, Hislop.

A bird used to visit this shore.
It isn't going to come any more.
I've come a very long way to prove
No land, no water, and no love.

Too many things have gone from us without being noticed.

A bird used to visit this shore.
It isn't going to come any more.
I've come ayaha, ayaha,
aaaaaaaaaghooey!

Hm. Hmn.

13: CATTLE MARKET

She sat in the exact centre of the back seat of a Rolls-Royce and idly turned the pages of a fashion magazine. She once raised her head to say a few discontented words to the driver, a young man wearing cowboy boots, jeans, waistcoat and hat who cannot have been me but he felt like me. She amused him, so he was not exactly her chauffeur, though she behaved as if he was. She glanced back at the magazine where she saw something interesting, I think it was an illustration. She read some words underneath it and was astonished. Her astonishment was so exciting that I wakened with this erection which has only just subsided. Oh I wish I had not wakened. That was nearly a wet dream, the first since boyhood days before I met Denny. I used to dream I was filling a fountainpen from a breast and wake up ejaculating. Who was that woman and why is CATTLEMARKET a magic word bringing feelings of deliciously exotic helplessness in the grip of deliciously exotic strength?

Remember. If you cannot remember, invent. The whole dream was inside the car. She was Janine, a rich Janine wearing CATTLEMARKET cowhide breeks. She discovered she was reading a story about what would happen when she left the car, hence her astonishment and my excitement. Yes, the dream is returning and so is my erection. (Excuse me sir) go away God.

Janine was never an actress, never a housewife, never had to work. Such folk exist. She has always been able to buy the things she likes but never likes anything for long, hence her accusing Jane-Russell-in-the-publicity-photo-for-*The-Outlaw* pout. Hence her love of tough, casual, slightly ugly clownish clothes expertly cut from eyecatchingly expensive material in order to suggest that she does not care a damn for her appearance. Hence her thick leather yellowbrown breeks (excuse me sir) be off, I'm busy with her thick khaki cowhide pants tied tight by a knotted white rope round so slender a waist that surely her bum CANNOT be plump enough to fill all that baggy leather but how tantalising if it is. Each trouserleg tapers to a snug little turnup cuff six inches above each naked ankle, no, no turnup cuff, a zip on each side keeps it tight. Feet sockless in white canvas sannies, no, sneakers, no, white canvas baseball boots without laces. I mean, they could be laced, they have eyeholes for laces but no laces in them stop grovelling at floorlevel soar HIGHER, remember Janine's slender waist with big breasts in white silk satin almost unbuttoned shirt no bra wide open collar at throat, then that sweet sulky face I know very well but her hair? A great cloud of blonde golliwog locks, not tightcurled but expanding her head as extravagantly as the breeks seem to expand her bum. And small diamond studs on her earlobes. Pause for breath.

(Excuse me sir) I will not. She leafs discontentedly through sumptuous magazine on her lap, *Cosmopolitan* or *Vogue* probably *Vogue* because she is bored with glossy pages of exquisitely posed and lit models advertising clothes/shoes/clothes/lipstick/clothes/hairspray/clothes/jewellery/clothes/perfume/clothes and Chef Gropier's surprisingly cheap little recipe for caviare, truffles and diced toadfish served on a blanched cabbageleaf. She sighs, looks up and asks the driver, "How are you feeling tonight, Frank?"
"Fine," he says, "why ask?"

"Because the last night we spent together was not fine at all from my point of view. You are a nice-looking guy, Frank, and as a masseur you have no equal, but I did not start meeting you socially because of your hands. I can rent those any time. Some of my best friends rent your hands. I go out with you evenings for the pleasure of those extra seven or eight inches, and of late you have been giving short measure in your delivery."

Frank grins and says, "Janine, tonight you will have more of those extra inches – more of everything – than you ever thought possible."

"Is that a fact?" says Janine sceptically, and yawns.

"It surely is."

"What did you say this place is called?"

"The Cattlemarket."

"It had better be good, Frank," she says, turning a page, "What kind of people use it?"

"The rich and the beautiful. You know some of them."

"Well it had better be good," she says, looking at an illustration on a back page between small adverts for sun-beds and French holiday homes. It heads an extract from *Sheriffs and Hookers*, a controversial new novel by Norman Mailer or John Updike. It seems to be a photograph of a patio party on a millionaire's ranch, but the clear edges of the figures, the supersmoothly graded tones and colours, the absence of wrinkles which ordinary strain imposes on most flesh and cloth all show it is a skilful airbrush painting based upon a photograph. Nearly everyone looks too handsome, too sexy, too laughingly cheerful to be possible, and nearly everyone wears cowboy boots, jeans and denim waistcoats. Even the women wear these, excepting several who wear denim skirts of the button-through or stud-fastened kind, some more, some less unfastened than others (excuse me sir) come back later I am being astonished/excited by women with button-through skirts more or less unbuttoned white silk satin shirts no bras and sulky apprehensive faces. Unlike the laughing tightjeaned cowboylike women who stand around with technicolour cocktails in their hands the skirted apprehensive women have their wrists handcuffed behind them (why not their elbows?) idiot it is anatomically impossible to handcuff someone's elbows behind them, the chain is too short (the police handcuffed Superb's elbows behind her) shut up you are trying to spoil my fun again, where was I when you interrupted?

Oh yes.

At first Janine does not notice these particular details of the illustration. They are in the background, and she is studying something even more peculiar in the foreground. In the foreground stands a woman seen from behind, her legs, her feet planted firmly astride astride astride on the patio flags. Since everyone else is looking at her she seems to be causing the gaiety of the majority, the apprehension of the rest. She wears hugely baggy khaki cowhide breeches tapering to snugly zipped cuffs above her slender naked ankles, the feet in laceless white canvas baseball boots (baseball boots cover the ankles) all right laceless white sannies/sandshoes/sneakers stop grovelling soar UP to the slender waist, are her breeks tied round it by a white knotted rope? Impossible to tell. Her waist is hidden by her arms and hands, the wrists being handcuffed behind her. Does she wear a white silk satin shirt? No. Above the waist she is completely nude. What is her hair like? Impossible to tell. The head is invisible because the top of the illustration is level with her shoulders. Only the pants and sneakers are familiar to Janine but the coincidence fascinates her. Being impatient with beginnings she skips a few paragraphs and starts reading the story a quarter way through. After reading a few sentences she finds they are giving her a queer woozy dreamy sensation. She stops reading and tries to make sense of it. She says, "Frank! Do you know Upman Maildike?"
"Who?"
"Upman Maildike. The novelist."
"Sure I know him. I've been drunk with him more than once. Why do you ask?"
"He has a story in this month's *Vogue*."
"What is it like?"
"A character in it has your name. He is also dressed like you."

"My God! What does this character do?"
"So far he is simply chatting up a chick."
"That could be me, I guess. What happens after that? Read it aloud."
But Janine has become too engrossed in the story to read it aloud.

The story is about a girl called Nina who works in the jeans section of a big department EXCUSE ME PLEASE store where she one day serves an eager handsome rich young guy who is buying cowboy EXCUSE ME PLEASE pants and waistcoat for a denim-only party being given by a rich friend who EXCUSE ME PLEASE I will not excuse you if I keep a tight hold on this small dream I will manage to pack all my obsessions into it Nina helps Frank choose these clothes for a denim-only party being given that night by a millionaire friend of his, the party is that evening, Frank is in great haste having received the invitation only an hour earlier on arriving home from an Alpine ski holiday. Nina is so charmingly helpful that Frank says, will she think him pushy and unchivalrous if he asks her to accompany him to this party? Because he is lonely and his friend's parties are always a lot of fun. And since Frank is charmingly shy and hesitant and rich Nina says, well, I have nothing planned so all right, and Frank says swell if Americans still say swell when they mean hooray, and he immediately buys for her, they need not leave the store for him to do so, a little button-through denim skirt which I INSIST THAT YOU HEAR ME, DID WE RIDE THROUGH THE VALLEY OF THE SHADOW OF DEATH JUST TO LET YOU TICKLE YOURSELF INTO ANOTHER WANK? Dear God, you know I need these absurd elaborations to fool myself into believing I can once again clasp the body of a woman. DID WE BREAK OUT OF THE DUNGEON OF DESPAIR JUST TO LET YOU TICKLE YOURSELF INTO ANOTHER WANK? I cannot change things overnight, God. WRONG. WRONG. WRONG.

Wrong?

Yes, on second thoughts I certainly can change things

overnight. Wait for me Nina, I have to do a job before you put on that skirt for me. Reach down to floor. Fumble under bed for suitcase handle. Got it. Pull out, lift up, lay on top of neatly folded clothes on bedside chair, I am glad I maintained neat habits on a night when they could easily have slackened. Open case. Remove notepad. Close case. Lay case on top of bedclothes on top of thighs, lay pad on case-lid as if upon desk. Take pen from breastpocket of good grey Harris tweed jacket hanging on chairback. Unscrew cap of Rotring Rapidograph with point four nib, a good designers' pen. Glance at digital-watch-calendar for time, date. And now, the truth.

7.50 a.m. 26 March 1982
The Blank Hotel, Greenock

The Installations Manager,
National Securities Ltd,
Waterloo Street,
Glasgow

Dear Reeves,

I am tendering my resignation as installations supervisor for the Scottish Region, and regret that I cannot offer the usual four weeks' warning before withdrawing my services. At the important I.B.M. meeting last night I suffered a minor stroke which forced me to withdraw before our business was touched upon. As you know, I am one of those frequently mocked individuals who are proud to have never lost a day's work through illness in their lives. In twenty-five years of service this is the first time I have jeopardised a National Security contract. This resignation ensures it will be my last. The cause of the seizure has still to be diagnosed (Liar) (I don't care) *but if the accountant needs a medical certificate before arranging my pension and severance pay I will contrive to produce one.*

As to replacing me, Eliot and Mitchell are obvious choices on grounds of seniority, but your best man is young Saunders. He is quick, skilful, inventive and still finds the work interesting. If promoted at this stage of his career he will annoy the hell out of everyone but produce invariably good results. I realise, however, that the company will probably promote someone from south of the border. From General Electrics to the National Coal Board more and more top jobs in Scotland are being given to Englishmen, presumably because those who run the country want key men who are more loyal to foreign bosses than to their colleagues and the public. But I may be mistaken. Maybe we native Scots are indeed a gang of stupid incompetents who lack the qualifications to manage ourselves. (You are getting overheated, cut that out.) (No, let it stand.)

I enclose herewith all schedules and documents relating to extant business. Should you or my successor need further information I may be contacted at my home in Glasgow.

Yours faithfully,
John McLeish

What can I do now? I have no plans, none at all. May I return to Janine reading Frank buying Nina a skirt/shirt etcetera? Does anyone oppose that motion?

Silence.

Right. Frank asks Nina, would you wear these when I pick you up tonight because this is an all-denim patio party. Nina asks, why denim? Frank blushes and says, well, the party has a theme. Has Nina ever been to, or heard of, a Tarts and Vicars party? She has not been to one, but yes, she has heard of fashionable masquerade balls at which the men dress like priests and their wives and girlfriends dress like prostitutes. Frank says, yeah, that's the idea, it's a British idea, and his millionaire friend who needs a name, Hollis will do, Frank's millionaire pal Hollis gave such a party once, and it was such fun that tonight's party will be on a similar theme, but more American. It will be a Sheriffs and Hookers party with a Wild West frontier flavour. The women are dressing like frontier whores and their escorts like sheriffs who are taking them into custody. Does Nina object to that? Nina laughs and says no! and anyway she sees nothing whorish in a simple skirt and shirt. Well, says Frank, Hollis finds these a turn-on and he is our host so the girls dress to please him even though there is indeed nothing whorish in skirt and shirt, though many of them add accessories that produce a very strong impact but there is no reason why Nina should compete with these, if she does not feel like doing so. He arranges to pick up Nina at her apartment in a couple of hours. He says he will not be alone – his friend Tom and Tom's wife Sherry will be driving down with them to Hollis's ranch, this story is becoming overloaded with new people but I need them to surprise me with new ideas which will keep me not quite able to foresee the end though it will inexorably turn into the usual dull old business. For twenty-five years my sexual daydreams and loneliness and drinking and work for National Security have propped each other up. Without the work the first three must increase until they destroy me. Could they fall into a looser order with room for something new to grow? No. Nothing new will grow in this mind.

Nothing new will grow in a mind containing a Cadillac containing Janine reading a story about Nina surveying herself in a full-length mirror. She has decided not to compete with other women by adding tarty accessories to the skirt and shirt. She wears these only, standing barefoot and stockingless, her face washed naked of all make-up, her hair unpinned and unclasped hanging loose behind her shoulders. No jewellery. No bra either, but though the shirt is semi-seethrough, the extra thickness of silk on the breast pockets prevents the aureoles of her nipples showing as more than faint darkness. And although shirt and skirt are decently fastened (skirt white denim with brass buttons shining like gold) she looks wonderfully lovely, young and enticingly defenceless. She is amazed by herself. If she appears like this among richer and older women who have dressed as outrageously as possible she will be the star of the party. But can she go outside like this? Why not? The night is warm and she does not mind some dirt on the soles of her feet. Nina is starting to interest me more than Janine does. The doorbell rings.

She opens and there stands Frank and Tom. She says, "Hiya!" and placed hands on hips, flaunting a little. "Like it?" she asks.

"Oh honey," says Frank, "you really are too much. You are now really *something*. Meet Tom, Nina."

Tom is well over six feet tall with a fierce black moustache, but a pudgy figure, a slight stoop and half-moon bifocal spectacles make him look like an absentminded bank clerk, despite a broad-brimmed leather hat, a leather waistcoat with a tin star on it, leather trousers, high-heeled boots and two thick belts creasing his hanging abdomen, one with a lariat and handcuffs hanging from it, one a cartridge belt with holster and pistols. Nina cannot take him seriously. His gravelly Texan drawl fails to disguise a voice naturally high-pitched and Eastern. He growls, "Nina Crystal?" and takes her hand.

"That's me all right!" she says. His grip of her hand tightens. He says formally, "Well, Nina, I have bad news for you. The new mayor has ordered us to clean up this town, so we are taking you and a few other bad girls a long long ride away from here to a place where you cannot tempt honest, cleanliving citizens. You will have no time to do that because you will be working very very hard for bad boys like me and my pardner Frank here."

She laughs and says, "I see the party has already started."

"Yep," says Tom, "and will last longer than you ever thought a party could. I now pronounce you hooker – and sheriff."

There is a sudden click. Tom lets her hand go and she sees the wrist is handcuffed to Frank's. Frank grins and tugs her out the door saying, "Walk, honey."

"Wait! I want my handbag!" she says, pointing to it.

"I'll get it," growls Tom, "you've other things to worry about."

"Your friend takes this game very seriously," she murmurs to Frank on the way to the elevator.

"He enjoys it more that way," says Frank. "So will you, eventually."

In the elevator they find the Bronsteins, an elderly couple from upstairs who have always (Nina feels) looked at her with grave suspicion because she is young, attractive and lives alone. They now stare at her with open mouths. "A fine evening, Mr and Mrs Bronstein," says Nina, but they do not answer and Nina finds it hard not to laugh aloud. She is full of confidence and merriment, excited by how much she will excite people at the party but taking none of it seriously, especially not her impossibly sweet, helpless, nude-under-two-garments self, certainly not that big slob Tom with his fierce moustache, dimly peering eyes, heavy guns and ladies' handbag. I like Nina. She reminds me of a friend I used to know, who?

Diana. I saw and heard nothing of her for ten or twelve years but when my marriage ended she began haunting me. I glimpsed her for half a minute in a remake of *The Thirty-Nine Steps*, and for slightly longer in a good but badly publicised film called *Country Dance*. Her voice occurred in radio plays I tuned into by accident. One evening I bumped into Brian in a loungebar in Irvine. He had a family now and worked as a speech therapist in local schools. He and Diana still corresponded. He told me that after the Edinburgh fiasco she had left Glasgow without completing her course at the Athenaeum. She went to London, auditioned for a part in one of Binkie's shows and failed to get it. She took a room near Swiss Cottage, bore an illegitimate son and managed (I cannot imagine how) to bring him up on money from the Social Security and from any acting job she could get, which at first was chiefly chorus work in cheap pantomimes and extra work in cinema adverts. Brian said she also got help from men friends. I thought he meant that she did a bit of polite whoring, so I was annoyed by his tone of mingled envy and admiration. I said, "Her son can't have much of a life."

Brian shrugged and said, "My children don't have much of a life either. Their mother and I give them a lot of attention and every material thing they need, but all the time they squabble over trivialities. The boy says he wants to be a rock star, but though he twangs on a guitar he refuses to take lessons and has no interest in any other music. The girl is slightly older. She wants to be a film star or a housewife. Nothing else strikes her as desirable. She has no interest in acting or drama and spends her spare time on fashion magazines, make-up, frocks, swapping clothes with friends, going to dances and gossiping about who kissed who. I met Diana's son last year and found him terribly impressive. He's cool, quiet and gentlemanly. He prefers the company of adults to children. His mother would like him to be an actor but he's determined to be a policeman."

This left me with nothing to say at all except, after a pause, "I'm sorry Diana is not a successful actress."

He said, "But she is! She has worked with most of the good British directors by now, and whenever they want to make a small part memorable with some extra humour or intelligence, she is one of a few dozen professionals that they know they can depend upon. She is a successful actor just as you are a successful electrician or engineer or whatever it is you do nowadays. Neither of you is famous but you've both always done what you mostly want. Unlike me."

I said crossly, "Why should a speech therapist envy an unimportant actress and an unimportant supervisor of security installations? I can tell you this for a fact: if you've ever cured one poor kid of a stammer you've done more human good than I've done in my whole career."

He sighed and said, "Yes, I suppose teaching is an honourable profession, even my branch of it, but my life has been wasted by an adolescent dream. I wanted to create companies which would hold audiences spellbound – I wanted to be magic. Our Edinburgh adventure showed what a fantasy that was. Whenever I feel depressed nowadays I suspect that my fairly loving wife, my averagely happy home, my socially respectable job, are consolation prizes for being a failure and a weakling."

He sounded exactly as if he was me. I could not let him get away with that.

"Brian," I said, "you were a great director! The whole enterprise was created by you. You made a company out of a lot of disgruntled people who often disliked each other and didn't particularly like you. We did astonishing things for you, things we could never have done for ourselves. I learned stage lighting and set construction, I became inventive because you demanded it. You goaded us all into a new kind of life and got us working together in a highly successful comedy, don't you remember? But you were best when things went wrong. You did not curse or blame us, you worked to repair our damaged egos. You would have brought the whole show to a highly profitable end if I had not suddenly removed your theatre."

Brian stared hard at me for a while, then chuckled. He said,

"Jock, I did not direct that show. You did."

I stared at him. He said, "As soon as you joined us you took us over, every one of us. You devised a lighting script which set the rhythm for everything we did. You built a set which decided every move we made. You recast the play with Rory in the lead and the play benefited, and when at last we met the Queen of England, I exaggerate, I mean the Queen of the Golden West End, you were the only one with the confidence to speak for us. You were a bit fierce and abrupt at first, then you relaxed and became jocose and condescending. You were very very funny, and though the Queen was not amused the rest of us were proud of you. But I stupidly lost my temper in a police station so you gave the show up as a bad job and that was the end. 'Well,' I thought at the time, 'the electrician giveth and the electrician taketh away. God damn that bloody electrician.' For a year or two I would wake up at night, grinding my teeth and actively hating you. You showed Helen and Diana what a weakling I am. You showed me what a weakling I am. I have no hard feelings about it now but it was a bitter pill to swallow when I was nineteen or twenty."

I cried out, "Nobody ever thought you were a weakling, Brian, especially not at the end. You and Diana and Roddy and Rory were the strong members of the troop, it was Helen and I who cracked under the strain. As for the lighting script, Diana and Roddy devised that – I simply told them what could be done and implemented their suggestions. And the stageset was what any first-year engineering student would have been forced to devise in the circumstances. And when I told you to give your part to Rory I was only voicing what everyone else had been saying behind your back for weeks. I said it out loud because I had an urgent private reason for returning to Glasgow and half-hoped you would tell me to go to Hell."

We were both astonished by these disclosures and drank deep while pondering them. I said, "It was all an accident – a wonderful accident. I wish it had happened later in life. The further I get from our time in Edinburgh the deader I feel. I am no electrician, no engineer, I no longer do what I mostly want. I am a supervisor. An inspector. A spy."

Brian said, "We were no accident, we were a co-operative. I suspect all good companies are co-operatives who won't admit it. I could never have admitted it when I was young, because I wanted to be cock of the walk. I wanted to be king. And Jock, for a while I was a king. It's true, isn't it? Two splendid girls loved me. For over two weeks I had them on alternate nights, nearly. I sometimes wonder, nowadays, if my imagination did not cook that up to compensate for sixteen years of solid monogamy, but no, it really happened, I think."

I said, "Forgive me for asking a delicate personal question, but how did you make love to she who eventually became Mrs McLeish?"

He said, "I will gladly forgive you for any question you ask, Jock, but I do not understand that question. Explicate."

I said, "One day in a tearoom, shortly before my marriage, Helen told me, with a touch of scorn which seemed aimed at myself, that your performance in the sexual act was, at a technical level, differently structured from mine. I have often worried, I mean wondered, exactly what she was referring to."

Brian shook his head and said, "I don't know. Everyone's lovemaking must have an individual twist but I doubt if mine is more twisted than most. I've always been too shy to attempt more than slight variations on the missionary posture. I may have been more experimental in my late teens but I doubt it. I was a virgin before Helen slept with me."

This news gave me vertigo. It still does. If Helen lied to me then twelve years of marriage were built on falsehood and the past stops being solid. I can put up with a lot of present misery if it is solidly based, but if I am wrong about my past WHO AM I? If the reality I believed in is wrong, how can I right it? What solid truth can we find in our mistaken heads? My head is a windy cave, a narrow but bottomless pit where true and false memories, hopes, dreams and information blow up and down like dust in a draught. Vertigo. No go. So go to Dianina I mean Janine in cowhide breeks in a Cadillac reading a CATTLEMARKET story about Tom Frank Nina crossing a pavement (sidewalk) sidewalk to a parked Packard (is Packard still marketed?) shut up Nina crossing a pavement (sidewalk) sidewalk to a parked Packard (is Packard still marketed) shut up Nina crossing a pavement (sidewalk) sidewalk to a parked Cadillac of course. This mind is inclined to twist into a spin so go more slow.

Bypassers stare at the far too theatrical scene as sweet, barefoot, nudeunderwhiteskirtshirt, loosehaired Nina crosses sidewalk between sheriff Tom, cowboy Frank. In back of Cadillac Nina sees what seems laughing foxy face of wicked little old lady. Frank unlocks cuff from his wrist, opens back door, relocks cuff on insideofdoor handgrip, then roughly, insultingly, embraces Nina, pushing hard tongue into her mouth, hard prick against her stomach. Released she gasps, "I don't like that."
He grins and says, "Tough", opens carfrontdoor, gets into drivingseat, slams frontdoor. Standing on pavement Nina yells, no, hollers, "Frank, I don't want to come."
He says, "But you will, you're part of the vehicle now", and starts the engine. Angrily she slides into the back seat and slams the door. She does not really believe the car will drive off with her chained outside it but she wants to escape the blankly fascinated stares of five or six male bystanders who watch her as if she was a film commercial for something they would dearly like to buy. She is almost glad when the car slides away from these gawping bastards though her heart thumps and a throaty, slightly gasping voice beside her whispers happily, "Hi Nina, I'm Sherry. Ain't you terrified, honey? Look what they done to me."
Foxy little Sherry has a wrinkled face which could be any age between thirty-five and sixty. Her wrists are both handcuffed to a handgrip near the roof of the car, she keeps wriggling against that point of bondage by twisting her body from side to side while ostentatiously crossing and recrossing a pair of unexpectedly beautiful legs. These are almost completely exposed in nearly unbuttoned denim miniskirt and under the torndownoffbothshouldersseethroughsilkshirt her small breasts are made perky by a black brassiere (could Sherry be a man in drag?) stop confusing me, she also wears whitewedgesoledsandalsnetstockingssuspenderbeltblack

Cleopatrastylewigbigsilverhoopearrings (come out of the sexy accessories Jock McLeish! We know you're hiding in there) GET THEE BEHIND ME GOD AND *PUSH* for Christ's sake if you psychoanalyse me you will discover you too are nothing but my imagination. Sherry says gleefully in her throaty stagewhisper, "Just see the mess I'm in! When they came for me I freaked right out, I yelled and struggled, they slapped me silly and dragged me here and tied me up like this. I admire how you can take it all so calm. But of course this is your first time so you don't know what's in store. Believe me these brutes will do everything they want to us when they get us to the Cattlemarket."

Keyword. Shift back to Janine reading it. Janine in cowhide britches in Cadillac driven by Frank to a place called the Cattlemarket realises she is reading about Nina in Cadillac driven by Frank to a place called the Cattlemarket where Nina will at last stand in a line beside a woman who is Janine. Vertigo. Janine feels the delicious exotic helplessness of being gripped and carried along by my imagination. She also feels great dread. If this is a dream she wants to wake but cannot. She stares at the back of Frank's head wanting to ask him a question, but not wanting him to know she perhaps has information of a matter he perhaps does not want her to know. He says, "How goes the story?"
She pretends to yawn. She says, "The usual sexist crap. Is this place you're taking me to a restaurant, a nightclub or a hotel?"
Frank says, "None of them and all of them. It's a comfortable ranch where a few likeminded acquaintances can have themselves a ball with no holds barred. You'll enjoy it."
"Good," says Janine in a small dry voice and reads on.

Sherry babbles, "Tell me, Nina, how easy do you come? Tell me truly because it's important."
Nina decides the whole thing is a joke she had better play along with. She says, "It depends on how much I like the guy, I guess."
Sherry says, "Then you'd better like the guys at the Cattlemarket! New girls are always popular and these guys fuck with their eyes wide open and they just won't let you go

until you come. And they have all the devices. They really do teach a dame how to surrender. My marriage has acquired a whole new dimension since I started going to the Cattlemarket. Tom and I would have separated long ago if a friend had not introduced us to it. Tom used to be so *feeble*."
Sherry is turning this into a comedy, I no longer feel strong and wicked as I approach what should be the POINT, CRUX, CLIMAX of the story, press on regardless. Nina says, "I'm sure Frank will keep me all to himself. I mean, that's why he arrested me."
Sherry says, "You've made a bad mistake, honey. Frank is no sheriff, Frank is a RUSTLER, a THIEF. Didn't he tell you? When he gets you to the market he'll either auction you or rent you to the highest bidder, Frank is cash-crazy, not cunt-crazy. But he supplies to the cunt-crazy and tonight he is supplying you."
At which words a chill of horror seizes Nina's insides what a cheap cliché stop talking critically don't divert me from the POINT CRUX CLIMAX, Frank says loudly without turning his head, "Pay no attention to anything Sherry says, Nina. Enjoy the ride."
Tom has turned round in his seat to stare hard and long at Nina which he does with evident enjoyment, and he says, "What I like about Frank as a supplier is, the dames he brings in just can't believe what's happening to them, yet he gets them delivering themselves in such very cute parcels. Remember the last dame he got for us, Sherry? The rich bitch in the leather britches. What was her name?"
"Janine," says Sherry, at which word – although I had intended to have Janine reading a description of herself standing half naked with her breasts, hair etcetera being fondled and lifted by various hands while various people discussed how, and how much, they were going to enjoy her – at which word the story must stop, because Janine has now been forced to see she is a character in it. *She realises it is her inescapable fate to be a character in a story by someone who dictates every one of her movements and emotions, someone she will never meet and cannot appeal to.* She is like most people, but not like me. I have been free for nearly ten whole minutes.

For more than twenty-five years before these minutes I was a character in a script written by National Security. That script governed my main movements, and therefore my emotions. How could I learn to love my wife when for half the week I never even slept with her? I made myself completely predictable so that the firm could predict me. I stopped growing, stopped changing. I helped the firm grow, instead of me. I became a damned chilly gentlemanly mildmannered selfcrushing bore like my father. No wonder Helen had to leave me at last, even though she loved me.

Helen loved me. I've just noticed that. She married me because she loved me. Partly consciously, partly not, she took great daft risks and told lies until she had so manipulated her father and my family and me that she and I were well and truly married. Nobody could do that without a power of love in them, why did I never notice it? When she turned away after we had made love, as if I had defeated her in a sullen combat, why did I never kiss her shoulderblades and say gently, "That was not all I wanted from you, though I liked it a lot. Turn to me again. Let me hold you."
That never occurred to me. I was too busy thinking, 'That was all she wanted, damn her, and now she has it, and I hope she's happy. Thank God I've work to do tomorrow that needs SERIOUS attention.' She must have been thinking the same thing but I was too rotten with pride to see it. Would she have refused affection if I had wept because our sex together was so quick and poor? Maybe not, because she loved me. Why did I not notice that? Why did I think I was cheap when Denny Helen yes Diana in her way yes Brian yes Alan yes Sontag and the editor were living proof that I was far more valuable than bastarding MONEY? I used to be surrounded by love, I floated upon it without seeing it and rejected it again and again. Now there is none left I can see it, distinctly. Or perhaps I now see it because for the last ten minutes I have been free. I am not predictable now, even though I have money and a tidy home of my own.

Will I start my own small business, if so what will it be? Will I buy a partnership, if so with who? Will I found a co-operative, start a theatrical company, join a commune?

Will I invent something? Will I retrain myself to be a farmer of cattle and crops, a farmer of crabs and kelp? Will I join a political movement? Will I get religion? Will I hunt for women through contact magazines and singles clubs? Will I marry again and have a family this time? Will I emigrate? Will I roam the world with or without a companion? Will I discover that I am a homosexual, a cool-eyed gambler, a carver of clock cases, a psychopathic killer? Will I die in a war, a brothel, a famine, a bar-room brawl or beachcombing in Sri Lanka or in the Falkland Islands or in some other remote souvenir of the Great Britisher's Empire? For I will not do nothing. No, I will not do nothing.

I see you, God, in my mind's eye. You are a naked old man stooping down from the middle of the sun, your beard and hair stream sideways like the tail of a comet, you are based on a print which became popular a few years ago. In the print you probe the space below you with forceps or calipers, but in my mind's eye your hand reaches down to me with the palm open. No wagging finger tells me what I Shall or Shall Not Do. You are saying, "Stand up son. You've fallen and hurt yourself, but we all make mistakes. Regard these thirty or so mistaken years as the end of your schooling and start anew. There's plenty of time. You're not dead yet. You're not even fifty."

God, I wish I could weep. I am free but miserable because freedom is useless to a coward. Bound or unbound, a coward is incapable of doing good to himself or others. My life has passed without one single brave good unselfish action. (You stopped Hislop.) Indeed I did but he was very frail at the time.

In the weeks after his wife's death he grew strange and shrunken. We would enter his classroom and find him sitting at his desk, elbows on lid and hands covering face. We would settle in our seats as quietly as possible and wait. Was he keeking at us between his fingers? Impossible to tell. We sat like stones until he cried out, without moving, "Take out your books!" and that was often the only thing he said to us before the bell rang for us to change classrooms, though we sat more still and silent than seemed possible for a class of forty-five children. We were terrified. We knew he was on the edge of doing something really mad, yet there was nobody we could tell. We had no evidence which would make sense to an adult.

One day he got up and wandered around the classroom spouting fine language like in the old days, but the words were jumbled together without sense.

"These I have loved, the rough male kiss of blankets, the moan of doves in immemorial elms, good strong thick stupefying incense smoke and jellies soother than the creamy curd who said that Mary?"

In a small voice the girl at the top of the class said, "Keats, sir."

"No, Mary," said Hislop with a sigh, "Keats did not say it, or Browning, or Tennyson, or Brooke. Mad Hislop said it. Poor old mad Hislop. Who said it, Anderson?"

"M-M-M-Mithter Hithlop thaid it, thir," said Anderson, who had a slight lisp when he got nervous.

"Stand up, Anderson. Say my name again," said Hislop, walking over to him, "Not mister. Nor sir. Just my naked name."

"H-H-H-Hithlop."

"Break my name in two," said Hislop very gently, "say Hiss and then say Slop. Say Hiss first, all by itself. Press the tip of your tongue tight against the base of your teeth and hiss like a snake."

After a silent struggle Anderson managed to say, "Hith."

Hislop sighed, produced his Lochgelly and flexed it between his hands. He no longer looked shrunken. Some gland was putting new blood and energy into him. He said, "Anderson, I am about to do something beautiful. Something that you will one day thank me for. Something that will make my name live for ever in the annals of the long town. On my gravestone I will order them to chisel the words, 'Here lieth the man who cured Anderson's lisp.' Lisp for me. Anderson. Say *lisp*. Distinctly."

"Lithp, thir."

"Oh dear. Say *stop*, Anderson."

"Thtop, thir."

"Worse and worse. I will not ssstop, Anderson, until you distinctly tell me to ssstop. Hold out your hands and double them."

Anderson did as he was told. Hislop did what we expected then said, "Say *stop*, Anderson."

". . . Thtop thir!"

"Hands out again, Anderson."

Etcetera.

He went on and on doing that foul thing while Anderson, face contorted and tearwet, sometimes whining, sometimes muttering, sometimes yelling, kept on saying it wrong *and kept on holding his hand out afterwards*. The rest of us sat petrified in a nightmare from which no awakening seemed possible because a teacher had gone mad. He had become mechanical. He was a machine whose governor had broken and which could only work by going on doing more and more of the same vile thing until I could no longer bear it and stood up and said, "He can't help talking like that, sir."

He gaped at me, did Hislop. He came over to me, the Lochgelly swinging by his side, and he stood in front of me and said words I could not hear because I was too occupied with my trembling. I think he ended with a command or a question for I suddenly felt the pressure of a silence which I must fill with some action or words of my own. Having no new ideas I said again, "He can't help talking like that, sir", and sat down, and folded my arms, and immediately felt a lot safer. Another teacher might have seized me by the ear, dragged me into some store cupboard and used the belt on me at random, but Hislop never touched people with his hands, only with the belt, and when this occurred to me I felt safe enough to become angry. I said, "You shouldnae have done that. You shouldnae have done that. You shouldnae have done that."

Each time I said the words it became more obvious that they were true, for Hislop should never have belted Anderson, and suddenly others were saying the words with me in a chant which got louder and louder, even the girls joined in and then we too turned nasty and mechanical. Our chanting accelerated, we lashed him with it. He retreated to his desk, cowered behind it in his chair, pressed his face on to the wooden lid and started punching the back of his skull with his balled fists, trying to smash himself out of existence. We fell silent at that. The door was flung open, the headmaster entered breathless, followed by the teacher next door. And Hislop looked up with a trickle of blood coming from a nostril and said in the voice of a tiny weeping boy, "O sir they wullnae lea' me alane, they wullnae lea' me alane."

We all felt ashamed of ourselves, and that was Hislop's last day as a teacher.

But I did right to stop him belting Anderson. Afterward in the playground the class gathered round me, again and again telling each other and everyone who joined us what Hislop had done to Anderson, what I said to Hislop, what they had all said to Hislop. A lot of them, yes, girls too, walked home with me and only went to their own houses when I entered mine. I had not become their leader in any way, they just liked being near me because they were glad I existed. They felt safer and stronger because I was one of them. They liked being near me because they were glad I existed. I was thirteen or twelve, maybe. I would like to make other people glad I exist before I die: Ach

Ach

Ach

Ach what's this?

Ach

Ach

Ach

Ach tears

Ach

Ach

Ach

Ach floods of them

Ach

Ach

Ach

Ach stop it

Ach

Ach

Ach

Ach stop it

Ach

Ach

Ach

Ach why stop it?

Ach

Ach

Ach

Poor Hislop

Ach

Poor Dad

Ach

Alan Alan

Ach

Where are you mother mother mother?

Ach

Denny Denny Denny Denny Denny
Denny Denny Denny Denny Denny
Denny Denny Denny Denny Denny?

Ach

Helen Helen Helen?

Ach

Sontag

Ach

The editor

Ach

The whore not Denny please God no

Ach

Me too, me too

Ach

Ach poor children, poor children.

We were all ignorant. We didnae know how to be good to each other.

Ach well

Ach well

Ach well.

Dry this tearwet face on corner of flannel sheet. Thus. I feel different. A new man? Not exactly the same man, anyway. What is this queer slight bright fluttering sensation as if a thing weighted down for a long time was released and starting, a little, to stir?

Don't name it. Let it grow.

Before I die I will make folk glad I exist again. How? Go away for a holiday and think about that. Lie on a beach under a warm sun. Drink wine, not spirits. The right sort of leisure will breed new ideas, revive old ones I have forgotten. It is ideas which make people brave, ideas and love of course. I will have a holiday, I will think, and I will return to the only place I am able to understand. I once thought I would have done better in London, or Cape Canaveral, or Hollywood even. I had been taught that history was made in a few important places by a few important people who manufactured it for the good of the rest. But the Famous Few have no power now but the power to threaten and destroy and history is what we all make, everywhere, each moment of our lives, whether we notice it or not. I will work among the people I know; I will not squander myself in fantasies; I will think to a purpose, think harder and drink less; I will be recognised by my neighbours; I will converse and speak my mind; I will find friends, allies, enemies if need be, and I (don't name it). Yahoohay, this has been an exhausting night, the longest of my life. I am not a massive man but I must be tough to have survived a night like this last. Hm. Hmn.

Janine is worried but trying not to show it. She concentrates on the sound of two unfastened studs in her skirt clicking with each step she takes. "That's a sexy noise," a childish voice says, and giggles.

'Act calm,' thinks Janine. 'Pretend this is just an ordinary audition.' And then she thinks, 'Hell no! Surprise them. Shock them. Show them more than they ever expected to see.'
Standing easily astride she strips off her shirt and drops it, strips off her skirt and drops it, kicks off her shoes and stands naked but for her net stockings. I need the stockings. A wholly naked woman is too dazzling so she stands naked but for fishnet stockings, hands on hips and feeling an excited melting warmth between her thighs. She is ready for anything.

I will stand on the platform an hour from now, briefcase in hand, a neater figure than most but not remarkable. I will have the poise of an acrobat about to step on to a high wire, of an actor about to take the stage in a wholly new play. Nobody will guess what I am going to do. I do not know it myself. But I will not do nothing. No, I will not do nothing. O Janine, my silly soul, come to me now. I will be gentle. I will be kind.

Footsteps in corridor.
KNOCK KNOCK.
A woman's voice.
"Eight-fifteen, Mr McLeish. Breakfast is being served till nine."

My voice.
"All right."

EPILOGUE FOR THE DISCERNING CRITIC.

EPILOGUE FOR THE DISCERNING CRITIC. You have noticed lines in this book taken from Chaucer Shakespeare Jonson The Book of Common Prayer Goldsmith Cowper Anon Mordaunt Burns Blake Scott Byron Shelley Campbell Wordsworth Coleridge Keats Browning Tennyson Newman Henley Stevenson Hardy Yeats Brooke Owens Hašék (in Parrott's translation, slightly shortened) Kafka Pritchett Auden cummings Lee and Jackson, so I will list only writers whose work gave ideas for bigger bits.

The matter of Scotland refracted through alcoholic reverie is from MacDiarmid's *A Drunk Man Looks at the Thistle*. The narrator without self-respect is from Dostoevsky's *Notes from Underground*, Céline's *Journey to the End of Night*, the first-person novels of Flann O'Brien and from Camus's *The Fall*. An elaborate fantasy within a plausible everyday fiction is from O'Brien's *At Swim-Two-Birds*, Nabokov's *Pale Fire*, Vonnegut's *Slaughterhouse-Five*. Making the fantasy pornographic is from Buñuel's film *Belle de Jour* and from *The Nightclerk*, a novel by someone whose name I forget. The character of Mad Hislop is taken from Mr Johnstone in

Tom Leonard's poem *Four of the Belt*, which he here allows me to reprint:

> Jenkins, all too clearly it is time
> for some ritual physical humiliation;
> and if you cry, boy, you will prove
> what I suspect – you are not a man.
>
> As they say, Jenkins, this hurts me
> more than it hurts you. But I show you
> I am a man, by doing this, to you.
>
> When *you* are a man, Jenkins, you may hear
> that physical humiliation and ritual
> are concerned with strage adult matters
> – like rape, or masochistic fantasies.
>
> You will not accept such stories:
> rather, you will recall with pride,
> perhaps even affection, that day when I,
> Mr Johnstone, summoned you before me,
> and gave you four of the belt
>
> like this. And this. And this. And this.

Brian McCabe's *Feathered Choristers* in the Collins Scottish short-story collection of 1979 showed how all these things could combine in one.

The most beholden chapter is the eleventh. The plot is from the programme note to Berlioz's *Symphonie Fantastique*; rhythms and voices are from the Blocksberg scenes in Goethe's *Faust* and night town scenes in Joyce's *Ulysses*; the self-inciting vocative is from Jim Kelman's novel *The Busconductor Hines*; the voice of my nontranscendent god from e e cummings. The political part of Jock's vomiting fit is from *The Spendthrifts*, a great Spanish novel in which Benito Pérez Galdós puts a social revolution into the stomach and imagination of a sick little girl. The graphic use of typeface is from Sterne's *Tristram Shandy* and poems by Ian Hamilton Finlay and Edwin Morgan.

Though too busy to be aware of the foregoing influences while writing under them I consciously took information and ideas (which she would disown) from a correspondence with Tina Reid, also anecdotes from conversations with Andrew Sykes, Jimmy Guy and Tom Lamb, also three original phrases of Glasgow invective from Jim Caldwell. Richard Fletcher informed and improved the book's electrical and mechanical parts. The fanciful use of light and space technology comes partly from conversations with Chris Boyce and partly from his book, *Extraterrestrial Encounters*.

Flo Allan typed all perfectly with help from Scott Pearson in the denser pages of chapter 11. Ian Craig, the art director, Judy Linard the designer, Jane Hill the editor, Bunge, Will, Phil and Tom the typesetters, Peva Keane the proofreader, worked uncommonly hard to make this book exactly as it should be.

And now a personal remark which purely literary minds will ignore. Though John McLeish is an invention of mine I disagree with him. In chapter 4, for example, he says of Scotland, "We are a poor little country, always have been, always will be." In fact Scotland's natural resources are as variedly rich as those of any other land. Her ground area is greater than that of Denmark, Holland, Belgium or Switzerland, her population higher than that of Denmark, Norway or Finland. Our present ignorance and bad social organisation make most Scots poorer than most other north Europeans, but even bad human states are not everlasting.

Finally I acknowledge the support of Mad Toad, Crazy Shuggy, Tam the Bam and Razor King, literature-loving friends in the Glasgow Mafia who will go any length to reason with editors, critics and judges who fail to celebrate the shining merit of the foregoing volume.

In retreat,
The Monastery of Santa Semplicità,
Orvieto,
April 1983

A.G.

1982 CRITICISM
OF THE FOREGOING BOOK

"1982 JANINE has a verbal energy, an intensity of vision that has mostly been missing from the English novel since D. H. Lawrence."

Jonathan Baumbach, *New York Times*

"I recommend nobody to read this book . . . it is sexually oppressive, the sentences are far too long and it is boring . . . hogwash. Radioactive hogwash."

Peter Levi, *The BBC Book Programme, Bookmark*

"On the strength of LANARK I proclaimed Alasdair Gray the first major Scottish writer since Walter Scott. 1982 JANINE exhibits the same large talent deployed to a somewhat juvenile end."

Anthony Burgess, *The Observer*

"Where LANARK was sprawling or self-indulgent, 1982 JANINE is taut, witty and deft."

Nicholas Shrimpton, *Sunday Times*

"I cannot rid myself of the notion that, despite its glaring faults, which do not exclude the modishly cryptic title, this work offers more hope for the future of fiction, considered as art and vision, than the vast majority of novels published since the second world war. The chief reason for this, albeit grudging accolade is that 1982, JANINE is about the world as it is rather than as it used to be . . . It's a pity . . . that Mr Gray is a late starter. If he were a young writer just embarking on his career I would, without hesitation, predict a brilliant future for him once he had dropped irritating mannerisms and, most important, refined and strengthened his prose style."

Paul Ableman, *The Literary Review*

"His style is limpid and classically elegant."

William Boyd, *The Times Literary Supplement*

"Gray is an authentically Rabelaisian writer, meaning not just that his work is bawdy and exuberant but that he is in love with the power of language to encompass life . . . Here is an original and talented writer, plainly in his prime."

Robert Nye, *The Guardian*

"There is a respectable school of thought which believes that the best thing to do with writers like Alasdair Gray is to ignore them and hope they'll go away. Well, they won't go away, and they take encouragement from the silence of their critics . . . Gray has been compared with MacDiarmid but, on closer inspection, bears a close resemblance to the Scottish buffoon, Compton Mackenzie. Those who have seen him on television will know the kind of chap he is. A vainglorious lout . . . the sort of writer who continually practises his speech for the Nobel Prize in front of the mirror. And he may well get to deliver it, for he is a profoundly reactionary penman . . . There is nothing here to differentiate 1982 JANINE from the cruelty, stupidity, and moral fascism to be found in trash like

'Suedehead', 'Skinhead' and paperbacks aimed at the young and uneducated."

Joe Ambrose, *Irish Sunday Tribune*

"I have read reviews of these books which make me suspect that the commentators had never read them. 1982 JANINE is not pornography but a thoughtful and sad study of the human predicament; to be trapped in a world where the little man, woman or country will always be exploited by the big bullies."

J. A. McArdle, *Irish Independent*

"If Alasdair Gray were a pornographer he would be rather a good one. He is not a pornographer, however. His power to titillate is betrayed by humour and pathos, the worst enemies of true porn. Humour is what makes the book bearable, though Gray's humour is very Scottish – that is to say, black."

George Melly, *New Society*

"As it develops, 1982 JANINE becomes a polemic of a good-hearted, old-fashioned kind, cheerfully enlivened by merry typographical japes, some of which need a magnifying glass to decipher, and including a sad little tale of true love lost through a young man's silly snobbery. But afterwards, not much remains. It is like a brilliant theatrical occasion that holds the audience riveted at the time but leaves them wondering, on the way home, what it all added up to."

Nina Bawden, *Daily Telegraph*

"The fragmented style may suggest Joyce and Beckett, but it becomes apparent that it owes more to the Scottish tradition which juxtaposes stark realism and wild fantasy and descends from Dunbar and David Lindsay, through Urquhart and Smollett to Scott, Stevenson and George Douglas Brown."

Seumas Stewart, *Birmingham Post*

"His fictions seem easily to inhabit all possible literary worlds, potent hybrids in a class of their own."

William Boyd, *The Tatler*

DK-7200 Grindsted
Denmark
July 26th 1984

Dear Mr Gray,

This is one of those boring letters where someone who likes your books writes to you to tell you so – so if that sort of thing gives you the creeps, ditch it! And, no, I haven't written a novel of my own, so I'm not writing to ask how to get it printed.

I bought JANINE on the knowledge of your name, and not because some hurried crit said it was pornographic. He either did this because he's only dipped into one chapter, or in the hope of stimulating sales and doing you a favour – perhaps both.

And my goodness what an enthralling book – the unities! – particularly the evolution of character. Marvellous! In 1949 I went to do my National Service, at Catterick, and one of my best mates came from Cotton Road, and we used to go to 'the jiggin'' at Rutherglen Town Hall. Also, my uncle Billie Barrie, of Kilsyth, was Chief Cashier on the Glasgow Corp. tramways, so there's hardly a mile of route, or an inch of ferry I haven't been on (in 1950/51) in either the one company or the other. So I could 'follow' you, and have the accents in my head.

Funny you remembered there were trams (most authors don't!). Getting off at Waverley, what I noticed about the Edinburgh cars was not so much their funereal colours – after all, lots of Corporation buses and trolley-buses down in England looked exactly the same – but how old they looked. Up in Aberdeen, one sizzled about in super streamliners; in Glasgow mad wee Irish girls who could only just see over the controls drove Coronation cars at 70 m.p.h. along the Paisley Road Toll at night – and then you got to Edinburgh, and tall, creaking cars, with an open front step, rumbled gently up, looking like something out of a Will Rogers silent film.

And Denny's never particularly articulate command of the language utterly deserting her in crises, and her reverting to keening or a primitive steam-whistle shriek. You certainly dredged up memories there (Dundee, 1953 – and I thought I'd long forgotten!).

Once or twice I thought you were betraying the Suspension of Disbelief conspiracy by talking directly to the reader (of course we really know this is only a story, à la Salman Rushdie) but I slowly twigged it was the dialogue with God. Sorry about that.

For chapter seven you claim inspiration from the programme note to Berlioz's Symphonie Fantastique – one of my favourite bits (bits? how many symphonies would like to be called a 'bit?') of music. Did you know that Berlioz, in his original programme (which he later swopped round the order of) took the note direct from Beethoven's Pastoral? Yes, well . . .

Thanks for a most enjoyable, and challenging, tour inside someone's very believable head.

Yours sincerely
David Clayre

GOODBYE

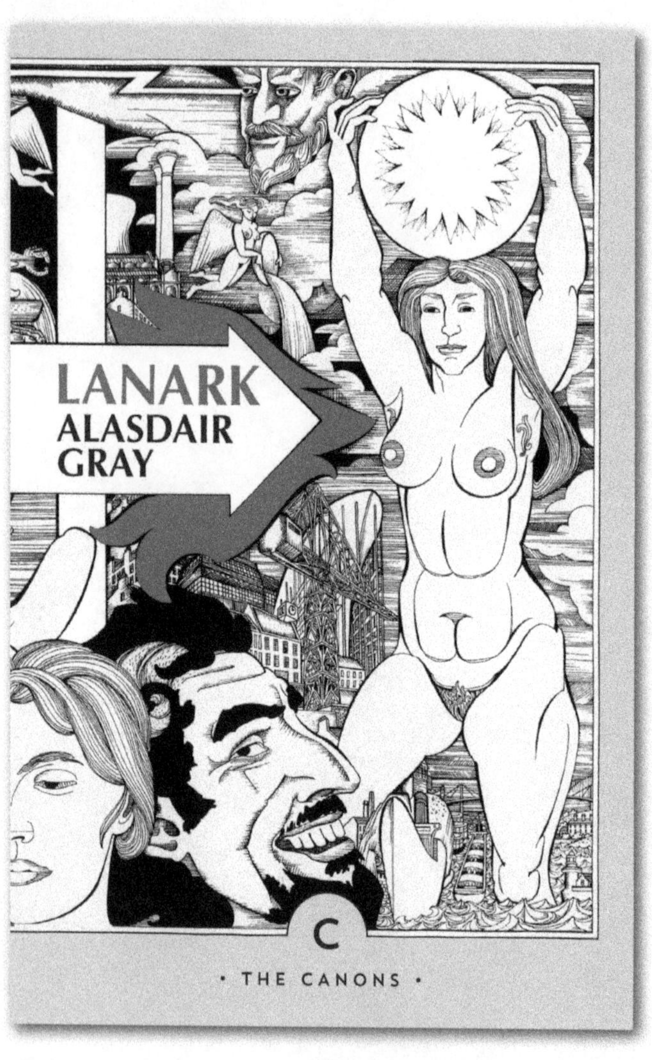

‘I was absolutely knocked out by *Lanark*. I think it’s the best in Scottish literature this century’ Iain Banks

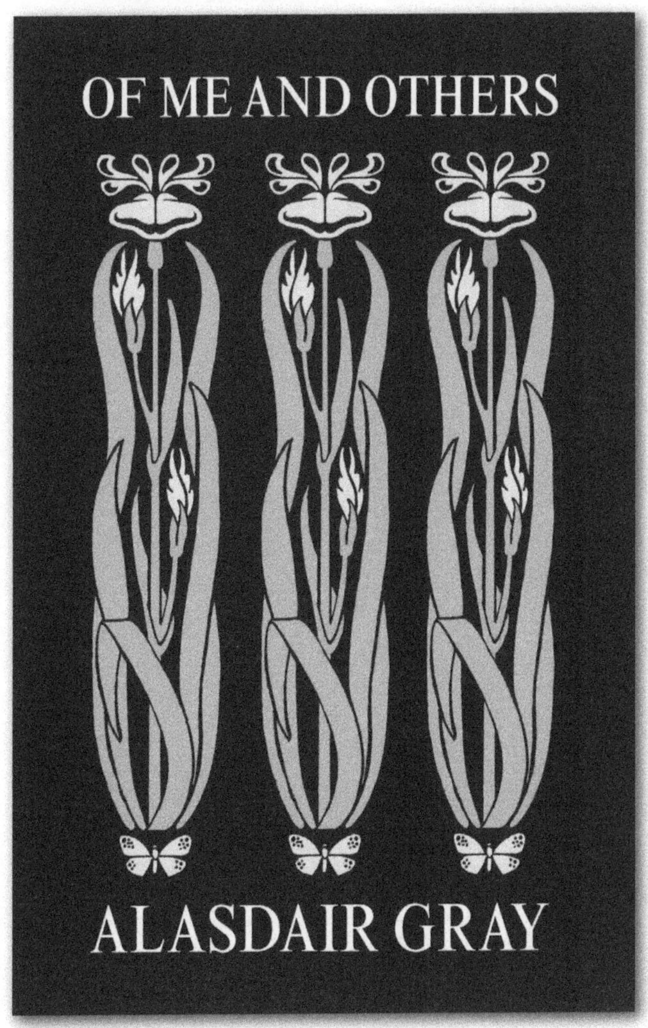

'Unbelievably inventive'
Ali Smith

CANON GATE

Printed in the USA
CPSIA information can be obtained
at www.ICGtesting.com
JSHW080933150424
61182JS00001B/2

9 781786 893963